BETH ASHER

THE WINTERHAVEN SOLUTION

In practical terms, Winterhaven was a working cattle ranch, where prime calves were raised for veal; there were comfortable cottages for the staff, a slaughterhouse, cows, chickens, pigs, geese, a tannery for skinners and hides to cure, and stables where Magnus kept his prize Arabians, and the hands their horses. Vegetables and flowers flourished in the rich coastal soil. A weapons range for automatic rifles offered the sharpshooters an ideal facility to practice. An infirmary staffed by a doctor who had been imprisoned for malpractice along with nurses like Noreen Porter, who had been discharged from hospitals, operated on a twenty-four-hour basis in case any of the men or their families needed emergency care. The children went to a kindergarten; afterwards to a private school on the grounds that had been accredited and offered instruction for the future members.

All told, about a hundred people dwelled in the Von Winters Valhalla. These men and women had been recruited from prison and some were former mental patients; a group of fanatical, dishonorably discharged soldiers had laun anti-government militia groups and joined him. Armed cells were embedded everywhere. They shared the Von Winter racial ideals and flourished with the seeds of hatred.

After Bruno's Directive for the murders of Jews before Christmas had been carried out, Magnus reduced the workload during the holidays. He knew when his troops needed a break to celebrate. During the frolicking at the annual Christmas party, Magnus handed out bonuses, gifts for everyone; he played with the children and presided over a sumptuous feast. This side of him revealed a man with a sense of humor, generous and approachable whenever anyone had a personal problem. He also hugged and kissed the numerous pregnant women, who carried Bruno's seed. Magnus displayed a paternal attentiveness to these loyal breeders who would deliver Winterhaven's future warriors. They would be his grandchildren.

With love

for

Bettye

and

Dr. Benjamin L. Cohen

ACKNOWLEDGMENTS

Unlike awards shows in which those presented with prizes are brazenly dragged, kicking and screaming, off-stage to ensure that a commercial can run on time, writers are given ample space and time to thank the people who made their voyage possible.

At an early stage when I didn't know whether or not to slash my wrists and abort my child, I was brought to my senses by two close friends.

LK and NSB made persuasive arguments and excellent suggestions that convinced me to carry on with my labors.

Joining this pair was my indomitable agent, Richard Curtis. He cajoled, criticized, calmed me down, and put some steel in my spine, insisting that I take this to term. I have Mrs. Curtis to thank for the title.

Rounding out this group was the woman who ultimately played the leading role in the life of this book. I was privileged to meet the novelist and editor Monique Raphel High. She agreed to edit the novel before any publisher dissed it. She brought to my work her generosity of spirit, insight, expertise, acuity, and a passionate commitment. She was relentless and her ideas invaluable. Whenever she radiantly smiled at me, I knew that I was in for more revisions and had to keep on truckin'. She is not a woman easily pleased. In a word, she was a marvel.

Her aide, Susan Chin, was also always there for me as a reader and came to my rescue innumerable times. I owe these two women an incalculable debt.

Robert and Dorothy Avery, my dear friends and early readers, filled me with encouragement.

At the final publishing stage, my editor, Marianne Paul, was of enormous help, pinpointing weaknesses and offering constructive ideas that enabled me to clarify my own thoughts and enrich the book. Roger Cooper has been a beacon; he paved the way with the tremendous team at Publishers Group West.

On a more somber note, Byron Preiss, the publisher, was killed in a tragic accident. As an observant Jew, the subject matter—my defense of Judaism against prejudice and anti-Semitism—was an elemental part of his life.

Finally, the reader may wonder why I changed some of the street names in Beverly Hills and locales on the Central Coast. The reason for this was prudent self-preservation. The principal activity in this environment is not gym attendance, any sport, plastic surgery, or weight loss, but frivolous litigation. I did not want to find myself at the wrong end of the street.

"The doer is always conscienceless; no one has a conscience except the outsider."

—GOETHE

THE WINTERHAVEN SOLUTION

BETH ASHER

ibooks

DISTRIBUTED BY PUBLISHERS GROUP WEST

A Publication of ibooks, inc.

Distributed by:
Publishers Group West
1700 Fourth Street, Berkeley, CA 94710
www.pgw.com

ibooks, inc.
24 West 25th Street
New York, NY 10010

ISBN 1-59687-154-7
First ibooks, inc. printing December 2005
10 9 8 7 6 5 4 3 2 1

Printed in the U.S.A.

PART I
VIENNA PRELUDE

Lust always died first in the blend of Rebecca's affairs, which had a furtive speed that never developed into passion or loitered around for love. At the Café Sperl, she swayed past the chess corner where a group of studious men, leaning over the boards, agonized over the time on their clocks before making a move.

She recognized a familiar face: the professor, the idol of the philosophy faculty. The mere sight of his long face launched a spiteful hangover. There had been little animal and less desire in him than in her previous hounds. His queen was fatally lost and he had no move.

Pressing on to the ladies room, Rebecca splashed cold water everywhere, and wiped off her smeared make-up with some tissues. Last night, she had played a concert in Graz, caught the train back to Vienna, met her friends at the U4 disco, and danced until closing.

She turned away from her reflection and thought she looked like a frowsy tart with her brazen breasts, the thicket of copper hair tangled down. On stage she had appeared angelic, younger than twenty-two, her lustrous red curls wound in a French twist. She had played supremely well—Scriabin, Granados, and Beethoven—a demonstration of the range of her repertoire and exquisite technique.

She had a voluptuous figure, not toned à la California. Her generous size and imposing height were in proportion—certainly for Vienna. Buxom adolescent women had a tendency to slouch, but with her grandmother in command, the rigors of posture and the carriage of the head—always tilted up—produced a match to Rebecca's pride. Her nose had a patrician, aquiline character, and her eyebrows were structured for the drama she always generated. She carried herself with the poise of a performer, and her sea-gray eyes, flecked with green, had a spicy candor.

In the hope of reviving herself, she would drink a triple espresso. On the way back to her friends' table, she stopped again at the chess corner. Idly staring at the café's stained-glass windows, the Rococo adornments, cherubs implanted in the ceiling, she rested her arm on a wrought-iron filigree railing. The Sperl was one of Vienna's coffee-house treasures, but despite the high-varnished walls, patches had become gummy, stained umber by a century of cigar and cigarette smoke. The café's clock hung so high that she had to raise her head up to see that it was 9:45 A.M.

At home, her grandmother and Herta, the household commandant, would be alarmed and argumentative about her staying out all night after playing a concert. As the breadwinner, Rebecca's throne and diva status were still shaky, and she expected another warning about the dangers of single women out alone.

"Move the queen or resign," she said impatiently to the professor's back.

The men watching the game scowled at her. He, however, turned and smirked, highlighting his excellent bone structure. This morning though, the Greek god's face was as bloated as a beer mug; he needed a shave and his teeth brushed. What could have possibly drawn her to him? Her impulse to conquer was nothing more than the illegitimate child of a short-term infatuation.

"Ah, Rebecca. Chess master as well as piano virtuoso."

Her last and final intimacy with a man old enough to be her father had ended brusquely. He had climaxed, then weary as a soldier in a trench, had snapped: "Well, I haven't got all night. I have an eight o'clock lecture."

In a feigned sign of atonement, he nodded to his opponent and tipped over his king. He rose and examined her with the pleasure of a connoisseur of fine antiques.

"I know you're addicted to champagne and I've got a gorgeous '90 Grande Dame. Would you like to restart *our* game—without a clock?"

"Think what the students will be missing. Your wisdom and wit. Hurry now, you'll be late for your eight o'clock."

"They're only on Thursdays," he said languidly, stretching his arms and cracking his shoulders and the crick in his neck.

"I'm flying to Los Angeles later today for my sister's wedding. Even if I wasn't, I'd suggest you find somebody else to screw. You get an A in philosophy and hypocrisy. In bed, an F. At that rate, the dean might call your parents in for a conference—if they're still alive. *Auf Wiedersehn.*"

She returned to the throng of musicians she'd been out with; some were dozing, others noshing, a few sober enough to be arguing about Beethoven's comment at the end of a composition.

"*'Muss es sein.'* "

"Yes, it must be so." Rebecca snatched a roll from the platter filled with smoked goose breast. "I've got to dash home before my grandmother calls the police and reports me missing," she said, starved and gobbling it, while the others sulked over coffee. She'd started smoking again and couldn't make up her mind whether or not to retrieve the pack she'd impulsively bought. With the prospect of a scene at home, she decided to take them along to settle her nerves and scorch her lungs for one more day.

"No salvation for hangovers," one of them remarked while Rebecca counted out a hundred new Euros.

"That's way too much, Becky."

"My treat."

"Safe trip...love to Miriam...."

"Ciao."

Kisses and good wishes accompanied her. She slung her clothes bag over her shoulder and picked up her make-up case, both primeval Louis Vuittons, as raddled with cracks as museum crocodiles. Chewing on her roll, she marched past the friendly waiters who had served her and her grandmother since the invention of coffee and she'd been a plump child with a lifelong investment in whipped cream.

The maître d' said, "Thank you for the tickets, Becky. I could afford to pay. But the Philharmoniker sold out for your debut."

Sold out. The phrase made her giddy. "Don't be silly. It was the least I could do." She stuffed her hair into a red wool beret, then slipped on her fine silk thermal gloves and over them, fur-lined leather ones.

It had started to snow angrily, and she caught a taxi and gave her address. As they drove through the heart of Vienna, the city itself resembled an elderly courtesan, deserted by everyone who had slept with her. She still had a wardrobe of baroque buildings on the Ring-strasse, but they were too grand and unfashionable for an old woman trying to make a comeback. Vienna was a rump, vagabond capital that had simmered too long in sour old wine. But Rebecca loved it. The music composed here still captivated audiences—as she expected to in a month—and would never die. It transcended its shoddy, corrupt history and its toxic affairs.

In Rebecca's apartment on the top floor of the house, two old women were sweating, even though the temperature never climbed above fifty degrees. In any event, the central heating had long ago suffered a paralytic stroke. Layered in thick sweaters, they flung them off and studied the problem. They took turns, first coaxing, and then struggling to remove a key from the safe. The drawers inside reeked of old cigars and rotting paper.

"I told you to destroy it," Herta carped at Rebecca's grandmother. The Benjamins's lifetime retainer was robust, domineering, a remnant of a feudal household, who had evolved into an indispensable family member and ruled the insolvent duchy.

"It's too late," Lilli replied, forlorn.

"I'll *tear* it up."

"No, no, Herta. I want to keep it...."

"Why?"

Lilli thought about it, as if considering an interpretation of music played by one of her students at the university.

"Damn-damn-damn," Lilli said. Her voice still retained an echo of youth, but her eyes were distant and bulged through thick bifocals. "It proves my innocence!"

With consternation, Herta's wide jaw flexed like a weightlifter's bicep. "Lilli, *you* were innocent."

Lilli Benjamin was a strong-willed, fragile woman whose austere manner concealed the tenderness within her. Once she'd been beautiful, but now her stooped posture—an occupational liability from years of playing the piano—failed to respond to exercise or a back brace.

The women halted before their beast: a matte, dark-green, chipped, Wilhemeinan-style safe. The dull brass plaque stated: MANUFAC-TURED BY H.F. PELTZ, 1895, DÜSSELDORF. It had been bought by Lilli's father because it contained a cigar cabinet. The key that Lilli had located opened the safe, but now it was jammed inside the lock.

Lilli dropped down on the messy sofa strewn with Rebecca's travel clothes. The folding and packing assignment the women had undertaken for her trip had come to a standstill. Lilli's vintage Mödler suitcase, used for heavyweight expeditions, lay haphazardly on its side, like a drunk in alley.

Herta paced the room with disgust. Miriam, Rebecca's elder sister, had always maintained a tactful order to avoid clashing with Rebecca. Since childhood, one had dropped clothes, the other collecting them without complaint. After Miriam had left for Los Angeles to be married, the apartment had become a slum, reflecting Rebecca's moods and tour events.

"Where is Becky?" Herta demanded, pointing a finger at an invisible criminal. "It's ten-thirty already."

"Let's have some fresh air."

As though about to negotiate a minefield, Lilli straightened up, took her companion's arm, and they guardedly found a path over coiled jeans and sweaters. Lilli pointed to the street below. Sleet gashed the pavement and roofs of houses; cars skidded and a troupe of motorbikes, noisily playing rap, spun out, adding a garish change to the murky atmosphere of Vienna in winter.

"The tour buses better not park in our driveway!" Herta spat. "Why is there a crowd—with police?"

Berggasse 19, Freud's consulting rooms across the street, had become a worldwide tourist stop for visiting shrinkniks and analysts seeking some useless crumb of inspiration from a visit to the room upstairs containing their master's couch. The museum shop did a flourishing trade in his books that would remain unread.

"Look at the weather, Herta—that's why Becky isn't home yet."

With snow ploughs grinding along the road over salt-cleared patches, Rebecca's taxi slewed over the ice at the entry of the Berggasse. She decided to get out and walk. It would be safer and she needed to clear her head. As she cautiously walked in her high snow boots along the Danube canal embankment, churning icebreakers blew their horns before bursting through narrow crooks, thrashing and shattering the blackened floes that had built up.

She looked up and realized that the snow had turned black and she attributed it to the centuries of pollution that had been ignored. For all its storied beauty, the Danube was a dump. When the winds came in early spring, the stench of decaying sludge on the banks saturated the air. She covered her mouth with her tartan scarf.

She took a short detour to d'Landsknecht, the friendly neighborhood *beisl* where the locals gathered for an early glass, greeted a few, then left with a steaming container of mocha which the owner topped off with a dash of cognac.

Heading down the hill of the Berggasse, she pulled up short amid a swarming crowd of angry American tourists. Swastikas had been spray-painted on the front door of the Freud museum. Above the lintels, a huge photograph had been pasted like a billboard advertisement of Hitler saluting SS troops in an open car; Himmler stood below him smiling smugly.

Sickened by the sight, Rebecca was, nonetheless, not surprised. Austria had become a fugitive state when it had embraced the Freedom Party. These powerful neo-Nazis were not shy about their preferences, and streams of them had paraded in their old SS uniforms in the city center to celebrate the millennium a month ago.

The visitors were protesting to a pair of bored policemen taking a token report.

"It's a good thing Freud got out while he still could," an indignant man was saying to the crowd.

The police were explaining to the staff and tour guide that they were not equipped with ladders.

Revived by the cold and brandied coffee, Rebecca angrily thrust herself in the middle.

"Telefonieren der Feueweh weiblich!" she demanded.

The officers ignored her.

"Yes," a woman tourist agreed, "get them."

"There is no fire," the officer said, looking fiercely at Rebecca.

Rebecca turned to the group, then with contempt at the officers. "I'll call them!"

"Fraulein...Benjamin, we know you...and where you live. It is a criminal offense to report a false incident to them."

"Punishable by a prison sentence," the other continued.

"You people are a disgrace. Get out of here!"

The crowd, encouraged by her mettle, jeered at the police, the pair taking to their car. Rebecca packed a snowball and flung it at the rear window. The tourists followed her example, pelting the car, which sped away.

Caving into exhaustion, Rebecca sadly said: "We're not all like them."

It was a miracle that her grandmother and Herta had escaped the ravages of the annexation with Germany. Fellow musicians had hid the two women in Salzburg. At the end of World War II, they had returned to Vienna and reclaimed the family property.

Rebecca crossed the street to the Benjamin house at Berggasse X. It was set back and had been built in 1900 in the Gothic revival style. Its once-creamy brick had turned a sooty dun color and was high-lighted with crazy-quilt reliefs of pigeon droppings that had hardened, forming intricate patterns.

Once inside, Rebecca shouted in the long entry corridor: "I'm home!"

She sat on the bench, eased off her wet boots and set her bag down. Her long wool socks were dry and she crouched low, passing the reception and music rooms. The house drafts were individual; they formed a cataract at the staircase. Trousers ballooned and skirts flew up to a lady's face, like drugged flashers at a soccer match.

She checked for the elderly women in the enormous ancient kitchen where the Aga stove kept the climate temperate. On a platter, a morgue of uncooked, pasty liver dumplings, salted marrow bones tied with string, had been stationed on the butcher-block. Herta's long-simmering beefy cabbage borscht bubbled with coils of fat globs. Rebecca skimmed it and wondered where the terrible queen of soups could be.

"God is good," she murmured, climbing upstairs to the apartment she now had to herself after sharing it with her Miriam for a lifetime. "Los Angeles tomorrow!" she trumpeted.

The sight of Lilli and Herta with their backs to her, before the open safe, puzzled her.

"Hello. I didn't want to scare you."

They both turned and blocked the safe under the eaves. After years of ignoring this useless object—apart from keeping a set of classics on top of it—Rebecca finally recognized its reality.

"I'm back with money....Two thousand euros!"

"Darling, we were so worried about you with this weather," Lilli said, going to her and kissing her ruddy cheeks. "You're so cold."

"I walked part of the way. The taxi couldn't make it."

"Couldn't you've called?—Your cell break down again?" Herta scolded.

"Is it possible for you ever to talk to me in a civil manner? I'm a grown woman, dammit, Herta. And keep your hands out of my personal things."

On defiant retreat, the commandant said, "I only came up to pack for you." This selfless rhapsody of guilt ladling was an unending theme. "I ironed your silk blouses and wanted to fold them properly.

"And I skimmed the fat off your soup, and turned the fire down, so we're even."

Shaking out her beret and blowing the mass of hair out of her eyes, Rebecca eventually located in her tote the check that she had received for her piano recital. She handed it to her grandmother. In turn, Lilli presented it to Herta, paymaster and magical auditor of the household accounts. Herta still blocked the safe.

"*Oma,* since you weren't with me in Graz last night I couldn't argue. I was paid in euros—not schillings—because of the currency change. How much is two thousand euros—in dollars?"

Quick as a fox, Herta said, "About seventeen hundred dollars."

Rebecca approached Herta. "Do I get a smile from you?"

She hugged Rebecca. "*Mameleh,* we worry about you."

Rebecca nodded. "I know. It's a mess across the street. The American tourists were raising hell."

"We saw the police...and..." Herta's words trailed off.

Rebecca related how the neo-Nazis had defaced the building. The women went to the window to observe the proceedings. A group of men had formed a human pyramid and two of them were aloft, tearing down Hitler's poster.

"Americans—bless them," Lilli said.

"They saved us," Herta agreed.

"I'll see plenty of them in Los Angeles tomorrow!" Rebecca exclaimed with exuberance. She followed the women back to the safe. "Now what's going on with that old slab of metal? Why's it open?"

Lilli's voice quavered. "When we came up to start your packing, I remembered my father used to keep annotated scores and first-night programs in here."

Herta shook the key. "We thought we'd have a look. Now we can't get the key out."

"Let me," Rebecca said.

She slipped off her woolen tweed pants and her sweaters. "Anything in there?" Rebecca asked, detached. One of her failings was the absence of curiosity, especially as it concerned other people's affairs. She lived by a simple motto: *Spare me your secrets....* Her dedication to succeed as a great pianist impeded more personal interests. She put on an old robe and went to the safe.

She jiggled and fiddled with the stubborn skeleton key.

"Herta, would you bring up some butter...and see if we have any straws."

"All right," the old woman said, mystified, abandoning her mulish ways.

While waiting, she and Lilli discussed her future and Miriam's. It all had to do with talent, and the natural indulgence tendered to genius, no mistake about that. Miriam had settled for second or third chair as a cellist; Rebecca, the pianist, had survived her prodigy stage with only a few minor breakdowns, and now tramped through the provincial cities of Europe as a guest soloist.

On March 21, Rebecca would have her official debut with the Vienna Philharmoniker. If it went well, there would be no more night trains to and from cities like Regensburg, Trento, and Graz, all crammed with earnest musicians who weren't up to her standards. The conductors she encountered were either nitpicking Asians or ancient maestros who might have been cloned from Einstein's old photos. The horde of them dedicated, yes, but first-class, no. After Vienna and conquest, she would be earning enough money to support the two old women without skimping.

Herta returned with a dish of butter and some thin bar straws. As though observing a magician or a scientific experiment, they gawped as Rebecca slid a buttered straw into the lock.

"I need a Q-Tip—In my make-up case."

She soothed the lock with the buttered Q-Tip and finessed the key out, locked the safe, and reopened it. With a smile, she pulled it out. The women beamed with childlike delight. Herta clapped.

"Well, how did you learn this?" Lilli asked.

"A janitor taught me. When you sent me to Oberlin for a year, I used to practice all night and my professor locked the keyboard. The janitor on the graveyard shift gave me a key that didn't quite fit. He took out one of those pats of butter they serve in restaurants—*et voilà*."

"Wonderful, Becky." Lilli picked up a batch of envelopes and stuffed them into the humidor drawers, then locked the safe. Shaking her head as she continued to test the lock, she said, "House deed, insurance policies in case the Nazis take over again...."

Rebecca laughed. "I don't care if they're love letters from Goethe or whoever, Oma...."

"We'll keep the cash and checks in there now," Herta said, turning to practical matters.

As the three women packed, they chatted affably about her trip to Miriam's wedding. Rebecca tossed in some jeans, which Herta refolded.

"Can we stop for a minute?" She waved them to the cleared section of the sofa. "Miriam sent me a First Class ticket."

"How in God's name do people pay six and a half thousand dollars for an airplane ticket?" Herta bleated.

"Miriam's future in-laws insisted. The Leopold family is wealthy. Now, *please*, let me go on. I'd like to cash in my ticket, change my reservation to coach, and the three of us can go to Los Angeles for Miriam's wedding."

"Out of the question," Lilli snapped. "We can't afford it."

"Correct, Lilli." Herta's pig-headed logic always strangled Rebecca. "Becky, your check from last night will just cover our expenses for February. We don't travel well," Herta informed her. "And I've never been a guest anywhere."

The absence of invitations did not surprise Rebecca. Who would have Herta? Rebecca's hangover brought with it a grumpy persistence.

"Miriam pleaded with *me*. And now *I'm* begging you to go with me!"

Lilli demurred. "My circulation is a problem."

"Lilli could develop blood clots in her legs from the flight!" Herta stated. "And then what...some emergency ward in Los Angeles with all the doctors treating children who've been shot?"

Rebecca ignored Herta. "Not that again, Lilli. Your circulation doesn't affect your teaching or correcting me when I get loose."

"Becky, you're an angel, and generous to a fault."

"Really? Not many people would agree with you, Grandma."

Lilli cradled Rebecca's head in her arms as she had since she could remember. The scent of her lavender hand cream washed over Rebecca and choked the odor of damp clothes, the fumes of old meals lodging in the elderly velvet drapes.

"We'd have to stay at a five-star hotel and *pay* for some dinners—do things properly," Lilli said as though admonishing a student's technique.

"It would be hard, Becky," Herta added, her tone soft and beseeching. "Lilli and I raised you and Miriam. Nothing would give us more pleasure than to be there for the wedding. But the Benjamin house has always had pride."

"And a sense of style," Lilli declared. "No matter what our circumstances, we've had a tone...the façade of elegance."

Rebecca remained troubled by Lilli's implausible excuse for remaining in Vienna. Miriam had assured her that she could stay with the Leopolds. Lilli was frightened by something and it wasn't Los Angeles or the United States.

With the emergence of a boozy sweat as a counterpoint to the headache from hell, Rebecca was anxious for a bath, always producing a Hitchcock film's moment of suspense. Would there be enough hot water? Would the ravens from St. Petersburg making their annual pilgrimage to the rotting mansion peck through the roof and join her indoors—as a pair had last week?

Rebecca decided to take her chances. The bliss of water, so hot it screamed, blotted the tarnished bathroom mirrors and reassured her that life would go on in some fashion.

The snowstorm in Europe had blanketed Rebecca's connection from Frankfurt. After almost a day and a half in transit, she was met by a wan but cheerful man at 3 A.M. Los Angeles time. He held a placard with her name printed in bold letter.

"I'm sorry to have been so late. Thank you for coming."

"It's absolutely fine, Ms. Benjamin. I'm used to it. Your sister apologized for not being here. My name is Robert." The chauffeur waved to another man, bulky and officious, with an earplug and wire peering up from his neck, also in a dark suit and tie. He guided the skycap and his trolley outside to the curb. "That's Frank with your bags."

Rebecca had never been to Los Angeles. Her three-year stay in the United States had taken her with Miriam to music schools at Oberlin in Ohio and Juilliard in New York. The sisters, scrimping on their scholarship funds, had had no money to travel. During holidays, they'd remained at school practicing.

Heaven might be filled with multicolored clouds, wisdom, gracious feelings, and spiritual love, but for Rebecca, paradise on earth, at this moment, resided in the gleaming Rolls Royce waiting at the curb in the middle of the night. The leathery scent of the backseat invoked a new respect for the virtues of wealth. Taking the Leopold family to dinner last summer had been a worthwhile investment. Her baggage aboard, money for a tip saved, she smiled in gratitude at the two men in the front seat.

"My name is Frank," the second man said, turning around, "and I'm Mr. Leopold's head of home security." He smiled formally at Rebecca as the Rolls purred into the night. "There's a liquor cabinet—soft drinks, nuts...yes, and cheese in the bar—so please help yourself."

"I'm very fond of cheese. Frank, thank you for handling my luggage and meeting me. Don't mind me babbling on. I'm so...so tired....But why do I need security?"

"Welcome to Los Angeles, Ms. Benjamin."

"Thank you. Please call me Rebecca," she said, opening a can of beer. "Don't waste your time being politically correct with me."

PART II
REBECCA

1

A virulent, hawking wind, worthy of the Beaufort Scale, whined and clawed through the gravesites and monuments of the Mount Jacob Cemetery in Staten Island, muffling the cries and keening of a crowd of mourners who had come to bury a loved one. As an act of respect for their loss, the relatives and friends, many of them flu-and cold-ridden, had braved the abrasive wet snow and tundra-like conditions that had descended on the river borough. Their cars, with headlights on, had followed the hearse slewing along the serpentine curves of Richmond Avenue to reach this resting place for the decedent.

The rabbi at the gravesite abridged his speech and ended with the ultimate tribute that could be said of a Jew.

"He was a *mensch*," the rabbi intoned. "And on this day, December ninth, Nineteen Ninety-Nine, God will receive and embrace Hyman Kugler because he was a noble man, honorable in business, loyal to friends, a devoted father, and a husband who revered his beloved Ethel. He was a faithful observer who kept the *Shabbes* and supported our synagogue—not just with money—but also with his time and the conviction of his enduring faith. Yes, a *mensch*!" the rabbi croaked, for he was losing his voice and wanted to terminate his battle with the elements, get into the family's heated limo, down a scotch in the backseat, and hurry back to the *Shivah*, a wake of dynastic magnitude.

"They ever going to leave?" asked a woman standing nearby, scrutinizing these maddening rites. She stamped her boots on the frozen ground in fury and for circulation.

"Not until someone thinks they're having a stroke and needs a doctor," her companion replied, his eyes concealed by dark glasses.

"Jews for you," she said, nudging the man. The couple stood beside a fresh gravesite, the dirt heaped in a pile, awaiting a new client. Their ages were impossible to estimate. The man was tall, had a coarse, black beard, and was dressed in a long coat, scarf, a beaver homburg and fur-lined gloves. He carried a stout, white cane with a protruding tip for the blind. The big woman, enjoining her arm in his, wore a voluminous full-sheared beaver, a muff, and a windbreaker to cover her *shaytl*, the wig worn by Orthodox Jewish married women to avoid attracting other men. But this devout woman, given the circumstances, went a step further and had covered her face with a black veil.

When the pine box was finally lowered—as a finale in keeping with tradition—the mourners dropped a piece of loamy gravel onto the casket that the gravediggers had chopped up like confetti for this purpose.

The couple at the gravesite listened to sneezes, rasping, and phlegmy coughs, and watched the scowling glares of the as-yet-uninfected group of mourners rushing through aisles of graves to their cars below. They only blew kisses, anticipating contagion, God forbid.

At three o'clock, Label Friedman, a recently ordained rabbi and Yeshiva graduate, made his appearance. Since vowing to perform a missionary role as part of his rabbinical commitment, he gave himself wholeheartedly to these itinerant duties. Christian ministers and Mormons always traveled far afield, so why, he reasoned, shouldn't he? He had taken the subway from Borough Park to the cemetery to offer solace to the lonely and grief-stricken.

God was everywhere and His surrogates, without consideration of recompense or praise, ought to serve these righteous causes. Still, if a mourner cared to make a small donation, Label would accept it and add it to the fund for other needy young men. Theirs was a holy calling, but, like cars, required gas in the tank. If no money were offered, Label would still pray with the bereaved. He frequently encountered solitary people: a wife, a husband, a child whose grief over the loss of a parent could not be assuaged in the temple or within the midst of family circles.

In the diffuse light, some distance away, he thought he could make out the hazy outlines of an isolated couple. With daylight eclipsing, like the sudden downward jerk of a window shade, the two human figures had become silhouetted in a ballet of shadows. Label Friedman dutifully approached them. They had already spied him. Virgil Hoyt and Noreen Porter had been waiting for him to arrive and tarried after Hyman had been put to rest.

Over the hillock of dirt, Virgil flicked his cane like a banderilla. "Get the waterworks going, Noreen," he murmured to his companion.

"You want hip-hop or rap?"

"Come on, cut it out."

On cue, Noreen, howling with woe, shook as her body canted over the empty gravesite. Desolation had found its purest voice.

Label heard her and now saw the couple more clearly in the gloaming. Anxious to serve them, he advanced, his galoshes slithering over the frozen ground like a seal's flippers.

"Oh, my poor, dear people," he chanted in a sweet, consoling voice. "It's so cold, you shouldn't still be out. Come, I'll say the *Kaddish* and you can go home...." He slipped his hand inside his overcoat and wiggled out his *tallis*, then kissed the silken threads of the prayer shawl.

"What are your names?"

"Virgil Hoyt."

The woman abruptly stopped crying. "Noreen Porter."

"I...yes, you're...Miss Porter," he replied, somewhat puzzled.

The names didn't sound Jewish to Label's ear. But nowadays, who knew? The cemetery's lamplights flickered on, but were blurred by dense virgas of snow.

"I thought...assumed...forgive me...you're not...?" Label had been prone to stammering all of his life and been mocked by his school-mates.

The teams of gravediggers had made their final pass and were driving their chugging, coupled, trolley carts. The embalmed echoes of Spanish complaints and curses about the weather blended in with sardonic bodega laughter. These disembodied sounds layered the deserted cemetery. Virgil waited until the last straggling cart entered the garage below and the electric door had closed.

Label patiently lingered for the mourners to explain their situation.

Virgil removed his dark glasses and his gelid, virtually colorless irises sent shockwaves through the young rabbi. They were such a hue of ashen gray that Label trembled. This man Virgil with the cane was not blind at all. Still startled, Label regained the discipline of his profession.

"And the name of the loved one?" he asked, suddenly wanting to run. The woman had sandwiched him against Virgil. He tried to squirm away. Virgil coughed, raising phlegm, and spat it. The spittle oozed over Label's face, the droplets like lice in his thin, patchy beard.

"Adolf Hitler!"

The contrived, unimaginable event, happening in real time, caused the young rabbi's heart to flutter and pulsate irregularly. His knees sagged forward in a prelude to fainting. Had he just heard correctly? But thinking was no longer an option.

Virgil struck Label with his right hand, encased in a glove loaded with spiked, forged steel knuckles. This spattered the bone of Label's nose and entered the cranium so violently that he dropped like a bull in a corrida's afternoon of death.

"I think he might be gone," Virgil said. "Shit!"

"No, he's just in shock," Noreen replied expertly. "...Virgil, we have to move! They're closing the gates, like a lockdown."

"I have a way out and I'm going to do this my way."

"What about cops?" Noreen asked.

"They're cooping in their cars, scarfing hero sandwiches and getting blow-jobs from crack whores. They don't give a rat's ass about these fucking kikes. Staten Island is one big mafia weather front in our favor. Get going with your emergency kit, nurse."

Noreen had once been a professional institutional nurse at sanctuaries for rich junkies, until various incidents had thinned her résumé to anorexia. She popped an amyl nitrate and force-fed it into Label's nostrils. His body jerked spasmodically as though on the verge of a grand mal seizure.

Virgil dug, clearing the lightly covered prep hole for someone's funeral tomorrow.

"Hit his knee reflex," Virgil ordered her.

Noreen's wig drooped over her eye. "What are you doing?"

"I want him alive and kicking."

"Why? I...don't understand."

"They have destroyed the world, *our* world," Virgil said, grunting, shoveling, clearing the space.

Something within Label Friedman's animal code of survival gave rise to recognition. His rattle became plainsong, an elemental fugue struggling to be heard. Through shattered teeth, choking and gagging on his own blood, Label resisted the shock of the attack. He turned his face to Noreen's with a deer's yelp.

She held up the Nazi handkerchief she had brought, with its gold eagle, its red and black swastika. She stuffed it in his mouth and handcuffed him.

Virgil hurtled him down into the hole in the earth.

Label's consciousness was not wired for this, or his worldly preparation, his prayers...any words of comfort.

Nothing.

He heard thrashing sounds of gravel shoveled over him. The pain from the blow drifted into a fleeting memory. He suffered, second by second, until the theory of what was a minute vanished. Time ceased.

He was being buried alive.

He could not scream. In a berserk, stuttering reflex, Label butted his head against the earth, which had hardened into frozen mud. Only a single word blazed like a neon sign through the splinters of his consciousness: *barschert*, fated.

Dirt, dirt, dirt, *schmutz*, he absentmindedly thought, *trayfe*, unholy. He prolonged the futile contest until his breathing, the suffocation, lulled him into the half-sleep of oblivion.

He listened in the cold earth, shovelful by shovelful, to his own death.

The activity had taken fifteen minutes.

Virgil, a time freak, was pleased by his calculations. He smoothed the top of the mound with a trowel. Noreen pulled out a large white bath sheet from her backpack. With the natural talent of a freehand artist, she spray-painted a swastika on it, using both red and black. It might have been like priming iodine on one of her previous surgical patients. Just in case the snow covered the spray paint, she planted a small Nazi flag on the grave, which Virgil stamped in solidly with his spiked glove.

Weaving down the hill to the locked gates of Mount Jacob, its Stars of David shivering under ice shingles, Virgil felt a spiritual elevation. He felt united with the leadership's goal of Heroic Realism: fighting for their cause against all odds, even though some thought it a lost one.

"Wait'll these spicks do their inventory tomorrow. 'I dig, you dig...¿*donde está el hoyo?*'" Virgil observed.

Noreen, a recent convert, was hit by a case of nervous giggles.

"How do you know all this?"

"Puerto Ricans are smart and do piece work, matching every hole they dig to a master chart that some office donkey puts on the computer."

"The sharpest are the Cubans. I worked with some of their doctors when I was on the move, running. I lasted six months in Miami before some bitch turned me in. They added an extra year in California for unlawful flight."

"It'll never happen to you again. You're under my wing, Noreen."

"I'm mad about you, Virgil."

Approaching the gate, Virgil once again assumed the blind man role; covered in snow, he staggered. His bereft female guide let out a scream of panic.

The gatekeeper opened the window a crack, nodding to the late, lost pair. He hit a switch to let them out and tilted back his bottle of Sam Adams, keeping one eye on the TV screen. They had the nerve to interrupt a Rangers game at the moment the Mighty Ducks were out in force, brawling a call against them for high-sticking.

"Damn," Virgil said, "I wanted to ask him the score."

"My wonderful sports junkie."

"And don't forget I'm the 'Grand Theft Auto' champ," he said with pride. He had mastered every war game marketed on Nintendo and PlayStation. "I can't get a money game at Winterhaven."

Noreen had trouble hearing. "Huh...what?"

The booming, automatic recording of the cemetery's welcome-departure spieled out a chorus of "Shaloms" with a chaser of incoherent Hebrew babbling. The racket trailed them to their van. Virgil took off his frosted glasses, opened the door, and immediately switched on the ignition.

Noreen climbed into the passenger seat. They quickly removed their facial disguises, and she clambered into the back, opened a make-up trunk for her wig and windbreaker, his beard, hat, and spiked gloves. She ran a comb through her short blonde hair, wiggled into a long, sheep-lined suede coat, and laid out his change of clothes. Virgil flicked the heater switch. He turned his head to watch Noreen, marveling at her meticulousness under such pressure.

She was a woman of palatial proportions, beef to the ankle, her frame bridled with large shoulders and steep breasts. Her blonde hair, boyishly short with no silly bangs, skin a leathery outdoor color, indigo blue eyes, arched eyebrows, devoid of innocence, gave her the imposing stature of a football coach. Her nose was substantial. A slight puttiness at the bridge magnified her "I take no shit" pugnacity.

But for Virgil the large, kissable, sensuous lips inspired him with thoughts of bedding the human equivalent of a lioness. Her growling laugh was a mating call. She was Thirty-five, give or take, four years older than him.

It had been nine months of unparalleled ardor with so much yet to discover about each other, their pasts. *Everything in its moment,*

Virgil thought. Soon he would confide in her about his successes and disasters, his years at Cal State Sacramento (SAC), the sister institution of Folsom...his background in cemeteries and allied endeavors.

For Noreen's part, she had not yet disclosed how her brief career as a surgical nurse had run aground when she had been charged with counting the instruments after an operation. In her haste to make a date with a horny resident, she had forgotten to remove a lap sponge from the patient's liver. The dead man's family and lawyers didn't forget and had traced it to her. She had been dismissed without references, a death sentence in her profession. In the fullness of time this piece of luck had brought her to the green pastures of mental health.

Before pulling out, Virgil kissed her, and her eyes became somnolent under his spell.

"Not fair to get me hot here," she moaned.

"That was just pure devotion, like kissing an Iron Cross."

"Virgil, you knock me out."

"Welcome to courtship, Nurse Noreen."

"Oh, God, I love you." She licked her lips. "Can I have pizza and something very sweet?"

"You bet." He looked at her voraciously. "And when I get you back to the motel, you're going to be my pie."

"I can't wait." She paused and stroked his shaved head. "I was scared. But I loved it," she admitted.

"You'll get used to it. We have a lot to teach each other."

"You seem to know a lot about cemeteries, Virgil."

"I'll tell you about it one day."

"This isn't the first time you—"

"...Let's change the subject."

The action that Virgil had executed at the cemetery had had its genesis at Winterhaven, the neo-Nazi commune nestled in central California where he and Noreen lived. Winterhaven had been conceived and created by Magnus Von Winter, who presided over its denizens. This elderly gentleman had been a protégé of Hitler's, and had escaped when the Allies had overrun Germany.

The Directive, however, had come from Magnus's son Bruno, a shadowy figure, who seldom appeared at the settlement. Yet the mere mention of his name inspired fear, even among the hardcore veterans like Virgil.

BETH ASHER

Bruno had ordered a national pre-millennium Blitzkrieg in selected American cities. It was to be a series of daring, provocative guerilla attacks. The most successful man would be promoted to the inner circle of SS apostles, and competition for this position was worth any risk. Virgil was determined that this day, Thursday, December 9, 1999, would go down in Winterhaven history.

Pulling into Richmond Road, snarled with shaky drivers on black ice, Virgil waited for the light to change. He looked back at Mt. Jacob and wistfully imagined he had been alive during the glory days of Dachau, leading a commando *Einsatzgruppen* in the great struggle of the Third Reich. Despite the success of today's operation, he choked back his emotions as he did whenever he thought of Hitler's gallant martyrdom. His sacrifice would never be forgotten by the men of Winterhaven. A rebirth of the pure Nazi culture would sweep away the Jews in the upcoming millennium.

Noreen sensed Virgil's mood swing. "You in the dumper all of a sudden?"

"No, no, I was just having a moment of silent joy."

When he made the light, she waved at the cemetery: "Happy Cha-nukah."

Virgil laughed so hard he almost lost control of the wheel.

2

Rebecca awoke unsettled at nine in the morning of whatever day it might have been, with a foul, jet-lag taste in her mouth and a stiff neck. During the airport ride, through an area called Culver City—what she imagined as Lower Austria—she had unwisely and greedily eaten a hunk of cheese, never a good idea without a radar device to locate her toothbrush. Frank had marched her through the grounds and a house that seemed to be a full resort, with lighted tennis courts and what appeared as a soccer field. She had been placed in a *wing* designated for important guests. Her bags were unpacked, clothes hung by two thoughtful maids who claimed expertise at pressing.

Miriam came into the bedroom carrying a breakfast tray. With a light flip back of her sassy straight-cut, reddish-blond hair and a heartfelt smile, Miriam, more slender and modishly angular than Rebecca, radiated innate warmth. She was the delicate fish course to Rebecca's big-boned roast.

Rebecca reached for a cigarette and was about to light it when Miriam shook her head.

"That's the only forbidden pleasure. You can fall down and drink yourself silly in the house, but the Leopolds don't allow smoking."

"Do they have drug dogs, like at the airport?"

"Sensors," she said with a laugh that brought out the mischievous, lighthearted manner and the life-lighting sparkle in her blue eyes. Rebecca was dazzling, as overwhelming as grand opera; Miriam was the muted, more refined, subtler beauty of the two.

Miriam set down the tray, yanked the covers off Rebecca, and hauled her to her feet. She reached up to her taller sister and smothered her with kisses and muscular squeezes.

"My big baby darling. I've missed you."

"Miriam, I've ached for you."

"You had Lilli and Herta."

"Well, you know how cheerful *they* are. I must brush my teeth."

"Good idea. What were you doing, chewing tobacco?"

"Don't get smart. Where's my make-up bag, toiletries...?"

"Just open the medicine cabinet—everything's there. We'll have coffee on the terrace." Miriam gestured, and Rebecca saw a radiant flash on her finger. "It's a little cool. But we don't mind that."

"Oh, my God—your ring is beautiful. I love solitaires."

"Three carats from Harry Winston. Scott wanted me to get a bigger one. I think the size is fine." She held it up and Rebecca nodded. "I don't like drawing attention to myself. Now, move."

Rebecca did her contralto gargling ritual, brushed her hair, spied a Jacuzzi tub with enough room for a quartet; a variety of L'Occitane gels and mousses—not the squinty hotel sizes—were stationed on a shelf, along with back brushes and loofahs still wrapped.

Accustomed to waiting on her younger sister without a grumble, Miriam ferreted through the closet searching her travel wardrobe. Amid gowns, Miriam dug up a coarse red plaid robe.

"Rebecca, are you moving here? There's enough room." She helped Rebecca on with the robe. "Yours?"

"Must be the professor's."

"Did he pack it for you?"

"Actually I think I stole it. It's become an unconscious farewell gesture of mine. Taking something from lovers I've dumped, before they know it's over."

Miriam was delighted by the news. "So the philosopher disappeared. No one could have a conversation with him without him telling you that you didn't mean what you were actually saying."

"It only took me a year to find out," Rebecca said, not tortured by the admission. "He'll find one of his student whores and deconstruct her mother or closest friend. He's addicted to *Chinatown*. He'll cook up something perverse for an orgy. Everyone's still sex-crazed in Vienna. It'll never change."

"For the life of me, I don't know what the hell you saw in him?"

"The absence of a threat. That's become my gold standard." She smiled at Miriam. "He always kept damn good wine and I loved his centrally heated bathroom...constant hot water."

Rebecca had little in common with men in her age group and her infrequent sorties with younger men proved to be a waste of time socially and in bed. She preferred older men; far from this being a search for a father figure, droning with a Freudian refrain, her attitude had a basis in logic. She valued experience and knowledge. And older men could be bossed.

"He was a shrub in bed and hardly ever waited for me. Worse yet, he was vain about performance. Aren't they all...? Actually he preferred theory, those ancient German bats we had to study and never understood, especially Nietzsche."

"Scott's not like that."

Rebecca beamed, dissolute in gossip. "That's not a bad reason for getting married."

"I'm crazy about Scott."

"Where is he?"

"Filling in for a cellist friend in Seattle. Three concerts and a chance to be short-listed with the symphony orchestra there. He'll be back this afternoon."

Rebecca opened the French doors. She sucked in the tang of newly cut grass and blinked at an interlacing grassy water ballet with mists playing over the Leopold estate: fountain mechanics and peeved gardeners were holding deep discussions with another squad of men erecting a marquee. She lit a cigarette and offered it to Miriam who sneakily took two rapid puffs. Miriam set down the tray on a wrought-iron table. Rebecca peered out at the expanse of lawn, the garden, a gazebo, a maze, waterfalls, fountains, all stunning but nothing left as nature intended.

"I know you said Scott came from a wealthy family—" Rebecca narrowed her eyes, "but this place looks like the Ritz Carlton."

"Just Jack and Paula Leopold's primary residence." Miriam peered up at the cloudless sky and her expression was part smile, part amazement. "Sometimes the lame and the halt fall into it. You're the one who's beautiful, I'm pretty, and you're the virtuoso performer...."

"And the king's son fell in love with *you*," Rebecca said with amusement.

"It's a miracle."

"Don't be ridiculous, Miriam. Every man was after you since I can remember."

"I was fading, beginning my descent."

"No, not at twenty-six. Maturing maybe. Your figure is fantastic. I'm a boxcar compared to you."

"Thanks, Rebecca," she said, amused by her sister's gifts of exaggeration. "We'll do for Beverly Hills, with all of the emaciated gym crazies."

In the distance, four people in shorts were running along a cinder track.

"Who're they?"

"Jack, Paula, and their trainers. Two cardiovascular miles, rain or shine."

"Barbaric."

"Wait till you see their gym, then you can talk about barbarism."

"A spa?"

"Yes, with a yoga masseuse on call."

"Miriam, tell me about the Leopolds' secondary residences," Rebecca asked with the avidity of a travel agent. "We have two old Jewish women grinding their dental plates and wearing overcoats to bed. After you left, I inherited Lilli's ratty mink coat—"

"That's a thing of the past, which I'll get to later. Jack has a penthouse in New York on Fifth Avenue. You'll stay there when you play Carnegie Hall."

"I'll play there when I'm asked."

"You will be," Miriam assured her. "When we all came to Salzburg to hear you, I flew in their private jet from their villa in Cap Ferrat."

"That's three."

"A house near The Ritz in Paris..." Miriam did a fancy ballet turn and laughed. "Oh, I almost forgot, the beach house in Malibu."

"Does Scott have a brother? I'll even settle for the black-sheep bastard." Dazed by the bounty her sister had secured, she continued, "Why didn't you tell me all this when we were at dinner in Salzburg? You were so vague about everything."

"You came late and sat between Jack and Paula. I couldn't very well give you their financial statement or list their properties. And whenever we talk on the phone, you're dashing off to a concert, or asleep—or not home."

Rebecca sniffed the air as her sister poured recognizable coffee, speckled it with flakes of chocolate and cream, uncovered warm croissants, and opened a jar of Forest Honey.

"Viennese coffee?"

"Julius Mienl ships on the Internet now. I remember how you hated the Greek coffee shops when we were at Juilliard."

They laughed disorderly, the two glories once again sharing guilt and admiration. It was as though they were back at the house in Berggasse, sealed under martial law at 10 P.M. by Herta. When the enforcer was asleep and not roused by a volatile apnea episode, the sisters would slip out to coffeehouses, pick up their dates, and dance to heavy-metal ecstasy.

"The year we spent at Oberlin was even worse. Icy Sundays in Cleveland, movies and diner meatloaf on white bread with canned mushroom gravy."

"The training there was good for me," Miriam said. "And I made some friends. They'll be at the shower tonight."

Rebecca brooded and her lips curled. "They hated me."

"You were fifteen and a little monster." She sighed benevolently. "The real reason of course was that you were a star and beyond all of us."

"Miriam, you're my Shield." Rebecca hunched up her shoulders. "I always wished I was you."

"You had the gift."

"So did you."

"I knew I would never be anything more than a player."

"A lovely one."

This was true and typical of Miriam, who was seldom given to exaggeration. Rebecca envied Miriam her trusting amiability and refusal to accept challenges. Their competition for musical supremacy had ended when Miriam, the cellist, was nine and she, the pianist, five. Performing was a blood sport for Rebecca. On this level, there was no room for mere talent, patience, or apologies. Professors simply cut students dead once they discovered that a gifted apprentice was not to have the chosen destiny.

Rebecca would become the soloist—give the recitals. Miriam would lug her cello on trains and buses, roaming from one chamber music group to another, and play second or third chair in provincial orchestras. For Rebecca, the perfectly tuned Bösendorfer Imperial awaited her onstage. Champagne and flowers afterwards.

As for Scott's skill as cellist, Rebecca decided to say nothing and had written him an effusive letter after she and Lilli had seen and listened to the hours of expertly engineered videotapes he had sent to Vienna. Lilli walked out while he was playing César Franck's "Sonata for cello and piano."

"I'm so happy for you," Rebecca said.

Out of the blue, she laid her head on Miriam's breast and quietly cried. As a child, Miriam had tried to replace their dead parents. She ran her fingers through the snarls of Rebecca's long red hair, soothing her. After a few moments, Rebecca wiped her eyes on the sleeve of the discarded philosopher's robe. She clasped Miriam's hand and kissed it. Once again, Miriam's silent serenity helped her emotionally. She climbed out of the crater of her mood.

"Miriam, I've become so hard—a horror."

"Great talent is never kind."

"Maybe you're right."

Below them, waving his sunglasses and shaking his head from side to side at the smoke curling off the terrace, Frank bowed his head.

"Good morning, ladies."

"Good morning, Frank," Miriam responded.

He headed for an army of men pounding metal pegs into the lawn.

"He's creepy," Rebecca said.

"Frank Salica's not a bad guy. He was a private investigator for movie stars with bad habits. Jack hired him to take over his security."

"He was overprotective when I came in last night." Rebecca's eyes followed him and she heard his abrasive voice bullying the contractor's teams. "Are you getting married at the house, or is just the reception here?"

"Both. Jack calls, the rabbi takes wing. Paula hates hotel food. She's been to enough charity banquets to work for the *Michelin Guide*."

"How do you get along with her?"

"She's been very sweet, maternal, sometimes pushy."

Smug with family pride, Rebecca said, "I'll tell you why...where could her son have met anyone like you, Miriam? Not here?" she jeered. "The rich girls we knew at school were boors, and patronizing. You're unique, a gem."

Miriam had met Scott at a cello competition in Toronto the previous year. She had finished second and he, even with his dazzling eighteenth-century, million-dollar Guarneri cello, had not placed. The wandering minstrels had joined forces with a chamber ensemble and traveled throughout Europe before alighting at the Salzburg Festival to hear Rebecca.

The wedding was scheduled for the following Sunday at a minute past midnight so that it would fall on Valentine's Day. Scott had chosen the date. In sleepy Austria, and the rest of Europe for that matter, Valentine's Day had not yet advanced to the furious commercialism of the United States. Just a matter of time, Rebecca thought.

Miriam's body became unnaturally still, as though tensed over a score to come in at the right moment. She preferred punctuality rather than nursing the mood of whatever she was playing, especially in a chamber quartet. For an orchestra her scrupulous early-bird entries survived in the glide of cellos.

"Rebecca, of all the people I trust, you're first in line. Of all the people I love, you are first in line."

"Yes, Miriam."

Without warning, blades of anger twisting her face, Miriam seized hold of Rebecca's shoulders. "I was depending on you! But you were too fucking busy to do anything for me!"

"What?"

"I *wanted* Lilli and Herta here for my wedding! You said, 'Leave it to me.' And I did. Our parents...the skiing daredevils...have been buried under an avalanche for more than twenty years. I don't remember them and I don't give a shit. I was five, you were a year old."

Seldom chastised, Rebecca lifted the hood of the robe over her face and briefly wallowed in the darkness.

"Becky, don't pull this with *me*."

Rebecca partially lifted the hood, sneaking a quick look, then pausing, as she would when playing and checking the audience's attention span. Miriam yanked it off. Her eyes met Rebecca's, angrily, then merged into compromise.

"Miriam, please, don't.... The fact is, Lilli's afraid of the United States. It's irrational. There's something very strange going on at home...." Agitated, Rebecca rose from the table, clutching the *grosser mélange* of Viennese coffee in the large cup. "Last week before my concert in Graz, I was alone in the music room, practicing...and I don't know how to explain this...but the *visitations* started again."

Miriam strangled her disappointment as she always did as Rebecca's bulwark. "I thought all of that had stopped."

"No, I just don't talk about it anymore." She stared into space. "I was playing 'Les Adieux' and I didn't sound like myself—the tone was Lilli's. And when I looked at my hands, they were hers. There were a group of men in the room whose faces I couldn't make out, with some women. Lilli was giving a recital. I just stopped, went upstairs to our apartment and thought, I'm tired, exhausted from all this travel and touring."

Miriam was uneasy. Her sister had suffered from these episodic fantasies since childhood. She claimed that she saw and heard the dead.

"Okay, I know you did your best to get them to come. Let's forget it."

"Thank you." She held onto Miriam and their lips playfully touched. Their sisterly goading resumed. "You are a bitch, though."

"And you're a slut."

"True once, and the more deceived for it." Rebecca waved her hands at the expanse of property. "Now look who's talking."

3

At five in the morning on Friday, December 10, yet another day in the endless celebration of Chanukah, Virgil and Noreen checked out of a Staten Island motel and drove to Brooklyn before the expressway traffic built up. She was his trusty navigator and studied the map in a dopey daze. Virgil, good as his word, had wrecked her.

She wondered if the cemetery murder had set off some highly charged sexual dynamic whose range of perversity lodged inside him. Was the act of burying someone alive such a turn-on? Best not to press him for an answer. He was all business again, grim under the beard and dark glasses; they had donned the Jew costumes before leaving.

The radio stations he kept surfing had no news flashes about Mt. Jacob, but there were other reports from around the country of attacks on Jews.

"In Dallas, two Jewish seminary students were severely beaten with baseball bats by unknown assailants...and their clothes spray-painted with swastikas...."

"We're getting a report from Chicago of a home invasion by three men dressed in SS uniforms who attacked a couple in their Lake Shore Drive home. The man was shot and in critical condition....

"This just in from Philadelphia: A Main Line home was set on fire and swastika flags were found in the mailbox....

"As I speak, our producers are putting together a distinguished panel to discuss this horrifying outbreak of anti-Semitism....

"We're now joined live by our sister station in Seattle. Reporting from Temple Beth-Israel is Lucinda Walker. What've you got for us, Lucinda?"

"Good afternoon, Ralph. As I stand in shock in front of this lovely old synagogue, now being guarded by the local members of the Jewish Defense League, I can only describe my own disgust at the vile graffiti and swastikas that were painted on this holy building. The police and FBI are inside the temple investigating this hate crime. According to a member of the congregation, the interior was defaced, as was the sanctuary. The Holy Ark where the Talmud scriptures are kept–"

"–Sorry to cut in, Lucinda–"

"Back to you soon, Ralph..."

"This is Ralph Parsons on WKOP for an instant weather watch update and we'll return to this major breaking national story from our AP feed and affiliates! It's sinister, frightening, eerie. Our panel and I will take your calls."

Virgil switched off the radio and smirked at Noreen.

"It's all chickenshit compared to what we did yesterday."

"Why are we heading back to Eastern Parkway?" she asked.

"Pearlman."

Noreen's nerves were jangling. "Pearlman, too?"

After the announcement of Bruno's Directive, volunteers had come forth. The country had been divided up into groups for these lightning strikes. The Winterhaven band of women seldom collaborated in an actual *Einsatz*. An action might involve wrecking a synagogue, a physical beating, planting a pipe bomb, shooting someone—murder.

Apart from maintaining the home and childcare, the women's working roles involved dropping anti-Semitic pamphlets in various towns, traveling as couriers with crank, meth, and ecstasy. They would make pre-arranged drops and collect money.

Until Noreen's arrival, none of them had been involved in a violent tactical strike. It was this very act of courage and daring that had drawn Virgil to her. Something beyond sweat oozed from her pores, a fetor of jungle hatred that scented her skin. Angry, Noreen was as deadly as anthrax.

When the areas of attack had been laid out, the cities targeted, only Virgil had picked New York. It was foreign territory to the rest of the corps, as indeed it was to him. But his credo was: "Aim High." If a statement were to be made by the new breed of Nazis, everyone, worldwide, would take note of New York. The Jew media was located there. Virgil had waited while the men argued about Los Angeles, everyone slaphappy about Hollywood. But New York remained unclaimed, until he'd stepped forward. If he was to become a *gauleiter*, a governor, and enter the charmed circle, his statement had to be the loudest, the clearest, the most violent. Promotion was never the ally of caution.

He and Noreen had flown into New York two weeks ago with a list of potential quarries. The rabbi was unnamed, but if they could put one down it would be like a Grand Slam in baseball. Virgil, with a long family background in entombment, had decided on a Jewish cemetery. Label Friedman had found his destiny in Virgil's home grounds.

Schlomo Pearlman, however, was on the top of the Winterhaven list. Virgil had been provided with his home and business address and phone number. Not that the home number was much help. All the Yids carried cells. The wealthy jeweler was a major contributor and fundraiser for Jewish causes and Israel; he was very vocal, leading rallies, writing articles.

Having followed him from his house on President Street in Brooklyn to the subway into Manhattan, up to his office floor in the diamond district on 47th Street, they had discovered he was a creature of habit. Every morning at eight o'clock, this swarthy, lardassed man, probably in his fifties, strode with vigorous, loping strides to the Utica Avenue-Eastern Parkway entrance of the IRT Subway and got off at Rockefeller Center in Manhattan.

Virgil parked the van in a lot near the station at a quarter after seven. The weather had improved, but they watched their step on the swollen, uneven sidewalks, moving over sheets of dirty black ice and through slush swamps clogging the sewers. They wandered into a bagel shop, already mobbed with men and women, jabbering in tongues. They got some coffee and hot onion bagels, cubes of rock-hard butter, and stood by the window.

At five minutes to eight, they strolled to the subway entrance and spotted Pearlman a short distance away. They tarried until they were just ahead of him, boinked their tokens into the slot, and shoved the balky turnstile.

The original plan had been for Noreen to shove him off the platform as the crowd jostled and the express train pulled into the station. Virgil would cover her move. But questions arose in his mind: Would the train be going fast enough? Noreen might shove the wrong man. Would someone in this bestial colony of beards spot her?

"It's not cool here, Virgil," she whispered. "What do you want to do?"

"Let's get him in his office and really do a number."

The idea appealed to her hardnosed, nurse's alertness.

"If he's carrying diamonds, I might get an engagement ring out of it."

With disgust, he said, "Diamonds from a Jew!"

"Let me tell *you* something, darlin', diamonds have no religion. They're *cut*, not circumcised by a rabbi."

Virgil had to give it to her, yielding to her mad humor of the moment.

The Californians could never get used to the noise level, the maddening cacophony of the subway. The IRT express screeching, blue and amber sparks flying from third rail, wintry, snowy, boots, galoshes squishing and squeaking. The platform seemed to heave, crammed with Hasidic Jews in beaver hats and frayed velvet-collar coats. The utter, noxious stench made him queasy.

This mass headed for Money Land: Wall Street and the diamond district. Virgil did his best to shield Noreen from the pushing and shoving during the rush hour. But he was helpless against these foul-tempered people, could not filter out the dank odor of wet coats, the vitriol of old sweat of unwashed people, the symphonies of coughing, sneezing fits, their colds, flu. As the crowd hurtled forward into the packed train car, Yiddish curses pealed from screeching, termagant females. Virgil regretted he wasn't escorting them to Dachau.

On another level, to get his mind off the surroundings, Virgil decided that this insult to his senses had a definite value. A Nazi officer had an obligation to test these polluted waters so that future preparations for the disposal of this refuse would be environmentally correct. The Chosen People, really, Virgil thought, huddled next to the immaculately hygienic Noreen, shivering, cupping the back of her leather glove over the sweat dripping from her upper lip. This must be what it was like in the boxcars. Hitler had failed to eradicate this blemish on humanity. Magnus and Bruno, with the help of the loyal guardians like himself, would succeed.

Jeweler's Row on 47th Street throbbed with hordes of men in Hasidic garments just like the outfits he and Noreen were wearing. In pursuit of Pearlman, they passed arcades of diamond merchants—with their greasy loupes pressed against their eyes like medical examiners—appraising diamonds, then pointing to their showcases to peddle their own lines. The shrieks of bartering spilled into the street. Not even the calves and pigs at slaughter on the Winterhaven ranch caused such a din as this rabble.

It was a relief when the couple entered the office building and signed a distracted guard's entry book. He, too, wore a yarmulke, but in the hubbub of the gift-giving Chanukah crowd he barely noticed the religious couple. Whenever they could, they averted their eyes from the snooping cameras and burrowed into the jam-packed elevator wall.

They got off at the seventeenth floor and wiggled through the dark, narrow corridor where more business was furiously being transacted. Innocent people could lose an eye with all the finger-pointing going on.

No one noticed them ring the bell at PEARLMAN DIAMONDS.

Schlomo saw them on his monitor. He was having coffee and an early sandwich of chopped herring on pumpernickel.

"Engagement ring, please," Virgil said into the dusty speaker beside the bell.

"You were recommended?" Schlomo asked, putting down his sandwich.

"The rabbi," said Noreen.

"Which one?" They hadn't been prepared for this and were silent. "Tell me, and I'll make a contribution...."

"I have his card," Noreen said.

"Fucking commission network," Virgil angrily hissed to her when the door buzzer sounded. The door closed automatically behind them.

"You're getting married when?" Pearlman asked, smiling. He had a napkin still tucked into his belt.

"The date's not set," she said, pinching Virgil's arm.

"Please sit down and give me an idea of what you're prepared to spend."

"A lifetime together," Virgil replied.

"*Halevai.* The love of God brings children, mitzvahs, everything."

Noreen was about to pass out in the stifling heat but could not remove her coat. "Could you please open the window? I'm feeling a little faint."

"Bride's nerves," Pearlman said with a good-fellowship laugh. He lazily stretched, then got up to grip the hasp. The window opened only halfway.

Noreen sprang up, blocking Pearlman, as he was about to take his seat.

"Did you ever think about what it would be like to fall out?" Virgil inquired, as though this were a scientific question about anti-gravity.

Pearlman was puzzled, but quickly parried, "No. Can I have your rabbi's card for my records?"

Noreen handed him several of Label Friedman's cards.

"We buried him yesterday," Noreen said, sucking in the cold air.

"*Amein*," Pearlman said, a sense of trouble marching into his mind.

"Alive, but not kicking...so's we could see," Virgil advised him.

Befuddled, the jeweler squinted at Virgil. His left hand moved to his sandwich and his right dropped below his desk to the alarm button.

"I'm getting a little...no, a lot confused."

Noreen hurdled behind Pearlman, pressing a honed straightedge razor against the soft wattle of his throat.

"Oh-ohhh, no. Please, *please*, I have a family. Take whatever I got, sell it, get rich. I'm covered...."

"We didn't come to rob you." She might have swallowed a fly. "We're not thieves—like you Jews," she said in a voice riddled with disgust.

Virgil struck Pearlman on the jaw, more gently than he had the rabbi yesterday when he'd been overcome by adrenalin. At the very moment of the blow, Noreen yanked away the razor. They had practiced these moves in the Winterhaven gym often enough.

Pearlman was stunned and immobilized. Together, they hoisted him to the window, arching his body headfirst through the window opening.

Noreen was feeling a rush. "Think he'll make it?"

"Asked the last sardine in the can."

For an instant, she was distracted. "Don't give me the giggles and break me up."

They worked in unison on this holy mission. It meant everything in their world at Winterhaven.

"Should I cut him, Virgil?"

"Don't bother."

Still conscious as his shoulders were drawn in and pressed hard against the yellowed cement ledge, Schlomo Pearlman, without his glasses, glimpsed distorted, moving specks dancing on the street below, the amorphous shapes of buildings, like melting wax from his Chanukah candles. He tried to form prayers, words, but they evaded him as he witnessed his own murder in a state of horrified incredulity.

Falling, plummeting into a nether world, the black hole of time without end sucked him into a final state of involuntary blindness and spontaneous abstraction. He no longer existed to himself.

Before leaving the office, Noreen quickly spray-painted a wall with a red swastika, then spread a gold handkerchief with its black swastika emblem on his desk, along with the last of Label Friedman's business cards.

"That ought to help New York's Finest," Virgil remarked, swaggering out with her.

4

"You ready to roll yet?" Harry Summerfield impatiently shouted from his bed, waiting for the hooker in his bathroom to pack her gear. "Taylor...Taylor Anne...? Taylor!"

He was anxious to meet Rebecca Benjamin face to face, and this challenge of dangerous new turf aroused him, and not the woman trying to get him up again. Conquest was his bubbly. "Rebecca-Rebecca" had been intoned like a fugue by her sister Miriam, and the Leopold family, for weeks now. The sycophantic sound of Miriam's voice was chalk on a blackboard.

But for a ladies' man, the scent of absolutely forbidden territory always beguiled Harry. His experience was more of a hindrance than a guide in the naked environment of emotional eruption. As an architect, form, not a developer's idea of function, was everything to him, and he didn't consider this superficial, but rather the essence of his artistic temperament.

Which of his techniques would work on Rebecca? Improvising or adapting his approach to her control? Their age difference made aggression the least likely approach. Umm, for a woman accustomed to fawning admirers, it made the most sense. Give the cat fish.

"I can't believe you're quitting on me," Taylor's half-heard voice registered.

Poking his head into the hall of mirrors of his bathroom, Harry stopped, almost remaining invisible, while he and Taylor surveyed her bare thighs, the supple configuration of her breasts and buttocks. This gym-worshipper had been blessed with a gene that gobbled up cellulite. Her skin had no declension of sunline creases and, at approximately twenty-six, she was still a grinning ash-blond pixie.

"Is that a hard-on I spy with my little eye?" Her coyness, the attempts at wit left him stone-faced, barely submerging a homicidal impulse to seize her neck and strangle her.

"No, it's a delusion." On his next trip to his local Barnes and Noble or Borders, he'd check the self-help section and see if someone had written a book on how to dismiss a hooker without tears or offense.

"I'll make it real again."

"Thanks, but you've abused it enough. I've got a fucking business meeting in an hour."

"Why aren't these people at church with their families?" she asked with such innocent disapproval that he started to laugh.

Her conversational skills revolved around the gym, trashy lingerie, church, and titanic erections in that order. For a moment he considered asking her why she didn't follow her own advice and go to church. But he hated to end their party on a note of sarcasm. He not only loved women, but also genuinely cherished them and supported their struggles. However, he had finished and wanted her gone.

Her Saturday-night stay-over had given birth to the horror of a ten o'clock Sunday-morning shave, a command performance at another lavish brunch. Jack Leopold, the moneyman behind his various architectural projects for more years than he cared to remember, had insisted. Harry had yielded; excuses wouldn't do.

"You sure?" She feathered his neck with genial, non-arousing, kisses, well aware of the missed opportunity. "I shouldn't say this, but I absolutely must: Harry, I'm positively crazy about you."

He was well prepared for this fragile pitch and looked through her, longingly at the shower; she mistook his POV for a change of heart. She had been prattling on during his war-games deliberations, and he surfed back.

"Now you've really given me something to think about."

"You mean that?"

"Since we met at...?"

"The Viking."

"Yes-yes." Like her, he didn't always tell the truth.

"I've only been out for a...year. I don't want to go on with the life," Taylor said, her twanging voice still hostage to Kansas prairies. "I'm in love with you."

Her unscrupulous lack of candor was evident to the connoisseur. She had a whore's whining past, without the guts to come clean. He knew he was the working girl's dream. How much longer could he endure her? More money, another thousand?

"Really, do you want me to arrange something—me!—with friends?"

In a last-ditch petition, she flicked out her tongue, which had the latitude of Africa. His weary silence dismissed this offer of military occupation. Now finally dressing, she slipped into her panties, and glided into her skirt, holding up her breasts in a final appeal before engaging the bra hooks, as though sealing an envelope.

"No, forget that."

Harry had never been inspired by college orgies when he'd been a young man during the hash-coked 'sixties at MIT. While his class-mates, none of whom had amounted to anything, had launched invasions of the Seven Sisters colleges, regaling him with their tales of explosive splatters of semen at Barnard and dope storms filling Vassar's dorms, Harry Summerfield had decided to become a great architect.

He was about five ten, trim, and well muscled with thick shaggy blond hair going to gray that he combed straight back. He had a broad shapely nose with a small flare, a spiny chin, and indigo-blue eyes of extraordinary acuity that gave him the air of a man relentlessly engaged in profound thought. Harry Summerfield's fine looks were magnified by this intensity, which dropped women to their knees. During the past few years, his sexual appetite had become insatiable. But pay as you go was the solution.

He fondled Taylor's face. "Let me work things out for now."

"Harry, my love, please, please, don't forget me."

"Never."

She entered his private penthouse elevator and pressed her freshly lipsticked lips against the glass before descending down into the actual world.

When she left, he leisurely showered, dressed casually in cords, green-striped Charvet shirt, a suede jacket, and loafers always without socks.

Architects needed to examine structural problems and attack them. He couldn't wait to test Rebecca. Was she soft soil where landfill would be needed? Granite? How deep would he have to dig to reach bedrock?

Miriam was already dressed and came in to find Rebecca buffed. She finished blow-drying Rebecca's hair and waited while she slipped on a denim shirt and the solitary pair of jeans Herta had packed.

"Yuck."

"Vienna's lousy flea market with a size-eight label and Nike knock-offs."

"We'll do something about that at Façonnable," Miriam said. "And get you some Mephistos as well." She looked at her watch. "We still have time before brunch. Becky, I've come to a decision and you're not going to be happy about it. Lilli will go crazy."

"You have my full attention."

"I'm going to suspend my career."

Rebecca thought she'd hear Miriam out before exploding.

"Go on...."

"Scott's an only child. We want to start a family as soon as possible. And our childhood—except for music—was like being in prison. What a life...the practicing, discipline, the house with those two women...! We were prisoners."

Rebecca knowingly shook her head. "You're pregnant."

Miriam had the glow. "I think so."

"How far gone?"

"I'm late—six weeks. My body's changing. No morning sickness. But you know me...I can do anything, go for a sail on the Danube in a storm without puking."

"And eat Herta's week-old goulash."

"I'm longing for it." She chortled. "I *must* be pregnant."

"If that's your idea of comfort food, then my diagnosis is schizophrenia, not pregnancy. Have you told Scott?"

"No. I thought I'd wait till the honeymoon. His parents are desperate for grandchildren."

"Let's please them." Rebecca sighed fretfully. "Is Scott going to continue playing?"

"Yes. I'll coach him, encourage him."

"Which conservatory did he go to...again?"

"The Curtis Institute in Philadelphia."

What was the point of arguing with Miriam about what she already knew? Displeasure would be futile. Scott could never perform with a major symphony orchestra. Rebecca's hidden diplomacy made an unexpected appearance.

She wrapped her arms around Miriam. "*Meine liebe Schwester*, I feel as high as you do. Ecstatic."

They strolled down the guest wing's backstairs to a rear entrance and through a pair of wide doors out to the loggia on which a Herculean barbecue took up an entire corner. There was a large round green baize table with chips in a walnut box and a pair of sports-bar, big-boy TVs: A rich man's nook to play cards with his friends, and grill hotdogs and hamburgers, while they boasted about their sexual conquests and got their stories straight for their wives.

A gunmetal Aston Martin Volante pulled up before turning out of their view.

"I love that car. I hope some idiot isn't driving it."

"No! You'll love the guy who comes with it. I've only met him a few times. Harry Summerfield, Jack's associate. He's one of the most famous architects in America. Rebecca, my baby, the Benjamin women will never have to worry about money again."

"This is my day to be astounded. Now get it out, tell me everything?"

"I have a pre-nuptial agreement."

Rebecca's laughter, this time not orchestrated for one of Lilli's cocktail parties with impresarios, rang out. "*Fantastisch*...How much do you get? And do I curtsy to the future *Prinzessin* Leopold?"

"No German or smoking at the Leopolds. Jack is a major supporter of the Shoah Foundation."

Rebecca's face drooped. "Do they keep a kosher house?"

"Lobster and oysters anytime you like."

"Well, I liked him to begin with. Now I truly respect him."

"Jack's a terrific host—you'll see—and a real good guy."

Miriam's demeanor abruptly changed and her jauntiness was weighted by an inexplicable gravity, which Rebecca attributed to the jitteriness of pregnancy.

"Jack's horrified by this outbreak of anti-Semitic murders. We all are."

Rebecca looked at her, puzzled. "Where, in Vienna?"

"No, here in the States....Didn't you read about it at home?"

Somewhat hesitant, Rebecca said, "No. We grew up with all this ugliness and hatred. That neo-Nazi bastard Jörg Haider and his Freedom Party still run things in Austria. They spray-painted the Freud Museum the other day!" She was furious. "Remember when he said Hitler had a terrific employment strategy and went to a party for Waffen-SS veterans?" She shuddered. "There's enough unpleasantness. If I see it coming, I look to the stars or stick my head in the sand. And, Miriam, we were hardly observant. We went to synagogue to say *Yizkor* for our parents on Yom Kippur."

"Things have changed for me. We're going to have a full-blown Jewish wedding."

"Klezmer blues—dancing on chairs. What, bride's night at the *mikva* for a pre-wedding bath. Come on, give me a break."

"No, they don't go to extremes. But they're serious and so am I, Becky."

Rebecca wanted to get back to crucial matters: money for the penniless Miriam. Her suspicions intruded. Contracts between rich men's heirs and financially deprived, innocent women, like her sister, always contained ominous clauses.

"What about this marriage settlement?" Rebecca asked. "Was it Scott's idea?"

"No, he never gets involved in his father's business. Scott is a pure musician. One of the things I love about him is that he's not a shark. He felt Jack was insensitive and they had an argument about it."

She firmly turned Rebecca to her.

"Now, pay attention: This is important. You see, Jack is so incredibly wealthy that most of his fortune is going to his pet charities. It's philanthropy on a monumental scale. There are billions involved! Scott received a large trust fund last year on his twenty-fifth birthday."

Rebecca smacked her lips as though eating truffles.

"Stop it, I'm not kidding."

"May I rub my hands together in pious rapture, Miriam? This is your finest moment of performance. It could mean chimney sweepers and central heating for Berggasse. Lilli and Herta will be dancing in the streets!"

"It will happen." Miriam remained focused as though following a complex score. "I went to a meeting with Jack and his lawyers."

Rebecca fell back as though about to faint at her sister's naiveté. "You didn't have a top lawyer, too?"

Miriam shook her head. "No, I felt it would be grasping."

"You shouldn't be allowed out by yourself."

"Shut up and listen. I'll be Jack's daughter-in-law in a week. I never want to be his adversary. Jack bought us a house in Westwood."

"How thrilling," she said with scorn.

"You'll see. We're going there this afternoon with Harry, and meet Scott there."

"Your pre-nuptial sounds like a death sentence. Remember when we were students how we used to read about the rich men dumping their wives without a penny?"

"Becky, Scott and I are marrying for love, not his money. But this is Los Angeles, and domestic algebra has to be done. Naturally, the main issues were divorce, length of marriage, children.... death."

Yet again Rebecca's apprehension emerged and her muscles tensed. Miriam, her gentle, big-hearted, older sister—a woman who never counted her change—suffered from a benign view of the world. She had allowed herself to be fleeced by a scheming businessman. To avoid unpleasantness and one of those marital fissures that begin as a paper cut before eventually enlarging into an abscess, Scott had passed the dirty job to his father. Scott would remain spotless, the artist.

"I'm listening," Rebecca grumbled.

"If Scott and I were to get divorced, I will be paid five hundred thousand dollars a year for ten years, and child support, when there are children. Tax-free. While we're married, I'll have an allowance of two hundred and fifty thousand. I intend to give a third to grandma Lilli and a third to you. If she were to die, then I'll make sure that Herta is provided for."

The cleverness of the apparently gullible Miriam filled Rebecca with renewed admiration for her sister. "And I worry about *you*...."

"I've always told you it was pointless."

Rebecca gasped. "Five million dollars! This isn't happening!"

"Yes, it is. It has! The documents were signed, notarized, and filed with the state."

Rebecca bowed her head, solemn within her elation. "To begin with, Miriam, I won't need the money after my debut with the Philharmoniker in March. I'll have bookings in Berlin, London, and Paris—if it's not a disaster."

"*Disaster!* That's impossible. Still, things do happen and I know it's been a terrible strain on you to support Lilli and Herta. So from now on, when you play, you can concentrate totally on the music and not the fees. Not that you haven't. But I know that you've been playing too often for too long." A hint of remorse crowded her pleasure. "All those miserable halls, gymnasiums. Dreck food at train-station buffets—when they were open. The years and places we've had to travel—"

"Let me stop you, Miriam. The experience was priceless. I'm glad I waited until I was seasoned. I've always had confidence and technique. But understanding and making the music part of you only comes with time."

For some reason, inexplicable to Rebecca, Miriam began to laugh wildly. "This you won't believe. When I was coming out of the ladies' room at the lawyers' office, I overheard one of them. He didn't see me and was bragging to his colleagues. He said: 'The Kraut took chump change.'"

"Oh, I love it."

Miriam's attitude swiftly altered to one of sobriety. "Rebecca, have you ever thought of being young, us—*us*—being young?" Rebecca was tentative and guarded. "I never have. We spent our lives as show dogs. If we made a mistake, or played badly, we'd be crucified at home. You always got the worst of it. Lilli was relentless. You're *my* baby. And now I'll have the money to look after you and give you a taste of freedom."

5

Magnus Von Winter and his son Bruno had disappeared from Europe, among the flight of refugees, in the late nineteen forties and made their way to the United States. During the postwar years in Zurich, Magnus had forged a new identity, made contacts, and eluded the most tenacious Nazi hunters. He'd studied everything available about America and decided to settle in California.

With a fortune at his disposal, he had bought thousands of acres of land outside of Cambria, and launched Winterhaven to continue the global battle against the Jews. Even though millions of them had been eradicated, they had, as usual, come out of the war with profit. They now had their own nation. It would be only a matter of time before they enslaved all the Arab countries.

Magnus had hired an army of contractors and built himself a stone replication of Himmler's Renaissance Wewelsburg Castle, outside of Paderborn in Westphalia. With a foretaste of demonology, the design component formed an isosceles triangle with three massive towers, a courtyard, but unlike the original, a moat and drawbridge over a trout lake to provide privacy and safeguard the estate. Its north-to-south right angles emphasized the care Magnus had taken to make his Antichrist statement. This ensured that light could not originate from the east, symbolically illuminating Christ's suffering and providing the first rays of sun.

In practical terms, Winterhaven was a working cattle ranch, where prime calves were raised for veal; there were comfortable cottages for the staff, a slaughterhouse, cows, chickens, pigs, geese, a tannery for skinners and hides to cure, and stables where Magnus kept his prize Arabians, and the hands their horses. Vegetables and flowers flourished in the rich coastal soil. A weapons range for automatic rifles offered the sharpshooters an ideal facility to practice. An infirmary staffed by a doctor who had been imprisoned for malpractice along with nurses like Noreen Porter, who had been discharged from hospitals, operated on a twenty-four hour basis in case any of the men or their families needed emergency care. The children went to a kindergarten; afterwards to a private school on the grounds that had been accredited and offered instruction for the future members.

All told, about a hundred people dwelled in the Von Winters' Valhalla. These men and women had been recruited from prison and some were former mental patients; a group of fanatical, dishonorably discharged soldiers had launched anti-government militia groups and joined him. Armed cells were embedded everywhere. They shared the Von Winter racial ideals and flourished with the seeds of hatred.

After Bruno's Directive for the murders of Jews before Christmas had been carried out, Magnus reduced the workload during the holidays. He knew when his troops needed a break to celebrate. During the frolicking at the annual Christmas party, Magnus handed out bonuses, gifts for everyone; he played with the children and presided over a sumptuous feast. This side of him revealed a man with a sense of humor, generous and approachable whenever anyone had a personal problem. He also hugged and kissed the numerous pregnant women, who carried Bruno's seed. Magnus displayed a paternal attentiveness to these loyal breeders who would deliver Winterhaven's future warriors. They would be his grandchildren.

But after the New Year's Eve celebration, in early January 2000, the dancing and *gemütlich* atmosphere abruptly changed. A sinister tension hung over the Winterhaven ranch like a louring weather front. It was rumored that he had gone to Vienna with Bruno. Upon his return, anxiety resurfaced, with unasked questions on everyone's lips. This apprehension of the unknown kept the community in a state of panic. But if any of the men became too curious, they disappeared without explanation and were never spoken of again. Friendships among the resident troops in this neo-Nazi realm were cautious; gossip was forbidden.

Virgil Hoyt found the situation rewarding and thrived on conspiracy. But for the majority, the tenor of paranoia was far worse than their years in prison. Behind bars, a man knew who could be trusted and which cabal or gang presented a threat. They learned what was expected of them, and the routine of the guards held few surprises.

Everything about the Von Winters, even Magnus's age, was cloaked in mystery. He sat a horse better than any of them and had demonstrated repeatedly he was the deadliest sharpshooter on the firing range. But what alarmed them more than any of these practical skills was Magnus's ability to appear and fade away at will. Where was he? And what disguise would he assume on any given day?

He was a magician, but the depth of his artifice suggested that his powers were almost occult. The most hardened criminals, paroled because of Magnus's intercession and support, quaked in his presence. Once enrolled in Winterhaven, these men and their women swore a blood oath in a mystical ceremony Magnus conducted. On these occasions, and in this role, he was the idealized blond SS Reichsführer in his well-cut SS uniform, the Iron Cross dangling, boots gleaming. His eyes were a cyanic blue, his voice silky, friendly. He had a strong lantern jaw, tight, fair skin, a broad nose, and sensuous lips. Then without warning, a stark irrationality would transform his features into something inhuman.

"You've waived all your rights. Your loyalty is to me and the cause," he would declare.

There was also a surreptitious, feral aspect to Magnus's behavior that terrified his followers, especially the newcomers.

Sometimes in the middle of the night, a man would be shaken from sleep and given ranch duty or ordered to drive down along the foggy highway to Cambria on an errand. Magnus would then blindfold the woman. Bruno, on a secret visit, would slip into bed with her.

Quivering with dread, wanting to please, these women never revealed what the experience had been like. But then during their first trimester a reward would appear with a card signed BVW: a Chanel suit; a platinum swastika pin; a Franck Muller *Lady* Conquistador watch. On the birth of a child, he would send a photograph of the latest trophy to Bruno to pique his interest.

During the trip to Europe, Magnus had purchased weapons from a new source in Amsterdam. His previous supplier, a man who made a market in unthinkable articles of trade and arranged depraved sexual exhibitions had recently had his head blown off in a hunting trip to Africa.

On an icy, windswept dawn Magnus took the Winterhaven field for maneuvers with his men. They were named the Bruno *Einsatzgruppen*. Ten four-men mobile killing units spread out in a pincer formation driving armored Humvees with new AK-47s and high explosives. In winter camouflage gear, they circled a reinforced concrete bunker, which they had built in his absence: its purpose, total destruction. They awaited his orders to attack.

Out of the mists, Magnus spied a burly single man running along the perimeter of the war-game exercise. He stepped out of his Humvee and raised his hand to halt the operation.

The man stopped in his tracks and saluted Magnus. "Tom Corley reporting, sir. I'm sorry to be late, but the infirmary just discharged me."

"It was your responsibility to be discharged last night. I checked the roster. You were fit."

"They gave me a sleeping pill."

Magnus leaned into his vehicle, pulled out a microphone. His voice echoed over the engines: "Everyone cease operations! Return to my vehicle and assemble!" Engines roaring, the armored unit circled him. The men, carrying their weapons, fell into ranks in front of him.

Virgil, given new responsibility, scanned the group. He saluted. "All present, sir."

"At ease," Magnus announced. "We have a malingerer in a combat sortie."

Dread, like a lethal virus, spread through the troops.

"The punishment for dereliction of duty is the firing squad. But since this is the beginning of our millennium, I'm going to make an exception with Herr Corley." A clear sense of relief rippled out. No one wanted to execute a comrade...except Virgil. Corley had paid the price for mouthing off to him when he had arrived and bore a livid brand mark across his back as a reminder.

Magnus smiled and raised his arms in an embrace of his men. "Come closer and form a circle around Corley and me."

A streak of sunlight struggled through the coastal cloud, and even from this distance the flutes of the ocean whitecaps were visible and their silvery streaks splayed with rainbows.

"Courage is our motto, so Herr Corley gets a chance to show us what's inside him."

Magnus slid his .357 from his side holster. He had lost faith in automatics during his days at Hitler's side. A crow nibbled nearby and Magnus shot it in the head. For a few moments, its torso wiggled and danced like a drunk, generating nervous laughter from the men.

Magnus opened the six-chambered revolver. "We have five shots left. Now I have to practice what I preach. I set the example, especially since I'm going to be guiding you on a new path." He spun the chamber, closed it, placed the barrel against his left temple and smiled at the shocked group.

Voices of the men bellowed, "No, no, *don't!*" Ignoring them, Magnus pulled the trigger and fired. They all heard the click and groaned with relief. Magnus reopened the revolver, rolled the chamber, and repeated this four more times, with exactly the same results. Yet he remained standing, and the expressions of incredulity and adulation on the men's faces made him laugh.

"Was this luck or destiny, gentlemen?"

"Destiny!" came the loud cry. "Destiny."

"Let's see what Corley's destiny is."

He spun the chamber yet again. He handed the .357 Magnum to Tom Corley. Despite the wispy rattles of the biting wind, the man was sweating and seemed in a delirious stupor.

"Don't be afraid. You see, everyone here had a choice when they joined: Trust God, or trust Magnus."

Virgil pointed his AK-47 at Corley. "You heard the order."

With a shaking hand, Corley raised the revolver to his temple. As his knees were beginning to corkscrew, Magnus shouted: "Act like a man. Fire it!"

The explosive sound of a single bullet acted as a more startling sound than the reports of heavy weapons during war games. Corley had blown off the side of his skull. The men, including Virgil, recoiled as though they themselves had been shot.

The Humvees were all equipped with stretchers, and Corley's body was placed upon one. "Do we bury him, or what?" Spence, the strapping blacksmith, asked.

"No, I've got a better idea. The exercise is suspended. Virgil, ride with me."

Despite the passage of decades, the immortal image of the man who was to become *der Führer* and Magnus's closest friend, even after his death, lived on in his consciousness. Adolf's face, his manner, and his compelling dignity were indelibly imprinted.

Magnus had first met Adolf Hitler in Linz during the sultry summer of 1930, where, at sixteen, he was already the star performer of a traveling circus. Hitler had come to his Austrian childhood city to attend a Bruckner concert, but he was also a devotee of magic shows. He took a naive glee in Magnus's legerdemain with cards, the way he pulled rabbits out of hats, his illusions, and his mind-reading talents.

Magnus wove through the benches and approached Hitler. Despite his mesmerizing ability when he made speeches, Hitler was reserved and shy. Magnus took his hands and pulled him to his feet; as he did, he brushed against him.

"Come now, show us the photograph of the attractive young woman," Magnus had said.

Flustered, Hitler tried to shake Magnus off. But Magnus's eyes were so penetrating that for an instant he was dazed. Suddenly, Hitler gasped. Magnus held up a snapshot so that everyone in the audience could see that it was indeed of a young woman. They laughed, while Hitler, with a sheepish smile, accepted his wallet and the picture back from this beautiful, dynamic, blond satyr.

At the end of Magnus's show, Hitler, intrigued and troubled, followed him back to his tent, fending off hordes of repellent Gypsies through the miasmic, shabby camp.

"What took you so long?" Magnus asked, wiping his sweaty forehead with a handkerchief embroidered with a swastika. "Were you afraid of me?"

"No," Hitler replied, taking the handkerchief from Magnus and wiping his own brow with it. "But I was astounded. Tell me how you could possibly know I was carrying a picture of my niece Geli in my wallet."

Magnus placed his arm around Hitler's neck. Adolf loathed all intimate contact, even shaking hands, yet he did not pull away from the young man. He was bewitched by his dynamic self-assurance. Magnus's long golden locks, and the ivory symmetry of his features, seemed to him as though Dionysus had been reborn. If ever there were an Aryan god disguised as a mortal, it was this boy Magnus. His hypnotic eyes tunneled through Hitler's secrets, his very soul.

"I'll think about it," Magnus said. "I've lived with these disgusting gypsies since I was born. But I've learned something from them and Beitel, the ugly Jew who owns this circus. I've watched how they barter: trade...trade...trade. I've been this Jew's slave since I was five. My parents trained lions. During a fire started by this Beitel, they were burned to death." The memory of it still incensed Magnus.

"Avram Beitel wanted to collect the insurance because attendance was poor. We'd had a summer of rain. Yet the Jews still made money in their stalls. I believe they caused this weather for the *geld*. For them everything is about money." Magnus held up his hands and sprayed them with sandalwood cologne. "My sweat still smells of burned flesh."

Hitler became solemn. "Yours, Herr Magnus, is a tragic story."

"Avram Beitel owed my parents thousands of schillings—and now, he owes me even more. So he makes sure I'm not allowed near the collection basket after my performances. Beitel has spies everywhere."

"Can I do anything to help?" Hitler asked.

"Trade. The man in uniform with pig eyes beside you has something I need."

"That's Captain Ernst Röhm. He's the leader of my SA Brownshirts, and the others are bodyguards. Now, what about him?"

"Captain Röhm is carrying a Luger Parabellum. If you could arrange for him to loan it to me, I'll be able to collect my money." Magnus paused and gave Hitler a sweet smile. "As a sign of my trust in you—before we go— I'll tell you how I knew about your niece."

"I'll wait." Adolf was entranced by the young man's confidence. "I trust you as well."

Hitler left the tent and returned with the Luger automatic. He handed it to Magnus. Before Hitler's eyes, the young man twirled it like a gunslinger in the old Western books that Hitler loved and occasionally still read. In an instant, the automatic vanished...but where? Intrigued, he followed Magnus outside.

Accompanied by six burly Brownshirts, swinging batons at the cringing gypsies and Jewish circus peddlers, Magnus, Hitler at his side, approached an ornate wooden wagon. It was boldly painted a peacock-blue and decorated with a gold Star of David; the masterly fretwork depicted Moses and the Ten Commandments, and the horseshoes of the *chai* symbol formed a relief. Before climbing up the polished mahogany stairs to the golden door of the wagon, Magnus spat on the Star of David; delighted, Röhm and his Brownshirts coughed and sprayed it with phlegm.

"Do you need my help to settle your score?" Adolf asked.

Magnus shook his head, climbed the steps, and knocked on the door several times. A bearded Jew with an embroidered yarmulke finally appeared. With a warm smile, he invited Magnus inside. Magnus flopped down on a tufted sofa covered in ruby-colored wild silk. The Jews had an eye for fine furnishings, he admitted to himself.

Avram, in his paunchy fifties, the hairs in his nose fluttering like flies, breathed deeply. He had been counting the day's takings, straightening rumpled bills, balancing discolored coins on a protective black velvet tablecloth so that his large, ornately carved Rococo desk wouldn't get scratched. He closed the canvas money sack, rolled into his high swivel chair, and smiled with affection.

"You were a marvel today, as usual, Magnus. I've asked the Linz *Zeitung* to take photographs of you tomorrow and write a story about your art and your courage."

"That won't be enough, Avram."

"We'll do more when we travel to Munich. The English Garden has approved a permit for us. Thousands of people will flock to see you."

"I want the insurance money you collected for the fire."

Avram gently turned away and picked up from a silver tray two gold goblets and the cut glass wine decanter. He poured wine, rose, and sat beside Magnus.

"Come, have some wine with me." He looked at his gold pocket watch. "I don't have much time. Sundown's in forty minutes and I have to be in synagogue with the family to begin the *Shabbes*."

Magnus glowered at him.

"What, *what*, my boy?"

"My mother and father died for you."

"It was their own fault. I told them, time and again, they were mad, making the lions do fantastical tricks. I begged them not to make them jump through the hoops of fire. But they wanted a new program. The lions were terrified, and Monarch knocked over the can of kerosene. I saw him with his mane on fire charging your parents, and then he ran to the others, setting *them* on fire." Avram's eyes drooped, and he pressed his hand against his heart. "In my nightmares, I still see all the fiery lions attacking your parents, then running through the fairgrounds...."

"Avram, *I* am your nightmare."

In a lightning-smooth motion, Magnus slammed the Luger against Avram's temple and pressed the trigger, but nothing happened. He pressed again and again, only to hear the hollow clack of metal jamming. Avram had fallen off the sofa in shock. Enraged, Magnus began kicking him over and over, flinging the Luger to the floor. As it clattered down, it suddenly went off, and Magnus, startled, jumped back.

Avram Beitel was moaning and in his abject terror, began to urinate. But the sour smell did not deter Magnus from packing up the money in the canvas sack below the desk. As he began to load the coins, he realized that they were too heavy, inconsequential in the grander scheme.

"*Wasser...Wasser*," the groaning Avram pleaded, trying to right himself on his elbows before collapsing again.

Magnus cupped his hands, filling them with the rusted and tarnished pieces of change, and sat down on Avram's flabby chest. As Avram opened his mouth for breath, Magnus thrust the coins down his throat. Avram gagged, and Magnus seized his lips, forcing them open, like a dentist. He grabbed a handkerchief, depressed the old man's tongue, grasping it with enormous power, until Avram was forced to swallow the coins. Avram's choking proved to no avail. The rasping melody of heaving congestion as he suffocated to death sounded the music of destiny in Magnus's ears.

Adolf had crept in and watched the last of this thrilling, macabre scene. Trembling, he wondered if he himself were capable of such courage. The glory of it...! Adolf wanted to touch, hold this young god. He had never felt so tormented and at the same time, besotted. He wrapped his arms around Magnus's neck, nudged his face forward, and kissed him passionately on the lips.

"I adore you!" he cried ecstatically.

Magnus was not a homosexual and suspiciously, asked, "Do you?"

Later, during the burgeoning progression of their relationship, Magnus learned to his relief that he was free to pursue his own thirst for women. Hitler's love did not encompass sexual possession. The eventual master of the Third Reich suffered from a birth defect called mono-orchism. He had been born with one damaged testicle and could never achieve an orgasm. But this condition caused a curious and inexplicable reversal of roles: The doting older man feared and loved by the masses fell under Magnus's spell. He invariably acted on Magnus's advice, relying on the younger man's judgment. The puzzlement within Adolf's circle over The Leader's behavior, attributed to his own brand of genius, was in actual fact covertly instigated by none other than Magnus. Armies of historians in future generations would ponder and speculate about Adolf's actions, but they defied analysis. For Magnus was the enigma the Führer took to his grave.

"You're an artist, Magnus, as I once was. I've never met anyone like you. Come, be with me," Adolf entreated him. "You'll warn me of danger."

"Is that all you care about?" Magnus asked softly.

"What more do you want from me?"

"Your love.... You can have mine."

"You'll have it, always. I swear," Adolf vowed, and then assailed by suspicions asked: "What is your actual family name?"

"Winthur. My family can trace its origins back to Albertus Magnus in the twelfth century! Can you do that?" he demanded.

This boy's powers of mystification overwhelmed Hitler, and his eyes filled with tears. This rabid, young anti-Semite's hatred rivaled his own; the affinity stunned him. As a starving artist in Vienna, he too had had to slave for Jewish peddlers who'd hawked his paintings and bled him with their commissions.

"*Mein Liebhaber*, you need a name that carries aristocracy with it. It shouldn't be connected to a Jew's circus. I have an ear for sounds, the impact words make." Hitler closed his eyes and his face became taut with concentration. "You'll be called Magnus Von Winter."

"I like that. With a capital 'V,' like the old, landed aristocracy from way, way back in time?...The purest of Aryans?"

"I wouldn't think of any other way to baptize a prodigy like you. The lowercase 'von' would only degrade you, as though your forefathers had been ennobled by some Kaiser along the way for money-lending or...providing gunpowder." Hitler's mercurial temperament altered and a roguish pleasure surfaced. "I'll pretend that I'm...an uncle of sorts."

"My uncle, yes." The elevation in status of a vagabond performer gratified Magnus. "I see things. If you let me, I'll be your guide."

"Yes, yes, Magnus...."

Outside the wagon, the SA guard waited and saluted Hitler when he followed Magnus down the wooden steps. Magnus scornfully handed Röhm back his faulty automatic and thrust the sack of money at him.

"There's Jewish *geld* inside this sack. It's for The Party.... Oh, and buy yourself a proper revolver," Magnus said. Then, to the assembled men: "Let's leave quickly. I'll guide you through the back woods. It's almost sundown and the police make their rounds now to check that no one's stolen the Jew's loot."

"...And that's why I never use an automatic, Virgil," Magnus declared when they had reached the "jungle" compound, separated from Winterhaven's castle. Magnus's abridged account had kept Virgil transfixed. The old man had omitted that his sleight of hand speed-loading the bullets required daily practice and was based on his experience with mass hypnotism, which was easier to perform than on one individual. As a crowd increased, so its perception and intelligence decreased. Magnus was as fit at eighty-six as he had been at fifty and had not lost his miraculous dexterity.

"You're the bravest, most gallant man on the face of the earth, Herr Von Winter."

"From now on, Virgil, you may call me Magnus."

In a barbed-wire building, two men with rifles waved, greeting Magnus.

"How's our family?" Magnus asked.

"They're happy, sir," one of the men said. A third man, with his back to Magnus, guarded the two while they chatted.

"Have they eaten?" Magnus asked.

"No, but it's time. They had deer and some lame calves yesterday...."

The air suddenly detonated with chilling growls and roars. A lion pride, hunting, moved closer. The female and her two sisters stalked forward from the high grass. Monarch IV, black-maned and imperiously roaring, stood high on a man-made kopje, his great head tilted up to the sky, defying the universe and demanding that it follow his commands.

The troops were already behind the fence, excited but timid onlookers in this spectacle. Two of them carried Corley's body to the entrance. The keepers opened the high steel gate to admit them, while a pair of crouching sharpshooters entered behind them.

The sounds of the rumbling lions reached a riotous crescendo when the corpse was dumped. The stretcher-bearers were unarmed, and sensibly, without cowardice, ran back to safety on the other side. In a blur, the lion pride streaked over to the carcass and tore it apart.

Magnus's voice carried eerily over the microphone: "A feast for lions."

6

The swans of Vienna had arrived for breakfast. Jack Leopold had seldom seen a more beguiling table arrangement even in Hollywood. The Benjamin sisters blotted out the Impressionist masterpieces adorning the walls of the dining room. He put his coffee cup on the mantelpiece, left Harry Summerfield standing by the fireplace, and opened his arms.

Rebecca never entered a room: its space received her. She gave Jack a glistening smile, stooped down, and allowed him to kiss her on both cheeks.

Jack Leopold had the Napoleonic presence of assured, powerfully built, fastidious small men, whose physical scale escalates, until they enveloped people and shrank them. Everything about him proclaimed mastery; his incisive emerald-green eyes consumed her, solved her mysteries. He had thick, graying sandy hair, an eagle nose, and a weathered color that hadn't come from idling around a pool.

"Welcome to our home, Rebecca," he said, beaming.

His wife Paula, taller than he, casually dressed in black pants, with a silver blouse and the panache of an Hermès scarf, waited for her husband's intoxication to wear off. She was somewhere in her sixties and made no effort to disguise her age; she was slender, still in possession of a regal beauty. She, too, had unmasking green eyes, harsh where her husband's might be playful. With the serenity of the mistress of the manor, she angled Jack aside, kissed and embraced Rebecca.

"Rebecca, it's a pleasure to have you. We hope this is the first of many visits." She shook her head in adoration, extended her hand to the smiling Aston Martin owner who was slowly approaching her. "This is our dear friend. Harry Summerfield, Rebecca Benjamin."

Harry gave a little bow, a courtier's derisive smile, at once familiar and icy, as if to suggest that the commotion attending her arrival had not impressed him. Rebecca found herself face to face with a handsome, patrician man who struck her as somewhat European and very pricey. He took her hand and lightly shook it.

"Hello. I'm Jack's hired hand. The resident architect. But I'm not looking for any more work. Your sister's more than enough."

"I'll talk to her. She never had anyone do anything for her. I'm happy to meet you."

"So am I. I'm a member of your American fan club. The tapes Miriam loaned me were sensational."

Rebecca froze and stared at Miriam. "What tapes?"

"The rehearsal tapes when you played at the Bösendorfer Hall at the beginning of January."

"Miriam, you didn't!"

"I asked Lilli to send them."

"Ladies, no musical disagreements," Harry said.

Jack and Paula, arm-in-arm with Rebecca in the middle, led her into the dining room.

She waited to be seated but was nettled. "The sound is fuzzy, asthmatic.... My grandmother has a prehistoric Grundig recorder and I played like an ox and clunked. They're just for us to listen to so I can make adjustments.... This is mortifying!"

"I get a similar feeling when Jack comes to my office and sneaks a look at models that aren't ready to be seen. But you were ready to be heard and certainly seen."

She was not yet placated and he realized that compliments were like lint on a black dress—to be brushed off. But he was delighted to have chased out Taylor. Rebecca was worth the shave. He decided that a flippant artists-united approach would work best. It was obvious to him that she knew how treacherously sensual she came across to men of all ages. For a moment, the Steinway grand, finished in figured Sapele wood, with its deep honeybee's-wing veneer in view from the music room, distracted her.

"Since I brought it up," Harry said, holding out her chair, "very indiscreetly—because I can't keep secrets—let me tell you, Rebecca, I've never heard *anyone* play 'Les Adieux' as lyrically as you did. And I didn't notice any blurring on the fuzzy tape."

"You wouldn't; only she does," Miriam said. "When Rebecca was eighteen she won the Rubenstein International Masters playing it."

"I milked it," she said. "You're not a music expert...Harry...just one in kindness." She bowed her head to her hosts, and then gave Miriam a curdled smile. "As you all are. Especially Scott. I can't wait to see him again."

"His flight arrives at one," Jack said. "I'm going to play golf and leave you to Harry at the kids' house."

"Can you believe how lucky I am, Becky?" Reverting to her teenage effusiveness, Miriam continued, "Harry's going to redesign it for us!"

"My wedding contribution," he said, without making it sound like a grand gesture, although everyone at the table—even Rebecca—was aware that it was.

The breakfast menu had everything on it that the best café in Vienna might offer: the kitchen staff deposited trays of caviar, smoked fish, bagels, breads, an array of juices, fruits, and grilled vegetables on a table, below a glowing Renoir picnic scene which dazzled her. Not the fact that it was a Renoir, but that it belonged. Miriam had not only found a wealthy family, but also one with impeccable taste.

"Is there anything special you like?" Paula asked.

"Just being here with you is special." She accepted a champagne framboise from a tray. "But I'd like to try your piano when I'm over my jet lag."

"We wondered if you'd ask," Jack replied good-humoredly. "We thought you'd like some down time from your schedule."

"She never stops practicing," Miriam said, rising from her seat opposite Jack and Paula.

"Scott's asked me to play something at the wedding, and I better get it right."

Miriam placed her hands on Rebecca's shoulders. With childlike adoration, Rebecca turned her cheek and rubbed it on her hand. She felt tipsy with happiness, even before she'd drunk anything.

"I have to admit I'm disappointed and upset that my grandmother Lilli and Tante Herta weren't up to the trip. But I have Rebecca here—" she stroked the brat's hair—"as my maid of honor. Rebecca and I lost our parents in a freak accident when we were barely out of diapers—at least I was—but now I feel that our parents have been reborn in you, Paula, and you, Jack."

"Please, Miriam, no tears before caviar," Harry said. Her gushing gave him acid reflux.

Unlike Rebecca, her sister's infernal kowtowing abraded his nerves. He had been bullied into redesigning the house Jack had bought for Scott and Miriam. A foreclosure in Westwood. Miriam, ever detail-minded and posturing, rankled him. If Jack Leopold lived in a tract house and Paula were making cheese dips, he wondered how she'd act. Money made bitches like her queen for a day, until, down the line, the husband wised up to the shrike he'd married and she had to be carried on a litter into divorce court attended by shrinks.

Rebecca heaped a portion of Beluga on her plate, the size of bird's-nest, and gave him a wicked nod. She liked everything about Harry, especially how offhand he was about himself. Middle forties, she thought, with a sonorous voice at low registers, and as slick as the philosophy professor in Vienna. She didn't ignore the fact that she was also besotted with cars. Rebecca's attraction to him and his Aston Martin, more easily given—since she was determined to drive it—progressed exponentially. Another older man, another nemesis, but this one possessed a grandeur unequaled in her experience of American males known for celebrating the three Ds: their dicks, dough, and drinking.

Food.... No more flat beer in dirty glasses with airport sausages. Rebecca tasted almost everything and ordered apple pancakes. She marveled at the Leopolds' phenomenal wealth. When Lilli had shipped them off, like basketball prospects, to the highest bidder, the penniless scholarship sisters had discovered that in America, life itself had all been about money.

After breakfast, Miriam gave Rebecca a brief of tour of the grounds—her digs for the next two weeks. Like schoolgirls crossing the street, the sisters walked hand in hand, with Harry and the Leopolds a short distance behind them. At the moment, Rebecca's feelings became ambivalent about Lilli's absence and Herta's carping. The old ladies deserved to be spoiled, a bonus for all the sacrifices they'd made raising the two of them. And yet, sharing these intimate moments with Miriam was precious, something Rebecca had yearned for. Selfish, perhaps, but the close weave between the sisters would inevitably unravel with Miriam's marriage and Rebecca's career.

"It's Eden. They're all great, Miriam. And they appreciate you."

"Don't make me cry, Becky. I'm so happy; I can't sleep at night.... Sorry, we've got to get a move on. It's Sunday and I don't want to keep Harry waiting. He's got his own plans. And we've got the wedding shower tonight."

Miriam went into high organizational gear. They followed Harry in Miriam's new gold Volvo convertible through Beverly Hills. After all the years of glamorous TV film footage, the village seemed small to Rebecca, the sightseer, passing designers' flagship boutiques.

"Why didn't you get a Ferrari?"

"And get carjacked to Tijuana to a chop shop...then have my corneas auctioned on the street corner...?"

"As usual, you're still more pragmatic than I am, Miriam."

Cruising down the Wilshire Corridor, stockpiled with highrises, with Miriam as guide, they turned into a suburban street called Lynbrook, cloven with small hills and dips.

"We're big-city girls; that's why I picked Westwood. It's not as fashionable as Beverly Hills or Bel Air. But we're just a few blocks from the main street. I can walk to shops—not easy in L.A. UCLA has concerts at Royce Hall, eighteen hundred capacity. Schoenberg Hall is more intimate. First-rate acoustics, and Scott can play with some chamber-music groups."

"Everything's finally working out."

"Rebecca, I'm sorry I hit the roof with you this morning."

"*Schatzie*, don't apologize. Look, we've known for years that Herta dictates everything. It never mattered what we wanted. She manipulates Lilli."

Miriam was silent for some time.

"What? Have I upset you by telling you the facts?"

"No...no, Becky. It's just that I've wanted to tell you something for years."

Rebecca prodded her. "Go on...."

"From an early age, I sensed that something was perverse. A shady element I could never figure out. I think Lilli's control over people is so deeply rooted—I almost want to say immoral—that she simply uses Herta as a screen. Lilli's the problem, not Herta."

Rebecca clutched Miriam's arm.

"There're always ugly secrets and role-playing in a house of women. That's the real threat—not men."

7

Virgil and Noreen were parked outside the Leopold estate munching cold Big Macs with the *Enquirer* pages epened over their laps. They had discovered that Harry Summerfield was the architect working on Miriam and Scott's house in Westwood. But his unexpected appearances, unsettled them.

"This guy's got more cars than I've had hot dinners," Noreen said with distant admiration.

"I'm thinking we should check with Magnus about him. He likes to get rid of people before they become problems."

Virgil and Noreen had been following Miriam for three weeks and were familiar with her routine. It had been tiring work, and some hands from Winterhaven had come down to spell them. But that hadn't worked out. The men, not used to the freedom of a metropolis, had become unruly. They'd brought in drugged lowlife Strip hookers to the furnished hotel-apartment the "Hoyts" had rented.

Virgil had ordered them back. No matter how violent or willing these ex-cons and former asylum habitués were, they needed the discipline and regimentation of Winterhaven. The true depth of the conspiracy was beyond this group.

Miriam took the familiar route to the house in Westwood. What disturbed Virgil was the new girl in the passenger seat beside Miriam. Previously she had carted along Paula Leopold; sometimes contractors and workmen turned up; or she met designer hustlers carrying big books of carpet and wallpaper samples.

The architect's Aston Martin was already parked in the driveway. Virgil stopped the van at the brow of the hill and made a U-turn, enabling them to watch what was going on.

"Do we know her?" Noreen asked.

"No. Get the video camera and do your tourist number. And go through your kit to make sure you've got everything you need."

"Yes, sir. I checked it twice already. Trust Nurse Noreen," she said with a half laugh.

"What's funny?"

"Oh, you. I just love it when you get all poker-faced."

"Murder is serious business," he said tersely.

When she rambled out with her camera, Virgil realized that the long break from Winterhaven, where their duties were carefully defined, had enabled them to truly connect. She was on call only for him and they had talked about marriage. They had even discussed a date. April 20th Hitler's birthday, would lend the occasion a righteous commitment.

Sitting behind the wheel on this quiet street in Westwood, Virgil reflected on his promotion. With it had come a raise in salary and expanded responsibilities. His entry into the inner circle thrilled him. Although Bruno's Directive—the Chanukah Blitzkriegs—had harvested worldwide publicity and nonstop cable TV specials of screeching Jews protesting, an attack of even greater subtlety and deadliness was needed, Magnus had explained to him as they'd watched the lions devour Corley's corpse.

"You and Noreen trumped everyone in the country with that rabbi and jeweler in New York."

In total, five Jews were dead: the pair in New York, and several rich nobodies.

"Thank you. It took planning."

"That's what Bruno said. We're both very impressed with Noreen as well."

Virgil's eyes glistened, his blanched skin flushed. He smiled with pride, revealing white but irregular teeth. Magnus recalled the long-legged bag of bones he had been, but years of weightlifting had bulked him out.

"During our trip to Vienna, Bruno and I decided to make you the new *gauleiter* of California. Every action in the state will be under your authority."

"What?"

Virgil was flabbergasted. He had expected relocation to a small state to organize partisans and malcontents fed up with the Aryan Nations and Nazi Low Rider movements. But nothing like this.

"You can count on me to serve our cause with honor and brutality."

"I'm giving you both the most important assignment of your lives."

After celebrating his elevation with Noreen, Virgil had opened up to her about his past. But he gave her an edited version. His was a story about hardscrabble farming families. A drought in the Salinas Valley had destroyed his father's asparagus crop and he had mortgaged the family's hundred acres to the bank; another bad-weather season had brought the Hoyts to their knees. Somehow or other the mortgage had found its way into the hands of a firm of Jew brokers and accountants who bought "paper," dealt in seconds and thirds, and eventually, had foreclosed on the Hoyts. The acreage had been bought by another Jew developer who had turned it into an industrial park.

When Virgil had been thirteen, with his two kid sisters in foster care, his mother, a local beauty, had run off to Mexico with a truck farmer. Father and son then went the rounds looking for work and had eventually found jobs as gravediggers. They'd worked cheaper than the unionized bunch and often at Jewish cemeteries up and down Northern California. "Just once, Virgil, I'd like us to put a live Yid into the ground." Finally, when his father had succumbed to lung cancer, Virgil, at seventeen, had gone back to school and worked in construction.

His career, such as it was, began after he took some night courses at San Joaquin Delta College. He did not want to be a laborer, or farm hand, and had studied business and bookkeeping. The students called it Jewish Engineering. Virgil possessed a sharp, probing intelligence, and his gentle friendliness made him oddly popular at Gold-Farber & Associates, Mortgage Brokers and CPAs. It was, in fact, the same firm that had foreclosed on the Hoyt farm, but in the intervening years, they had foreclosed on so many farms that his was hardly a memorable case. This was his first real position requiring skill.

These Yids had some deal with a big corporate agri-business. They used to pay the wetbacks by check and they had a check-cashing outfit. They'd discount the checks because none of these people had any ID. It took him a year to find a chink in the firm's accounting procedures, and he began to systematically embezzle money from the firm. He invented an imaginary force of itinerant workers and cut checks for them. More pressing than his quest for a stake to start his own business was the sexual obsession he had developed. Virgil had fallen in love with Howard Farber's fourteen-year-old daughter.

In Virgil's heaven, he would be empowered to count the downy golden hairs on Sarah Farber's entire body. He might have abominated the sect, but, he had to admit, they did produce luscious females. He saw Sarah occasionally when she accompanied her father down from the main office in Sacramento to the Stockton outpost.

The office manager, a hulk of flab, had a long history of instability and alcoholism; the two female bookkeepers were beset by problems raising their kids and, consequently, seemed to spend half their workdays petitioning the schools to reinstate their vagrant brats. Even though Virgil was the fourth link on the office chain, Howard Farber would always find something generous to say to him.

"I really like your attitude, Virgil. Coming in Saturdays."

"Well, Mr. Loudon has had a shaky pen, lately. And the gals have Little League, then the Wal-Mart to hit, and I don't mind picking up the slack."

He received raises his second year and was earning twenty-six thousand a year—plus another fifteen from the fictional workers. He never messed with the state or IRS withholding, concluding that the very payment of taxes would eliminate any inkling of misappropriation. He opened an account in a Stockton wetback S&L, using a real social security card and counterfeit driver's license from a dead man. To the tellers at the "We Cash Payroll Checks Instantly" bank, he was simply another load who took half his check in cash and deposited the rest.

Virgil's *float* always chaperoned an excursion into Stockton's hooker precinct. In their dusky cribs, and for a price...well, they'd let Virgil do his thing and forget about it.

But no matter which señorita Virgil selected, when he closed his eyes, she mutated into the golden Princess Sarah. This image of the perfect mate entailed a drive past the Farber house in Sacramento. Sometimes he would catch sight of his beauty, but mostly, he staked out the house at night, until he was able to predict the family's routine.

The following year, in the middle of a warm summer night, he crept into Sarah's bedroom while she was asleep and kidnapped her. He drove her to an abandoned auto body shop whose accounts he had once serviced outside of the Pollardville Ghost Town. She was never seen again and he did not become a suspect.

But Howard Farber eventually tracked the embezzlement to Virgil, and he was given four harsh years by an indignant Hispanic judge.

At Cal State Sacramento (SAC), the sister institution of Folsom, Virgil, used to getting on with people, considered his time well spent. During his tenure, bodybuilding and the support of Magnus Von Winter created a blade. Virgil dispensed hate literature for the emerging Nazi Low Riders: Jews and Blacks and Orientals did not belong in America and should be deported. Virgil was elected president of SAC's Nazi groups and wrote fervent tracts proclaiming their superiority.

Posing as the benevolent head of a prisoners' aid society, Magnus traveled to various prisons in search of recruits. At SAC, he encountered Virgil, filled with anger about the Jewish conspiracy that had taken over the world. Magnus found the young man a suitable candidate for Winterhaven training. He plied Virgil with gifts of food and hired an attorney for his parole hearing, who persuaded the board to commute his sentence.

When Virgil was discharged he lived like a prince, doing the books at the Winterhaven slaughterhouse and learning the trade of tanning. He loved the Nazi indoctrination classes and knew that his moment would eventually come.

"Virgil, Virgil." Noreen was tapping on the window of the van and roused him from his trance of glorious deeds.

He climbed out and stood behind her. She was still shooting the video of Miriam and the new woman, chatting together outside a gabled two-story old red-bricked house lofted on the crest of the corner. Wayward ivy grew up the walls to the chimney.

"Their voices carried," Noreen informed him, "and they were speaking German."

"Maybe she's a girlfriend from Vienna. Let's get back out of sight."

8

The sisters walked up the steps past a small garden; the front door was open and they could see Harry inside. The pine floors had been marine-varnished and were covered with plastic. They passed through a long entry hall and into a large living room, swimming in natural light from a galaxy of French windows, which led to a broad expanse of garden filled with mature oaks. Harry looked up from blueprints spread out on a workman's table in front of a fireplace.

"All this space..." Rebecca said, squeezing Miriam's arm.

"We've got over four thousand square feet. It's going to be a family house."

Harry smiled at them. "Come on, I'll take you through and show you what I plan."

As they followed him, the front door opened. Scott, harried, burst in.

"Hi. I hope somebody can loan me forty bucks. I took a cab from the airport and I forgot to go to an ATM. The driver's holding my cello hostage outside."

To everyone's laughter, Harry pulled out a wad of cash and handed two twenties to Scott, who rushed down the steps. He was back in minutes, carrying his cello.

"Becky, you remember my financier fiancé," Miriam said, kissing Scott.

He then turned agilely and roped Rebecca in his arms, kissing her with enthusiasm.

"I'm thrilled to see you, Rebecca."

"Me, too, Scott. I don't know how many times I've been in your position in Vienna." She looked mischievously at Harry. "Unfortunately, I didn't have Harry to bail me out, just two old ladies screaming at me while they emptied their purses."

He moved to Harry and gave him a bear hug. "Thanks."

"It's okay. I'll just add it to your father's account. Scott, I was going to take the ladies on a walk-through."

Rebecca couldn't remember when she had been with a family group whose sweeping warmth and affection cast aside any thoughts of conflict that invariably arose or lay hidden. It wasn't simply that Miriam had found her soul mate, but along with it—despite the Leopold fortune—such a tenor of benevolence. She wandered last in line; Harry took them upstairs, pointing out the details of expansion for children's rooms, the master suite, and an addition to the terrace overlooking the garden for a rehearsal studio with a skylight.

"From the standpoint of acoustics, it would be better to have it all wood, but you don't want to be shut in. You can see the sky, treetops, and when you have kids, you can keep an eye on them and still practice."

"That's great. We can build another studio in the yard later on if we need it," Scott said, looking at Miriam, who nodded.

"The other thing is that I don't want to redo the exterior. I could tear it down and build you something modern and arty. But then you'd have neighbors and cars stopping to gawp."

"Yes, let's keep it low-key," Miriam said, curling into Scott.

"Right," Scott agreed, "the last thing we want is everyone to know that Jack Leopold's son and his wife moved in. It'll be a new experience for me—living without security people around. I guess in my parents' position—and with a house like theirs—you need them. But Miriam and I just want to be what we are—a couple of traveling musicians."

Scott's modesty and thoughtfulness touched Rebecca. He had a roguish, hippie quality, with his slick hair in a ponytail, and a raggedy beard and moustache. He had deep green eyes, his mother's broad nose, flashing white teeth, and chunky fingers. He was brawnier than his father, five-seven, about Miriam's height, but a good five inches shorter than Rebecca, the tallest and most self-conscious member of the quartet.

"When do you think it'll be ready?" Miriam asked.

"I'll have one of my people at the office pull the permits and put on our top contractors, Miriam," Harry said, disguising his exasperation. Like all architects, especially one of his genius, he hated to be prodded. "If you think of any more changes, let my office know."

The couple headed down the stairs and began a loud dialogue in the kitchen.

"....I'm not going to get in the middle of one of your mother's campaigns," Miriam was saying. "I can't stand her taste...."

Harry guided Rebecca to the terrace, and the burst of bright northern light made her squint for a moment. He handed her a pair of sunglasses. "You'll need these in L.A."

"Thank you.... I couldn't find mine."

He slipped them on her. "Keep them. I've got a spare."

"No, no, but thank you."

He was silent for a moment. An odd, tingling sensation had over-taken him when he'd placed the sunglasses on Rebecca's face. His very sensitive olfactory nerves picked up a rare feminine essence that aroused him. She gave off the scent of something wild, almost reminding him of a walk through the damp woods.

"I'll be leaving for Tampa in a couple of days. And won't be back until the wedding."

"Tampa? Where is that?"

"It's a lovely city, with natural beauty, on the west coast of Florida. I keep forgetting you're not American and don't know the country. Your English is perfect."

"I suppose...with an Ohio whinny and some New York gutter in it."

"Not so I'd notice."

He saw through her disingenuous modesty. She was luscious, a challenge for a sexual craftsman like him, definitely worth the trouble.

"Are you taking a vacation there?" she asked.

"No, I'm building my dream project for Jack." Harry experienced a surge of affinity with her. "You're a brilliant pianist, Rebecca, so you'll understand. You create music, I sculpt space. I've always believed that an architect creates temples, an artist just paints them. This complex will house a theater, museum, concert hall, a gigantic shopping center, naturally. There'll also be a park on the bay and tropical gardens."

It took her a moment to grasp the enormity of his undertaking.

"That sounds incredible. My grandmother's also a pianist and in her day, a great one. But she loves all the arts, and Vienna is an architectural wonder. She used to take Miriam and me to all our grand buildings on the Ringstrasse, and quote something from Goethe: 'I call architecture frozen music.'"

"Yes, I know the line. Look, this will keep me busy—and out of trouble—for at least three years.... Who knows, some day you might play there."

Her interest peaked. "This is all unbelievable." She did a ballerina turn, her hair swirling. "You *are* serious. My head's spinning."

"I have that effect on people.... Rebecca, are you going to be tied up with Miriam *all* the time?"

"I'm not sure." She loved to create uncertainty, make a man hit his marks. "We'll see. Maybe she'll want to do some things on her own...or with Paula."

"Why don't you persuade Miriam to look at more paint samples for the house together with Paula and truly bond?" There was an edge to him that intrigued her, and he knew it. "Can you have dinner, lunch—a drink with me?"

"Ummm," Rebecca hummed, ambiguous, enjoying the prelude to the game when the low register in a passage tiptoed out before it was fully developed into a theme. Filling in the riddle of temptation had always offered possibilities.

"Can I drive your car?"

"Sure, that's easy," he said, unable to suppress a laugh. "I'm still like a kid about them, too. I have four more." He took a chance, wrapping his arm around her neck, and she playfully nuzzled him. He was that rare man who'd never had his face slapped.

"Want me to list them in any special order?"

"Harry, your Aston Martin will do just fine."

9

For once punctual at seven o'clock, fresh from a nap, and Visine in her eyes, Rebecca came downstairs. She couldn't believe the scene unfolding before her: a Japanese chef was displaying his Samurai dagger artistry for the Leopolds. Sushi prepared at home made her giddy. Scott left the table. He was in warm-ups and looked sleepy.

In the background *Sixty Minutes* with Mike Wallace had begun. "What a blessing, he's not doing a number on the lead and mercury in raw fish," Scott said. "Sunday nights are our exotic dinners," he explained. "Chinese, Thai, Indian."

"How monotonous," she said with a laugh. "But maybe I could get used to it."

"Hello, gorgeous!" Jack shouted from his observation post alongside the chef. "This was flown in from the Tokyo market last night."

"It's Omega Three for the week. Want a taste?" Paula asked.

Behind her, in a sleek navy silk suit with a bright yellow ruffled blouse, Miriam caught hold of Rebecca as she was about to advance for a tasting.

"We've got dinner."

"Have fun, ladies." Scott gave Miriam a drowsy hug. "'Bye, babe."

"Male strippers, Miriam?" Jack asked.

"These women are depraved musicians, so I don't know what to expect," she said.

"Do you want Frank to run you over?" Paula asked.

"No, thanks, I'm in love with my new car."

Fifteen minutes later, the sisters sauntered over the bridge from the parking lot of the Hotel Bel-Air. They paused for a moment to watch the illuminated swans gliding on the pond below.

"What a place to get married," Rebecca said.

"Too humdrum for the Leopolds."

"When we were kids and everything at the house was so somber and I used to get depressed, you'd say, 'Don't worry, we're destiny's darlings.'"

Miriam held Rebecca close. "I was right, wasn't I?"

Six old schoolmates, four from Oberlin and a pair from Juilliard thrilled Miriam. They were sitting on sofas in the warm, mahogany paneled lounge before a roaring fire. The sisters went round, kissing the women before sitting down in armchairs.

Champagne was opened and toasts made. Carrie and Joanna, two sleek lipstick-lesbian violinists from Oberlin, had joined the Cincinnati Chamber Symphony. Rebecca, the child prodigy, had accidentally caught them in bed when she'd had to deliver a score from Miriam. It had caused an uproar, and neither of the women had forgiven Rebecca for what they'd considered spying. Miriam had patiently tried to buffer Rebecca's shock, and sensitively enlightened her about sexual orientation and the need never to be judgmental. It was a lesson in tolerance that had served Rebecca well. Miriam's presence eased the coolness of her reception.

"We've been hearing all about you," Carrie said. "The Wunderkind."

"It's no surprise," Joanna noted. "We knew you had *it* even when you were a brat."

"Thank you," she replied and passed to the pair of wives. In piano competitions, Rebecca had scorched the older women. They were first-class accompanists, but nothing more, and had married fair-to-middling musicians, like Scott.

"It's babies and the occasional call for a fill-in," a plump, amiable Kate said. "I'm teaching composition part of the year."

"That sounds like a full life, Kate," Rebecca, at her most diplomatic, responded.

"I brought my latest one with me. He's eight months old...with colic. My husband's babysitting at the hotel."

Rebecca was in her element with vintage champagne, the absence of a schedule, and a vacation at the Leopold estate.

"I'm so proud of you, Rebecca," Maureen, slender and a fussy musician, said, hanging onto her. "After you won the Rubenstein, I thought you were ready to come out."

"My grandmother insisted I wait. My repertoire wasn't strong enough to suit her."

"Is she still teaching?" Kate asked.

"Yes, at the conservatory. But she's been booted up to emeritus."

While Miriam was flooded with chatter, Rebecca moved on to the two former Juilliard students waiting for an audience: one a sonorous French horn player, the other a flautist. Both had befriended Rebecca during her two years in New York at the Wilson Residence Hall. They'd cooked together on a Coleman stove, traded dirt, and armed Rebecca with Trojans before dates.

"How's my favorite tart?"

"Still not in your class, Norma."

"Hah, not in bed, that's for sure. Rebecca, we read about your playing at Salzburg last year. The reviews! When are you going to play here?"

"Vienna first, according to Lilli's plan, then see what offers we get. She doesn't care what I think, she just wants to soak everyone."

The sisterhood, such as it was, Miriam's bridesmaids, had finished their third bottle of Cristal when they wobbled into the elegant, peach-colored dining room. They sat at a large round table, embowered with roses and peonies. An imperious waiter introduced himself. His credentials were worthy of Dr. Kissinger and the Dolder Grand in Zurich: the specials followed, everything "napped" with some kind of sauce, and soufflé orders were demanded of the tipsy women.

After they sent him on his way, Miriam tapped her glass.

"I'm so grateful to have you all here. I know it hasn't been easy with your schedules and family obligations. So thank you...." With her breasts inflated with pride, Miriam felt the tenderness and cama-raderie. "We've all had to put up with Rebecca. As her first and prin-cipal martyr, let me say it was worth it. She'll have her debut in Vienna with the Philharmoniker on the first day of spring. Mehta will conduct—"

"—We'll see if I'm in the mood," Rebecca piped in, ripe with good will. She squeezed Miriam's hand under the table, then glanced over at the food. "The maître d' is deboning Dover Sole. I'm having an orgasm!"

"I told you not to bother with the sushi."

By ten-thirty, dazed, a little drunk, her eyes drooping, and unable to contend with a rebound of jet lag, Rebecca whispered to Miriam. "Sorry, I'm fading."

Kate was beside them on her cell phone, anxiously explaining to her husband, without success, how to handle their infant. "Okay, I'm on my way," she said, hanging up and glumly looking at Miriam. "Forgive me, but I have to leave now."

"Kate, will you give Rebecca a lift back?" Jack Leopold had reserved and of course paid for dozens of rooms at the Beverly Hills Hotel for guests who were flying in for the wedding. "Tower Way is just a couple of minutes from the hotel." She quickly drew her a map with directions and the home phone number. "Maybe I should call the house and they'll send a car for you, Becky."

"No, no, it's no trouble," Kate assured her. "Don't let us break up the party. You guys have a good time."

"We'll be fine." Rebecca leaned down, kissed Miriam, and said, "Watch your drinking."

"I will.... Kate, come to the house tomorrow with your husband and baby, say about twelve. You can have a swim in the indoor pool, play tennis, and use the spa. You'll meet Scott and we can all have lunch together. He wants us all to play together one night...."

"Sounds great."

Rebecca lovingly stroked Miriam's hair. The combination of fatigue and exultation made Rebecca emotional and she had tears in her eyes.

"We *are* destiny's darlings."

10

Shortly after midnight, with goodnight kisses, the six remaining women huddled together under the hotel's green canopy. A sharp-edged wind screeched through the canyon and the treetops flailed, while their cars droned in the driveway. Miriam, with a dreamy smile, took a last look over the stone bridge, but the swans had taken cover.

"Your Volvo's here...."

Miriam handed the valet twenty dollars for their cars. "Thanks, but Mr. Leopold already tipped me," he said, holding the door for her. "Do you know your way, ma'am?"

"Yes. Perfectly."

Miriam inhaled the luxurious new-car leather smell, slid in her seatbelt clasp, and with a last merry smile at the hotel, turned right out of the driveway down Stone Canyon Road. With no traffic, she'd be at the house and in bed with Scott in ten minutes. Two double espressos that had counteracted the champagne and wine wired her. She zoomed down the road when she saw—

—A crying, partially dressed woman lurching into the road in front of her.

Miriam hit the brakes at the narrow Strada Corta Road intersection on the left, just before Sunset Boulevard. Instantly, she slipped the gear into park, put on the emergency, and released her seatbelt. There were no streetlights at the junction and she flicked on the brights. She thrust open her door and rushed to the woman, still weaving and moaning in pain.

She wore only a bra and panties and had clearly been attacked and dumped here.

"Let me help you!" Miriam cried, reaching toward her. "I'll call nine-one-one!"

Suddenly—the woman straightened up, swung her fist at Miriam's jaw, and knocked her to the ground. Stunned, Miriam tried to right herself, scraping her knees, then stumbled to her feet and lost her left shoe. Her heart was hammering in her chest.

Behind Miriam a man loomed out of nowhere. She reeled in shock when he pressed a long-barreled gun into her right eye.

"Hands behind your back," he ordered, viciously jerking her right hand behind her. He snapped a pair of handcuffs on her wrists.

"What are you doing?" she gasped, unable to control her breathing and the terror engulfing her.

"Shut up!" the woman commanded her. She had slipped on a long, dark coat.

They dragged and pulled her into the back of a black four-door van. As Miriam's shock gave way to a sharp, pervasive dread, she screamed. The woman punched her again. As Miriam fell back, the woman yanked up her skirt and ripped at her hose. She dug her powerful fingers into her Miriam's thigh and jabbed a needle into the soft flesh. Miriam gave a strangled moan from the sting.

On his knees, the man swiveled from the driver's seat and reached over the headrest. He seized Miriam's head in a powerful vise. With his fingers gouging her windpipe, he slapped a thick piece of duct tape over her mouth, then tossed her back like a gym bag.

With the assignment completed, the man turned to his accomplice and congratulated her: "That was like an Oscar de La Hoya haymaker, Noreen." He drove down to the light on Sunset Boulevard, turned right, and headed for the 405 Freeway. "I better watch my step with you," he said with a wise-guy grin.

She bowed her head genially. "Thank you, kind sir," she said. Then, seriously: "You put a roll of quarters in your palm and swing from the heels. I told you I had plenty of experience with the crazies at my old institutions. The real bad ones are heavy-duty. You get an eighty-pound girl on crank, she can be ferocious. Miriam was a pussycat."

Hearing her name, Miriam was overwrought with confusion and strained to remain conscious, but the drug with which she had been injected was already making her drowsy. Her swollen jaw ached. When she ran her tongue over her lower teeth, they were loose and jagged. She couldn't stay awake. Slumped in a corner, she peered at the blurring lights of oncoming cars before sinking into a stupor and blacking out.

The persistent rapping on the door startled Rebecca and rescued her from a tortuous dreamscape. She wasn't sure if she had imagined the sound or if it were actual.

"What...?" She switched on the bedside lamp and looked at her watch. "Yes, just a minute." The knocking grew louder. "I'm coming." She opened the door, expecting Miriam, but instead, scanned Scott's drowsy, heavy-lidded eyes.

"Sorry to disturb you. Is Miriam in here with you?"

"No, Scott, no."

They stared silently at each other for a moment.

"No? Her clothes aren't in our bedroom. I thought she didn't want to wake me and might have stayed with you."

"Maybe she's still out with the girls."

"At four-thirty in the morning?"

Rebecca, befuddled, tried to shake herself out of her sleep haze.

"Where could she be?"

Scott stared at her. "I don't know. I'm worried. Her car isn't in the driveway."

"Does she usually leave it there?"

"She always parks in front. Robert puts it in the garage in the back with the rest of the cars."

"Is anyone up to ask?"

"Two of the night staff are in the kitchen. They say she hasn't come in." Scott poured himself a glass of water from the pitcher on the nightstand, then dipped a handkerchief in it and rubbed it on his face. "I tried her cell before I woke you."

Rebecca shivered and found a sweater that she slipped over her nightdress. "Maybe the phone's not working. It happens all the time."

"It's fine," Scott said, his voice hushed with apprehension. "We both have each other's code and all I got were my own messages."

"Let's call the.... the...."

"The Bel-Air. I did. The valet's still on his shift, which ends at eight. He said Miriam left alone about midnight after the rest of the group. That's why I came to your room."

"Let's throw on some clothes and drive over. Scott, give me five minutes." She thought quickly. "Have you told your parents?"

"They're still asleep. I don't want to upset them."

11

Miriam awoke, groggy, with stabbing pains in her jaw, and sickened by the odor of urine. Her panties were soaked. She tried to remember the attack. Where was she? How long had she been unconscious?

Splintered visions danced through her mind of a woman in the road.... She'd been hit very hard. The woman was now sitting in front of the van with the man and they were turning off a dark main road, possibly a freeway. The tires ground over a metal grate. They came to a gatehouse where an armed man greeted them and opened a barrier for them.

High steel razor-wire fencing enclosed the property. Miriam saw and heard cattle and horses, smoke coming from the chimneys of black and red houses, high lampposts with stark halogen lights shining through the misty pastures. She had never been on a ranch and felt completely disoriented.

The car stopped again, this time to let a herd of calves cross over a metal-ridged platform fording a stream. To the left of her was a hut where a large fire blazed, and a group of men were wrestling calves to the ground. A tall, bearded man in a leather apron was branding the animals. Their agonized mewling terrified her.

When they finally crossed over a drawbridge, she observed a building that mystified her. This edifice might have emerged from Europe's medieval past. It was a castle of some kind, a bizarre Gothic design. She thought she had stepped back in time and crossed the threshold into another world, an ancient preserved quarter.

Disbelief intensified her trauma. For a second, she wondered if the hulking woman had given her acid, and a drug trip was causing these hallucinations. Miriam had never tried anything but the occasional joint years ago.

The van stopped under a porte cochère in front of the stone building, lit by wall torches.

"Want me to take her tape off, Virgil?"

Naming the man introduced a new level of terror to Miriam. Before they had been bestial criminals, nameless monsters. But now that she knew them as Noreen and Virgil, her fear entered a realm that soared beyond her experience.

At the same moment, she had a promising insight: These people had conspired to kidnap her to collect a ransom from Jack Leopold. It was obvious, or else why would they have abducted a total stranger? They had carefully planned this, shadowing her for days, weeks. They had accomplices. How much was she worth...five, ten million?

"Sure. It doesn't matter if she yells her head off here," he said.

Miriam screamed as the tape was torn off. Her lips were raw; her mouth throbbed; bleeding welts extended from her ears, to her jaw.

Wrenched from the car, she was revived by the sudden rush of bitter, wintry air for an instant. She staggered and was bullied ahead to an entrance. She couldn't believe her eyes. A man in a black SS-uniform with a swastika armband on his jacket raised his hand in a salute to the couple, who returned the gesture.

"You guys are something special."

Miriam could no longer focus. Her body gave way and she fainted. She was dragged backwards by her cuffs and did not hear her host's greeting.

"Welcome to Winterhaven, Miriam. My name is Magnus Von Winter."

12

Frantically speeding along Sunset Boulevard, Scott kept up an uneasy chatter that alarmed Rebecca. "I'll take a shortcut through the Bellagio Gate to the hotel."

He kept barking the names of streets as if his route mattered to someone who might just as well have been in Brazil. It was now five-fifteen, according to an all-news station whose freeway traffic and weather conditions were spewed out by a chatty helicopter pilot cracking asinine jokes. This was her first and she hoped last experience of performance weather. Winding along empty, curving streets, she at last recognized the parking lot of the Bel-Air.

Several members of the hotel staff and two valets were already outside, all displaying morose expressions. As they got out of the car, a man in a blazer came forward.

"Mr. Leopold."

"Yes."

"I'm the night manager."

"Do you have any information?" Rebecca blurted out.

"We contacted our security people—Bel-Air Patrol—and they found a gold Volvo convertible down on Stone Canyon at the intersection of Strada Corta. The doors were open, but the battery was dead." He pulled out a pad. "California license BMB8433." He pointed to a valet. "We sent Eddie down and he still had the parking ticket when he took her car and identified it."

"Have you called the police?" Scott asked.

"Security did."

"Which station would handle this?"

"West Los Angeles Division. They're located over on Butler—just off Santa Monica Boulevard. You know the Nuart Theater. It's a few blocks past that on the south side." He fell silent in shared concern. "Please let us know how she is."

Once they were back inside the car, Scott's head drooped and they sat dumbfounded. Rebecca thought he was about to cry. He seemed shrunken behind the wheel, like a boy pretending to be an adult and fearful of the consequences. She pressed his arm with support and affection. "I'll be okay," he said, turning out of the driveway and down Stone Canyon, passing newspaper vans lofting newspapers over the gates of manor houses.

"Rebecca, I have a difficult question."

"Yes, what?"

His words came out in a torrent. "Did Miriam mention anything about being unhappy? Calling off the wedding? Maybe it got to be too much for her. My parents? Was there a guy in Vienna she was secretly in love with? Maybe she met someone here or when we were on tour—?"

"No, no, no!"

She was deeply shaken by Miriam's disappearance, but it would be irresponsible to reveal now that Miriam thought she might be pregnant. She could not betray this intimate confidence. When Miriam returned, it would be her place to tell Scott.

At the junction, a police car light flashed, and a tow truck operator was rolling out a cable. Scott pulled into the side street and sprang out with Rebecca.

A young officer eyed him warily.

"I'm the legal owner of the car," Scott said, producing his driver's license. "The pink slip is in the Volvo's glove compartment—or should be."

"Did you get stuck, or what?"

"No, my fiancée was driving it home last night after a party at the Bel Air Hotel."

"She left their parking lot at about midnight," Rebecca said. "I'm her sister."

"Did she contact either of you and say she was having car trouble?"

"No," Scott said, "it was running fine when the valet brought her the car at the Bel Air."

"Hang on for a couple of minutes."

The policeman dashed over to the tow-truck driver and took him aside. The driver dropped the cable and went to the side of the black and white. When he resumed work, he was wearing latex gloves, as was the uniformed policeman.

"I phoned this in," he informed Scott moments later. "Mr. Leopold, just to be on the safe side, we're going to impound the car."

In the chilly morning, Rebecca felt the sweat gather on her neck. "I'm confused," she said. "Would you normally do this?"

Frank Salica, with an erection the girth of a slugger's bat handle, reached over for the phone. Sitting on top of him, the Leopolds' lissome, naked yoga instructor, opened her eyes. "Yes, Scott.... *what*? Miriam! West L.A. Listen, just go there and don't talk to anyone or file any reports until I get there. Uhh...Give me thirty."

Claudia rolled over with displeasure.

"Do we have to quit right *now*?"

"Yeah, Scott's in trouble for a change."

With every tendon, ligament, and muscle throbbing, Frank shuffled to the shower.

"Frank, do some Third Eye meditations and Crown Chakras, you'll feel like a million."

"Claudia," he groaned, "you did me in. Now grab your leotards and Kama Sutra creams and I'll catch you later."

Dressed and weaving through traffic in his big BMW, he decided not to take a Percodan. Miraculously, thanks to Swami Claudia, he had regained the use of his limbs; his autonomic nervous system functioned without pain and the back spasms he had suffered from for years had vanished. He had a clear head from his night of alcohol abstinence, tea drinking, and orgasms. When he saw Scott and Miriam's succulent sister sitting on a bench with cups of coffee-machine acid, he knew exactly what happened.

Scott hadn't done his homework. Big bucks or not, the bride-to-be had taken a walk for a catnap with some Hercules. Women, the best of them, possessed baffling behavior patterns.

"Relax, Scott. I'll find Miriam. My crew is the best there is."

Frank hit buttons on his cell phone, jabbered descriptions of Miriam to them, and waved to actual detectives with badges who passed by him with repugnance. With Scott dozing on her shoulder, Rebecca's confidence reached its lowest ebb. She doubted if Frank could find a cockroach in a Chinese restaurant.

13

Two women thrust a naked Miriam under the heavy blast of a shower in a communal bathhouse. She regained consciousness, but was so overcome by the savagery of this harrowing nightmare that she found herself surrendering to the instinctive timidity of her childhood. Cowering in the recess of the wall, she could not stop sobbing. The shower was finally turned off and a bath towel flung at her. She dried herself with her back to the women, and then wrapped the soggy terry cloth around her.

In a black SS uniform, the woman she recognized as Noreen strutted through the door.

"Put these on." A pair of blue-striped trousers and shirt were tossed at her.

"I don't understand..."

"Don't open your mouth."

The shirt was coarse and badly stitched with a J and a yellow Star of David on the right-hand side. Bewildered by this and the callous treatment of the women, it slowly dawned on Miriam that she had been taken hostage by an insane group of neo-Nazis. Several years ago, like every Jew in Austria, she had been repelled by the election of Jörg Haider and his so-called Freedom Party. It was a sadistic, fascist, neo-Nazi organization, and the nation had been ostracized by many other civilized countries. In Vienna, there had been marches, rioting, and street fighting between vicious bands of skinheads and the rival socialists. She imagined she might be outside Vienna, the captive of one these extremist groups, which intended to collect ransom money. It was beginning to make sense. Without a shred of doubt, she had been taken somewhere in the countryside of Austria or Germany. That was the only logical explanation.

She couldn't still be in the United States. She had been drugged and only awoke when she'd arrived at this castle from the Middle Ages. She was certainly in Europe. And yet everyone spoke English. How could this be possible?

Her mind was swamped with fragmented scenes. Playing in a concert with Scott somewhere in Germany—Dresden? Was Rebecca in California? Where were her college friends from the Bel-Air party? Had someone drugged her drink?

Everything became more chaotic when she was marched through a winding stonewalled passage. She glanced sidewise at Noreen. Miriam had no recollection of what had occurred after she had gone to assist Noreen on the road. Her short-term memory had failed.

She arrived in an immense chamber with very high ceilings; the wall was pregnant with tapestries, paintings, and glass showcases filled with axes and swords. Full suits of crested armor were stationed in the corners of the room.

Standing on a platform, an elderly, distinguished-looking man was addressing an attentive audience. Above him, an enormous swastika hung on burnished eagle-headed pegs.

The man gestured to her, held out his hand, summoning her to the platform. She gazed at him, virtually mesmerized by his cavernous eyes. He nodded to her and turned back to the room.

"I've decided to resume an agenda that has always been very personally close to my heart. And with this in mind, our units throughout the country have been informed to identify suitable candidates. I'd counted on my son, Bruno, but he's been occupied with other urgent matters."

The men listened, enthralled. Having learned Adolf's techniques of mass psychology, when to pause, keep people waiting, in order to titillate them, Magnus seized hold of Miriam and shook her.

"This creature standing before you is a Jewess! Her name is Miriam Benjamin. She was about to be married to the son of a billionaire Jew. This means she would be breeder and a powerful one. Now we have Virgil and Noreen to thank for capturing her.

"She will have the honor of inaugurating our new facility. It is my hope and belief that it will be used for thousands of other Jews—women and men."

There was thunderous applause and shrieks of pleasure from the spectators. Magnus found his moment. His group had needed a dramatic theme to inflame them.

"Again, welcome to Winterhaven, Miriam," he said with a broad smile. "And to our Jewish Bride Program."

14

By noon, under a raw, gray drizzle, uniformed police, and helicopters, along with hundreds of volunteers from Jack Leopold's office staff in Westwood, were swarming through Bel-Air. They were going door to door and searching the wooded areas. Surrounded by hordes of TV interviewers with microphones and cameras crews, Rebecca, Scott, and his parents were making statements on camera on what was referred to as "Breaking News." A publicity-shy billionaire and his bereft family were center stage. Colored still photographs of Miriam flashed on TV monitor screens.

When Rebecca finally broke away, she headed for the family Rolls Royce where Robert the chauffeur mournfully stood by the rear door.

Frank was on his cell. He clicked off and turned to Rebecca. He had decided not to tell the family yet that Miriam's handbag had been found inside the car and one of the cops had bagged a woman's left high-heeled Prada. Someone, probably Rebecca or Scott, would have to identify these items.

"I put the FBI on notice. But it's too soon for them to get involved."

"Why is that?" she asked.

"They need a ransom note to give them federal jurisdiction."

Now it all made some sense to Rebecca. At the same time, she developed a spark of optimism. Naturally, the kidnappers would demand millions from the Leopolds. They would pay it, and Miriam would be returned.

"Should I call my grandmother in Vienna?"

"Nothing she can do. Why upset her? Wait a minute. Maybe Miriam contacted her."

Rebecca nodded, unconvinced. "This is so horrible. I don't know if I can lie to her about it."

"Do it! We know Miriam didn't catch a flight to Europe from LAX yet."

"How?"

"I notified the INS." She stared blankly at him. "Immigration. When we get back to the house, we'll check to see if her passport is still there. Scott must know where she keeps it."

Emerging from the crowd, she saw Harry Summerfield. His features were rigid, set in an ominous cast. He took her hand and led her to his car.

"I thought you were leaving for Tampa."

"I cancelled my trip when Jack called. Let me take you back to the house." He tried to smile, but his mood had also become forbidding. "You can drive the car, but I don't think it's a good idea just now."

"No, it's not."

She succumbed to the wave of compassion that she felt radiating from him. She held him tightly and wept in his arms.

15

It was nearing ten at night in Vienna when Lilli came to the phone. In the background, Rebecca heard Barbara Karlich, the Oprah of Austrian TV, interviewing someone. Lilli hated to miss this show and her voice was gruff. "If it had been anyone else, I would have asked them to call back. How are you, Becky?"

"Just fine. Everything here is beautiful. The Leopolds are very thoughtful and loving. Are you and Herta all right?"

Rebecca was in the Leopold TV room, a showcase to just about everything produced by Bang and Olufson, even to the sculpted telephone. Harry was behind the wet bar mixing Bloody Marys. He held up the tabasco and Rebecca nodded, signaling with her fist to keep spiking her drink. One of the kitchen people, now reduced to a skeleton staff, brought in a tray of sandwiches.

Rebecca tried to remain calm and matter-of-fact, "Oma, have you spoken to Miriam yet?"

"No. But I do want to talk to her. Put her on."

Rebecca's body grew limp and her head fell back on the chair. In the doorway, a group of uniformed policemen and detectives from West Los Angeles listened in.

"I thought Miriam would have called you by now."

"Not a word. But you know brides...." The receiver thumped. "Herta!" she shouted, "Did Miriam call when I was out? No, Rebecca. I just got home from a faculty dinner a few minutes ago. They keep slashing my teaching assignments. Saves them money. Never mind. How is my darling, Miriam?"

"Very happy."

"Is her house ready yet?"

"No, it needs some work." Harry handed Rebecca the drink, and she mouthed a thank you. "The architect thinks they can move in by June."

"Is Scott there? I'd like to say hello."

"Everyone's out."

"Rebecca, I should have come. I'm filled with remorse about my decision." She appeared to be waiting for another invitation, but Rebecca resisted the trap. "Well, your circulation problems are real."

"I know, I know. Have Miriam and Scott call me at my office tomorrow. I'll be in at eight so that should be a good time if they're up."

"Yes, yes, love to you and Herta. *Auf Wiedersehen.*"

She hung up, took out a cigarette, and was about to light it, when Harry shook his head. "Take your drink outside and smoke it there."

"I was going to quit...for good."

"Maybe this isn't a good time."

Scott came into the room. His despondency had intensified. He slumped down into a leather sofa and nervously flicked through Miriam's passport before laying it on the table beside Rebecca.

She idly picked it up, turned to the photo, and remembered the summer afternoon several years ago when they had both gone to take their pictures before getting their passports renewed. They had joined a group of wealthy music lovers for lunch at the Three Hussars. Miriam, always solicitous and conscious of the cost, had ordered a prawn salad and nudged Rebecca under the table when she'd started with Osietra caviar and gobbled it up in her blinis. She'd followed with their saddle of veal, the most expensive dish on the menu.

Afterwards when they'd window-shopped, strolling down the Kärtner Strasse, Rebecca had dragged her into Humanic, one of the city's finest leather shops.

"I don't like stores that I can't afford," Miriam had said, becoming fractious.

"Pick out something—a bag, a jacket."

"Oh, stop it, Becky. Herta dumped your credit cards in the morgue."

"When you went to the ladies room, I agreed to play at one of their deadly evenings."

"No...you didn't?"

"An hour of Mozart and Brahms. And I insisted on cash."

"You're so tacky."

"Ten thousand schillings." Rebecca sniggered. "Whores don't take checks. How about that black evening clutch in the showcase? You could feed a horse oats with your handbag."

Miriam was euphoric with this unexpected gift. She waltzed with Rebecca out of the shop. Once back on the street, she became flustered.

"God Almighty, they're late at home with the utility bills again. If I strut in with a shopping bag from Humanic, it'll be a night with the Gestapo. Herta goes through my drawers all the time."

"I'll hide it. She doesn't go through mine any more. I caught her when she was about to throw out my Today sponges. I told her very nicely that I would poison her and bury her alive in the back garden if she ever opened my drawers or my closet again."

The lovely afternoon with Miriam surrendered to Scott's ululant voice intruding on Rebecca's musings. "Miriam wouldn't have left me."

Her future brother-in-law's behavior irritated her. Rebecca despised men who bleated; they struck her as craven. Perhaps this was the legacy of Rebecca's upbringing in a household of women. She and Miriam had learned how to cook, iron as well as any professional laundry, garden, perform heavy work, go to the tool shed, and fix anything rather than call some handyman who'd fritter away time and their money.

She joined Scott on the sofa, cuddling him in her arms, while looking at Harry whose eyes focused directly on hers, with cloudless hunger. He silently waved goodbye.

"Never. Never, Scott. She adored you."

All at once, the hall resonated with a squall of voices, raucous and tearful; bodies appeared, small and large, intruding on the chamber music of lament. Police, electricians, technicians bustled through the room.

Kate, who'd given her a lift last night, carried her baby in a backpack.

"Rebecca, I didn't have time to get a towel when the cops came to the hotel. Can you get one? I've got to nurse Noah."

"Yes, yes, of course."

The Leopolds arrived. Paula slouched and flustered, her doleful face pinched, shaking her head. Jack Leopold, resolute, his squatness and barrel-chest giving him the commanding presence of a general. He projected an aura of confidence and acted as though he were at a board meeting.

"Now, everybody, please pay attention. I'm sorry that these circumstances are so alarming. But that's a fact. This is my wife, Paula. If there's anything special you need, food or whatever, she'll arrange it. I asked the police to bring you here, rather than the station for interviews. If you need to make a call, use your cells, or you can have ours. But don't pick up any of the telephones in the house. The police and the phone company are setting up wiretaps. This gentleman,

Frank Salica, is our personal security man. He'll act as our liaison with the police."

"From what I understand, Rebecca and—" Frank looked at a list—"Kate Miller, could you raise your hand until I can put a face to everyone?"

"I'm Kate." She held the hand of a pale-faced, solemn man. "And this is my husband, Edward."

"I was babysitting our son while Kate went to the party for Miriam."

"Thank you, sir. Kate, you and Rebecca left the hotel at about ten-thirty."

"Yes, I drove her here. She didn't know the entry code to the house."

"Frank, I let them in," the chauffeur, interjected. "I spoke to Rebecca and waited until Kate left."

Frank studied the intent faces of the people in the room. "Exactly who were the last people to see Miriam?"

The women raised their hands and each explained how they had all embraced Miriam in the Bel-Air parking lot and made plans for the following day.

"When we got back to the Beverly Hills Hotel, we went into the Polo Lounge for a nightcap and stayed for about an hour," Carrie informed him.

"We were still wound up and kind of curious," Joanna elaborated, clutching her partner's hand. "None of us had ever been to the Polo Lounge."

"We had Irish Coffees, said goodnight to Norma, and went up to our rooms. Carrie and I live together in Cincinnati and we shared a room."

"My husband's playing two concerts and is due to arrive on Friday," Norma said.

Frank adopted a concerned but detached attitude during the questioning, but he too was alarmed. "Did he call you last night?"

"No, he's on the East Coast. He was playing in Boston last night. By the time I got to bed, it would've been five in the morning there."

"After you left the Bel-Air...anybody...? did Miriam contact you during the night? Call or email?"

The subdued, remorseful, negative responses filled Rebecca with foreboding. Who had lain in wait for her sister? A kidnapper, rapist...killer? Occasionally she heard about such things in Europe when criminals or terrorists were involved. But the average person—even women—seldom worried unduly about safety. Obviously, sensible people didn't roam the streets or dangerous neighborhoods at night. Of course, girls in the drug scene sometimes went missing. But children weren't dragged from their beds while their parents were asleep as had happened in America.

By late afternoon, Jack's personal assistant arrived from the office along with his public relations staff and three attorneys. Jack with his wife, Harry, Frank, Scott, and the chief of detectives went to another wing of the house and closed the doors. The detectives had installed surveillance equipment on Jack and Scott's home computers and at the Leopold office. Additional phone lines were in place because the press had already found the family's unlisted numbers.

Miriam's six women friends were in other rooms, giving statements to the police. Kate's baby, apparently not used to the strange surroundings and the weeping women, played a malicious counterpoint, howling all afternoon.

Rebecca was interrogated for three hours about Miriam's possible enemies in Europe, or if she knew of some man Miriam had broken up with, who harbored thoughts of revenge. Had there been a teacher, a professor, a rival whom she considered an enemy? At the end, Rebecca concluded that it was all a charade. The conscientious detectives were as much in the dark as she was. No letter or phone call demanding money had been received.

As she was finally about to leave, Rebecca thought that the day could not get worse, but it did. Another detective opened an attaché case. Sheathed in plastic bags, it held Miriam's clutch purse and the Prada leather pump they had discovered earlier. She understood only too well the significance of this discovery. They had also bagged the contents: Miriam's wallet, cash, credit cards, a heart-shaped compact and lipstick.

"Does this look like your sister's handbag?"

"Yes, it's hers. I bought it for her in Vienna a little over two years ago." She peered at the shoe. "It's her size, a six. She was wearing it last night."

"Thank you for your help, Ms. Benjamin."

As the night wore on, Rebecca sank into a listless daze, then went upstairs to her room with a bottle of Grey Goose. She poured herself a stiff drink and restlessly walked back and forth through the large suite. What could have happened to Miriam? Had a mastermind sexual predator who'd left no clues attacked her? Or was she the victim of a motiveless crime?

At daybreak, bleak and frosty, Miriam was rammed along by Virgil and Noreen over the drawbridge connecting Winterhaven to the main road of the property. The blue-striped uniform made out of a burlap-like material itched; with her hands shackled, she couldn't scratch. Behind them, a procession of chanting men marched in military unity.

Spirals of light illuminated a gleaming, oddly shaped steel building. Towering, spiked gates were open and the engine of heavy machinery churned. Miriam vacantly stared at flashing red warning signs.

NICHT OFFEENEN (Do Not Open)

LEBENSGEFAHR (Danger to Life)

Magnus opened the gates and pointed to a brass sign above the entrance.

TOPF UND SöHNE

"This is an original trophy sign from the firm I commissioned to built the crematoriums at Dachau."

Miriam had become deaf and mute and her mind was bleached of all memories. She existed in a nightmarish purgatory of nothing-ness—non-being.

Time, her surroundings, and space itself had lost their meaning.

16

Some time before six in the morning, Rebecca was awakened from a twilight sleep by heavy knocking on her door. Still dressed, she tumbled out of bed and lurched to the door. Harry Summerfield, eyes bloodshot, rumpled and unshaven, glumly handed her a folded section of the *Los Angeles Times*.

"Do you want to come downstairs and join us for coffee?"

She took the newspaper and stared at him. "Yes, all right, thank you."

She was afraid to ask if there had been any calls about Miriam, but realized it would have been the first thing he would have mentioned. Even with her vision blurry, she recognized a small grainy photo of Miriam and slowly read the article.

TUESDAY, FEB 9, 2000
SEARCH BEGINS FOR MISSING WOMAN

A 26-year-old woman, presently residing in Beverly Hills, who was on her way home from a wedding shower held for her Sunday night at the Bel-Air Hotel, has vanished, police said. Miriam Clara Benjamin, a native of Vienna, Austria, is 5 feet 7 and weighs 125 pounds, with light chestnut hair and hazel eyes. She was driving a gold 2000 convertible Volvo C 70, which was found abandoned on Stone Canyon Road, California license plate BMB8433.

She was last seen by a valet parking attendant at midnight getting into her car at the hotel. She is to be married on February 14 to Scott Jason Leopold, son of Mr. & Mrs. Jack Leopold. Mr. Leopold is chairman of the J-L Development Corp.

"We're all in a state of shock," Scott Leopold said. "My fiancée is a very responsible woman and for her just to disappear like this doesn't make any sense. She knew her way around the city and speaks flawless English. She's a cellist and we were going to play at a chamber group with friends this week."

Anyone with information about Ms. Benjamin's whereabouts is asked to call West Los Angeles police at 310-575-8402.

There were Danish pastries on the sideboard buffet and it was help yourself. Frank Salica had taken charge of the household staff and gardeners. They were all out searching the Leopold estate again. Rebecca saw dozens of people on the grounds walking in a horizontal line.

Jack and Paula hugged Rebecca. She made an effort to control her emotions, but tears escaped and she wiped them with the sleeve of her cardigan.

"How's Scott doing?"

"The doctor came by and gave him sleeping pills." Paula's haggard face revealed cold fear. "Rebecca, I should tell you that Scott had some problems in the past. He had a breakdown when he was seventeen. It was from the pressure he was under with all the recitals and trying to get into a top conservatory."

Rebecca realized that tact had made an unusual appearance in her life. She had not mentioned that Miriam believed she was pregnant. This would have only compounded the situation and caused him greater pain.

"I twisted a few arms with the FBI," Jack said. "If there's no word or contact, they'll get into it tomorrow. Without a ransom demand, they insisted they needed forty-eight hours, and a request from the brass at Parker Center. That I fixed. We need specialists, and the L.A. police aren't up to it."

Rebecca suddenly seized hold of an idea. "The new house in...?"

"...Westwood," Harry said handing her a cup of coffee. "I took the police there and we searched from top to bottom."

In desperation, Rebecca continued to grapple with her impulsive suggestions. "What about hospitals? Maybe Miriam banged her head in the car, blacked out, had temporary amnesia, and some stranger took her to a hospital. She left her bag in the car. They wouldn't know her real name."

Jack squeezed her hand affectionately. "The cops already checked that and the logs of all 911 calls."

Their serene common sense enraged Rebecca. "I won't accept that she's dead!" she shouted.

Paula draped her muscle-toned arm around her shoulders. "Of course not! No one's suggesting that, darling." Struck by a brainwave, which she hoped would soothe Rebecca, Paula said, "Our rabbi is coming later."

"I don't want any rabbis," Rebecca protested. "We're not ready to sit *Shivah*."

"Calm down, Rebecca. He was scheduled to talk to the kids and take them through the prayers."

"I'm sorry. I can't think straight. Maybe this maniac will call and let Miriam go. Let me tell you something about my sister. She may seem accommodating and soft. But she's strong-willed and no one ever pushes her around. She was raised by two very difficult women and I wasn't exactly whipped cream. Miriam is a match for anyone. She's smart and she can be tough."

She rushed outside, sucking in the damp air, and lit a cigarette, already fed up with her surroundings and the Leopolds's maddening regulations. She stubbed out her cigarette in a planter and returned with her mind made up. "I'd like to borrow a cell phone and your least expensive car, Jack."

"Where do you think you're going?" he asked in alarm.

"And a map of Los Angeles."

"Robert will take you wherever you want to go."

"Thank you. But I don't want to be driven around in a chauffeured Rolls Royce." She hated herself for sounding so huffy. "Sorry, I..."

"Come on, I'll take you." Harry immediately took charge. "I've got a Range Rover with a navigation system and a phone."

She rushed up to her room, yanked a leather jacket out of the closet, and picked up her bag. As she was about to leave, Jack walked her outside. Unwittingly, their gaze roved to the workmen unloading tables and chairs from trucks for the wedding. The white marquee had been completed—fit for royalty—and emblazoned in gold lettering with MIRIAM and SCOTT, the Star of David above their names. For a moment, Miriam's abduction was veiled by the sunny splendor of optimism.

Jack handed her a cell phone. "Zero One is my cell, zero two, my office, zero three, the Beverly Hills Police Department. Rebecca, I'm troubled because I feel responsible for your safety. Now please don't take this in the wrong way. I understand your frustration. But you've lived in a cloistered world of music and concerts. Miriam and Scott also have. And I would imagine Lilli has. You don't know what's out there...the madness and violence, the rage that drives people in their *everyday* world. Stay here. This is your sanctuary."

In spite of his warm manner, Rebecca recognized that deep within Jack Leopold the elements of nature and experience had united to produce a core of ferocity that inspired fear in those who really knew him. He had not become a billionaire through acts of chivalry.

She kissed him with affection. "Miriam is right. You are a prince."

He was insensitive to flattery. "Some of the time. Rebecca, now don't let me worry about you, too. So be sure to call in."

"I will."

They drove to Harry's apartment, talk radio and idiotic callers displacing conversation. Rebecca had expected the celebrated architect to be living in a mansion. Instead, she found herself riding up a private elevator to a condo on the Wilshire Corridor that she'd passed with Miriam. It was, in fact, a penthouse with a roof garden; apart from the masterly drawings on the wall, the fine Bose sound system, and elegant furnishings, it insinuated modesty. There was, however, an antique Bechstein piano, a good one from the turn of the century. He led her into a designer, stainless-steel, Poggenpohl kitchen that might have been a showroom model. Except for making coffee with the most exotic Capresso espresso machine she'd ever seen in a home kitchen, she couldn't imagine it had ever been used.

"I'd offer you something," he said, opening the fridge, "yogurts...no, they're dead. Wait, there's a wheel of Stilton from an old client in London who sends me one every year from Fortnum and Mason. I hate Stilton."

"Let's swear eternal friendship. Stilton makes me sick, too." She glanced around. "I don't know why I thought you'd have some unbelievable house."

"Actually, I do. A country place. I've been too busy to get up there much. Maybe when Miriam comes back, while you're still here, you'll visit."

His phone message light flickered and calls continued to come in, but he ignored them. He went behind her, his hands on her shoulders, and walked her into the living room, sitting her down in an Eames chair.

"Let me clean up and I'll take you down to the garage."

She had to get off the subject of Miriam. "Are you married?"

"No."

"You're getting over a divorce?"

"Nobody wants me." He winked at her. "I'm still single."

"In Vienna, women would be throwing themselves at you. You'd need armed guards to protect you."

"I'll have to put Vienna on my must-trav-to list."

"No yearning for children?"

For once he seemed puzzled. "I like kids, but you've got to raise them."

"What a pity to end the gene pool."

"Maybe not." Again, he was taken aback and she realized that he might be impotent and she had tactlessly raised a sensitive topic.

"Actually, I've been a disappointment to my father.... I made a lot of false starts." He moved closer without crowding her. "I guess with all the traveling I do, it's been hard to meet the right woman. Someone *I* wanted to marry."

She recharged the female detection mode. "I'm sure you've had plenty of candidates. They must be all lighting candles and holding vigils."

He laughed. "That's probably true." He turned away from her. "But you see, men like me hit a certain stage and just stop thinking about it. Years ago, it might have been an issue. Meeting a woman who'd make my life crazy, agonizing. That would've been a challenge. Sure, there were women I might've married. No question. And it's got nothing to do with being an architect or who I've become. Or money, and that's relative when you're a Jack Leopold."

"What about your mother?"

He flushed with anger. Again she had hit a hot spot.

"They've been divorced for years and she's one of those self-centered women who never gave a damn about me. Whether I lived or died."

"Sorry, I didn't mean anything. Just curious about you."

"Look, Rebecca, I'm like most guys, struggling with their uncomplicated crap."

Interesting spin, she thought, *deprecating himself.* Another philosophy professor, fucking with her head. But at least Harry was brilliant, and had endearing traits and might prove to be honorable. His body and face appealed to her. No mats of hair drifted out from his shirt collar, nor bulging muscles, but more importantly, he did not ooze with the pugnacious superiority of the men she'd known at home. Harry Summerfield was confident of his identity and didn't have to make claims for himself.

"Make yourself at home, I won't be long."

Agitatedly, she wandered through his apartment, settling in his studio where she examined drawings on a drafting table. He had a wall-to-wall collection of oversized architectural books in anchored maple bookcases. On a huge worktable encased in Plexiglas, she saw a miniature model of the Tampa Art Center. Wondrous glass pyramid shapes, and concentric whorls of copper braided the structures; everywhere light glowed and long outdoor walkways serpentined around the structures. His imagination was breathtaking and she realized that his seductive, offhand manner camouflaged a man of genius.

His collection of classical CDs was fastidiously alphabetized by composer. An old French writing table had a book open to the photograph of Louis Kahn's Kimbell Museum in Fort Worth, Texas. There were no framed degrees, awards, nor photographs of people or pets on the walls. He was a solitary, private man and the shade of mystery intrigued her. He simply wasn't a typical American male. He clearly had a dedication to his work and this conveyed a spirit of kinship. And then, snooping in a random way, she concluded that Harry was a lover of women, probably the wilder the better. The world of rich men was so transparent that she laughed to herself to get her mind off Miriam. She knew how short-lived the loyalty of males was. Yet there wasn't a trace of a woman. Just the monastic set-up for speeches she'd heard before, implying, "You're the one."

She was startled when a middle-aged man and woman, unannounced, walked into the study.

"Oh, so sorry, Señora," the man stammered.

"Is Señor Harry in home?" the woman asked.

"Yes, he's getting dressed."

They nodded, unfazed, apparently accustomed to strange women waiting for him. The thought of it made her smile. The high priest did have a sex life. She heard Harry's voice, left the study, and stood at the entry to the kitchen. He was wearing velvety blue cords, a turtleneck sweater, black Birkenstock sneakers, and had a leather jacket slung over his arm. She liked his youthful, casual style but sensed that nothing about his clothes, his demeanor, and his behavior was uncalculated.

"I would have bring food," the woman said.

"Sorry, Marina, I forgot to call you and Carlos."

"We think you in Tampa," the man said.

"I go shopping?" she asked.

"Yes." He now noticed Rebecca. "Anything special you like to drink—Diet Cokes, beer, mineral waters, food?"

She hadn't planned on a sleepover yet and realized that no matter how her impulsive inclinations eventually played out, she would remain with the Leopolds.

"No, thank you. Just the car."

"Okay." He turned back to the woman. "The usual list. Whatever I can eat cold."

In the elevator the terror returned, and she clung to him, struggling within, as she was about to break down.

"Harry, will I ever see Miriam again?"

"Yes, yes." He held her in his arms and soothed her. "She'll be back."

In the garage, his cars occupied four spots: A Bentley, Jaguar, Ferrari, and the Aston Martin. Rebecca got in the driver's seat of the Land Rover. Harry explained how to use the Becker Navigation System and the *Thomas Guide*. She loved mechanical information.

"I have two questions, Rebecca. Do you have a driver's license? And where are you going?"

"I have an international license, valid for California. I'm going to drive to the Bel-Air Hotel and around the neighborhood."

"Okay. Have you ever driven one of these?"

"We have a Volks bug and I've always driven a shift. I also have my own Vespa."

He shook his head skeptically. "A motorbike."

Her attitude became defensive. "Yes. Motorcycles, too. I've been using a friend's Harley for years." He gave her the impression that he had acted in haste. "Drop me at a car rental."

"Don't be so touchy. I don't give a damn about the car. I use it get to sites when I'm working in California. What I do care about is you having an accident."

"I'll be careful and bring it back in a few hours."

"You can use it as long as you like and drop it off at Jack's."

"Not the Aston Martin?" He began to laugh and she reached over and kissed him on the cheek. "You're becoming my white knight, Harry. They' va been very rare in my life—just Miriam."

"I'm flattered....Rebecca, one last thing, don't pick up any hitch-hikers, male or female, young or old."

"You have my word. I really appreciate this."

"Here's my card. My office is in Century City at Fox Plaza. If you have any problems, call me."

She switched on the ignition, and lights, slipped the gear into reverse, but as she was about to back out, a van pulled up and parked behind them. Harry reached over and blew the horn, but the van didn't move.

"Jesus, with everything going on I forgot...."

He flipped open the glove compartment and took out a handgun. Rebecca gasped, then turned around. The van hadn't moved.

"Is something wrong?"

"Nothing, nothing." He reassured her, "I get up very early and drive to sites—miles out of L.A.—in the middle of nowhere, and you never know what you're going to run into."

She shook her head nervously. Harry held the gun up. "It's a Glock 21. Austria produces the most beautiful women and the best automatics." He slipped the gun into his belt. "Is this creep ever going to move? Hit the horn again."

He left the passenger door and walked to the black van. A man leaned his head out. A woman sat beside him.

"I was waiting for your spot," Virgil said.

"Don't park here. These are private." Harry pointed. "There's a visitor's section there."

"Thanks, I must've missed the sign."

Standing behind the Rover, Harry signaled Rebecca out of the spot. She opened the window, looked at the backs of the couple waiting by the elevator.

"Are you going to be all right?" she asked.

"Just fine. I'm armed and dangerous. Now you watch yourself, Rebecca."

17

Rebecca located the street off Sunset Boulevard leading to the hotel. Yesterday—which might have been measured in months—it had been choked with police cars and volunteers searching for her sister. She parked on Strada Corta; there were only a few cars and a gardener's truck. The yellow police tape tied to some trees was already down and flapped in the wind.

Throughout her life, Rebecca had had what she believed to be visitations. As a child, Lilli and Herta had dismissed them as imaginary. She would catch fleeting glimpses of people she knew were dead. These specters appeared to her during her waking hours and defied the boundaries of time. Rebecca had actually witnessed her parents', skiing accident and located them frozen under the cataract of ice with others who had been swallowed up in the avalanche.

Only Miriam believed her, but in recent years these phantoms had seldom been mentioned between the sisters. Rebecca herself never claimed that she possessed psychic powers or second sight for fear of what others might say. She could not explain how this process occurred.

As with her musical talent, this power flouted all logic. It was best not to try to delve further into the arcane mysteries that surrounded it, but to accept that sometimes, she would be taken on a visit beyond the realm of the here and now. Whether curse or blessing, it was hers to bear.

Rebecca walked up Stone Canyon along the narrow verge under its canopy of trees, the branches flailing. Slowly, she came back downhill, until she reached the intersection.

—Suddenly it was dark. Shadowy figures were darting out of the bushes.

—A woman was stopping her car.

—She left the door open and was racing now...to help someone....
Rebecca screamed, "Don't, don't go!"

All at once these shapes dissolved and daylight returned.

Rebecca spent several hours in Bel-Air wondering if Miriam was attempting to contact her. She phoned Jack several times, but there had not been any word from the kidnappers. By mid-afternoon, she got back into the Rover and drove through the UCLA campus and into Westwood Village.

She parked and walked around, passing movie-theater complexes, donut shops, and student fast-food hangouts. She was astonished not to find a single bookstore in a university neighborhood. She felt dizzy and realized she was ravenous. She stopped at a middle-eastern restaurant, where she ate an enormous lamb Shwarma sandwich, which she lathered with hummus and hot sauce.

She set the navigator to the Leopold address on Tower Way and was amazed, childishly pleased, by its user-friendliness. The Rover was like a tank in traffic. Parked outside the Leopold estate was an armada of media trucks, with helicopters buzzing above. Men and women with cameras and microphones banged on the windshield, until she opened the driver's window and explained to a police guard who she was.

"Get one of the detectives to give you an ID badge."

It was almost six when she reached the house. She peeked into the living room, where well-dressed strangers in casual attire were whispering over drinks and hors d'oeuvre as though this were a reunion cocktail party. Several people turned in her direction and a woman pointed at her. They must've been friends of the Leopolds who had come to offer support.

Harry took her aside. "I never should've let you out alone. We were getting worried."

"It took me ages to get into the house. I called your office. Your assistant said you'd already left."

"I had some meetings with my team. But I couldn't get any work done. I must've been crazy to let you drive around by yourself."

"I had to retrace Miriam's steps. I believe two people took her. A woman with a man."

He backed away from her, troubled and perplexed. "*What!* How could you know that?"

There was no point in elaborating or describing her vision. "I can't explain.... I have episodes and see people. Sometimes I hear their voices."

Harry stared at her, not certain what to believe. "I don't understand."

"Nor do I."

For a long moment, he found himself at a loss. "Would you like a drink?"

"Okay, vodka with ice." She was back on track. "How's Scott doing? I want to see him."

"He's in the music room with his parents and the TV people."

Scott had secrets and Rebecca wondered what they were.

Jack was convinced that the only thing that the public understood or cared about was money. He was live on camera with local TV, flanked by Paula and Scott. Rebecca watched him.

"It's very simple," Jack was saying. "If anyone knows where Miriam Benjamin is or can give the police any information to locate her *alive*, that person or persons will receive one million dollars." He held up a signed check. "If that person needs work and isn't involved in her disappearance, he or she will also be offered a lifetime job with my company."

The camera moved to Scott, and the interviewer asked him for a statement.

"My fiancée never harmed anyone. She's a brilliant musician and she's brought pleasure to people all over the world. Miriam, we're still going to be married on Valentine's Day...."

Tears surged down Scott's face; the camera cut away from him and flashed a photograph of Miriam.

18

Jack's strategy had become national news and appeared in papers throughout the country, along with a full-page ad featuring Miriam's photograph. TV stations also ran it, and talk radio offered the police phone number and a hotline. Everyone at Jack's office, his advertising agency and public relations division, had put aside his work to blanket Los Angeles with posters of Miriam. The police and the FBI were inundated with hundreds of calls revealing sightings and leads.

That evening, in an effort to take everyone's mind off the situation, Rebecca sat apathetically at the Steinway in the music room. It had been four days since she had touched a piano. She tested the keys and pedals. Although it was not quite the unblemished sound to which she was accustomed at home, it had a fleshy ripeness. Her small audience was made up of the Leopolds, Harry, who had postponed his trip to Tampa, and Scott, unshaven, taciturn, and wearing mismatched clothes; he seemed in a trance.

"Why don't you play something for us," Harry said affably. "It'll take everyone's mind off the situation."

Miriam had a passion for Scriabin, and Rebecca decided to play his "Piano Sonata No. 10." Scott came to life and moved only a few feet away to observe her technique. When she finished, he bowed his head. He slid beside her on the bench, tearfully leaned his head on her shoulder, and she kissed him.

"When we were at Salzburg, we weren't able to see your hands."

"Lilli should have gotten you house seats." Rebecca frowned and gave a brittle laugh. "She must've sold them."

All conversation ceased when Frank slipped in and took Jack aside. Accustomed to handling crises in his business, Jack's authoritative manner deserted him. He closed his eyes and his face seemed to contract. Paula rushed to him. Scott looked up, paralyzed with fear.

"The detectives outside just told Frank that they've found something–" he broke off, and leaned against Paula.

"We're going to drive to a synagogue in Sherman Oaks," Frank advised them. "Please, everybody, let's not jump to any conclusions."

Harry's stolid demeanor had also fractured. "We can all fit in my Rover...."

"Robert's got the van outside, Mr. Summerfield. You can come with us, or drive. Here's the address."

Rebecca wobbled to her feet. "Harry, I'll go with you."

Led by black and whites, sirens piercing, and an unmarked car of detectives, Harry followed the van over Coldwater Canyon and eventually turned onto a street called Valley Vista, which wound around until they reached Kenter. He turned into a floodlit nest of police cars. At the edge of the scene, TV crews were already churning their cameras.

He pulled over beside a cordon of police. "We're family members."

"All right, sir. Park in the synagogue lot."

They wove through a crowd and were stopped behind yellow police tape with the Leopolds and Frank. Police photographers were massed ahead, shooting still photographs and a video of a body beside a large orange dumpster.

"Frank, do they know if it's Miriam?" Scott nervously asked.

"I'm trying to see if I recognize anyone in this crew who'll let us see the body."

He signaled a detective who had questioned Rebecca. The men spoke for a few minutes, while everyone waited apprehensively.

When he returned, Rebecca's dread turned to anguish.

"Just Scott and Rebecca can come through, Mr. Leopold."

The two of them, clasping hands, were cautiously led on a perimeter, passing detectives and technicians on their knees, planting evidence flags, preparing molds for footprints and tire tracks. Up ahead, men and women in jackets and IDs from the coroner's office were talking to detectives beside the body.

A detective briskly asked, "You the sister?"

"Yes."

"And you?"

"I'm Scott Leopold. My fiancée, Miriam Benjamin, was the kidnapped woman...."

"I see. Officially, we have to make the ID at the coroner's office. But they haven't bagged the body yet. Follow me. And *don't* touch anything under any circumstances."

Spotlights illuminated a body in a striped blue outfit. Scott hugged Rebecca with relief.

"It's not a woman!" he cried with relief. "He's bald."

They moved closer to the semi circle of police. The face of the dead person appeared to have Miriam's profile. But this couldn't be her.

"Can you show me the right hand," Rebecca tearfully asked a gloved forensic technician.

As she leaned forward, the saliva in her mouth dried and she thought she might be swallowing her tongue. The ridges of calluses on the fingertips stood out in bas-relief. A mental picture emerged of Miriam smoothing them with a pumice stone. A rancid, gassy stench arose from the body. The head had been shaved, and a blue tattoo number, still raw and scabbed, crossed the livid forehead.

"It's her!" Scott screamed and ran through the police cordon like a lost child.

Rebecca winced, clutched her stomach, turned away, then back to make sure she hadn't imagined the scene. This vision of what had been human and beloved no longer existed, except as a turbulent nightmare, a darkened, hypnotic delusion that had mutated into something grotesque, beyond imagination.

The physical pain Rebecca suffered had a crippling penetration, spreading like a sudden fever throughout her body. Her arms and legs became heavy, the faces of people around her lost their forms, lique-fying into viscous beads. She staggered back, then keeled over and hit the ground, deadened by the radical shock.

19

The macabre facts of Miriam's murder emerged several days later in an onslaught for which no one could have been prepared. Driving with the Leopolds to a tallow gray office building in Van Nuys, housing the courts and law enforcement agencies, Rebecca imagined she was in a Third World country.

In the office of a Deputy District Attorney, filled with investigators, she stared out of the window to the street directly below swarming with unreadable signs in Spanish and Arabic over fast-food restaurants, cut-rate furniture shops, indented with gun stores, pawnbrokers, and rows of bail-bondsman boutiques flashing pink and orange neon signs.

A somber, middle-aged man by the name of Ed Whitney, with coffee-colored bags under his dull eyes, came in carrying a stack of folders. He was trailed by several investigators. He shook hands with them all.

"I'm sorry to bring you folks such unpleasant information. I have the coroner's report. Frankly, everyone is mystified."

Rebecca became alert. "In what way?"

"It is Miriam Benjamin, isn't it?" Paula asked.

Whitney's eyes rested on Scott, whose nose was wine-colored and dripping. Rebecca had seen him using coke after Miriam's body had been identified. She had pleaded with him to stop and he had physically thrown her out of his room.

"Yes, it is. Ms. Benjamin was not sexually molested. Her engagement ring is still missing, and we assume it was stolen. Now...she was pregnant and that accounted for the blood stains on the burlap underpants she was wearing." Despite delivering bad news to families for twenty years, Whitney was shaken. "The medical examiner estimates she was in her sixth week and miscarried some time during her ordeal. It's hard to pinpoint the exact time. We're treating this as a double homicide."

Scott fell into his mother's arms, but Jack remained unflinching.

"Miriam told me she was late and might have been pregnant. She didn't want to mention it to Scott or you and Paula before the wedding," Rebecca admitted. "It *was*...a piece of good news she wanted to save." Her voice tailed off.

Scott staggered to his feet. "Excuse me, I have to go to bathroom."

"Sit down, Scott," his father shouted, aware of why he wanted to leave. "We all have to face this and not cop out."

"I won't be much longer," Whitney advised them. "We sent the concentration camp uniform she was wearing to the FBI lab. They've matched it to one used in a Nazi death camp called Gusen in Austria." He was incredulous. "Apparently, it's genuine.

"How these neo-Nazis got hold of this clothing, we have no idea. But the really baffling part of this homicide is the cause of death. Frankly, we've never encountered anything like it in the United States. This is an anti-Semitic hate crime without parallel.

"According to the toxicology reports, Ms. Benjamin was gassed with cyanide. But it's not like the gas used for the execution of convicted killers in this country. This is a chemical called Zyklon-B—the same compound produced by the Nazis and used during the Holocaust in the death camps."

Rebecca wondered how to ask a logical question. "*How* can this be possible?"

Jack, also bewildered, broke in. "There must be some twisted reason for this. The way it was planned. I think Miriam was hunted...."

Ed Whitney remained blank-faced. The roomful of investigators mirrored his look of complete puzzlement. "The reason all the pathology reports came in so quickly is that there was virtually no decomposition. They kept her body refrigerated so that everything would be easy for us."

Rebecca shuddered as he continued.

"We've decided not to release this specific information about the Zyklon to the media. We hope whoever has this—they're pellets apparently—won't unload them. When we catch up with these people, and if they've still got a supply, it'll provide invaluable evidence for the case. No matter how you're tempted, or what journalists may promise you, don't disclose this."

Jack Leopold, overcome by this revelation, continued to nod his head like a doll on a spring.

Rebecca wiped the tears from her eyes. "This just doesn't make any sense," she insisted. "Miriam and I are from Vienna. We don't have any Nazi enemies there—and certainly not here."

"Do you think a group is involved, Mr. Whitney?" Paula asked.

Whitney turned to the detective lieutenant in charge of the invest-igation.

"We're convinced of it," the man replied. "No single individual could have kidnapped Ms. Benjamin, then driven to an elaborate gas chamber he would've had to build some time previously, and commit-ted this murder by himself. He had to have help. We're looking for a very well-organized cadre of neo-Nazis."

"*Neo-Nazis?*" Paula echoed, outraged. "Is there any connection to the Jews who were murdered in New York last year before the holi-days? Weren't these killings called the Chanukah Murders?"

"We don't know. The FBI's office in New York is dealing with those."

Whitney nodded to the detective, and he resumed. "Thanks, John. We're going to petition the court to seal this, because it may interfere with the investigation," Whitney said. "We'll tell the media that the cause of death is still undetermined. But we must mention the Nazi elements. After that, since this falls under the Federal Hate Crimes statute, the FBI and a federal prosecutor will take over the case and have jurisdiction. But of course, we'll continue to work with the fed-eral authorities." He paused, spent by the catalogue of horrors. "I think it'd be best to exclude the fact that Ms. Benjamin was branded...post mortem...with a swastika."

20

In the early evening of February 13, 2000, a Sunday, at a time when the bride and groom and their family were to have been photographed, the bubbling young rabbi who was to marry the couple stood in the center of the Leopold living room. In a sepulchral voice, he led a large group in the *Mourner's Kaddish*. The mirrors and paintings had been draped with black sheets. The *Shivah* for Miriam had begun.

That afternoon, Miriam had been buried at Forest Lawn Cemetery in the Leopold family mausoleum. Rebecca and the bridesmaids had gone to Bloomingdale's in Century City and bought black dresses on Friday, rather than keep their appointments at Chanel, where Miriam and Paula had selected their gowns. The women stood near Rebecca, crying, bereft.

Lilli and Herta had been flown in from Vienna by Jack's private jet on Friday. Their skin sallow, eyes hooded with tears, they stood holding Rebecca's hands and chanting the lament with the congregation of the Leopolds' friends, none of whom Rebecca knew.

"'Yeetgadal v' yeetkadash sh'mey rabbah
"'Amein.'
"'May His great Name grow exalted and sanctified
"'In the world that He created as He willed.'"

For Rebecca, the scene possessed a hallucinatory quality, a hollowness that Scott personified. Tortured, he stood between his parents, who were physically supporting him. If he needed drugs, Rebecca thought, he was entitled to them. This tragedy abrogated logic or reproach. To her surprise, he had come clean with everyone and agreed to begin tranquillizers that night. The family doctor was nearby, keeping watch.

Harry solemnly gazed at Rebecca, then on what seemed to her an impulse, he thoughtfully took charge of Lilli and Herta. With himself in the middle, he put his arms around the waists of the shattered, elderly women. His actions struck her as benevolent and gallant; she lost sight of them as new arrivals of Leopold friends stopped to commiserate with her.

In the music room, Harry assisted the ladies to a long sofa beside the piano.

"Are either of you on any medication that would prevent you from having a drink?"

"We're on everything," Lilli said.

"Herr Summerfield, a good cognac won't kill us," Herta said longingly, contemplating cut-glass decanters that might have been plundered from the Spanish Main.

"And that's what you'll have," he said with a smile.

Lilli nudged him. "Deep amber liquids always catch Herta's eye for beauty."

"Even without my glasses."

It was obvious to Harry that he must avoid mentioning Miriam, unless they brought it up. It was up to him to divert them and harvest Rebecca eventually.

"You're in luck. Jack bought a bottle of 1874 Hardy Perfection cognac at an auction. You can't see it, ladies. But I know where it is."

"We deserve to be spoiled," Lilli said.

"Yes," Herta agreed, "if not now, then never."

"You know where the best stuff is," Lilli said with admiration.

"I do. Because I make the best buildings."

They seemed almost alone and oblivious to the hundreds of people whose numbers could barely fill the space in the Leopold mansion. Lilli took off her fogged glasses and Harry cleaned them with a cocktail napkin. He straightened them on the bridge of her nose, and as an expert on structure, appraised her features.

Rebecca's facial structure was more Nordic than Lilli's, but there were traces of Rebecca. She, too, had once had a full bosom, the natural curving insinuations of natural beauty.

"Thank you." Lilli also examined him. She would admit that she had a weakness and an eye for good-looking, well-dressed men. She touched his sleeve. "A Brioni."

He was surprised and delighted. "Correct."

"It's the cut. And the way the buttons are sewn on the cuff. I knew a man—long ago—who had his clothes tailored either by them or Kitor."

"The dueling Italians."

"Yes, but the beauty of Italian swordsmen is that they never draw blood."

He was enjoying her humor, albeit engendered by disaster. Harry found this older woman charming and with a razor-sharp mind.

"They insult each other brilliantly as well."

"That they do. They're also craftier than the French in a negotiation, and not as nasty when they steal," Lilli said with the familiarity of a professional.

Harry laughed and carefully poured three snifters.

"And what's your opinion of Americans?" he asked.

"Bullies. Childish. Rude. But very generous despite their manners. Now tell me why you design buildings, Herr...?"

"Harry—and I'll call you Lilli if I may."

"Yes, do. What made you choose this?"

He sighed, somewhat startled by her insistence.

"I was building little houses even as a child. At the beach with mud, out of sticks and logs in the garden, with blocks at home. Everyone said they were very well done. My father always encouraged me." He had a sudden flicker of anger. "My mother abandoned us. Now it's your turn...."

"What a pity—her loss. Rebecca and I began the piano at a very young age. I played at five, Becky at three, with more brio. I found melodies, she composed them."

"Really."

"She has absolute pitch and could have been a composer. But there's no money in it. Performance pays. She was a natural like Mozart, a genius. And her hands are phenomenal. Look at her broad palms, and densely fleshed fingers. They're shaped like spatulas. But the most extraordinary feature is that her little finger is almost the length of her middle finger."

"And that's an advantage?" he asked, intrigued.

"An enormous one. God designed them." Lilli continued with her expert's lesson. "You see, Rebecca can play a range of notes effortlessly, without exerting the tension of stretching that gives most pianists nightmares.

"And with all these natural gifts, she's utterly careless about her life." Lilli brought out her handkerchief and snuffled. "Miriam had to be the one to die," she said, unaware that she was implying that the wrong sister had survived. "She was too good to live...."

"Lilli, taste this cognac," Herta suggested. "It's wonderful. How much did Herr Leopold pay for it? A fortune, I'll bet."

"Ach, Herta, will you just stop this and drink as much as you like."

Herta turned her head and stared at a painting of a nude. Refilling her glass, she got up and peered at it. "It says Goya. Can it be real?" Lilli hissed. "Impossible woman."

"Yes, it is a Goya," Harry said, his manner patient and mood turning affable.

Lilli leaned over and spoke softly. "Her nerves are gone. We're both devastated. I've had my tragedies. But this is the worst of them."

Soothing her was beyond him or anyone for that matter, and she seemed to respond to his delicacy, the tacit sympathy when the unspeakable was the occasion for their meeting.

Rebecca had to escape from the assembly of strangers offering condolences. Human faces blurred, their voices jarred her nerves. It had become unendurable. She looked around for Lilli and stopped at the entry to the music room. She stared at the piano. Without warning, she heard an otherworldly sound. It was a music tone in the middle voice and unquestionably Miriam's cello.

Rebecca nodded, then murmured, "Yes, I will."

She walked to Lilli and Harry. He rose immediately and offered her a seat. A waiter brought another glass, and Harry poured her a generous cognac.

"I need it."

"We started without you," Herta said, leaning over. "Drink it slowly, Becky. Herr Summerfield said it cost a fortune. And leave some for us before bed. That's a Goya behind you, and I saw three El Grecos, a Van Eyck, too."

"The Renoirs, Matisses, and Cézannes are in the next room," Harry advised her.

Rebecca touched Harry's hand, suggestively and affectionately, and, in his view, corroborating her progress to his bed. He leaned over to Rebecca and smoothed her hair.

"Lilli is brilliant, like you. A treasure."

"You're an astonishing man, Harry."

Watching this interplay, Herta said, "*Him*, you couldn't bring home to the Berggasse?"

"He wasn't in Vienna, Herta."

As though making signs to a stubborn dog, Lilli pointed to the other room. "Go, go, visit Cézanne."

"You'll come for Rebecca's debut with the Vienna Phiharmoniker?" Lilli asked.

"I wish I could."

"You can't believe what he's building in Florida. I saw a model in his apartment."

"Maybe she'll perform in the concert hall I'm doing in this complex."

Rebecca smiled sorrowfully at him, then laid her head on Lilli's breast. Lilli shivered, struggling with tears.

"I'm going to play something for Miriam."

"Yes, yes, it's right you should," Lilli said.

Harry's eyes were fixed on Rebecca, and he finally fully grasped her emotional wound. As an only child, and a perennial loner, the bonds of family had never taken root in him. Rebecca stood up, then fondly touched his face. He stared at her with adulation.

"I'll be back in a minute. I just have to wind down."

The mourning guests were not quite so glum, chitchatting with drinks, and roving around the enormous buffets, the tubs of caviar, platters of lobster tails, the chefs slicing filets, fixing omelets, amenable to all requests.

Herta roved around the buffet like a soccer goalie checking the turf in front of the net. Blinking with astonishment at the extravagance of this feast, she returned. "My God, this looks more like a wedding banquet than a funeral tea."

Without ostensible disapproval, Harry explained. "In a way it is. I was having a business meeting with Jack when he got a call from the wedding caterers. Paula had prepaid them...months ago. Since there wasn't going to be a wedding, Jack traded with them."

"What a clever man. He must be a delight to do business with," Lilli said without concealing her contempt.

"I'm sure in your early performance days, you've seen better...in Vienna."

"Not since—" Herta began, then caught herself—"well, *I* haven't."

"Shall I have a waiter fix you ladies a plate?"

"Just pile mine with caviar and gravlax. I'll have the filet afterwards," Herta said.

Lilli glared at her companion. "Nothing for me, thank you."

Rebecca returned and nudged Harry aside; he nodded at her. In the din, he tinkled a glass with a spoon until the clattering and voices fell silent.

"Friends, all of you, Paula's, Jack's, and many of you mine...we've been brought together for an appalling occasion. Instead of celebrating Miriam and Scott's wedding, we've been summoned to the bride's funeral. Lilli Benjamin, Miriam's grandmother, is here. She was one of Europe's great pianists. This gift has been passed on to her granddaughter, Miriam's sister. Rebecca Benjamin would like to play a tribute to her sister."

Rebecca, in performance with an audience, always relied on her professionalism. She looked at the throngs of people, putting down their plates without clattering silverware, but clasping their drinks. She gazed straight at them.

"This is one of my sister's favorite pieces. And it's appropriate."

More people crowded into the music room and were impatiently hushed. When Rebecca sat on the piano bench, the spectators looked at her with respectful sympathy. Lilli and Herta, standing, had moved closer to Harry. Rebecca beckoned the crying "bridesmaids" in their black dresses and had them group around her.

"This is a French piece by Ravel and it's called a *pavane*, which is a stately, formal dance that was performed in courts. Many of you have heard 'Pavane for a Dead Princess.' I'd like to dedicate this to my sister Miriam. She'll never be lost to me, or forgotten."

Rebecca's arms angled from above. Her cupped hands extended and fondled the keys; the powerful fingers stroked the keyboard with balletic and eloquent movements, arousing sadness and a deep mixture of emotions. She played with delicacy and fluency, the flow in both hands. Using the pedals softly, she let her body sway as she articulated the mournful melody, poetically carving and shaping the notes so that the effect became three-dimensional. Tears streamed down her cheeks, and she structured the music with tonal brilliance and a palette of emotional coloring that revealed her technical genius.

When she concluded, the guests were weeping. She nodded to them and made her way to Lilli and Herta.

Harry intercepted her. "You're marvelous. Is there *anything* I can do?"

"No. Thanks for being so lovely to my grandmother and Herta."

"It was the least I could do."

"You're my nero, Harry."

"I'll try to be," he said, carried away by such conviction that he was stunned and appalled by the liability of his own sincerity. For the first time in his life, he'd become captive to a woman.

Supporting her grandmother, Rebecca and Herta slowly walked up the stairs to their rooms.

Jack caught up with them and managed a poignant smile to Rebecca before kissing her hand. "Ladies, if there's any way I can make your visit with us more bearable, please tell Paula or me."

"Thank you for your kindness, Jack," Lilli said. "I think we need to be alone with Rebecca."

After dumping Miriam in the Valley Synagogue lot, Virgil and Noreen let their curiosity get the best of them. Behind the wheel of the black van, Virgil curb-crawled past cop cars, stretch limos, fleets of Rolls Royces, Mercedeses, and clusters of uniformed chauffeurs, smoking and jawing about missing the Lakers game. They were awed by the Leopold estate. It was lit up like the movie premieres and award shows they had seen only on TV.

"Think how many Jews we could have killed tonight if we'd brought down some plastique," he said wistfully.

"I'd have laid out the fuses," she said.

He laughed and chucked her affectionately under the chin,

"Love you, babe. But I don't think we're into suicide missions—yet."

21

Lilli and Herta had been given a corner suite of rooms down the hall from Rebecca. It was spacious and beautifully furnished, with a grand view of the illuminated, serpentine gardens and fountains. The wedding marquee had been struck like a film set, the rows of chairs removed. Nothing remained of the outdoor chapel where Miriam and Scott were to be married at a minute past midnight. Rebecca's mind wandered; the stretch of ground now seemed barren and resonated with mocking hostility.

"If you want tea, coffee, the staff will serve you twenty-four hours a day."

"Coffee, perhaps," Lilli said wearily.

"More of that cognac for me with my coffee, if you don't mind, Becky."

Rebecca responded with an embittered laugh and ordered coffee and sandwiches. "Miriam had Julius Meinl ship their house blend from Vienna for *me*."

"No," Herta said, then bit her lip and sobbed. "And now our *Liebling* is dead...."

Lilli's head sagged into the black lace neckline of her dress. "Viennese coffee for *us*.... How typical of Miriam."

"It's all so strange, Oma. I went to see the police and the prosecutor before you arrived. Miriam's murder makes no sense to them. It's an enigma." She threw up her hands. "Neo-Nazis in California? They have some of these people in motorcycle gangs.... This is so bizarre! They believe Miriam was stalked by a group. We all keep asking why—why *her*? What could she conceivably have done to make them her enemy?"

"America is filled with madness," Herta said. "But I'm glad to see you finally met a gentleman. Mr. Summerfield treated us like family."

"Yes, I must say, I liked him very much." Lilli walked shakily to the bed, where her battered briefcase lay. She opened it and removed an envelope.

Herta scrutinized her with catlike intensity, then furtively shook her head. "For God's sake, Lilli, don't do this! Nobody should ever know."

"What?" Rebecca demanded, bolting up. Lilli strummed the envelope over her fingertips. "Does this have anything to do with Miriam?"

"I doubt it," Lilli replied.

Rebecca shook her head. "Was this what you were hiding in the old safe in our apartment?"

"Yes. Herta said I should destroy it. But I couldn't...." Lilli shuddered. "It's about my past...." Her voice choked. "For years I tried to imagine it hadn't existed."

Herta wrapped her arms around Lilli and buried her head in her chest.

"It's so dreadful, Becky," she bleated. "Lilli is good and this makes her look like a monster."

"Herta, Herta, I must do this." She sadly turned to Rebecca. "You see, Becky, I wasn't quite truthful about my reasons for not coming to the wedding. I was overwhelmed by terrible anxiety. It had been weighing me down. It made me feel unworthy. But in a more practical sense, I wondered if some element from my other life might somehow emerge here." Lilli took a handkerchief from her sleeve and wiped her eyes. "Herta and I talked about the situation endlessly. And we decided to remain at home."

Rebecca knew that if she insisted, her grandmother would refuse to disclose what this issue might involve. She opened the terrace doors, walked outside, and lit a cigarette. A troop of valets was pulling up cars for the mass of departing guests.

"Put your damn cigarette out and come inside," Lilli ordered.

Rebecca rushed back. Someone was knocking on the door. A kitchen staff man wheeled in a trolley. "Would you like me to serve you, Ms. Benjamin?"

"No, thank you, we can manage."

When he left, Herta said, "Just like home." She poured them coffee. "What a family. They live like royalty."

"They behave a lot better, and they're kinder," Lilli said. She sat down opposite Rebecca in a deep armchair, and handed her the envelope. "I won't keep you in suspense any longer, Rebecca."

The envelope bore the crest of one of Vienna's finest hotels. Rebecca took out three sheets of paper.

Wien
Januar 2000

Meine Liebe Lilli,

You will undoubtedly recognize the handwriting. I still use the Platinum Mont Blanc pen. It is the same one that signed the order saving the lives of your parents and Herta when they were about to be sent to Mauthausen for resettlement. I've often felt that people like you ignore the monarchy of chance to their detriment. And if not for me, you would have died as well.

I spent the night at the Palais Schwarzenberg in the grand suite. When I awoke, I reached out to hold you in my arms. Your fragrance, the very texture of your skin, still finds its way into my dreams. You made a lasting mark on me.

You see, Lilli, this is all something of a case of happenstance and deserves an explanation. Our son, Bruno, brought along the Neue Kronen-Zeitung newspaper when he came to celebrate the millennium with me. He thought I might be amused by the local gossip and also read the obituaries in Vienna. Little did we realize that this innocent, thoughtful gesture on his part would, only days later, bring us back there.

Bruno was totally ignorant of your existence, just as I was. I expect you also thought I had died. On his third birthday, when he expected you to miraculously appear, I finally told him you had been killed in the war. He was inconsolable. I explained that American Jews had bombed the hospital you were in and you had perished. And that's what I believed. So he grew up motherless. I decided never to remarry. With Adolf as our best man, I could hardly imagine a replacement for either him or you.

Bruno insisted that we make this trip. He was obsessed by this article about you and the Benjamins: your parents' music publishing business and, of course, your granddaughters: Miriam, the bride-to-be, a cellist, and Rebecca, whose performance we attended. But more about that in a moment.

Our magnificent son was deeply troubled about the taint of Jewish blood coming from your side. I reassured him and explained that you had been adopted and were raised in this venomous faith through no fault of your own. Well, it doesn't matter. Truth has a shaky history: It never saved a marriage or won a war.

However, he did want to know how you felt about him. He couldn't understand why you had never attempted to find him. I finally told him the facts. You had tried to miscarry, abort him, with Herta's help, and had no feelings at all for the sacred life that would emerge. He was enraged by your behavior, your abnormal hatred of him.

In escaping from Germany with our newborn infant, I was forced to disguise myself as a Jew, and this filled me with self-loathing. I even tattooed myself with a Dachau camp seal. I claimed I had escaped and become a member of a partisan group. I had already bought a house years before in Zurich and shipped all of my furnishings and mementoes there. The journey from Wien to Bodensee with Bruno was difficult—even for me.

We stayed for several days at the Hotel Johanniter-Kreuz. I took you there once for a romantic weekend. When I regained my bearings, I hired two local women to drive with me and our son to Zurich and reconstructed everything: You remember that one of my specialties was Usweises—identity papers, disguises and disappearances. I assumed a new role.

I met with the bankers I had cultivated and was treated royally. And why not? I had a fortune. However, it was clear to me from the outset that the future for us would be in the United States and not South America. When Bruno was four, we emigrated.

I wish you'd learned something from me. The Jews were never meant to survive. Study your history. They were outcasts thousands of years before Christ; their corrupt rabbis arranged Christ's murder; they, and they alone, created insoluble problems for every society they penetrated. They were always intruders whose treacherous manipulations and propaganda, and their lust for money, brought them the retribution they deserved.

Do you think that everyone is hostile toward them for no rational reason? Even today, ask yourself, why is the entire world prejudiced, and will be forever? Pick up any newspaper in any language, switch on the TV, and read and hear about their ritual slaughter of unarmed people in the Middle East.

Why does every nation harbor intense feelings of anti-Semitism? It's for the same reason they hate and fear disease. Only the Nazis came close to curing our planet's lethal poison. The Jews are Satan's tribe, the aliens on earth. Even before the Nazis, every country segregated them in ghettoes. The Jews have the same effect on people as a dog with rabies, and for this reason, they must be eliminated.

And we squandered the opportunity. Had Adolf followed my advice, the war could have been easily won. The male Jewish work force was educated, many of them in professions: doctors, scientists, mathematicians, and skilled craftsmen who could have been employed under our supervision. The flower of their creative people fled, emigrated or was put to death. Country bumpkins and Röhm's drunken SA thugs couldn't take their place in industry, pure Aryan or not.

There were hundreds of thousands of Jews who loved Germany, considered themselves Germans. They also believed in our expansion agenda for Lebensraum. They fought in World War One with distinction. Many gave their lives for the Fatherland. It was this Third Front, the concentration camps that cost Germany the war. The matériel, rolling stock, railways, camps, food, fighting men used as guards, the planning, construction, energy, all of this wasted our resources. Even in death the Jews undermined us.

And what did we gain from the Holocaust? Nothing! Six million Jews dead. Meaningless in the larger scheme. Once the war was over, and the men had served their purpose, that was the time for a total, worldwide eradication program. Instead of carrying out his imbecilic, Frankenstein experiments at Auschwitz, Dr. Josef Mengele should have liquidated the wives, brides, and sterilized all of their women once they reached puberty. We would have had zero population growth of Jews and a work force that was dynamic until they all died. Israel never would have come into being!

Even now at 86 (and you at 77) I can't help reflecting about our meeting.

It seems only yesterday that Adolf and I drove down from Berchtesgaden one sunny July afternoon and saw you perform for the first time at the Salzburg Festival. You had an aura even then—airs, I thought at first—billing yourself simply as Lilli, no last name. We'd never heard anyone ever play like you. Adolf and I were entranced.

What a fateful meeting that was, even now, for me, despite the passage of more than sixty years. When we came backstage, he never suspected your household was Jewish, and I made certain he never found out. Thus, his esteem persisted, along with his admiration.

On a Sunday afternoon, Bruno and I went to see your granddaughter Rebecca here in Wien at the Bösendorfersaal. Her playing was sublime. I'm looking at her photograph on the program—she is you. She's only twenty-two and I'm sure she'll have a brilliant future.

When she played the Chopin Nocturne, I imagined myself back in time. The hubris of memory...I can never forget the period before the war when Adolf, Goebbels, Himmler, Göring, Bormann and their wives and ladies would come to one of our sumptuous Sunday high teas in the Berggasse.

You were my wife, playing the piano with divine fire, and our witty, ravishing hostess. It makes me smile when I recall that I was harboring three Jews: Herta, baking cakes for Adolf in the kitchen, and your parents, hidden in the special apartment at the top of the house.

During Rebecca's recital, I kept an eye on you in the adjoining box. At the interval, I called your name, but you ignored me and did not recognize me. I was the "blind" man with the white cane. Later, at Rebecca's party in the wine bar, we sent the owner over to offer you a bottle of champagne, but you declined without thanks. You were too busy promoting Rebecca with some vulgar impresarios. Your voice still has a fine, insinuating timbre, and despite age and unquestionable infirmity, there was a quiet eloquence about it that still echoes in my mind.

You'll be happy to know that Bruno is flourishing. Naturally, he's dedicated to the Nazi cause and its future supremacy. He is a celebrated artist in his own right; he has inherited this from you, the mother who never wanted him, but who had him because I willed it. If you could only know him, you would be proud, and you would like him, maybe even love him, as I do. He, too, was quite taken with Rebecca. Unfortunately, we won't be able to attend her debut with the Philharmoniker and visit you—this time.

    dein,

    MAGNUS

At the bottom was the wax seal from the ring Adolf had given him.

22

Rebecca finished reading the letter. The pages fluttered in her hands. Her skin had turned ashen.

In a voice, overflowing with nausea, she asked: "Who—*who*! Is Magnus?"

As if talking to a bill collector in Vienna, Herta furiously spat out her words.

"A *dybbuk*."

"What? Don't double talk me, Herta. I've had enough. *I* don't understand."

"A monster, an evil spirit who takes control of a human body. That's what Magnus is! And he made Lilli suffer."

Rebecca thought she had sensed his presence: since childhood, a faceless figure had chiseled itself into the steep landscapes of her nightmares. Yet, whenever she was on the verge of coming face to face with this phantom, she would awaken. Perhaps this had caused her visitations. She had no way of knowing.

"Herta, you're not making any sense," Rebecca insisted, turning to her grandmother. "*You* tell me."

"When I met him with Hitler, Magnus was twenty-four, I think. He had silver-blonde hair, a perfect, straight nose, a carved chin, deep-set, steel-blue eyes, and he was wearing a silk, Italian bespoke white suit, with a red shirt and a black tie decorated with a swastika." She bowed her head. "He was the most striking man I'd ever seen.

"Hitler fawned over him, pulled his sleeve, held his hand. They had a very odd relationship—not gay, really—I don't know. Hitler was like an indulgent father, flaunting his beautiful son, his idol. He was everything Hitler wasn't. He had been given a post. When Adolf mentioned it, he smiled or gave a little laugh. 'My Minister of Identities and Hearts.'"

Lilli caught her breath and averted her eyes from Rebecca's.

"Magnus had an astonishing hold over Hitler."

After that meeting in Salzburg, Magnus had courted Lilli with honeyed intimidation; she'd had to cope with flowers, dinners, and threats. She was then a virginal seventeen. Vienna's reputation for sexual freedom became anarchy under the Nazis. Women of every faith were prey.

During this period she learned that Magnus was, of all those in the inner circle, the most rabid anti-Semite. He wielded enormous personal power over Hitler. The other ministers always deferred to him, even though he was the youngest and most unofficial of the lot.

"Some of them—Göring of all people—stood in awe of him. Himmler himself was terrified of him! Magnus was Hitler's pet, and nobody dared disobey him. You have no idea how clever and ruthless he was. I actually heard him shouting at Hitler!

"Well, some months later, I became Magnus Von Winter's mistress." Lilli fortified herself with Jack Leopold's brandy. "Then—the unspeakable happened. We went through a bizarre blood marriage ceremony, conducted by the SS at a castle in Wewelsburg. I don't know if it was legal. You see, Becky, there was no real law anymore, only whatever the Nazis decreed.

"After the ceremony, Magnus took me to the crypt. He told me that I had been received under the 'Plinths of Doom' and I would be spared because I was now totally under his protection."

Although she loved her grandmother, Rebecca was infuriated. "I can't believe you actually knew Hitler and Himmler...*them*?"

"Yes, yes, I did."

"That *he*...Hitler was your best man and came to *our* house in the Berggasse?" Rebecca asked, appalled.

"All too true, and he came frequently."

A cold sweat drenched Rebecca. "But you were a Jew!...Weren't you? Were you really adopted?"

"That was another lie Magnus invented for himself and for the son he stole from me. Of course I was—I am Jewish!"

Rebecca remained confounded. Lilli's resolute attitude did nothing to clarify her concerns.

"You have to understand, Rebecca, in my time I was a STAR. *You* know, there are different rules for us. I'd performed in Berlin, Salzburg, Paris, and in Vienna. Even after the annexation of Austria into the Third Reich, Hitler remained a provincial music lover from Linz, and *I* was playing for him in my home. My talent awed him.

"In our circles, Adolf was still a nobody. He'd been a vagrant, living on the streets and in shelters in Vienna. He was anonymous. Adolf? He would never have thought to question me. And by this time, Magnus had all of our papers, birth certificates—everything official—changed. I materialized as Frau Von Winter. My parents, your great grandparents, Leon and Elise Benjamin, and Herta too, all became Aryan. We were untouchable."

Rebecca shook her head mournfully, too shocked to express her wrath. "Are you telling me the truth?"

Herta's indignation gave her features a frightening witchlike configuration from Rebecca's *Grimm's Fairy Tales* of demons.

"You think Lilli would admit something like this...if it wasn't true?"

"Herta, please, she's still a child and doesn't know."

"I resent that," Rebecca said.

Lilli's body sagged and seemed to crumble. "Yes, of course, it's all true. The fact is, I was forced to play Hitler's favorites—*Liebestod* from Tristan, all of Wagner—and he would burst into tears."

"Oma, I don't know what to believe."

"Why don't you just listen for a change?" Herta insisted, casting her eyes at Lilli who had the stricken pallor of someone about to have a stroke.

"That summer, '39, Magnus ordered the Gestapo to have the Vienna gas corporation cut off supplies to all the city's Jews. They were using more than anyone else and the city was losing money on them. And do you know why the Jews weren't paying their accounts...?" Herta bared her teeth in rage. "They were committing suicide!"

For a moment, the three women withered in silence. Herta poured herself and Lilli more cognac. Rebecca looked at the two wretched old women, and her emotions roamed from sympathy to aversion. She could not find a balance, and her judgment of their behavior, especially Lilli's, became contemptuous.

"We had gas because of Lilli's influence with Magnus. I was fourteen, apprenticing as a baker in Lilli's parents' house. The Gestapo was going to send me to Mauthausen. I was *selected*—put in the SS brothel there! The Nuremberg laws were pure hypocrisy. The SS constantly tortured Jewish women and loved young virgins."

Herta's phlegmy gasps forced her to spit into her handkerchief. She stuffed it her handbag, the clasp snapped open.

"They would drag me to the basement of the house and rape me. The smells of the men's sweating bodies...."

Kissing Lilli's hands, she continued: "Lilli pleaded with Magnus to allow me to live—and here I am."

"Please, Herta, don't." Lilli sighed and snarled at Rebecca. "Americans like Jack would call this a trade-off. My parents were also going to be shipped there to work in the stone quarries at Gusen. When prisoners were too sick to dig, they were flung into ice-cold showers in the freezing weather and their bodies were dumped in the Danube. They rotted in the spring thaw."

An instant flash of the black snow falling when Rebecca had returned to the house after her night out struck her with the force of an anvil. Pollution was not responsible for this chemical reaction: the souls of the dead were clinging to an audience in tune with their suffering.

Herta's fingers struck her chest with anger and self-contempt. "To think that I used to bake those sickening, sweet dumplings—*Kaiserschmarm*—and cream cakes for Hitler...! I wanted to spit in the cream, poison it, but there were SS guards watching me all the time."

On April 20, 1945, Magnus had left the Führer bunker in Berlin—arm-in-arm with Albert Speer—after Adolf's fifty-sixth birthday. The war was lost. But the intransigent old guard, like Goebbels and his family, remained in the bunker, planning their suicides.

Magnus had arrived in Vienna the following day because he had learned that Lilli was in labor. An SS doctor had been assigned to her.

"It was torture." Lilli had regained her composure, but her voice retained a stark, festering anger beyond consolation. "Maybe I would've been better off in a death camp. Herta and I had done everything we could during my pregnancy to abort the child."

Herta cupped Lilli's face in her rough hands. "Do you remember what happened when you took the Ergot pills?"

The women had not spoken of these matters for decades.

"Yes," Lilli replied gloomily. "They had the chemist's name on the box. A squad went to his shop and chopped him into pieces. After that, the women guards never left us for a moment. Even when I was in the bath! Bombs were shattering buildings all around us. Yet Magnus was composed. There was a deranged audacity about him. His personality...?

"The doctors thoroughly examined the newborn baby and declared him healthy. Magnus had him bathed, wrapped in blankets, and took him. I was relieved, even grateful. He leaned down and kissed me. For once in all the years I'd been with him, he was subdued and said:

'Adolf failed me. He was the wrong man....I'm sorry to say goodbye to you, Lilli. But my son and I will never be safe be with you. No matter where I go, you'll find a way to betray me and kill our child....'"

Rebecca was sickened by the absence of maternal warmth or concern about the loss of her son.

"You were his mother! I don't understand you, Oma. Didn't you feel anything for your own baby?"

Lilli removed her glasses. Her watery, bloodshot eyes glowed with ferocity. "In bed with Magnus, I stopped being myself—it was the only way I could survive. I became a dead woman. To me, this child, was born dead. A spawn of my own dead body by a man who bred death all around him."

Herta's face pinched with wrath. "If you'd given birth to a child by the man who raped you, tell me, Becky, how maternal would feel?"

"I don't know!" Rebecca had never been able to repel Herta's assaults. "I don't know."

"No, you don't. There's a lot you don't know, Becky. *You can't imagine!* Lilli was the prisoner of a sex degenerate. Magnus would have the SS women guards strip for a show and have them carry Lilli to the bedroom and they would watch and—and—join—"

"Stop! Stop!" Lilli shrieked.

The women had reached the point of disregarding sounds on the estate. The firm knock on the door seemed normal and they ignored it. Then it opened in slow stages. Eventually, they turned to the partially hidden figure, standing there.

"I was in my car, but I had to turn back to see if you were all okay. Do you need anything?"

Rebecca sprang up. "Harry..."

"You're a treasure," Rebecca said, relieved by the interruption.

"You certainly are." Lilli rose with effort and joined Rebecca at the doorway. "I'd very much like to hug and kiss you. But I always give or catch colds."

Terminating the intrusion, Herta pulled the women away from Harry and regained her habitual hostility to the world.

"You'll visit us in Vienna to hear Rebecca play," she suggested in the same manner she used when the butcher demanded payment. "Good night, Harry, we appreciate your interest in our family."

23

No matter how much cognac Herta swigged, Rebecca could find no way to shuck her off. With her face as rough and unyielding as an oyster shell, she remained. All through her life in their house of women, Rebecca had never been able to dominate this bully. Nonetheless, she forced her grandmother to resume.

"...And don't tell me you're too tired. I won't accept it."

"As you like."

Lilli had left the hospital several days later. Vienna was in chaos: with unceasing Allied bombing, it became an inferno; fires never stopped, snipers shooting, Americans storming in with tanks. Putrid bodies piled in the street. Her parents were desperate to get out of the apartment where they'd hidden for years.

"My parents fled. They didn't care about the bombing. I grabbed hold of them on the Berggasse—in front of Freud's building, of all places. They'd been shut away for years, imprisoned in what became your apartment."

Rebecca wondered if the grisly history of the house had somehow combined with the presence of the Nazi hierarchy and her grandparents' tortured spirits. Had this become implanted in her psyche and made her a receptor?

"Bombs and explosions were everywhere, and my father said to me: '"This is music only the Americans could play for us."'"

Lilli began to struggle and walked out alone to the terrace. Herta signaled to Rebecca to let her rest, and she nodded. When Lilli leaned over the rail, Rebecca became worried and rushed to her. She cradled her grandmother against her. Cars coming and going, barking voices and furious, blinding lights illuminated the estate in the madhouse of a murder.

"My parents found their way to Der Ringstrasse and were caught in a firestorm attack of American bombers.

"After the war, the surrender—Herta and I had to *prove* we were Jews. We had no papers. Those we had had been forged by Magnus, and we burned them."

After leaving the hospital, the two women had returned to Berggasse. The house had not suffered serious damage.

"We had no gas, electricity, or water. The SS servants were gone, but left behind some tins of food, so we didn't starve. We spoke English, which made things easier with the Allied Occupation forces. They didn't doubt that we were Jews.

"We never mentioned Magnus. Anyone who might have known what had happened was dead. Gassed. Or had gone insane. Those who survived, and knew the family before the affair, vouched for me. Musicians I'd once played with helped me. Then for the next three years—'48, Herta—?"

"I think so, Lilli."

"I worked in cafés and hotel bars, coffeehouses, playing any kind of music, popular ballads."

"And weddings," Herta said with a grimace.

Rebecca listened, spellbound, and finally uttered the words: "Cafés—*you?*"

"I was a woman in disgrace, and I deserved nothing more. Herta worked in a bakery in the Kaiseralle, where the prostitutes bought their bread. We scrabbled and scratched. The city was in ruins—a sewer. The Allies were busy chopping up Berlin and Germany. Vienna was ignored, a stepchild."

Rebecca had begun to understand that there was more at stake for her than her career, and yielded to her primary instincts as a woman. Lilli's suffering had become her own.

Lilli reached for the bottle of cognac and filled her glass before handing it to Herta.

"I met a Swiss-Jewish gentleman," Lilli continued. "He was an auctioneer and also had an import-export firm. We were married in 1949 and your mother was born the following year."

Tears glimmered in her eyes. "*My* daughter Erika—*your* mother—was a genius. She could read at three. She enjoyed listening to music, but never wanted to play. Your grandfather and I spoiled her. Yet she never became difficult. Even as a child she had a gift for science and math.

"When she was ten, Karl and I divorced. No *Sturm und Drang*—all very civilized. He emigrated to the United States. He'd met a younger, less damaged woman, an American, and he wanted to marry her.

"We parted without raising our voices. He was an absent father, but wonderful to your mother. He traveled to Europe at least once a year to see her. He'd take her skiing to Gstaadt and St. Moritz. Erika was a fantastic skier."

Rebecca tried to sift through the fragments. "Did my mother know anything about your previous life?"

Herta snorted. "Heavens, no. Lilli and I lied to her."

"Your mother was studying to be a physicist. When she was twenty-two, she married one of her colleagues. Your father—ah, I adored Frederick. He was a charming, patrician man with wild, red hair—that's where you and Miriam got your coloring. He and your mother always talked about the universe having eleven dimensions—something about string theory."

Rebecca's parents had gone on a weekend's skiing trip to Innsbruck.

"Herta and I were delighted to look after you and your sister. Miriam was five and you were just a year old. As I said, your mother was a daredevil skier. Frederick was just as reckless. It's a mystery to me, why intelligent people take such risks."

They had skied the expert slopes at Innsbruck on new powder.

"There was a mammoth avalanche. They, and dozens of others, were lost. Swallowed up by the snow. Search parties had to wait days for the snow to stabilize. But it was futile. Even after the thaw, none of the bodies were recovered."

For years Rebecca and Miriam had not discussed their parents. It was a subject that their grandmother found too depressing. In time, the sisters' curiosity had dissolved. But occasionally Rebecca had seen them embedded under the ice.

"For Herta and me, it was like yesterday. We had no time to grieve because we had you and Miriam to raise. To avoid red tape, I legally adopted you because the government paid larger benefits to Jewish orphans, and so your name was changed to Benjamin. And there you have it, Becky."

Deeply troubled, Rebecca folded the sheets of paper from Magnus's letter and inserted them back inside the envelope "You never answered my question. Who was Magnus actually? "What was it about Magnus that made him so powerful?" Rebecca demanded.

"He was a sorcerer," Lilli declared.

"He was from another world," Herta said. "To this day, I really believe that, Lilli."

"I don't. He was a magician. He spied on me constantly. He wore disguises, followed me to cafés. Sometimes he'd be a cripple begging for handouts. He'd appear as a woman, stooped over and bent in a wheelchair. I never knew what to expect...."

"I was terrified," Lilli admitted. "Even when I was forced to be with him—intimately—he remained inscrutable."

Herta shuddered. "Magnus was Hitler's divining rod, his soul, and Satan's architect of death. He was not simply his protégé, but more like a guide."

"That's true. You see, Rebecca, socially, Adolf was entirely different from the frothing madman shrieking at the Nuremberg rallies, or what history made him out to be. He was reserved, awkward with women, so very polite that he seemed almost servile. He seemed—dare I say it?—cultured. But in the way that people who have no real confidence in themselves behave. He never discussed politics or the war. It was a refuge for him when he was out of Berlin and wanted to escape from his flunkeys at Berchtesgaden."

For an instant Rebecca felt a surge of hatred for the two women who had raised her. Everything in their lives had been constructed on deceit. Now that it was out in the open, she became convinced that Miriam's murder was the result of their duplicity. She glared at them. "Are you sure you never told Miriam?" she asked.

"How can you possibly suggest Lilli would do such a thing?" Herta replied.

Rebecca sprang up furiously. She had come to a decision and now placed the letter inside her handbag.

"*How?* I believe Miriam's murder was Magnus's revenge to punish Lilli. Miriam wasn't simply killed out of the blue by some neo-Nazis. There had to be a reason for torturing and degrading her in just such a way!"

"What...what are you going to do?" Lilli asked.

"I'm going to show it to Jack Leopold and make copies for the police."

Herta drunkenly stumbled toward her. "You can't! Don't you realize how that would compromise Lilli? She'd be humiliated and dismissed from the conservatory!"

Rebecca scowled at her. "It's a little late to worry about *this* family's reputation."

24

The two old women left very early the next morning before anyone stirred in the household. Robert, the chauffeur, explained to Rebecca that he had been called at four o'clock in the morning and driven them to Lufthansa at LAX.

"I told them that Mr. Leopold would make the arrangements. But—"

"...There was no arguing with them."

"Exactly." He handed Rebecca an envelope. "Your grandmother left this for you."

On fine notepaper embossed with the name Leopold she read:

Rebecca, Liebling,

I haven't stopped crying and can hardly see what I'm writing. We can't stay. Please come home. You have to prepare for the most important event of your career, your very life.

Nothing will bring our Miriam back and she, more than anyone, would have wanted you to have this moment. Do you remember when you were a little girl and we would go to the Phiharmoniker, and you and Miriam said some day you wanted to perform there? I took you aside and said, you would. You play better than I ever did, my darling girl. My emotional calibration was often feigned by circumstances. Yours is real, instinctive. A gift to the universe.

You have five weeks before your performance on March 21. There is some confusion now (which I couldn't go into) about Mehta's availability. There's talk that Bernard Haitink might step in as a favor. He is touring with the Berlin Phil and also has to mount his "Tristan" for the Royal Opera House. So nothing is firm, except your performance as soloist.

You must practice your program and be prepared for the rehearsal dates with the orchestra. They begin on March 4, no matter how the conducting issue is resolved.

Forget about me. I'm finished. But disclosure will ruin you...your entire future. Please, please, consider this.

You're only 22. You have choice. I didn't. I saw your anguish and understand your feeling that I betrayed you. But I was a prisoner and I don't mean to ask your forgiveness. I

will have my day before OUR GOD. I am a JEW and whatever
happens to me, I accept without complaint.

What happened to me was fated—Barschert. Please, please,
Rebecca, don't sacrifice yourself. This is a situation beyond
human jurisdiction.

OMA LILLI

Scott's lamentable abuse of the cello emerged from the music room.
It sounded as though he were taking out his anger and sorrow on a
Bach partita. When Rebecca stepped inside, he was naked, oblivious
to any human presence. Right before her eyes, he slipped off the chair,
snapping the neck of the priceless Guarneri cello as he fell, clinging
to its strings. He splayed on the Persian carpet, the strings dangling
like spaghetti. The metal music stand had keeled over with him,
releasing a loaded syringe and spewing its venom.

Rebecca immediately felt his pulse and shouted for help.

Jack, unshaven and in pajamas, rushed in, followed by two staff
members.

"Oh, shit, he promised!" Torn between fury and concern, Jack
ordered someone to fetch a robe and blanket. "I'm so sorry, Rebecca.
I thought all this was behind him." He shook his head in despair. "He
was clean with Miriam. She gave him some backbone. I just don't
know what to do anymore."

She had hoped to discuss the letter with Jack, but Scott's condition
made this impossible. She had to pick the right moment but realized
that she was now having misgivings.

"We need to support him and each other," she said.

"Rebecca, you've been a godsend. Lilli and Herta did some job
raising you girls." Jack had lost something of his godlike stature, the
attention to detail he brought to every situation she had seen him
encounter.

A wheelchair was brought in and Scott was strapped into it. Jack
instructed one of the staff to call his drug counselor and the pilot of
his jet. Scott was being sent to a drug rehab retreat in Minnesota.

"Times like this, I can't stand the sight of him." Jack clenched his
jaw. "I was forty when Scott was born. Paula was convinced that she
was past it at thirty-eight. So we treated him as a miracle from God.
Now look what he's become."

The furrows of Jack's large oval face hardened into tight grooves and Rebecca detected an element of the implacable industrialist who carved cities and factories out of deserts. "My son is a third-rate cellist, and a junkie." He picked up the cello, looked at it sadly. "We bought this in London for him after he graduated from Curtis. Scott had to have the best."

Like doomed prisoners, they wandered around the expansive room, the walls adorned with original editions of scores from Brahms, Tchaikovsky, and Stravinsky that she hadn't noticed amid the splendor of what she now thought of as the Villa Leopold. But the unity of this contemporary version of a Renaissance family had imploded.

"I'm thankful Lilli and Herta aren't up yet to see this."

"Jack, they left for Vienna very early. Robert took them to the airport."

He was disconcerted. All of his plans were in a shambles. "Why? They could've gone in a private jet."

"They're in shock. It's better for them to be at home."

He walked with her into the deserted dining room, now immaculate, the table leaves removed and reduced to eight places.

"Have some coffee with me." He looked at his watch. "Paula took an Ambien and won't be up for a while."

"Jack, may I stay a little longer with you? I can't face going back yet."

"Yes, sweetheart, we love having you here."

"I just can't leave with all of this unresolved. I have to find out something definite."

"You don't have to explain. I'm not satisfied with the way this is being handled by the police or the FBI. I can't believe there isn't a single lead. I've had Frank hire a team of former detectives. Let's see what they can come up with." His eyes screamed with an angry luster. "Money motivates people—lots of it." He paused suddenly. "Forgive me, I've forgotten when you have your debut in Vienna...?"

"The first day of spring."

"You have to practice, don't you?"

"I'll try to."

"Is our piano okay for that?"

"Yes, I'm happy with it. It needs a tuner to make a few adjustments for me."

"Paula will call him. Rebecca, you played so beautifully. I kept hearing the music all night long, even in my dreams."

They drank their coffee and Jack strained for a smile. He began to cry. In his pain and confusion he no longer seemed to be the great man, but simply a feeble student of life who could not find his way through the maze of paradoxes that had been thrust at him.

"This whole situation is all so crazy and out of control. Where's my daughter-in-law? My girl Miriam. She's supposed to be honeymooning with Scott. She's murdered before her wedding; my son's on the skids, shooting junk." He picked up his cup and it trembled in his hand. "I feel lost. I mean, Rebecca, don't take this in the wrong way, please don't. Does anything make sense? I'm rambling....

"Last night, I walk Harry out to the car to get some air and try to focus and concentrate on the present. I've got to get my mind back—talk business where I feel secure. Harry's utterly depressed, and this worries me. He's my closest friend. But I also have a billion dollars invested in Tampa. Now out of the blue, he starts talking about *you*. Says that you're the loveliest woman he's ever met. He tells me this after we sit *Shivah*. He's older...but in great shape. You can't imagine how many women have been in love with him, and he's always walked away. He's crazy about you."

"Maybe I've been too friendly. I do that. Harry's a sweetheart. I've always wanted an uncle like him, and now I have two."

25

With the unveiling of March, marking the end of Rebecca's third week in Los Angeles, Miriam Benjamin's murder had dissolved into the polluted air quality of Los Angeles—another crime statistic; there was hardly a mention of it in the papers, and only an occasional reminder on the local TV stations. Jack's marketing people had, however, put together a cable commercial that ran in conjunction with booming ads for mattresses, CD compilations of noted gospel singers ("Unavailable at stores"), and free plastic surgery consultations. Jack's million-dollar reward was still in place, along with a hotline number to call in case anyone had information.

Magnus made certain that everyone at Winterhaven watched tapes of this plaintive appeal to determine if anyone had succumbed to this inducement.

Chuck Avery, a flabby, middle-aged sloth of an FBI agent, had an office in the stark Federal Building slab in Westwood. He had been put in charge of the case. He was constantly at odds with the Van Nuys detectives, as well as Frank Salica and Rebecca herself.

Avery thought the ad a waste of the Leopold resources, and many of the callers—unhinged insomniacs and greedy, clairvoyant trouble-makers—had nothing in the way of reliable information. He and his team had assembled a massive file on known members of the Aryan Nations and the National Alliance, which they pored over whenever Rebecca showed up.

"Please have a seat, Ms. Benjamin." His schoolmaster politeness irritated Rebecca. "Can I get you something to drink?"

"No. Mr. Avery, you told me you'd call me. Last week, I gave you the name of a man who might be involved."

He looked at his notes. "Oh, Von Winter. We ran a check on him in our files, Interpol and the Austrian State Police."

"And...?"

"He's not on any list of war criminals."

"Did you try to contact any of the Jewish groups I suggested?"

"We put out inquires on the Web to worldwide Holocaust organiz-ations. In fact, I called the Museum of Tolerance here in Los Angeles to find out if they could assist us. They were very helpful and put their resources at our disposal."

Rebecca felt a burgeoning optimism and, for the moment, dismissed her misgivings about Avery and his file readers.

"They contacted the Wiesenthal Center in Vienna and Paris. I'm sorry to say that nobody has any record of Magnus, or Bruno Von Winter." He referred to his notes. "Now Magnus is the man you claim was a friend of Hitler's. And he threatened your grandmother during the Nazi occupation of Vienna. Forced himself on her?"

"Yes, constantly. Our housekeeper, Herta Schwarz, would have been sent to an SS brothel if my grandmother...you know what I mean. They were terrified of him."

Chuck Avery slowly dropped his official mask and exuded sympathy. "It was the worst wor of all. My father served in the infantry and was wounded in the Battle of the Bulge. He told me things.... The Nazis were inhuman." He sighed and she was encouraged. "Rebecca, let's get back to this situation you brought up. I can find out from the consulate, but maybe you'll save me the trouble: How old is your grandmother?"

"It's a family secret, but I'll tell you. She'll be seventy-eight in June."

Avery put a TUMS into his mouth and chewed it. For once, he fumbled and seemed to lose his way among the strangled vines of the Benjamin dynasty. "I wouldn't have guessed it. She sounded much younger when I spoke to her. And certainly with all her faculties. I caught her before she was off to the conservatory to give a lecture."

Rebecca's head snapped back. "You spoke to her?"

"Last night. I know you and Mr. Leopold think we're a bunch of morons, and you've hired private detectives. That's your legal right. But for the moment, let's skip that. I asked your grandmother if she had a photograph of Von Winter, or could give me a physical description of him."

Rebecca brightened. "Well, Mr. Avery, you *are* making progress. I apologize if I've underestimated you."

"Look, this is a bit awkward." He began shuffling papers again. "Often, something happens when you've had someone you love so viciously murdered—without any logical motive. People lose their emotional stability and begin to imagine all sorts of things." His phone rang and he told his assistant he'd call back. "To get to the heart of what I'm trying to say, Rebecca, sometimes people make things up, and imagine events, to help themselves over their difficulties."

"I'm a bit confused. What exactly are you implying?"

"With your grandmother's consent, we recorded the conversation. Would you like me to play it for you?"

"No, that won't be necessary. I'll take your word."

Avery's attitude softened and he looked at Rebecca with avuncular compassion. "She's never heard of the Von Winters—Magnus or Bruno."

Rebecca swayed back on the chair and was overcome by a swell of nausea.

"Are you okay?"

"No, I'm not."

"Your grandmother asked me to pass on a message. She'd like you to return to Vienna to rehearse for your concert. Personally, I think that would be a good idea."

26

Position was everything to Lilli and always had been. Her standing in musical circles had to some degree enabled the sisters to leap over competitors for scholarships, though essentially, their own talent had brought them to the forefront. While practicing Brahms' "Piano Concerto in D Minor" at the Leopold house, without concentration or pace, Rebecca thought angrily about the predicament into which she had been thrust and where her loyalties belonged.

Miriam's death gnawed at her constantly, coloring every aspect of her being. Music, her career itself, struck her as a selfish indulgence. How could she go on, actually perform, as though nothing had happened and Miriam hadn't existed? The lust for fame and the good life that success would assure her no longer dominated her drive. It bore a hollowness, a triviality, while the specter of Miriam haunted her day and night.

It became a question of what—apart from music—was actually important to her, and this itself was new territory. She had no doubt as to what advice Miriam would have given her: *Go back, play brilliantly, and enjoy the moment.* Rebecca slumped over the Steinway, brooding over what to do, when Jack came in.

He had told her at breakfast that he would try to have a normal working day. He slung his briefcase on the sofa. It was unnecessary to ask about developments. Someone would have called her.

She charged over and kissed him. "Let's have a drink, shall we?"

"I'd love one."

"Let me do it."

"I'm easy. Paula was disappointed you didn't go out to the beach house with her."

"I feel comfortable and safe here. And I wanted to see you...to ask for your guidance."

Every room downstairs had a wet bar and she poured them both Grey Goose vodkas on the rocks in the Baccarat tub glasses he preferred. A silent kitchen staff-person delivered a tray of dim sum and Peking duck pancakes with dipping sauces.

"Scott's improving daily."

"That's terrific."

"His doctor said that the key to his recovery is to keep him out of California. Scott likes the Midwest. He feels he fits in. Maybe he'll wind up there."

"I didn't do well there. I was too young at Oberlin, and my hormones began to explode." She waited and he began to relax. "Jack, I have to make the most serious decision of my life, and you're used to that, I think, in business."

"I may've made some questionable ones today. Harry needs more money for the Tampa Art Center. The structural engineers have modified their plans."

"I'm sure you'll work it out." She placed her hand on Jack's. "I trust you, and Harry as well. I wish he were here, too. He's so easy, as only smart people can be."

"That's a fact."

"I have to perform in Vienna in sixteen days...."

"Are you ready for it?"

She became indecisive. "Technically, I'll play well. But psychologically—I'm not sure."

"I can't help you with that."

He brought the bottle of vodka and made them more drinks and they tumbled into a warm father-and-daughter camaraderie that she had never before experienced.

"My philosophy professor told me that before people make a decision—a choice—they endure anguish, despair, and forlornness."

Jack laughed, touched by her naïveté. "Every guy does that to get a woman into bed."

She shook her head ruefully. "I fell for it."

"You miss him, you want to go back to perform and see him?"

"Neither," she said harshly.

"Then stay."

"Even if it involves destroying some people?"

He grew pensive. "Let's for a second ignore the profit motive in big business. Sometimes when I buy a piece of property—land—I have to get rid of the locals' houses or small operations to build something larger...commercial and more functional. In a real-life sense, the issue then becomes one of changing the destiny of human beings. Suppose I give the people more money than they ever could have made. Let's say, because of this money, their marriages break up. At the same time, I deliver jobs for new residents who can send their kids to college, pay off loans, or whatever. We can go on forever about the implications. Every issue has a nuance of morality connected to it. You make a decision and live with the consequences. It's always been that way."

She tried to measure her words. "Jack, what if I told you I may have information about the man who murdered Miriam, or assisted in it." He stared at her, confounded. "And that someone close to me might know about this? It would cause the person great pain if I revealed this."

He pulled away from her, startled. "Are you sure of this?"

"Not entirely. I'm not an investigator." She had a change of heart. "But intuitively, I'm certain."

"I had Frank fix some clerks in the LAPD, and he got access to national computer files. We're trying to determine if there've been cases similar to Miriam's. Old, unsolved murders that were buried or ignored. The point is, Rebecca, I've pulled out all the stops." His eyes assumed a level of controlled ferocity that intimidated her. "Does that answer your question?"

"I'm going to give you a letter. But please promise me that you'll respect its confidential nature. No one—not the police or Frank—can ever know about it."

"I never accept conditions that restrict me from acting." His face went taut as a drum. "Are we clear on that? Now, make up your mind."

She handed him Magnus's letter and rushed out of the room.

Rebecca had no way of anticipating what Jack's reaction would be, but she had uncovered a deposit of merciless inflexibility in him that made her apprehensive. Even the warm yellow tones of her suite, so beguiling when she had arrived, now struck her as sickly and poisonous.

At eleven, she put on a denim jacket and slipped out of the house. She had seen Frank leave a stucco cottage behind the tennis courts several times. His BMW was parked outside. She peered through the window; the TV flickered without sound and she heard his laughter. She rang the doorbell—infernal chimes.

He loped to the door, awkwardly tying the belt of his robe. Just as he opened the door, the crabby edge of a woman's voice resounded: "Not now, goddamn it!"

"Hey, quiet!"

Frank's hair sloped over his brow, sweat leaked into his eyes, and he was out of the breath. "Rebecca?"

—"I'm sorry to have disturbed you, Frank."

"Is there a problem?"

"Yes, in the bedroom!" The woman pressed her body against the wall and peeked in.

He turned. "Claudia, will you cool it?...Sorry, what can I do for you?"

"I didn't mean to interrupt."

"You can call me directly from your room. I'm one-one."

Rebecca had lost her European gentility and didn't care about barging in on lovers. "I had to see you, Frank."

"Oh...all right, come in, then."

The steamy, aroused woman reappeared, wearing a tangled blood-red Samurai kimono. Claudia Atkinson, personal trainer, masseuse, and yoga spiritual guide, offered her a glass of red wine. The room was redolent of clammy sex and hashish.

"I really shouldn't have interrupted you, Claudia. I'm sorry, but this is urgent."

Claudia, apparently placated, nodded to Frank. "It's okay, you've been through hell."

"Yes, I have." Rebecca turned her charm on Frank, concealing her lack of conviction. "Mr. Leopold told me how ingenious and resourceful you've been, gathering information on cases like my sister's."

"I've been putting my back into it."

"We talked about the progress you've made. Since I lived in Oberlin for a year, then in New York for two years, I thought if I looked at your files, maybe I'd pick up something. An obscure name. A fact that only Miriam or *I* would have known about."

Eager to be rid of her, he agreed. "You've got something there."

"We all have to work as a team."

"For sure. Give me a minute...I'll put it all together for you."

"Thank you, Frank."

As soon as he left the room, Claudia assured her that except for occasional periods of relaxation, Frank was on top of things.

"Listen, Rebecca, if you ever need a massage—or want to do some yoga—or talk to someone, I'm here for you, honey."

Frank returned, carrying a thick folder that he handed to her. He had swabbed back his hair and tried to disguise the flavors of Claudia with a splash of nauseating aftershave.

"Lots of it is in police terminology, raw intelligence, reports, and crap that I haven't had a chance to go through. If anything catches your eye, make a note, and we'll talk about it."

Escorting her outside, his attitude became conspiratorial.

"Rebecca, this isn't just confidential, it's top secret. Lots of people could get into serious trouble—prison—if it was traced back here. I mean, everyone in this house. Is that clear?"

"Thank you, Frank. I would never betray you. This is your time off—now complete your mission."

He stood in the rich, wet grass, watching her walk away and straining to hear her what she was saying.

"'Welcome to Los Angeles, Ms. Benjamin.'"

Rebecca left Kinko's where she had copied and collated the swamp of police paperwork, then returned to the Leopold fortress. Armed guards now patrolled the property day and night. She was escorted to the house by a security car with two men who opened the front door for her. For some reason their presence did not reassure her. At the rate things were going, she'd need a photo ID.

The kitchen staff, always on call, also irritated her. Why couldn't she simply go to the kitchen, and fix herself coffee and a sandwich of leftovers? At moments life this, the very nature of wealth itself restricted her freedom and imprisoned her.

She opened the terrace doors of her sitting-room, put a towel down before standing on the Directoire writing table, and disabled the smoke detector. She tossed her clothes in the bathroom hamper and wiggled into pajamas, which smelled of lavender. Somewhere in the entrails of the Leopold palace, a Hispanic maid had washed and ironed them, polished her boots, turned down the bed, and brought in bottled water and a carafe of coffee.

No wonder Miriam, accustomed to helping Herta with the house-keeping drudgery, had felt an irresistible desire for this way of life, even if it entailed nursing a third-rate musician whose lonely act of rebellion was to become a drug addict. The severity of her judgment brought tears to her eyes.

As a student of musical composition, Rebecca knew that for the first time since she had arrived she had a measure of control. Frank Salica, master detective, had, like a lazy teenager, thrown dirty socks under the bed. These sloppy files, like the police themselves, operated in bedlam. Rebecca's parents had been physicists and their daughters had inherited their tidy, analytical minds.

Reading the hodgepodge of national reports of murderous rapes, dismemberments, and questionable suicides until five in the morning produced a thin harvest.

Would there be any parallels, a congruence? She placed the wormy, suspicious ones in a separate pile before packing them all inside her music score case. Her eyes gave notice, and the cold coffee couldn't keep her awake as she fell into bed, numb.

27

An insistent knocking on the door roused Rebecca. She still had no notion of the time or day and finally mumbled: "Come in."

A maid poked her head in. "Mr. and Mrs. Leopold asked if you could please come downstairs as soon as possible."

Rebecca hurriedly washed her face, brushed her teeth, and ran a comb through her hair before scurrying into the breakfast room as the grandfather clock in the hall chimed ten o'clock.

Rebecca's natural exuberance made a rare appearance. At last, there would be news about Miriam's murder. The killers had been caught, confessed, and the family might have a moment of liberation. They could not rejoice—Miriam would still be dead—but retribution was at least part of the contract that society could extract.

"Good morning. How was the beach, Paula?"

"Sit down, Rebecca."

Paula's voice had a hostile, metallic peal and for once she was not coiffed but scruffy, wearing a rumpled sweater over jeans and dirty sandals. Jack's glasses were angled on top of his head and he hadn't shaved. His eyes were closed and his mouth contracted with a starkness that made his lips vanish. When he opened them, he waved at the houseman.

"Please don't interrupt us for anything—and close the door."

Rebecca helped herself to coffee and sat, frozen. "Did they find him?"

"No, but we found something even were werer," Paula shot out. "To think Scott might have married into a family like yours...! We're deeply sorry that Miriam's dead, but in way, we've been spared."

"My God, what we only discover about people," Jack said. "It never crossed my mind to have Lilli's background checked out."

"I see," Rebecca said, conquered by panic.

"Do you know what happened to my grandparents, my aunts, my uncles—_their_ children?" Jack asked rhetorically. "They were shipped to Belsen, Dachau, Auschwitz. My mother's brother was the only one who escaped. When he arrived here, he had one hand and one eye. Camp guards had chopped his hand off with a meat cleaver and stuck a poker in his right eye. They left him for dead, but somehow he survived. But he went mad and committed suicide because the Nazis had put his pretty little daughter and wife in a brothel!" Jack could hardly breathe through the turbulence of rage.

"Please, please, Jack," Paula cried, trying to calm him. Rebecca looked sidewise at her, hoping she might have an ally.

"I have to get it out, Paula."

Her throat closing, Rebecca stammered: "I can't excuse..."

But Jack raised his hand. "Rebecca, shut up! Now listen to me good. While Lilli was playing the piano for Hitler and screwing this Magnus, human beings—Jews—my family!—were being tortured and killed by the SS!"

Paula now joined the attack. "Or let's ask that Nazi servant Lilli travels with to bake us Hitler's favorite pastry."

Jack thrust the envelope with the letter in Rebecca's face.

Paula shook with wrath. "This whole Benjamin family is poison, Jack! The way they've sucked us into their filth."

The Leopolds were now talking to themselves as though Rebecca were not present.

"...Scott, bless him, was an innocent." Jack screamed—"and fuck the drugs!"

"He lifted up a rock and he thought, *we* thought, he was going to marry into a decent Jewish family.... Aarrgh, I can't!"

"Paula, you're wrong! Lilli couldn't help what she did. She was turned into a whore, a sex slave. She was the victim of a monster," Rebecca protested.

"*Really.* Well, according to Magnus, Lilli isn't even Jewish. None of you are, if the mother isn't," Paula insisted.

Rebecca was accustomed to the highly strung tempers of conductors and tried to imagine herself rehearsing with one of them. "We *are* Jewish. Magnus lied to his son. And Miriam never knew about this! I only found out when Lilli came for the funeral. That's when she showed me the letter." Tears sprang to her eyes. "I wouldn't give it back. I thought it would help with the case."

"Help the case?" Jack regained a semblance of control. "Rebecca, if you show this to the FBI, you'll be deported. And frankly, that wouldn't be a bad idea."

Jack turned away from her and again spoke directly to Paula, sympathetically. "Our government and police are running themselves ragged, working day and night, to find out why somebody paid back a girl from a Nazi family. There is *no* mystery! Maybe it was a Jew who lost his family and wanted retribution. *I* fucking well do!"

Paula clasped his hand and held it her lips, then hugged it to her cheek and added fuel. "And who could blame you?"

Rebecca had never been subjected to such a wounding personal attack, and she clamped her hands over her ears defensively, like a child. She was too shocked and frightened to cry.

"Could Miriam have told Scott about this, and maybe that's why he relapsed?" Paula asked.

"We'll never know, honey, because we won't ask him."

"You're right." She looked at her sporty Chopard. "It's now ten forty-five, Rebecca...." The phone rang and Paula picked it up, listening for a moment. "Thanks, Carmen." She hung up. "Rebecca, your stuff is all packed. Don't shower or anything. You will be out of this house in fifteen minutes. The houseman is upstairs waiting for you. He'll take your bags down, and a cab will be waiting."

Rebecca wobbled from the table. The Renoir on the wall seemed to be crooked, celebrating a picnic that had never occurred. The room, the Leopolds' faces, smudged into vague outlines. Objects appeared to take on a supernatural force, flying through space.

Jack seized her roughly by the arm. "Wait a minute, sister. Do you have the key to Harry's Range Rover?"

In a tremulous voice, Rebecca searched her mind for words. *"Ich nicht haben der Schlüssel."*

He recoiled. "We speak English here!"

"They always revert to German!"

"I gave the key to the security man last night. Please—Paula...Jack, you've made the most serious mistake of your...."

".... I don't think so!" Jack bellowed. "By the way, I had my travel department cancel your ticket back to Vienna. Let Magnus and his son pay your way back. Now get the fuck out."

28

Rebecca lost all sense of time. Still in a state of shock, bewildered, and lost, She had asked the taxi driver to take her to a reasonably priced hotel in the neighborhood. She had no idea how long she had been in the room at the Renaissance Hotel. It was located at the rump end of Beverly Hills. She didn't remember much more than that when she woke up naked in bed.

She hadn't unpacked or eaten. She called the desk and learned that she was beginning her third day there and that it was Wednesday, March 8. The room rate was $145 per day and the reservation manager wanted to know how long she planned to stay. She told him she couldn't be sure.

The Leopolds' accusations played a mutinous antiphony within Rebecca's consciousness. The sound of their voices jumbled into atonal madness. It was as though music had never existed in the world. The Leopolds' faces continued to dissolve and rematerialize into a swollen mass of undefined flesh, until they were transformed into demonic masks.

Rebecca took a bath and sat in the tub in a deadening torpor, until the water turned cold.

She was not in Vienna, leaning over the kitchen sink with Miriam or Herta about to rinse her hair. The instability of silence alarmed her and she suspected that she was having hallucinations. She pulled herself up and realized she must wash her hair in the shower.

Afterwards, in a daze, she blew out the hair dryer; an irritated hotel engineer, with a squealing pager on his belt, brought in another one.

She undid the clasps of her suitcase and realized how perfectly everything had been packed. Her bras and panties had been ironed. She ripped the backing off a new pair of hose and, dragging herself to the window, squinted in the marshy glint of faint light. Winter afternoons always disclosed the masked somberness that lay within a city, its hovering secrets more palpable to a stranger.

Where were her music scores? In a panic she rushed to the closet and found her briefcase, bulging with folders. For a moment she wondered where these unfamiliar papers had come from. She emptied the contents on the bed. Pages and pages of official police reports tumbled out, along with shocking coroner's photographs of Miriam, and her piano scores.

Miriam had a shaved head and a swastika on her forehead.

Springing back, Rebecca screamed.

She fell onto the bed and after a few moments, struggling to control herself, she finally thrust herself up, squirmed into black wool pants, a green turtleneck sweater, a long suede coat, and black loafers. Her large travel handbag contained a passport, address book, make-up, and her wallet.

She counted seventy dollars and two hundred euros. She'd check her VISA limit, but thought she'd be fine with American Express. Herta always paid their bill promptly.

After a pancake breakfast in the hotel restaurant overlooking a small deserted pool, Rebecca was desperate for air. She picked up a map at the desk and was given directions to the local park, which, she was told, had tennis courts and a jogging track.

The main street east to west was called Pico Boulevard. Walking west down a humpback hill, she passed a 76 Station with a market called Owen's behind it. She turned south, a right turn on Roxbury Drive. She had expected souvenir shops with racks of postcards and bric-à-brac, but nothing suggested that this was in any way a tourist area.

Her head slowly started to clear when she reached the Community Center entry of Roxbury Memorial Park. Under morbid aqua composition umbrellas, seniors were arguing about misplaying cards in their Bridge games. Rebecca stopped to pick up some leaflets and local papers for something to read.

She passed a children's designer plastic playground populated by mothers, Hispanic nannies wheeling baby carriages, and ruthless children establishing their territory in a sand pit. The smell of grass, burgeoning flowers, and a grove of Chinese Elms, cedars, oaks, and budding lindens, brought to her senses a topical reunion with Vienna. She thought, of the lush Belvedere in her home city at the onset of spring where she and Miriam used to idly walk.

The memory of Miriam assumed a physical presence guiding her, and Rebecca did not feel quite as isolated and lost. Miriam's strong, encouraging voice and soft laugh chimed in her ears. Rebecca with

Miriam in her head wandered through Roxbury Park for hours, until Rebecca realized that the park was not in Vienna.

At the market, She picked up the L.A. Times, a sausage sandwich, a bottle of Stolichnaya, peanuts, crackers and Brie, chips, a lemon, beer, and soft drinks. As she left with her shopping bags, a domed, reddish stone building caught her eye on the other side of the street, and she crossed over.

She read the name.

THE SIMON WIESENTHAL CENTER'S MUSEUM OF TOLERANCE

God had revealed Himself and directed her to this hotel, this walk, and this location, which honored the timeless slaughter of her people. There was no doubt in her mind that Miriam lived on, in some form. Her sister had disclosed that she existed in a dimension of time and would be piloting her on an enigmatic journey, a pilgrimage that had a design and purpose.

It was just past eight in the evening when Rebecca called Vienna. Herta answered the phone. Her shrill, despotic voice was filled with a litany of accusations. "Where have you been? We were in a panic and thought that madman murdered you too! How can you be so selfish and irresponsible? Yes, I know only too well—"

"Stop screaming at me, dammit! Put Lilli on."

Lilli picked up the extension. Her stertorous breathing made Rebecca uneasy.

"Will you ask Rebecca what she did to cause this catastrophe?" Herta demanded. "Or should I do the dirty work?"

"Please, Herta. I can't bear any more of this," Lilli implored her.

"Tell me! What's going on, Oma?"

A gruel of sweat surged down Rebecca face, as she listened, stupefied by her grandmother's account of the events.

"I called and called the Leopolds' house. But could only get through to a rude servant. He wouldn't give me Jack's office number—nothing. He said Paula and Jack were away, and hung up on me. There was no explanation, no letter, nothing."

The Leopolds had re-opened their family mausoleum at Forest Lawn, removed Miriam's casket, and had it flown to Vienna, with all the regulatory documentation. The casket had been delivered to Berggasse X that morning.

Miriam now resided embalmed in the music room, along with her cello.

This act of cruelty, the vindictiveness of misunderstanding Lilli's circumstances, brought out Rebecca's resolve to fight.

"Bury her at home—in the garden. Yes, that's a good idea. Beside the greenhouse. Call my friends—even the professor. They'll all be discreet and there won't be any legal problems."

"I see," Lilli said, resigned to new, contemporary horrors as well as those of her past.

"Don't hurry home, Rebecca. We managed to survive before you were born and we will again," Herta said before slamming down the receiver.

"Becky, I'm still on the line." Lilli sighed. "Listen, I'm trying to cope with Miriam dead and not crumble completely." A suspicious delay accompanied this, before Lilli regained her wits. "Having Miriam home is better than her being thousands of miles away in a crypt with those Leopolds. This idea of burying her in our garden makes me feel better."

"I feel the same way now."

"Can you send me the phone numbers of those friends of yours? That philosophy professor and his students will have to do." Lilli shifted her desk lamp and rustled sheaves of paper.

"Becky, I did the best I could in my negotiations. But a date is a date...especially a debut with the Philharmoniker." Lilli's voice trembled with the intensity of a requiem. "I caught the posters in time. They were about to print them. *You*—your performance—has been cancelled."

Rebecca would have fallen if she hadn't been sitting on the bed.

"Please bear with me. In Zaragoza, there's an opening in July."

Lilli again fumbled with her scattered notes and there was a small noise of objects falling. But her grandmother was always careful with the miniature bottles of Johnny Walker Black Label, which were duty-free gifts from traveling students.

"Becky, didn't you win a competition there? You like Spain. It would be outdoors. An afternoon at the public pool. Let's see, they'll have 'An audience of at least two thousand...'"

"They sent an offer—fifteen hundred. I'll fix that. We're at the beginning of negotiations."

"Please don't bother. I can't...I'm in no condition to perform. I haven't been able to practice properly...since I saw Miriam."

"Yes, yes, I understand." Lilli's breathing had a strangled rasp. "I assume you showed Jack and Paula the letter from Magnus?"

"I did."

"I thought as much. And the FBI man who called me? He won't gossip...?"

"Who knows?"

"Oh, Rebecca...no one who wasn't me could grasp what I—never mind. I would never expect sympathy for my actions." Rebecca's silence revealed confirmation. "When are you coming home?"

"I'm not sure."

"Make it soon. We used your American Express for our tickets back. Herta can't pay this month's bill."

Herta was back on the line, indignant, contradictory. "You must come back immediately. You have to earn, Becky. Don't be so selfish!"

She was tired and disgruntled about being the family meal ticket. Her childhood and youth had been swallowed by the need to provide for everyone.

"Herta, I'll do the best I can."

"Get off the line, Herta...." Rebecca heard the familiar slam-down. "Darling, we love you." Lilli's voice was a beehive of honey. "Stay in touch."

"Yes."

"Oh, Becky, I've been told there's a glorious cathedral in Zaragoza. Paintings by Goya...I'll work on these people and get them to pay. We'll get through this."

"Goodbye."

Rebecca lay face down on the unmade hotel bed, banging the mattress, trying to drown out the sound of her unremitting cries.

"Miriam, I'll be with you always."

29

By Friday, still shaken, and with charges mounting for her room and the hotel restaurant, on impulse, she called Harry Summerfield. She did not expect to be able to speak to him and was surprised to hear his voice; he even more surprised to hear hers.

The patient pursuer, convinced he had missed the screw of a lifetime, had just returned from Tampa. Jack had warily avoided discussing Rebecca or her whereabouts.

"You're still here...! I thought you'd gone back to Vienna. I said to myself, either she's too busy signing autographs, or I didn't make enough of an impression for a call or an email."

"You made an impression. I'm in Beverly Hills."

"Really? What happened?"

"It's rather involved."

"Lunch? I look like hell. I got in from Tampa at five this morning and rushed to the office. If you're not embarrassed being seen with me—"

"Or you with me."

"Where are you?"

"Wandering....How about outside of somewhere?"

"Gucci on Rodeo. A half-hour?"

"Fine, I know where it is."

"I'll drive the Aston Martin so you'll recognize me."

There was a lustrous warmth in the old bricked courtyard of Il Cielo where they were lunching. For a moment, the waiter's Italian accent and the glass of chilled Vernaccia created the impression that Rebecca might have been in a Tuscan *albergo*. In his denim shirt, jeans, and rumpled tweed coat, Harry had something reassuringly European about him. He didn't mind her smoking and his blue eyes revealed something beyond a predatory sexual interest.

Harry studied her. Rebecca possessed the feminine characteristics of old vanished societies. Never in love, he was entranced by Rebecca and how often he found himself thinking of her. With women, he had always been in command of his emotions so that nothing could develop into devotion, since this might lead to absolute commitment.

But Rebecca had taken possession of him, insinuated herself into his mind, and he realized that this might lead to recklessness.

Unlike the women in previous affairs, Rebecca seldom went out of her way to please him, or anyone, for that matter. He had enjoyed the company of intelligent women, but never anyone so gifted and completely her own person. Although she did her best to conceal her real feelings of weakness, he was touched by her fragility.

"Now don't take this wrong way, but you can stay at my place. I don't know your hotel. I guess I've passed it enough times. It's really not for you Rebecca."

"I'm on a budget."

"Can I get personal? Are you short of money?"

"Not exactly. But things are a bit tight."

"What about the concert in Vienna?"

"I had to cancel."

"That must've been painful for you. It's not my world, but were the promoters—whatever they're called—angry? Did you hurt your prospects?" he asked, concerned.

She nodded, finished her wine, and the waiter was quick to refill her glass.

"No question, I've ruined myself professionally."

"Couldn't Lilli manage the damage-control?"

"No, sometimes it's hard to decide whose side she's on." She shook her head, ambivalent about Lilli. "And besides, murder, death, plague, it's all the same to an impresario. You're unreliable. They write you off." She sipped her wine and puffed on her cigarette. "But, Harry, emotionally, I couldn't go through with it. I don't know how it is with architects—or men, in general—but losing Miriam this way just drained me of everything. You start out with ambition—nothing can stop you from achieving your goal—then life *finds* you and blows up everything. And what you do? Your old goals, just don't seem important anymore."

He held her hand and she touched it to his cheek.

"I'm sorry, Rebecca. You're so gifted. But people have to make career decisions, even if it goes against them." His smile was filled with encouragement. "You'll come back. *I* believe in you."

They skirted over the Leopold situation. Clearly, he had no idea of what lay at the root of the quarrel. She thought it unlikely that Jack and Paula would discuss Lilli's Nazi background with him or anyone else. The truth would be embarrassing.

"Harry, can I trust you?"

"Only with your clothes on."

"We'll see."

She laughed and in a way felt an attraction to him, but it was fraternal, benign, and she could not imagine being intimate with him. She wasn't about to become his mistress or a trophy wife. He was like a wise family friend who brought the best wine, a jar of caviar, and retailed the latest gossip. He was someone to take along to a concert, or lighten up a dinner party. Lilli had a collection of these armpieces. The prospect of an actual physical relationship with him or any man would have been perverse and impossible for her now.

"I had a problem with Scott." Her story unfolded over the rich lobster ravioli, which she ate ravenously. "He was using coke and I tried to get him to stop. Stupidly...you can't reason with people doing drugs."

His expression registered scornful disgust. "They've had problems with him for years."

"Did Jack mention it?"

"Oh, he'd never talk about that to anyone. He keeps family affairs to himself."

Rebecca was relieved that Lilli's past still lay buried. She related how she had found Scott naked and barely conscious.

"Miriam's death would have set him off. Not that he needs an excuse." Harry continued to lash out, surprising Rebecca, and at the same time pleasing her. "After all, look at him: he's a mediocre musician with a billionaire father and an adoring mother. In Beverly Hills, it's a recipe for disaster. How could he not become a drug addict? The thing is, Miriam had him under control. That's one of the reasons why Jack and Paula were so enthusiastic about them getting married. They did everything to encourage Scott. Your sister would be his keeper."

Miriam had omitted this aspect of their romance.

"I see. It's none of my business, but I got the impression that you and Jack were the closest of friends."

"We're business associates...friends, I suppose. Under his gracious exterior, Jack's my bad dream. He's an extremely hard and demanding guy. I never lose sight of the fact that he finances what I'm building.

He controls the consortium of banks and every division in his company: from the industrial sector—factories, dams, shopping centers—to the residential. The art center and concert hall—all the other interlocking parts in Tampa—will cost more than a billion dollars. It's all his money this time. Not many people would personally develop and finance a project on that scale."

After a moment, she said, "He's no one to have as an enemy."

"Come on, Rebecca, don't be cute."

"I was being sardonic."

"You don't want to ever find out how dangerous and unscrupulous he is."

After a Tiramisu and espresso, they waited for his car outside. He tipped the valet ten dollars, which seemed overly generous, but she supposed this was not unusual for such an expensive car in Beverly Hills.

Harry held the door for her. "Where can I drop you?"

"Are you sure it won't be an inconvenience?"

"Oh, stop, come on, Rebecca."

"It's a small street in Beverly Hills." She pulled out of her briefcase Harry's *Thomas Guide*, leaned over, and showed him where she had marked the place. "It's a cul-de-sac. Oh, and, you can have your guide back."

"Keep it. I've got more." He put on his rimless glasses. "Sycamore Place? I actually don't know the street. As an architect, I should—it's expensive property—a lane between Charleville and Durant."

In five minutes, he was driving past the gnarled, towering rows of budding sycamores on an old-world street, with an admixture of Spanish-style *fincas* and redbrick Queen Anne and Georgian revivals. They all had well-tended gardens and small lawns. She pointed to a lush two-story, ocher-painted duplex, sheathed in ivy with blue-flowered wisteria vines serpentined around its entry pillars. Above the downstairs apartment, there was a balcony with an array of clay flower pots on a broad balustrade. A flame-point Himalayan kitten stood sentry above, motionless.

"It's that one, 99 Sycamore Place."

Harry was puzzled by her refusal to share her plans with him. He came around and clutched her as she got out. Rebecca squirmed away and grasped his hand. She held it tightly for a moment. The magnetic field she emitted sent electric waves through him. He was unnerved and jerked away from her as though a snake might have bitten him.

"You gave me a shock."

"Blame it on all the Stoli I drank last night."

His macho sensations resumed the invasion, still flowering with erotic fantasies. He recognized she was faltering, treading on the precarious edge of the mountain. He smelled conquest. She was about to throw her hand in. Come home with him. He'd strip her down, slaughter her with his tongue, and have her screaming when he thrust inside her, and the pleasure became theirs. Rebecca was the complete woman for him: exquisite prime beef on the hoof. His obsessive hunger and desire for her had become bottomless, beyond any architectural obstacle he'd encountered.

"What *are* you going to do?" he asked, troubled by his reaction.

"I intend to find the people who murdered my sister—and kill them."

"*What!*"

Harry's face stretched tight and he gripped her shoulders, livid with frustration, frightened by the madness of her quest.

"I'm pleading with you, Rebecca. Don't do this to yourself! I can protect you. Come down to Tampa with me." He released her. "You can stay with *me....* I'll find you a place on the beach. You can be alone and work this out.... Then go back to Vienna."

She appreciated his loving concern, but it had the impact of a light rain. "Harry, I adore you. You're a wonderful man. Like a hero in all the American movies I saw when I was a teenager. *You* are the real thing, though. But I can't let go of this."

"It's senseless and dangerous."

"I don't have a choice. Playing the piano used to be my life. But now I'm at the crucial point. I can't turn, I can't move. I'm locked in. *Miriam* asked me to do this. She *pleads* with me all the time."

He was becoming frantic, a condition he despised in men and women. How could he make her understand what was at stake? Common sense, logic, had no place in this situation. Slowly the revelation surfaced.

"Rebecca, do you play back that last night you were with Miriam?"

She froze. "I do! All the time," she said, incensed.

"If you'd been driving back with Miriam that night...? Do you think you'd still be alive?"

Her mind wandered as he continued his lecture. His voice had a piercing, intimidating tone, and reminded her of Lilli's carping when she had played badly.

"...Or would the two of you have been murdered? Do you remember what Miriam looked like?"

"Please, stop, Harry. I only see the old Miriam I love."

"I'm trying to save you!"

"I'll be all right, Harry."

She thanked him for lunch, the use of his car, and his helpfulness. She held him tight before kissing him on both cheeks. He pressed closer against her, feeling her plush breasts against him.

An elemental anger overwhelmed Harry. "For me, women come, and go. I've never told anyone I cared really. But I'll be here for you."

"I'll remember that. Just support me. And I don't want your money."

"Rebecca...."

"Harry. Good luck with Tampa." She began to laugh and the sound was so pleasing it was almost unendurable for him. "With someone like Jack, you'll need God on your side, and I'll pray that you live to tell the tale."

She watched him, with a hint of regret, driving his beautiful Aston Martin out of the cul-de-sac. She had never felt so despondent and at the same time calmed by the unexpected sound of Miriam playing the cello.

30

Rebecca's appointment was for three o'clock and she wove through her briefcase before she found the page she had torn out of the *Beverly Hills Courier*. She had five minutes to spare and strolled by neighbors out with their dogs who watched her with curiosity; a few nodded.

A thickset woman with short blonde hair and a belligerent attitude was walking an exuberant dachshund. The dog had been a gift from Magnus—the pick of his new litter. Noreen Porter quickly twisted her sparkling diamond ring so only the platinum band showed.

"Are you lost?" she asked.

"No, I'm not. Thanks."

"Okay, come on, Dort, we're going home."

"Hello, Dort. I've never heard a dog called Dort."

"It's short for Dortmunder. That's a German beer," the woman said, slipping on latex gloves, and opening a baggie.

Rebecca smiled. "Ah, yes, an icy Dortmunder. You're so fastidious with your gloves and sack."

The woman glowered at her. "Maybe *you* like to walk through shit and bring it home. We don't!" she said, heading to the coiled outlet of the street.

Unprepared for this slap on the wrist, Rebecca morosely strode back to 99 Sycamore Place. She realized that wherever she went in Los Angeles, severing connections was characteristic of the people who lived here. There would be no open arms to receive her, and if she wanted to survive, she would also have to freeze out everyone.

Under its mellow pastels, its unnerving, seasonal greenery and seams of sunshine, Los Angeles revealed unstable geography and a coal-mine hardness in which no canary could survive. The paradox she recognized was that the fragility of its ground supported a transient, disconnected society waiting to be defined and which might be buried alive without warning. The city's lurid voluptuousness, impregnated by rap, drugs, and sleazy sex, embedded rootless people searching for an explanation, but not a meaning.

Before ringing the doorbell, she looked again at the newspaper ad she was answering.

Female companion sought by elderly woman. Must drive.

**Medical & household assistance required.
Rent-free apartment in upper duplex for the right lady.**

A once-beautiful woman, with sallow skin, purple veins scheming out of her flesh, and a short black wig, eventually answered.

Rebecca entered a world of startling collector's beauty and thought the woman listing on her Malacca cane, with its unusual, carved jade handle, might once have been a museum curator or owned an art gallery. A pair of Chesterfields in lime-green velvet faced each other beside a lively fire. Between them stood a glass table, supported by four carved metal elephants. The room was painted a light, warm chrome yellow. For an instant, Rebecca was mesmerized by the grace of the furnishings.

"My name is Rose Fleming. I've made the tea...always Earl Grey, brewed, never tea bags." She pointed in the direction of the kitchen. Rebecca put her case down on a glass-topped wrought-iron art deco table beside a matching pair of ruby armchairs. "Unfortunately, I can't carry the tray in but I haven't reached the stage of having to suck my tea out of a saucer yet."

"I'll get it, Mrs. Fleming."

"My name is Rose...and I never wasted my time in a marriage. There's Devon cream, scones, jam, *miel de lavande*, if you're hungry."

"What?"

"Lavender honey from Provence."

"*Je comprends*," Rebecca said. "I'm just overwhelmed by your astonishing taste—your eye. I speak French."

Rose Fleming silently watched Rebecca serving the tea. The girl knew enough to place the cozy over the teapot.

"This is fine Sevrès, an old pattern," Rebecca said with a bleak smile.

"You're very young to know about things like that."

"We had a service like it once at home."

Rebecca put her milk in after she had poured the tea, and Rose, vigilant, approved.

"I have a nurse who comes in daily to give me injections. I'm an old piece of spoiled meat to her. We don't like each other."

"If she shows me how, I'll give you the injections."

"Can you cook?"

"Yes."

"I don't have much of an appetite. Maybe because the nurse brings in awful goop from the supermarket and nukes it. I enjoy soups. They're easy for me."

Rose Fleming removed her glasses and her eyes were a piercing peacock blue. "I'm too sick and rich to bother with a tenant for the upstairs apartment. And I want to fire the nurse. Now tell me why a young woman as good-looking as you—and with taste—would want to do work like this?"

"I need a place to live."

"Are you pregnant?"

Rebecca threw back her head. "Absolutely not."

"What did you do before this? Do you have any special skills?" Rebecca fell silent. "Is that an embarrassing question?"

"No. I'm concert pianist. I've decided to take a long break. I don't want to perform."

"Really? Where's your family?"

"I have a grandmother in Vienna. That's where I'm from."

"Vienna. I'd never know it. Your English is rainproof."

"I have a good ear. I went to school in the States for three years. By the way, Rose, I have no references or friends in Los Angeles."

"That makes two of us." Rose hesitated. "Forgive me, that's a lie. I do have one. An old Irish lawyer I used to sleep with. Hard to believe a woman like you has no one."

Rebecca pondered this. "Oh, there's an architect I know. Harry—Harry Summerfield."

Rose grew animated. "Of course I've heard of him. Frank Gehry and Summerfield are the two most prominent architects in Los Angeles."

Sniffing her, the kitten Rebecca had seen outside nestled in her lap, and she stroked him.

"Do you have clothes, or do I take you as you are?"

"They're back at the hotel."

Like one of the detectives she'd met, Rose continued to ask direct questions, but this time they were not humiliating, implying that Rebecca might have had a secret lover. Rose insisted on getting some air and climbed the steps with Rebecca's help to show her the apartment.

It was comfortably furnished, functional, and enormous, containing twenty-two hundred square feet. The bedroom overlooked a large back garden with roses in bloom, lilies, a flowering pear tree, and was shaded by the splayed branches of more sycamores.

"I have leukemia, Rebecca. I'm dying," Rose said. "Are you up to it?"

Rebecca held her gently, feeling the fragile structure of what had once had been a stunning woman.

"Yes. I won't leave you or let you down."

Later that afternoon, after Rebecca had brought her bags from the hotel and met the nurse, she sat on the edge of Rose's bed, glancing at the attractive feminine room with its fine antiques, a table with old snuff boxes, and Meissen figurine lamps.

On the opposite wall, Rebecca was astonished to see a poster-size photo of a man crooking a rifle and standing over an enormous dead lion.

"The great love of your life in Africa, Rose?"

"Yes," she said, wiping back tears on her robe sleeve.

"Oh, forgive me. I didn't mean to upset you."

"Doug will always be everything to me."

"When did you lose him?"

"After he went to Africa."

"Africa? My God. Your travels. What a life you've lived."

"He's alive—barely."

Rose's voice vaporized, but her blue eyes retained a degree of righteous outrage and passion that surprised Rebecca.

"Douglas Horne is my nephew. He's on trial for murder in a city called Dar-es-Salaam in Tanzania. The prison conditions there are brutal."

At a loss, Rebecca tried to comfort the distraught woman. She tried to imagine the man's circumstances. But this was suddenly displaced by images of the horrors Miriam had endured in a gas chamber.

Douglas Horne would be the perfect man to explain murder to her: He had committed one.

The light sharply refracted on the photograph of the dead lion, and bands of a rainbow formed. Miriam's face flickered in the photograph, then slowly, but clearly manifested itself. Her sister stood behind the hunter looking at her. She nodded and smiled at Rebecca.

PART III
HORNE

1

On the evening of February 10, 2001, Douglas Horne approached the customs line at LAX. He knew they'd be waiting for him and had spotted him the moment his passport had been stamped. It wasn't difficult: he was six-five, hadn't trimmed his beard or moustache for a week, wore a baggy safari suit, wide-brimmed hat, stained with mustard and red wine, and Dr. Marten's hiking boots encrusted with mud. He pretended that he hadn't noticed their interest. He hung back, hoping they wouldn't hassle someone who looked as though he'd just ridden hard and put away wet.

Damn, he couldn't smoke and tossed the last cough drop into his mouth. Rules, everywhere, rules. He pushed his cart forward and waited for them to make a move. When it was his turn, the customs man stared at the five long canvas cases for a moment, then shook his head with disapproval. "Some people want to talk to you."

Two men in suits, not expensive or cheap but shiny and badly creased, discreetly flashed their Alcohol Tobacco and Firearms badges. One of them, forties, blonde buzz cut and bulked out, but not as big as he, said: "Mr. Horne, would you come with us, please."

"Sure. I hope you're in the mood to buy me a martini."

He had read the export laws before bringing his guns through. In fact, he knew all the hunting codes because that was a prerequisite before he could get his original license. He could no longer hunt big game after the incident and he hadn't troubled to have it reinstated. There'd been no point. He was persona non grata in Tanzania. He'd had enough of nosy officials, mercenary lawyers, and corrupt judges whose only interest seemed to be in making eye contact with the pretty young jurors at his trial.

The agents sandwiched him, one in front and one behind. He caught sight of some others from their team, trying hard not to stare at him. The shorter of the agents opened a door and nodded. As he walked into the room, he had no intention of giving them a hard time. He was happy to be home, and too weary for games.

In the small, sweaty office, the fluorescents buzzed and a couple of them flickered, biting his eyes. He expected to be strip-searched, but the agents were careful not to get too close to him. It still puzzled him that grown men could do such shit jobs, but they did them in every country, were proud, pensioned, and respected.

"I'm Agent Dawson," the small man volunteered.

Horne opened a tattered crocodile briefcase and presented his passport, licenses, and arms manifest signed by a consular official in what was serving as the outpost for the American Embassy in Dar-es-Salaam, which had been bombed by Al Qaeda terrorists.

"Douglas Horne at your service, gentlemen," the former safari guide and hunter said, mocking himself a bit.

It was as though he were at the bar of the Mount Kenya Safari Club charming dubious clients who really preferred their lions on TV, their women in Victoria's Secret chemises, and Masai servants tripping over themselves with bottles of Cristal.

"Do representatives of the ATF smoke or drink?" he asked. "Are you allowed?"

"Not at the moment." The blonde man seemed somewhat surprised by Horne's levity. Usually people were agitated—fumbling for their lawyer's phone number.

The two men pored over Horne's documents like exterminators looking for bedbugs. It had been a slut of a year for him and he hoped that now that he was back home, his life would improve. Although he loved the United States, Horne felt no great loyalty to its minions after they had let him turn to blue mold in prison before sending a consular slug—dumber than rat shit—so that he could be assigned a lawyer at his own expense. Nobody liked the Americans in that part of the world: they were lordly, uninformed, and couldn't even bother to learn Kiswahili. Horne had lost native friends in the embassy bombing.

The blonde guy finally introduced himself, Agent Somebody. He touched the gun cases and coyly asked, "Now, what've we got here?"

"Why ask me? Open them and look." Horne was immediately sorry he had ragged him. "I don't mean to be a ballbuster. I've been in transit for two days and flying for the last twenty hours. Where the fuck am I?"

"LAX," Dawson said. "Look at your ticket."

"Normal people don't travel with all these guns," the blonde guy said.

"Normal people don't hunt big game," Horne said.

"My God," Dawson squealed, "never seen anything like this, Tony."

"Holy shit," Tony, the blonde, said with covetous admiration and alarm.

Horne tilted his safari hat over his eyes to kill the murderous lights. "Not exactly one of your pea-shooting .38 Specials."

"No, it's not," Tony said, in the dawn of respect.

"It's a Holland and Holland Royal Ejector .500/.465. The Arabesque-style scroll engraving is a Holland trademark. This double rifle is used with .500 grain soft-nosed bullets for lions. Full metal jacket for elephants and rhino. It holds two shots. A gift from one of my grateful clients. You guys have the papers and the provenance."

Tony's Midwest farmboy could not be repressed. "You've shot lions?"

Dawson was clearly intimidated. "What if you miss?"

"I guess we wouldn't be having this conversation if I had."

"How long will you be staying with us?" A voice sprang from a microphone behind what Horne knew to be a see-through, dark mirror pretending to be an innocent, smoky window.

Horne's eyes were too raw for him to raise his hat. "Do you always ask American citizens how long they're staying?"

"Mr. Horne, you've been out of the country for twelve years and just been acquitted in a murder trial. You come through customs with five very big guns...and an assortment of handguns. Your firearms papers are in order, but we have to check a few things."

"How'd you get these jobs? Ever try to enlist...Marines, Navy...? No, I guess not."

"What are you planning to do with these weapons?"

Horne grunted. "Lock 'em in a closet. Unless there's big game in Beverly Hills."

"Well, you can understand our concerns. You come back after all this time with an armory."

"You don't have to worry about me."

"I want those rifles taken apart," the voice demanded.

Horne shook his head, but exasperation would not help his cause. He quickly disassembled the rifles. There was .22 BRNO, Czech-made, used for small game with a five-shot detachable magazine. He had acquired this years ago. No bill of sale. What had he traded? A live King cobra. Then he held the stock of a .30/'06 caliber Winchester model 70. This was a gift from the retired hunter who had trained him. It held four cartridges. In another case was his Safari Grade

SAKO from Finland, with a five-shot drop box magazine and which used 4.375 H&H cartridges. Finally, he unzipped the last weapon, and in seconds, field-stripped a semi-automatic M4 Super S.90 Benelli shotgun.

"What's that one for?" the disembodied voice asked.

"When people crowd me, I just start firing." He couldn't resist goading them. "You and your families and the nation can be safe now that I'm back."

His strategy worked. Dazzled by his assurance, they hustled him and his arsenal to a taxi at the strip of the dirty sidewalk.

"How many lions did you shoot?" the chief agent asked.

"I don't remember. Fifty-sixty. None for sport. I only took rogues—mankillers." Horne felt as though he were back in Dar-es-Salaam, being questioned by a police inspector. "As for the other kills, I lost count a long time ago. I worked the game reserves in the national parks as a ranger during elephant culls. I also had a couple of seasons when a band of rhinos were crazed by a virus."

"Well, you can understand our concerns."

"Oh, stop the bullshit. You know damn well you don't have to worry about me. It's sixteen-year-olds with Uzis in crack houses and kids settling scores at schools."

The brief recital gave Horne a second wind. Now that he was home from Africa, maybe he should stop thinking about conspiracies. It was just that his experience from an early age had smoked out a venality that seemed the very twin of incompetence whenever he encountered people working for the government. In Africa they were all corrupt; in America they hid behind the public-safety mask.

On a cell phone, a sullen Russian cabby was brandishing his fist in the air, screaming. He eventually opened the trunk and hoisted Horne's gear into its greasy innards. He stared at the gun cases but did not touch them and watched Horne lay them in the back seat. Brusquely, he now hung up and started paying attention to what was happening.

"Is this your address?" Dawson asked.

"Yes, yes."

"Is this a house or an apartment?"

"It was my aunt's home, and she left it to me. Okay now, girls, can we all go home?" Horne turned his attention to the driver. "Keep off the 405 and don't be using that cell phone while you're driving me, Tolstoy, or I'll get very angry with you."

"Yes, I understand. Where we going?"

"Beverly Hills, 99 Sycamore Place."

Horne had the driver stop at a convenience market on Venice Boulevard. The cold honeycomb rain cut through him and he looked up at the opaque purple heavens skywritten with ghostly fumes of car exhausts. Blue-black dirt and mud mottled the grimy Coca-Cola clock outside and it was a test of his eyesight to unveil the actual time which had been a mystery to him over the last few days, or was it months?

It was only eight-thirty in the evening. He'd lost track of these radical time changes. L.A. had welcomed him with a rousting at the airport and a vinegary February winter evening. All the mart had in the way of food were gummy takeout trays. This place reminded him of the corrugated iron-roofed *dukas* on the roads outside Arusha, with their music videos featuring screeching sitars. The dusty shelves contained a few bottles of some off-brand vodkas labeled in Hiero-glyphics. He settled for a six-pack of Beck's along with a crushed carton of Marlboros.

When the cab nosed past a deserted Rancho Park—the tennis courts he had once played on—and turned off Motor to Pico, cars were woven in dreadlocks all the way to Beverly Hills. Passing by Twentieth-Century Fox, Horne was grateful for the familiar landmark. Murky, rain-spattered billboards glowed with photos of TV shows and movies he'd never heard of and would never see unless he were imprisoned again.

The cabby turned into the graveyard of Century City where new buildings had sprung up like poisonous weeds in this architectural wilderness. In its sterile towers, computer monitors shimmered inside offices over the heads of corporate slaves still at their tasks.

They drove past Beverly Hills High School and Horne said, "Pull over, Tolstoy."

"My name is Serge, and this is not the address."

"I just want a few minutes."

Horne got out, shrouded in the shadowy mist over the school field. He had run miles around the track and, when he looked up, the old smokestack over the oil well still hissed fumes. It had been decorated with some kind of fabric design. Maybe instead of teaching the three Rs, the students were quilting.

He sneered at that monument to wealth and education, Beverly Hills High School. He had spent his tormented senior year there: a transfer, friendless and feared for his quirky moods, his excellence on exams, and his refusal to get involved. Even the pumped-up jocks had given him a wide berth; afraid he'd kick their asses in public.

Horne smoked a cigarette and waved the driver back inside the cab.

"Now take it slow, it's tricky to find." Horne was excited about returning to familiar terrain. "Take the second right and I'll guide you."

Sycamore Place was a murmur of a lost, secret world. If someone weren't looking for it, he'd be unlikely to find it. The trees were sturdy, like elephants surviving the wounds of old enemies. Horne noticed that a number of formerly single-family houses had been gouged into nests for singles on Robbins and Durant. This would be a likely scenario when he unloaded his aunt's home. The cab driver turned into an alley, twisting around blind curves, and eventually reached a cul-de-sac with a low-tolerance for U-turns. In England such a street was called a mews.

For Horne, absent for a dozen years, the street had grown even more beautiful in the rain. It accommodated stout ivy-covered houses: some of them Queen-Anne-like mansions, alongside red-brick Georgians. His aunt's lazy Spanish gem had been designed for dreamy summer coolness before air-conditioning.

All the houses were presided over by an entourage of dynastic gnarled sycamores, planted in the thirties during the childhood of Beverly Hills. The trees were now about sixty feet high. When he'd first moved into his aunt's house, he'd been sixteen. The gray, rough knotty trunks were what he had imagined elephant trunks would be like. Despite his time in Africa, these thoughts had woven their way into the permanent tapestry of his illusions.

A chill of pleasure quivered through Horne when the cab stopped at the house. He lowered his head and eased his stiff legs out. The fickle rain had tapered to an unthreatening drizzle, and the sky through the stripped, barren trees bore a vermilion cast. He looked at the lighted upper duplex. From the open porch upstairs, he heard piano music, a murmuring of voices, and wondered if there were a party going on.

"Don't touch the cases. I'll take them out."

The driver nimbly lifted out the leather bags from the trunk and placed them under the eaves of the downstairs patio. Horne, distracted, sheltered his gun cases in a lean-to against the front door and again wondered what was going on upstairs.

"Thirty-four dollars and here is receipt."

Horne peeled a fifty off his skimpy roll and handed it to the driver. "Keep it."

2

The burled walnut door of his aunt's apartment had a weathered varnish glaze, and the black wrought-iron spikes enclosing the spy hole had been newly painted. He opened the screen door, tried the keys, and discovered both locks had been changed. At his feet was the tenant's idea of stationery: a shirt cardboard with a note.

WELCOME HOME, MR. HORNE. PLEASE JOIN US UPSTAIRS.
REBECCA

Fatigued, he dragged himself up the steps to the upper level of the duplex and glanced around for the hammock where he would drift through summer days, drinking beer and listening to Vin Scully's silky voice urging on the Dodgers. Robust wooden tubs filled with herbs and flowers were everywhere. The huge, angled living room was crammed with people. In what had been the dining room at the rear, a grand piano now stood. Irritably, he pushed open the door and entered unnoticed. Everyone was listening spellbound to the woman at the piano. All he could distinguish through the crowd surrounding her was a nimbus of long coppery hair, finely meshed in sinuous curls masking her face.

He was hardly an expert on music, but he could appreciate the caliber of the pianist. He had no idea what she was playing, but it was melodic and emotionally moving. She was mesmerizing, worthy of a concert hall.

His eyes roved through this apartment he, his mother, and father had frequently stayed in, before his parents had disappeared in Africa. Now the place was unrecognizable, foreign to him. It had been repainted a ripe apricot; the high ceilings, moldings, and wainscoting as well. Sumptuous Old World furnishings, sofas with cane arms that looked as though they came from a museum, had displaced TV tray tables. Delicate porcelain lamps—rare antiques, he suspected—were everywhere. A French grandfather clock in working order anchored the entryway; an English barometer stood on a maple wood chest.

"What the...? "

His Dodger and Lakers pennants had been ousted by a collection of paintings in ornate gold frames, geometrically spaced like a gallery.

Horne wondered why people bothered with phony copies or reproductions. He knew a little about art and thought one resembled a Dutch master. Others possibly some Renaissance painters whose names and certainly shaky provenance he could hardly identify. There were bronze sculptures of figures that might have been Greek or Roman.

Walnut floor-to-ceiling bookshelves, many of them filled with German history and memoirs of Nazis, burrowed against sets of the classics in Moroccan bindings with raised gold lettering; along with them, shelves were leased to music scores and obscure 78s in albums by someone named Lilli.

His past with his parents had been obliterated. It was as if someone had moved a European setting into Beverly Hills. Horne was bewildered, disoriented, overcome by powerlessness.

For a fleeting instant the woman's face, inhabiting another world, became visible. The hunter's eye glimpsed a young woman with sculpted features vanishing under the thicket of flying hair. Blocked by the other guests, he, too, was caught up in her mysterious circumstances, a kind of delirium. He watched her hands pausing, gliding, soaring on the keys and her artistry seemed to reach a sublime level. He felt the transient dizziness of exhaustion.

Something nudged him and he looked down at a Flame Point Himalayan cat marking him with his head. When he stooped to pet the cat, it darted behind a tapestry of rich golden figured drapes.

Horne, running on jet lag remote, joined in the applause.

"Nobody plays Brahms like Rebecca," said a well-built, smartly dressed man, worrying his long blonde hair back into place. "Are you a musician, too?"

Horne had no idea what the man was talking about. "No, I just flew in," he replied, the lights, like spiders, knitting webs in his eyes. Horne had floaters and his vision became a wasteland of cloudy images.

Extending his hand, his jacket sleeve bobbed up, exposing gold-button Tiffany cufflinks: "I'm Harry...Harry Summerfield." He had a friendly, cultivated voice. "Where're you from...Mister—?"

"Africa. My name is Horne, okay?"

"Funny, Rebecca never mentioned you. I thought I knew her all her friends. Did you meet her there or in Europe?"

Exasperated, and immune to diplomacy, Horne snapped. "What the fuck's going on here? I never met the lady and she didn't know I was coming in. Does that explain it?"

Ignoring Horne's hostility, Harry was not cowed by Horne's size. "No, you'll have to do better, or leave. This is a private party."

"Shit, I live here!"

Harry was stumped. "What? With Rebecca?"

After the airport welcome, Horne's temper got the best of him. "Listen, my friend, let's draw straws to walk her cat another time. This was my aunt's house—mine now. I just want to get my key and crash."

"I am sorry."

"Forget it. I haven't slept for days." He observed guests putting cash into a crystal bowl beside the piano. "What is this all about? A fundraiser...or what?"

"Not exactly. It's the anniversary of her sister's death—a remembrance evening for her."

And now Horne was defensive and at a loss. "Forgive me. Jesus, I had no idea. I'll be living downstairs. I just want to get into the apartment."

"So you're her landlord, I guess." Harry said, calibrating the circumstances. "Oh, hell, I'm sorry, Mr. Horne. I just flew in from Tampa myself and haven't had much sleep." Harry's blue eyes were sympathetic. "I met your aunt several times when Rebecca moved in. My condolences."

"Thanks."

Through the mill of people, wiping the sweat from her brow with a towel draped around her neck, Rebecca spied Horne and closed in on him. She wore a mauve velvet blouse with matching pants. She moved boldly, unself-conscious of her imposing size and height.

She extended her strong fingers and clasped his hand in her steamy one. Her sweat drizzled on him. She had something of the dominant confidence of big women and might turn mean if she didn't get what she wanted by the time she hit thirty. In Africa on safari he'd seen his share of them, snapping like Great Danes at husbands who hadn't fulfilled them.

"Mr. Horne, I'm Rebecca Benjamin."

"Just Horne, no mister, and it's a pleasure to meet you finally."

"I couldn't come to the airport or I would have. It was impossible to cancel this evening."

"That's okay. When Aunt Rose's letters were still getting through, she mentioned you often. I appreciate your being with her at the end."

"I loved Rose. She was a real *woman*, brave and high-spirited. Let's get you settled. I'll take you down. I had to get new keys. We had an attempted break-in. As soon as the ghoul squads read an obituary, they hit the place. Pity you weren't waiting in the dark to welcome them with one of your big hunting guns."

Her attitude was unexpected. "I'm well-known for my hospitality to intruders."

"I'll bet," she said with a husky laugh.

Her fiery hair, damp and darker up close, settled over fair, flushed skin with freckles lightly dotting her cheeks; her eyes were a penetrating gray flecked with green, and she had full smiling lips and a snooty, arched nose with a full bridge. Horne guessed she was in her mid-twenties. As a hunter, he was sensitive to the spoor of animals. Even sweaty, Rebecca smelled like just-watered grass. He was enthralled by her talent, which bred this self-assurance. She was weaving through guests, tugging him along, while she was kissed, kissing back, accepting congratulations on her recital, and playing herself down.

"...You're very generous but I hit some sour notes," she informed her admirers. "I really must practice more. Back in a few minutes."

Outside, she took Horne's hand, like a teacher guiding a blind child. "Loose step. I called Armando and he'll be here ASAP. He's your aunt's man for all seasons. You must be exhausted."

"Yeah, I'm done in."

She unlocked the door, switched on the entry light, and tried a lamp. "Cranky timer on this guy. I'll add it to the list."

She picked up two of his gun cases and set them in the corner. He carried in the others and went back out for his bags, scooting them down the slick, shiny wood floors.

"I wasn't sure of your exact arrival—yesterday, today, or next week. They were really ugly at the prison when we tried to contact you. I don't know what kind of people do those jobs."

"Unskilled," he said, amused by their viewpoints toward authority.

"Feelings have become acquired skills. Who knows about genes? Maybe they started life without them, confiscated at birth. The embassy people—attachés or whatever their imperial titles—they couldn't be bothered either. Look, Horne, my guests won't be staying much longer and I'll tell them to tiptoe out. I've finished playing for tonight."

"I'm fine. Don't worry about me."

To Rebecca his bravado seemed like a piece of elastic; he found himself unable to sustain it. Gaunt, with bleak hollows below large, pale-blue eyes, he might have been a mansion blighted by indignant storms and stunted summers, his height and size virtually eroded. Horne had been rendered into a brittle ghost of the man she had seen in Rose's photos of him. Prison had confiscated something of his youth.

They were in the kitchen and she opened the fridge. "I picked up some bread, milk, and coffee from Trader Joe's, cheese, pâté, sausage. Well, you get the idea. I also assumed you might like a drink."

She opened a kitchen cabinet stocked with vodka, Patrón tequila, scotch, Jack Daniel's, and cognac.

"What, no scented candles and chardonnay?"

"I wondered about that and got a Chablis."

"Putting you on."

She was flustered and her regal bearing drained away. "You sure? I wanted your homecoming to be perfect...with Rose's death, you being in prison, and the two of you frustrated by the separation."

"I knew she was dying and I wanted to be here with her. She was my connection to—" he shook his head —"it doesn't matter."

"She talked a lot about you and your parents." The mistress of music lost the security she had displayed at the piano. A sense of kinship drew out her unconscious, palpable sadness. "She said you were her—well, not exactly her son, but her son. I don't mean to babble and be emotional."

He wondered where she had gone to school. Her pronunciation occasionally changed. Underneath the polished English, like the skullcap below a wig, he detected a faint accent. Possibly Scandinavian or German. But this wasn't a safari orientation where such questions were asked as a matter of politesse, a warm-up, a way of checking things out, particularly identifying cowards. He could always sniff them out.

"You're fine, Rebecca."

"You'll have to adjust to life in Beverly Hills again."

He shook his head. "I don't think so."

"We'll see. I really want you around." People were trailing down the steps and calling her name. "I have to go. Dump your dirty clothes in the hamper. I'm doing a load in the morning and going to the cleaners. By the way, our keys are mates. I didn't want to spend Rose's money on Chubbs and thought I'd let you decide whether you want to change these."

"Rebecca, you're a saint."

Her buoyancy evaporated.

"I'm Jewish and there are no saints; just people everywhere searching, asking themselves questions, investigating, trying to find their way. We have a lot to talk about. Your aunt's memorial, for one thing. I didn't want to do anything without your permission. They had these nasty little urns. Her ashes are at the mortuary."

"I'll get them. Rebecca, were you with my aunt when she died?"

"Yes. She insisted on signing herself out of St. John's, and I brought her home on Christmas Eve."

"How long did she last?"

"Two days. She didn't want nurses or anyone. Afterwards, I called the doctor, her lawyer, and the mortuary."

"Was she in much pain?"

"I don't think so. I gave her the morphine shots."

He caught himself, refusing to give in to the menace of his loss. "She was the last of my family."

"I know. Rose wanted to hear music. I carried her upstairs and made sure she was comfortable on my sofa. I played Rachmaninoff's 'Prelude in C Sharp Minor.' It was her favorite piece."

Horne was solemn but composed. He had lost his combativeness the moment he had entered the apartment. In its place, the tenderness of the lost boy emerged.

"She was very lucky to have you."

Rebecca nodded. "So was I. Rose told me it was a bubbly quartet in the old days. You, her, and your parents."

"We never stopped laughing. It was a ball for me. I could drink within reason, have a couple of hits on a joint." He shook his head sadly. "Paradise. I'm still looking for it. Oh, well...thanks again for everything."

"I'm glad you're back, Horne. Sleep well." As she was about to leave, she turned. "I have a favor to ask: Will you teach me how to shoot?"

Her request surprised him. "I don't think you need to worry with me around."

Across the street, a veil of fog shrouded Virgil Hoyt prowling near a lamppost with his dachshund Dort. He didn't like the idea of this stranger moving into the apartment below Rebecca. It was inconvenient and would prevent him from using the spy hole he had drilled when he'd broken in after Rose Fleming had died. He and Noreen had been in Beverly Hills for months, watching Rebecca. Magnus considered her a threat, but apparently, it was too soon to eliminate her. Virgil heard voices, a man with Rebecca, but couldn't make out his features.

Harry waited for Rebecca on the steps of her apartment. He kissed her hand with adoration. It seemed to him that she had been playing only for him.

"Your performance broke my heart tonight. But you know that."

"It was for Miriam. She broke everyone's heart."

Nipping a potential rival before he climbed over the fence and hosed Rebecca's garden, he said, "I met your new landlord. He was rude, angry—a real pig."

"Aren't they all? But pigs are supposed to be smart."

"One of those sunless people."

"Maybe he's got a bad conscience.... He was a big-game hunter in Africa."

Harry decided to decapitate the competition. "Killing animals. Just what Beverly Hills was missing."

She was always pleased to see him, but his unpredictable schedule made it difficult.

"Harry, how long will you be here?"

"A couple of days to try and get Jack out of my hair." A group of professional mourners from the synagogue, led by a rabbi, had arrived for a *minyon*. "Can we get together without a crowd?"

In his apartment in Tampa, he had awoken that morning with a naked lap dancer beside him, hating both her and himself. At the last moment, he had flown to L.A. to see Rebecca. She was always in his thoughts: distracted at meetings, on the site, he was haunted by the ghost of her.

"Yes, of course."

"Fine. I'll call you." He hardly knew how to approach her any longer. He had hoped to break her down, but she still resisted. She'd kept him dangling for a year and played him with the same confidence as her piano. "Rebecca, this is no life for you. Whenever I come back from Tampa, and see you on the run, it hurts me. You're playing atrocious chamber concerts with people who aren't fit to turn the pages of your scores." When he came home, he would be her chauffeur. "You're ruining everything you struggled for in Vienna."

She was suspicious and infuriated. "Have you been in touch with Lilli?"

"Yes, I've spoken to her a few times," he admitted.

"She lied to me about that. I only hear the truth from you."

"We're worried about you."

She resented Lilli's surreptitiously discussing her life with him. "Don't be. I don't need any help from her! And Harry, I'd like you to keep out of our family issues."

"I didn't mean to interfere." He was chastened. "But how are you surviving?"

"I have some other work that pays pretty well." He seemed unconvinced and glared at her. "By the way, how's *your* patron—Jack?" she challenged him, her chin jutting out defiantly.

"We're getting along beautifully. Mutual hatred. The job's running late because of El Niño. But he ignores it and blames me instead."

"Lorenzo and Michelangelo," she quipped, but he was not amused. "You're not always right. The Medici loved art."

She gave an embittered laugh. "True. I can imagine what a great help Jack is to you."

"He'd like to fire my ass. Only he can't."

"Good for you." Sharing an enemy endeared Harry to her. "I'm getting closer to the people who murdered Miriam," she confided.

He was startled and concerned. "Really? Call the police, or should I?"

"No, I prefer to handle it without them."

She kissed Harry on both cheeks and quickly pulled away to discourage any prospect of intimacy. Rebecca's touch set off a wave of craving and he wanted to seize her right then and there, drag her back to his apartment, tear off her clothes, and demolish her. Always deeply aroused by her, this time he had the foresight to have his outcall specialist Taylor with one of her friends on standby. He'd ordered the most titanic redhead she could find.

Even with this insurance, he knew they could not replace Rebecca. His attraction to her transcended the physical. There was her extraordinary range of talent, her independence, and an indefinable, magical essence she alone possessed. Even though he was youthfully middle-aged—some thirty years older—he had discovered that Rebecca was his equal, and worthy of him. He had become a casualty of passion, taking himself prisoner. Rebecca had mutated into a mysterious infection, the metaphor for his condition.

"What was the collection bowl for?" he asked.

"My investigation."

3

After a long shower, and a soulful blessing of his native country's bathrooms and water pressure, Horne settled in the living room with the bottle of Patrón and a lime. Awaiting trial in Dar-es-Salaam, he had spent six months in solitary on a lice-infested mattress; water came once a day in a rusted can, accompanied by a tin mug of bug-filled gruel; afterwards he was granted fifteen minutes outside where he dumped his wooden shit-bucket in a sludge pit filled with rodents.

The only way to catch up on sleep would be to drink himself into another time zone. The familiar, but strange, surroundings unsettled him. Dead people, his family, inhabited the rooms. The dark wooden floors had been polished and revealed old reflections. He touched his aunt's treasures out of affection for a bygone time. Sitting in one of the Chinese red suede Dominique art deco chairs, he placed the bottle on the glass-topped Leleu table. He remembered Rose's exhilaration when she had brought the furniture back from a Paris trip. He gazed at the silver-framed photos of what once had been a family, his lost family, and found himself in the wasteland of depression.

As he squirted some lime into his mouth and banged back a triple shooter, he heard a vehement, eerie chanting coming from upstairs. After a few minutes of this wailing, he parted the curtains and observed Rebecca accompanying a group of people. The street light revealed bearded men in black slouch hats and long black suits tipping their hats to her. They climbed into a van on which a Star of David was painted, and he watched it pull away.

Horne took the bottle into the bedroom and sprawled out on the bed. The sheets were blue and crisp, scented with lavender.

Rose Fleming, his mother's sister, had been an astute business-woman and had bought this large duplex some time in the late seventies. After leaving her position at Bullocks, she had opened a high-fashion boutique in Beverly Hills. She'd snapped up many of her old customers, who demanded personal attention and rushed to see the new, designer clothes she would bring back from Paris and Milan.

His aunt had been a woman with a generous but whimsical disposition and a preternatural horror of marriage. Not exactly a feminist and not exactly *not* one was how she used to describe her position. She loved men, but wanted them at a distance and kept in their place.

No kids for her, nor picking up a guy's dirty underwear. She cooked for her lovers, took them to bed, then satisfied herself, and sent them on their way. She had never permitted a second toothbrush, a plaid sports coat, or a pair of trousers to take up residence in her closets. Rose Fleming was easy to be with so long as everyone knew she was the law.

This duplex had been Horne's home for the two years before he had come to Africa to search for his parents. It was a regular stop during his childhood when his parents had come south for vacations with some new half-baked business idea for his brilliant aunt to finance.

His parents, Bonnie (née Fleming) and Keith Horne, had been impenitent and casual borrowers. They had metabolized the sixties, smoking lots of dope while roving through America, landing in the Northwest, enlisting in cause after cause: his father, a coffee-house protest-poet and singer; his mother working short order or baking. The pair of them forever taking college courses of some kind, none of which ever led to financial stability. How he had loved these mad adventurers.

Ultimately they'd settled in Eugene, Oregon, with other kindred spirits. Anarchists, socialists, soapbox howlers scornful of big business, and anti-government mutineers. Every day, leaflets for some pet obsession would be distributed, announcing meetings and requests for anyone who didn't mind being chained to a tree or spending nights in sleeping bags to make sure that nobody agitated bird nests.

Horne had been born in 1969 at the hollow-eyed end of his folks's hippie period. Rose, Bonnie's older sister by twelve years, had given her and Keith the down payment for a small house in Eugene.

"You have a baby, you can't be screw-ups forever," Rose had told them. "Now get your lives together. I'm bailing you out for Douglas's sake. He must have a home! Don't you let *us* down."

The crazy-quilt educational courses Bonnie and Keith had been taking at community colleges wherever they roamed had finally paid off. They were masters of matriculation when it came to grafting transfer credits from obscure schools so that they counted toward a degree.

When Horne actually got to know his parents at about age eight, his father had become an eloquent, pony-tailed, high-school geography teacher—an Africa specialist, adept at Swahili, no less, defending "the cradle of man/womankind," and a connoisseur of the frequent name changes of its countries. Ask him about King Leopold and the Belgian Congo if you wanted a non-stop earful of the horrors of slavery.

Bonnie, less voluble but a wizard baker, had opened (thanks to Rose's largess and faith) a pre-Starbucks coffeehouse, which featured her pastries and breads, poetry readings, and music on the weekends led by Keith and his band, the Zanzibars.

Horne cherished the mysteries of his parents and their ministries of belief, the infinite capacity for kindness they displayed and unmasked in others. Even now, fifteen years later, he remained haunted by their disappearance.

As he dozed in Rose's lavender-scented bed, a flashing image of their sunny faces embraced him. But then bizarre sounds coming from upstairs intruded on his somnolent memories. Was someone crying, or was he imagining it? He reached over to the night table and found a pair of airline earplugs before drifting off.

Like a foul bora wind, the *visitations* had returned with Horne's arrival. Rebecca had no way of controlling these illuminations and inner flashes. The figures of Miriam and other dead women soared through her mind, suffocating her. In bed at last, she sobbed, smothered by these visions.

4

The smell of coffee woke Horne. He was disoriented. He seized his big Sako, which he'd loaded with 4.375 H&H cartridges when he'd awakened at four in the morning. The Lalique clock on the cane bedside table revealed it was now ten o'clock. He heard the kitchen door to the back garden close.

Stiff and stretching, he clambered over to the window, slid back the curtains, and watched the pianist from upstairs—Rebecca—folding clothes in the lighted washroom. Marauding under the sycamores in the alleyway, a high green truck thundered through the bleak ashen morning, fork-lifting garbage bins before slamming them against the wall like a backboard.

Rebecca carried a wicker clothes basket back to the kitchen. Horne quickly yanked on a terrycloth robe. The owner of Sycamore Place felt more like the rusty, bust-out ex-boyfriend of a successful woman who'd dumped him for greatness, and, out of pity, was giving him a squat. He put down the rifle. Tired as he still was, he had to cope with a rod of steel. God, he'd like to have Rebecca beside him.

She regarded the rifle without fear. "Good morning. I promise not to harm you."

"Force of habit." He crooked the Sako in a corner of the wall. "I've spent thousands of nights in the bush. Garbage truck surprised me. If it had been just you, believe me, you would've gotten a different reception."

She ignored the come-on. A year in L.A. had polished Rebecca's icy detachment to a flawless cut diamond. Shorn of tact, never her strongest asset, she had acquired a supercilious toughness in this environment. There was no one to do for her, no one to trust, and she refused to become enslaved by hypocrisy.

Only Rose Fleming had been a gem. Harry had become a magnanimous friend, but she was wise enough to understand that the interests of older men and younger women seldom coincided. She was not about to fuck for bucks. In fact, every elemental sexual impulse she might have had had dropped to thirty-two degrees.

Re-learning life at twenty-three had been a challenge. No longer the diva in demand, she filled in at concerts as a player; she scrounged, and valet parked at private parties and druggie clubs where her "*real* big tits" were her principal asset for *real* big tips.

"The central heating makes a racket when it starts up, so I didn't turn it on."

Taking charge, Rebecca had something of an autocratic disposition, but it wasn't displeasing to Horne. The age question arose: her smile creases meager; sun had not touched that freckled ivory skin. As for make-up, he was surprised by the lack of it.

He shuddered from the chill. "Jesus, you could hang meat in here."

Horne turned on the gas switch, flicked the firelighter, and the big fireplace barked into flames. He remembered the thermostat was in a corner of the dining room and slid it into the seventies to take the chill off. The bearish furnace growled. Rose's antique collection in the armoire jangled in alarm.

"Whoever buys this place can put in a new unit," he said, standing by the vent and relishing the warm air. "They'll probably gut it. Shove in more units, like the rest of the neighborhood. This was all one-family houses when I lived here."

"But Sycamore Place has been preserved. Rose and the neighbors battled with the city council when they were ready to approve condos."

She poured him coffee. "Just black, thanks,"

"*Eine Grosser Schwarzer.*"

"What?"

"A big black. I have a Viennese blend. My grandmother sends it to me."

"Rebecca, I'd drink anything after the mud in prison."

"I've got warm croissants and English rough-cut marmalade."

He felt encouraged by her readiness to please. "Great. I guess Rose told you what I like."

He'd been a reader all of his life and in prison books had been plentiful. He'd read a biography of Graham Greene who, when he had been interested in a woman, would simply say, "I'd really like to fuck you." This approach not only saved time, but also avoided pointless warm-up conversation. For the fortunate author it had supplied hundreds of volunteers. Horne, however, preferred a more courtly approach—as long as it was brief.

"Who needs the Beverly Hills Hotel with you here? My manners have deserted me. Good morning, Rebecca. For a while there, I actually didn't know where I was. I forgot to sleep with my compass."

She looked at his drawn, hollow-eyed face. The spark she had seen in Rose's photos had been extinguished. In its place, she sniffed mating banter and was disappointed.

"You'll adjust." She hesitated. "We all do...I had no idea you were planning to sell the house."

"I hated living in Beverly Hills." When Rebecca ignored this with busy work, he asked, "Is that a problem?"

Under the brackets of his aunt's copper pans, the perfect woman ignored his question and began folding his jeans and pairing his thick hiking socks on the large butcher block, the way station for the family barbecues in the old days. Every scratch and scrape on it represented some facsimile from his past, now the beyond. Fleeting memories churned through his mind: Keith making the martinis, Horne, a little stoned, drinking his beer allotment, Rose tossing salad, the shrimp boiling, Bonnie seasoning the prime rib, the kitchen filling with the aroma of rosemary garlic bread in the oven and Neil Young's "Crazy Horse" on the stereo with his father accompanying. The quartet's days of plenty were gone.

5

While he unpacked, his shabby clothes gave off the rancid odors of animals, DEET, oil, guns, and himself. Horne decided on his strategy: don't spook or crowd Rebecca. She'd be skittish. From time to time, he inadvertently looked up at her as though plotting a route map under a flashlight from his Land Cruiser.

Rebecca possessed abundant assets. Underneath the densely patterned big-bucks sweater, she filled out a black turtleneck tucked into baggy jeans, which made woeful work of the table of contents on display last night. This woman didn't need to advertise her assets on a billboard. He had been totally bummed out on arrival. He hadn't paid attention to her bosom. A blunder, which he blamed on jet lag.

At heart, he could not relinquish the juvenile aspect of wanting to touch what he saw. Issues of his dick had not been on his mind for some time. He'd been crammed in a cell, with infrequent court appearances, until the judge, diplomats, and witnesses had been rounded up. Horne's was not a DNA case. Until then he had considered himself *unrivaled* when it came to assessing people, judging character. A notable exception, of course, was the Dutchman he had shot after tracking down the rogue lion threatening the camp.

In the warm kitchen, he buttered up the croissants, lashed them with marmalade, and made a mess at the snug breakfast table overlooking the garden, brightened by his aunt's patches of sweet William, violets, pansies, poppies, ranunculus, tulips, snap dragon, and primrose that he had tended. He decided he ought to shave before asking her to fluff his pillows, spend the next ten days with him, build a treehouse, teach her how to nurse a lion cub, and make a documentary about it.

"Where exactly did you meet my aunt?"

"She ran an ad for a companion in the *Beverly Hills Courier.* I needed a place to live. We liked each other immediately." Her face clouded. "She told me she didn't have much time."

"You were living in L.A.?"

"Not exactly."

He was puzzled. "When was this?"

"March of last year. You'd been arrested and she was despondent."

"Calamities run in pairs."

"That's a little glib," Rebecca snapped. "For some people, just being in the wrong place is a death sentence."

He couldn't recall the last time a woman had put him down. "I know a lot about bad timing, madam, or would you prefer 'Fraulein?'"

She didn't respond to the taunt. "Let's move on, shall we?"

Once she lifted the clasp of a worn, but fine, black leather briefcase, his plan for a spontaneous seduction was gone; she removed a long, striped, gray account book and a file of envelopes containing receipts. Without looking in his direction, she tossed the car keys and garage opener on the table. And along came the DMV pink slip.

"I was using Rose's car and had it serviced."

"How'll you get around?"

"I have a bike."

In spite of her commanding manner, he saw that her determination was built on a thin foundation of bluster. As a big game hunter, he had a wide range of experience with people who wanted to test themselves. A wave of unexpected tenderness swept over him. "Why don't you use the car when I'm not? Take the spare key."

"No, thanks, I can manage."

"What was she driving?"

"A Lexus 400. It's ten years old but in excellent condition."

Desire again furtively intruded. It was as if an assassin with a garrote were strangling him. He was the captive of her sensuality and had the hard-on from hell.

Oh, to be in Arusha now at Madam Begawan's brothel. He heard her sweet trill, "Would your friends like to open some of my new purses?" she'd ask Horne when he'd brought in some of his horny, married safari nuts who'd had a week of martyrdom in tents with their old ladies and were dying for a whack at black satin. The guys had stuffed their wives with plenty of cash and plastic and dropped them at the local markets to unearth native artifacts with his guides.

"I heard some odd sounds last night. Reminded me of the way the Masai hum or chant before a burn. Exactly what was all that about?"

Driven by a monsoon of desire, Horne had blundered. He had committed mistake number one. Hold a pat hand and don't ask anything; asking a question is a sign of male insolvency.

"How do you mean?"

He bungled on. "I don't know...it could have been a dream."

Rebecca's demeanor advanced from aloofness to vigilance. Her expression became a bay of somberness, altering the symmetry of her features into something jagged.

"People were crying. We came to the end of the *Shivah*. That's your version of a wake. But you wouldn't know that," she informed him in such a patrician manner that he took umbrage.

No gym bullies with pumped-up bodies ever scared Horne, and now she was behaving like one of them. They always failed, because fear was stillborn in his nature. He had seen too much of death to be intimidated.

"Why should I care? I'm not prejudiced. It doesn't matter to me."

Still distrustful, she nodded. "Well, knowing Rose, I hoped you weren't. But you can never tell. What you heard was the Mourner's Kaddish. The Jewish prayer for a dead parent, a dead child, a dead family member—even a dead friend. The rabbi was *davening*. That's Hebrew for praying." She covered her face with her hands. "We were all...wailing."

Horne didn't know what to make of this disclosure. Displays of emotion compromised people and often repelled him. He stuck the other croissants in the toaster oven to crisp them up. He loved being back in America with small conveniences that everyone took for granted.

His bones ached and his right shoulder was sore. Horne imagined he could see the pin that held the joints together after he'd been gored by a Cape buffalo while learning his trade. An alcoholic English surgeon had repaired it. It was nothing short of a miracle that his gun bearer and trackers had stopped the bleeding and carted him miles back to Arusha when the Land Rover had run out of gas.

Notwithstanding the housewife act Rebecca assumed for his benefit—croissants, washing, and clothes-folding—Horne knew he was out of luck. This would be a consolation breakfast without a follow-up at this stage. No spontaneous roughhouse with the supple pianist. Well, he'd patiently spoor for her. When she was exhausted by pursuit and realized the way nature worked—primitive and enduring—she'd relent to the male, lie down in the bush, reconciled to the inevitable.

With his best "Welcome, safari travelers," Horne trotted out his sympathy sonata, the way he would have for lost luggage. "I'm sorry I intruded on you and your friends."

"You didn't intrude. You had to get into your apartment."

189

She was industrious again: tidying, nervous, touchy.

"You don't have to do that. It's been a long time since I had a crease in my pants. I'll hang up my clothes. It could develop into a gym exercise for me."

"I like things tidy. First the *Hausfrau*, then the artist. It was bashed into me by our housekeeper. 'Let Herta do it.' My grandmother Lilli and she used to quarrel about it. But I'm not exactly fragile. Herta wanted to train my sister and me so we'd know how things should be done. Survive. We even learned to cook against my grandmother's wishes. God forbid the pianist or the cellist should break a nail or get our hands burned."

"This is wonderful. You can cook and clean." He laughed, trying to disarm her. "Suppose I do the hunting and bring the meat home." His clumsy attempt to brighten her mood failed. She was disheartened and he decided that any move on her might definitely be premature. "Oh, by the way, my guns don't need dusting."

"I won't touch them!"

"That's good—don't," he said, without being rude.

She was chastened, nonetheless, disagreeably staring through him.

"I didn't expect to arrive and have someone actually playing the piano. Hearing you was spectacular. I don't know a lot about classical music. But I like some of it."

"Good for you. I'm very relieved."

Indifferent to the care of her hands, she rinsed the dishes under scalding water before putting them in the dishwasher. "I apologize, Horne. My nerves are shot."

"Mine, too."

"Thank you for your compliment. But this wasn't a celebration. And a recital isn't the proper form for mourning." Now she sounded foreign to him. Like a German. He couldn't quite get the hang of her yet. "It was for my sister, Miriam, to honor her life, rather than mourn her loss. Some people I've met came by. I wanted to commemorate this disastrous occasion and the end of the mourning period."

He listened intently, ostracizing thoughts of a screw. Her grief embraced him.

"It was also to show my Miriam that we would never forget her. I promised her."

He nodded. "I see," but the situation was still unclear to him. "What actually happened?"

"You don't really want to hear about this."

He played along, but she was unconvinced. "I do. Come on, let's be friends."

"Horne, let's just get through this. I've kept your aunt's records and I'll show you precisely what I had to spend. I have all the cancelled checks. Here are the IRS and the State FTB payments. The grocery bills from Gelson's market. Medicare and AARP statements."

He pushed away the ledger, the papers burrowed in envelopes, dated and coded. Rebecca was definitely a German who'd lived here for a long time.

"Rebecca, tell me what's going on?"

He'd allowed her to reverse roles. Let her think she was driving.

"My sister was murdered!"

In his eyes, she, the prey, detected surprise. For a moment he was speechless, disabled by the declaration. "Oh, sweet Jesus."

"I came over here for her wedding and ended up identifying her body. You see, I was about to have my debut with the Vienna Philharmoniker, then go on a concert tour." Rebecca's teeth gouged her lips. "There will never be a tour or music without Miriam."

Subdued by this revelation, Horne hardly knew how to continue this startling conversation.

"What happened to him—the fiancé?"

"Scott Leopold had a nervous breakdown. He was a musician, a cellist like my sister. The truth is he ran away like a skunk, and his parents decided I was toxic." Rebecca shook her head and her hair flew in every direction; she whacked it back.

Trying to visualize the situation, Horne foraged through his own bitter memories. "Yes, yes, I understand—a little."

"I decided to stay on in case the police found the killer. I thought it would take a few weeks...oh, I can't explain. You've got your own problems. I'm involved with the Center."

He was baffled. "Center of what?"

"The Museum of Tolerance. I'm a volunteer docent there. It's dedicated to the Holocaust victims of the Second World War. There are exhibits of the Warsaw Ghetto and footage the Nazis took that show what the concentration camps and the death camps were like. It's connected to the Documentation Center in Vienna started by Simon Wiesenthal."

He couldn't find a thread. "Nazis? I don't quite follow the connection between the Holocaust and your sister."

"Miriam was found outside a synagogue in the Valley." She stared fiercely into space, then turned away. "Neo-Nazis murdered her. I'm not afraid of them. Maybe if *two* sisters from the same family are murdered, the FBI might get off their asses."

During his years in Africa, Horne had seen all manner of grotesque slaughters among the tribes, but he was nevertheless appalled. Searching for his parents, he had come across missionary nuns, dismembered. Hutus and Tutsis in their continuous civil war in Rwanda were notorious for their brutality. But he was in Beverly Hills, and this kind of savagery struck him as fantastic. Nothing made sense when confronted by the enigma of murder.

"There's another aspect to her murder that the police haven't disclosed. I can't either. But I'm convinced there's a link to other cases."

"There are other cases like this?"

"Yes, absolutely."

"I'm really sorry, Rebecca. You've been through hell."

"Damn right I have."

"How're your parents coping?"

"They died years ago. My maternal grandmother, Lilli, raised Miriam and me. And Herta, who's like our aunt." Horne dashed to the toaster oven to rescue the croissants before they seared. "I shouldn't be discussing any of this with a stranger. Let's get this accounting over with."

His attraction to her gave way to sympathy. "I understand you being upset, but don't get pissed at me."

"I'm pissed at everyone. I shouldn't be here, doing this." Her eyes became glacial. "I'm trying to control my fury at everything—the whole universe."

"Don't include me. I can't do anything about catastrophes and misfortune." He too had become short-tempered. "I've had my own. Leave Rose's stuff. I'm sure you haven't beat her out of a dime." The hunter in pursuit had found a trail to her. "Come on, talk to me, Rebecca. I'm on your side."

She was disarmed by his sincerity. "Are you, really?"

"Completely."

Finally a luminescent smile appeared that made her infernal quibbling endurable. Of course, she was an artist, and temperamental. She shoved the accounts book away. Horne, the expert, had succeeded in getting her to open her basket of snakes.

"The killer hasn't been caught! And these murders have been going on for years."

"Where're the cops been in all this?"

"They're busy with their pet gang trials, drive-by shootings, drug dealers, police corruption. You name it. Los Angeles is a hellhole. If my sister wasn't a *foreigner*, like some illegal alien, they would have had a task force combing every inch of the country."

"Isn't this all supposed to be some kind of federal hate crime?"

"Ah, you try talking to the FBI, Horne. Maybe you'll have more luck that me." Her beautiful, commanding hands were raised in anguish. "There's been a worldwide rebirth by neo-Nazis everywhere. There are over two thousand hate sites on the Internet—and the trend is growing."

He leaned closer, enveloping himself in her scent. "Were all the women Jewish?"

"Yes, and from different states. I have the files, but the police aren't interested. They've written me off as a crackpot."

"Cops for you. Show them your evidence."

She shook her head. "It's not possible."

"Why?"

Her expression assumed a sad, transcendent dreaminess, which made her even more ravishing. His initial lust yielded to his sensitive side and he was moved by her tragedy.

"I've been in contact with the girls during their journey. Their souls are in the process of a transmigration. But sometimes they communicate with me."

He had witnessed her artistry, been charmed by her competence, amazed by the meticulous bookkeeping, knew of the care-giving to his aunt, but now he was stunned.

"How's that possible?"

"I can't enlighten you about that...because I don't know myself how it happens." She closed her eyes. "These murders are all the work of a *dybbuk*."

He couldn't keep up with her. "A *what*?"

"Satan sends the souls of evil dead people—demons—and they take over living persons. They're responsible for these murders. There is a man by the name of Magnus Von Winter. He was Hitler's protégé and his closest friend. Magnus has a son who I believe is also involved. His name is Bruno."

"This Magnus—he's alive?"

Her face became pinched with grief. "Yes. He's in his eighties. But I'm sure he changed his name years ago."

"Why would he want to kill your sister?" Horne threw up his hands "...and these other women?"

Rebecca retreated, reluctant to disclose the truth. "My family had a connection with him."

"I see," said Horne, but he didn't see. In fact, he felt like a blind man in an unfamiliar room—totally at sea. He was lost in the tangle of her conspiracies.

Horne damned his luck. His last poker game—before taking out the Dutchman and his party on safari, pre-murder trial—when he'd been holding a full house—aces and queens—he'd lost to four kings in a Texas Hold-'em game at the Planters Club. An entire season of savings had gone down the drain. Though not prone to superstition, he was beginning to wonder if the planets were somehow aligned against him.

"In Africa, you'd have people believing that you can contact spirits." Horne's deep, resonant voice had calmed safari camps when lions rushed through the site. This morale booster, he hoped, would work like shock treatment for the woman, or at least establish a sympathetic alliance. "Here, in the West, I imagine it's difficult."

"Not for me," she stated.

Nobody could cope with this level of folly, irrationality. But he owed her a debt on Rose's behalf, and he gave it a shot: Bloody Marys and a steak at the Palm might enable him to glue her tiles back. Better yet, Trader Vic's for lunch, where he'd feed her a few Zombies. Hunting, he had always been sure of himself. His courageous optimism triumphed over negative experience. He laced her up in his all-knowing hunter's smile, prepared to listen to tall stories from prospective clients.

"Let me get cleaned up, Rebecca. We'll whip through my aunt Rose's stuff whenever. I'll take you to lunch."

Flicking him off like a big green horsefly, "Thank you, Horne. Maybe another time. I have appointments and meetings," she said briskly, making it clear that she wasn't some maid to bang when the dryer went down and overtime kicked in.

She smiled at him finally with warmth and took his hands in hers. His hopes for a resolution were high even though his mind was cluttered with desire. To prolong her departure, compliments always worked.

"Your English is perfect—no accent."

"I spent time at Oberlin with Miriam, then we studied at Juilliard. I'm sorry to have imposed...please don't be angry with me for laying all my troubles on you."

He couldn't chart the R.P.M. of her mind. "Of course not." He always concluded an unsatisfied hard-on courteously, implying that a middle-of-the-night call would be promptly answered. "Look, I'll be here for you."

Having whetted his appetite, she strutted and stretched. "We'll see."

They shook hands. He walked her out to the alley garage. Thoughts of romance gave way to solace, an unholy combination for a male in heat. Bike? He'd imagined her pedaling a Schwinn, unconcerned with traffic or direction. Instead, she saddled a big Harley, nimbly revved the engine to a fine hum, and blew smoke in his face.

Americans never appreciated the conveniences of their homeland until they returned. But he was starting to luxuriate in them. While shaving, trimming his beard and moustache close, he realized that he had not walked into a concert last night, but a séance.

No, out of the question, he couldn't hit on a wacko. It would be despicable...or maybe not...? His concept of honor, and acting on its code, was sometimes inconvenient, yet inescapable for him. He had lost too much to reverse direction at this point. Still, the second-best poker of his life was like Rebecca's demon.

"Oh, Lord! Losing with a full house, give me a break, deal me a winning hand."

Thirty minutes later, the bike was back, roaring outside his window. Clean and trim, he maneuvered all six feet, five inches of the renewed Horne into trousers and a denim shirt. He opened the door, his arms ready to receive her. They all liked to be coaxed into a change of heart.

She shouted, "I forgot: I'll be back late. Please feed my cat. You have *our* key. And don't shoot *him*. I've changed his name from Lucky to Glück. He was your aunt's and I adopted him."

"That's terrific, so he's bi-lingual," Horne said. "I'll teach him a little Kiswahili so he can work safari tours. We'll sign him up with Disney. He'll be a big hit in Arusha."

Finally she laughed. Like some vision from space, red scarf flying in the wind, helmet visor down, she might have been taking off for a black hole to save Earth. Still, he felt better about his prospects—the possibilities—for trusting a strange man with a beloved cat was as precious as a wild joker in poker.

6

At one, wearing his frayed safari jacket and boots, Horne strolled past Sycamore Place's fashionable houses. The trees were healthy, ivy on the Georgians groomed to a fare-thee-well. It was still nippy but power walkers brushed past him. The Friars Club was still in place—gin rummy and comedians. Walking to Century City, Horne encountered huge derricks, the size of container steeves at African wharves, dominating Santa Monica Boulevard. He squinted at the Peninsula, a toy-sized hotel, new since he'd last been in Beverly Hills. Stretch limos and Rollses were thick as mosquitoes during the migration. He strode through a detachment of bellhops and parking valets nursing Euro-trash cell-phoners into their Jags and Mercedeses. Almost every man he passed had spiky hair slicked with pomade and wore crocodile loafers.

Yards of sleek marble delivered him to the dark mahogany bar. He felt at home in such places, until he saw the bartender ring up ten bucks and change for a fucking Bloody Mary. He decided he better get the new lay of the land and avoid tourist ambushes or he'd be broke before nightfall.

His appointment with his lawyer was for two-thirty and he headed for the Hamburger Hamlet on Century Park East, only to find that it no longer existed. He wound up at the Century City food court, now renamed Westfield Shoppingtown. Bullocks was now Macy's and he didn't recognize most of the stores in the open-air mall. Inside at a food counter, his turkey was actually weighed on a scale before the counterman made a sandwich. It had the flavor of wood shavings.

Amid tribes of clerical workers and retail drones wearing nametags, he read the *L.A. Times*, studied the sports section, especially news of the Lakers, only to discover they were not playing at the Forum anymore, but at a place called Staples Center. Magic and Kareem were no longer on the team. Talk about being out of touch. There was no might-have-been about it; Horne was a lost tourist who had arrived in a foreign country.

Thomas Haggerty, the Irish ferret and senior partner, welcomed Horne into a majestic office awash in emerald-green in a tower overlooking the Los Angeles Country Club. He had been Rose's lawyer, sometime lover, and finally, cruise mate.

"Never fuck your tenant, then they live rent-free. Lawsuit if you try to evict them. Political incorrectness these days can cost a guy millions. Homeowners' policy doesn't cover landlords for fornication, fellatio, or sodomy with the female. Gays, I'm not sure about. In your case, Dougie, it's immaterial. Lady Rebecca beat you to it. That's five hundred dollars' worth of advice in under a minute. I charge that for an hour now, without having to hike to court Downtown."

A handshake and embrace accompanied this reunion.

"What's this all about?" Horne was eased into the favored client's green leather wingchair just below the wall of photos of Haggerty in foursomes with Palmer, Nicklaus, and Trevino.

"Rose's will, which I drew up with Bob Mayer. He's our new managing partner, and I figured that when a Fleming wouldn't listen to an Irishman, I'd send in the scholar-rabbi. Bob's celebrated persuasiveness was to no avail. Rose wouldn't budge."

Horne's head was reeling. "Look, Tommy, I was rousted by the fucking ATF at the airport after forty-eight hours of roaming bars and hassles to get back to my *own* country."

"Big guns give them the shakes."

"I'm a hunter, or used to be. I arrive at the house, and a concert is in progress. Huh? This morning, I hear from Rose's tenant—now mine—there's some annual wake."

Tommy Haggerty picked up his glass bowl of signed golf balls and jiggled them. He'd had wonderful days playing Links courses in Scotland and wished he were in a pot bunker at St. Andrew's.

"Rebecca, she bewitched your aunt."

"She's done a pretty good job on me, too. Viennese coffee and croissants from the finest piece of ass I've seen in years. I can't wait..."

"—Keep it zipped, in the stirrups—put a saddle on it. I just told you, she's *an untouchable.*"

Horne reluctantly agreed that Rebecca would require the patience of trackers.

"Sifting through her bullshit, she nursed Rose and hung in with her until the end."

"All true...but...now, oh, wait, maybe you'll need a Talisker single malt or any alcoholic beverage of your choice."

Tommy got up and selected one of the old harlots from his selection of putters, an ancient wooden gooseneck that had kept the yips away.

"Simply glorious having you back, Dougie. I knew you'd be able to prove self-defense against that bloodthirsty Dutch beast. That boy I hired for you took Triple First honors at Cambridge. And I made sure he could do the tribal juju stuff for juries, just like our Master Cochran. University of witch doctoring."

Tommy hit his intercom. "Adele, hold my calls, and please be a darling and bring in the real stuff and two glasses. Yes, my client and I are indeed starting early." The tray appeared shortly after, while Tommy pored through files. "Thank you, dear." Haggerty poured immense shots.

"Well, 99 Sycamore Place is legally yours. In the current market, it's worth about two million—possibly a bit more: location, double lot. Someone can tear it down, build it out, and have himself a ten- or twelve-thousand-square-foot aberration. Bowling alley in the basement, whorehouse within reach, pool on the roof. Never mind."

Horne sipped his drink, reassured. "That's a mood elevator. I aim to head up to Oregon, check in with some friends. Maybe buy a decent boat. Do some charter fishing. I don't know. I'm not sure." Horne's yearning for the sea was part of his youth. "I love that whole coast. I just want to get the hell out of Beverly Hills."

"Sounds like a plan, and would be if the circumstances weren't—dare I say—perverse and intractable."

"I've got fifteen, come on, hit me with a six."

"You're sure you want this card...? Let me hand you the bottle and pour your own."

"Tommy, stop—enough!"

Haggerty, counsel to the great and famous, put down the putter. His hands were shaking badly.

"Too many three-footers, Doug. You have what is known as a *sitting-owner-tenant*. Rose left the upper part of the duplex to Rebecca. She can't sublet, assign, or have a stay-over, husband/lover, either sex, whatever her inclination, or have children reside with her. The Viennese cat, Cluck, whatever, is included in this eccentric Faustian Pact."

Horne shouted and the lawyer backed up.

"Whaaat....?

"Please....In short, laddie, the upper portion of the house is legally Rebecca's, until she decides to leave or die. My best-case scenario is that she quitclaims it to you. Perhaps you could fuck her to death, provided you've got a notarized document granting you carnal rights of passage. Mike Tyson for a witness won't do. Actually, heed my advice, and don't, *don't*, don't abuse the cat."

Thunderstruck, Horne flooded his glass with more whisky. "Why, why the hell—if Rose was of sound mind—would she do something so crazy?"

"She was of sound mind, I can assure you. That's another reason I had Bob Mayer with me. He's dealt with any number of our collection of deranged clients."

"Tommy, this is *me*! My future and my life, the Dougie who went to Dodger and Laker games with you and my dad."

"Rose was closed-mouthed about her bequest. All she would divulge to us was that Rebecca had a mission. When I pressed her, Rose said, and I took this down, 'When you get to know my angel, Rebecca, you'll understand why I made this decision.'"

"That's bullshit! A wacky classical pianist sandbagged her! Rebecca was on deathwatch with a woman suffering from leukemia. I know this kind of Euro-trash."

"You're wrong, Douglas. Rebecca's not trash."

The veins in Horne's thick neck pulsated with blood-rage. Haggerty had known him for a long time, but now came to realize that this once-quiet, imposing loner boy was capable of deadly violence. Even murder.

"Oh, you're defending her now! I've known hospice workers in Africa who gave up their lives nursing everything from sleeping sickness to AIDS. They're saintly people. This is fraud. Rebecca's a con woman."

"A very beautiful one, Dougie."

Horne was in grief. "I lost my hard-on."

"Kill her with kindness. If you put her in an adversarial position, it'll just be legal fees for you. Teams of feminists and their tribe of lawyers working you over. L.A. is a *corrida* and I've kissed litigation goodbye."

"Shit! What the fuck am I going to do?" Horne waited.

"Sometimes silence is a lawyer's best defense."

THE WINTERHAVEN SOLUTION

An unexpected financial solution—sent by God—brightened Horne's horizon. "Tommy, if it's worth two million plus, and has no mortgage, can't I borrow against it?"

Haggerty's fretful sigh was not encouraging. "You could if you had a job and some hope of handling the debt service, say on half a million, which, plus taxes and low interest, might run about six thousand a month."

"*Six thousand?*"

"I'm afraid lenders aren't sympathetic to the unemployed indigent. They don't accept lion heads for seconds."

Frustration blended with fury, and a choking sensation subdued Horne. "Tommy, did you investigate Rebecca? Say, she's a felon, or wanted, escaped from prison." He pounced on an idea: "A bughouse."

"It would complicate things. But in the end, you'd be bald like me. Felons and crackpots may inherit property."

"But surely Rose could be protected from a swindle."

"No evidence to suggest this. Rebecca knew nothing of this until I informed her."

"What was her reaction?"

"She cried bitterly, blessed Rose, and told me she'd light special Jewish candles for Rose.

Horne's eyes had murderous intent. "She's a specialist in prayers for the dead."

Haggerty clucked in agreement. "Her sister was murdered."

"That came out with the buttered croissants she so thoughtfully fed me. I've lost more than a step. I'm ogling her tits while she's laying out Rose's medical receipts."

"It happens—even to old lawyers. In any case, you were in the toughest prison in Africa and there was nothing you could do about Rose's decision."

Just this side of full-throttle hyperventilation, Horne strode back and forth before the vast window framing the golf course below. Hackers were hitting mulligans by the pound.

"What do we know about this woman?"

"Not much. But...I must admit when she had me to the apartment, I had tears in my eyes when she played Schubert's 'B-Flat-Major Sonata.'"

201

Horne was outraged. "That's her gimmick! She plays the piano, shoves her tits in your face, and fans the air with her hair. She seduces every guy with a dick."

Haggerty was not tempted to disagree, but he was an expert handler of bereaved clients.

"Try talking her into vacating. Maybe pay her a percentage of the sale money."

"Tommy, I am dead broke. I'm on the fucking balls of my ass."

"Come clean with her. Negotiate. Maybe she'll bite. I know she hasn't got a quarter for a parking meter." He pulled out a sheaf of papers from a file. "Here, Rose paid for her furniture to be shipped from Vienna...24,700 dollars and change—and another 2,000 dollars for special handling for her piano. Oops, let's not forget the insurance premiums with Lloyd's for her hands."

"What! Are you serious...?" Horne bellowed. "I've never heard such bullshit!"

"She's a *concert* pianist," the lawyer explained. "It's not a frivolous safeguard."

"Is there a deductible for a fucking hangnail?"

Haggerty believed in breaking bad news all at once and not saving the worst element just as the client was leaving. This was a method of merely deferring malpractice suits from clients who whined, "You never told me...."

"Let me complete the last leg of Rose's voyage to insolvency: She was also sending by wire transfer—two thousand a month—to Lilli Benjamin, Rebecca's grandmother, who lives in Vienna. This is helping the woman survive, or she'd be on the street."

"You forget anything, Tommy?"

"No, that's how Rose busted out."

Looking down from the office to the street, Horne experienced vertigo, the first time this had happened to him. He had faced enraged bull elephants carrying two hundred pounds of ivory, wounded lions, leopards that had sprung at him from trees, never flinching or taking a step back. But now a sense of dread enveloped him. He had been away from the wiles of civilization; Los Angeles was the actual jungle—not Africa—and he felt lost.

"I don't know what to do."

"Doug. Cheer up. A lawyer, who lends a client money or, for that matter, carries him, should be disbarred for stupidity and incompetence. But as my godson, Dougie, you have a rich godfather. Go down to City National on the corner. I'll have Adele call first thing in the morning. She'll explain that you're my client, and money will appear. Will ten thousand see you through the month? And a VISA with ten thousand."

"With Bloody Marys ten bucks at a bar, I'll have to drink at home. Sorry, Tommy. Yes, of course. And thanks." Horne's thought process was suffering from weather fronts, episodes the Weather Channel referred to as "inversions." Horne pressed on with the monomania of a prospector panning for gold. "What about Rose's money from investments and the sale of her boutique?"

"Gone. It was spent on the noble purpose of searching for your parents when you were at Beverly Hills High. Last, but hardly least, our saintly Rose paid your legal fees in Africa. Bribes were part of it."

"What for?"

"So that your jailers didn't make an Irish stew or have you tartare. They haven't heard about Mad Cow disease or that toast points are necessary."

Homicidal thoughts sprinted ahead of Horne. He might have been tracking a lion that had killed someone in a village, a maddened beast.

"I'm lost, Tommy."

"But not disfigured." He handed Horne a bulky envelope. "Rose's papers, insurance policy, copy of the will and some personal stuff Rebecca got out of the safety deposit box."

Horne was inconsolable. "She had the key to Rose's safety deposit box?"

"Keys to the kingdom."

"I'm in shock.... Tommy, will you at least have dinner with me?"

He unpeeled a roll of hundreds and handed Horne a thousand in cash.

"Wish I could. I'm heading to the gym."

Bereft, Douglas Horne, gored on the Serengeti by a Cape buffalo, a man who had nursed a pride lion, wanted to weep. "I've been royally screwed."

"Not necessarily. You could easily rent or lease Rose's apartment for five or six thousand a month furnished, short-term—forty-five hundred long-term, unfurnished. Go, move up to the Northwest and live like a squire on that. It'd bring in fifty-sixty big ones p.a."

"Hardly enough to start a fishing business. Six months in prison in Dar, and now this."

"By the way, you'll be happy to hear that I did travel to Arusha on my own dime after I saw you. Your case was moved from Arusha to Dar because the Tanzanian government is so broke it doesn't have enough money to hold court there. The judges and 'prosecutors' haven't been paid for years."

With a contented smile, the elfish lawyer recounted the legal hurdles over which he had galloped for his client's freedom.

"I visited The Begawan establishment—your friend, the madam—for assistance. She was very concerned about you, but more importantly, she helped to put me in touch with her *colleagues* in Dar-es-Salaam." Thomas Haggerty struggled to console his client, a young man he loved, and whose quest for his parents he had supported. "I brought Rose's last bucks for bribes—just in case our Cambridge barrister fell short. You play poker. Rose was down to the green after that, and she was dying."

"It was a clear case of self-defense with that degenerate Dutch-man—"

"Let me interrupt you: There are no virtuous causes in a murder trial, especially in a foreign country." Haggerty paused, licking his lips. "I had to *get to* people and visit a whorehouse in Dar to get the job done." Haggerty snickered. "After suborning and bribing people, it's not my fault that I had a wonderful time with the satin purses. Justice isn't an issue anywhere. Deep pockets are all that count."

Horne, embittered by blighted hopes, dragged the lawyer up to the roof garden and sat with him. "If Rebecca should die, what happens then, Tommy?"

Haggerty had heard this suggestion before, from legions of piqued clients.

"Ah, you're thinking *mysterious* disappearance. It won't work. I know you're serious. But don't act rashly. Sooner or later cops'll find a body part somewhere...Malibu, her teeth in Death Valley, the head on the beach of the Kahala Hilton...wherever. And while you're settled up in Portland, or an island, some guy with a pounded beefsteak face will knock on your door." Describing the tenacity of detectives' ingenuity was a useful tactic for a client on the verge of violence. "Laddie, the cable channels cover that every night. Hours of detectives and forensic experts. Your face will be unforgettable. Not easy to get away with murder these days."

Horne opened his arms, beseeching tribal gods. "Tommy! What do I do with this bitch?"

"Settle. Confer. I'll do the haggling." He smiled. "My nickname is the Hag."

They walked toward the roof door. Two security men waited for them with their guns drawn.

"You okay, Mr. Haggerty?"

"Fine. I was just having a legal conference. Trying to persuade my client that suicide is not the answer to his problems."

7

On Santa Monica Boulevard, as demonic drivers honked through the foggy dusk, Horne stopped to watch two women screaming out of their windows and threatening each other with road death. What was going on with his life: some karmic calamity, an El Niño of the spirit, an unspecified, obscure feng shui edict he had ignored? The Serengeti and its wildlife, the jungle itself, were known elements to him. He could survive, flourish there. The treachery in Beverly Hills presented greater dangers than Africa.

At home, impervious to the rain slanting in, Rebecca's plump cat was at the window on the floor above him, meowing and scratching the screen.

"Hey, Suck, there's a clause that says you can't use window screens for a manicure. Eviction. No notice. Read the small print."

He climbed the stairs, unlocked the door, and was confronted by the outraged ball of hair that won the stare-down. Swiveling his head, he directed Horne to the kitchen. On the counter was an unmarked jar, which Horne determined was fresh chopped liver. A note from madam provided instructions.

PLEASE GIVE GLÜCK WATER FROM THE ARROWHEAD COOLER. THE TAP WATER CONTAINS ARSENIC. THANKS,

R

Horne fed the cat, put water in the china bowl from the cooler, and roved around the apartment, unable to unleash his fury. He lifted the lip of the piano and considered smashing the keys with his fist. There he collected another memo from the mistress of the castle.

DON'T EVEN THINK OF TOUCHING THE KEYBOARD!

Horne's bellow shook the room before lapsing into a dismal sound of futility. Like a dying animal, its feeble, terminal howl completed his humiliation.

"I need a fucking witchdoctor."

Horne had an aversion to spying and had no intention of rifling through Rebecca's personal effects and papers, or examining her lingerie, but he found himself drifting through the apartment, resentfully casting hostile glances at the abundance of possessions.

He had no notion of what these furnishings and paintings were worth. He wouldn't recognize a Beidermeir clubfoot if he tripped over one. Her bedroom held no fascination for him. If she arrived this minute and crooked her finger at him, he'd tell her to start packing.

What had begun as flirtation and instant attraction had disintegrated into repulsion. After six months in prison in Dar, he'd been ready to poke anything female that morning. A warm body attached to a sumptuous redhead would have done him just fine. But she was a cheat, a grifter, and he despised her deceit. Africa was full of lowlifes like her: German hookers fresh from the Frankfurt meat market scrounging for dope; English remittance men who screwed the native girls and kited checks. The mere thought of this cagey swindler's flesh repelled Horne. He regarded Rebecca as a squatter. The Masai would already be saying prayers over her body if she pulled a stunt like that in Africa, he thought. He'd read Ardrey's *The Territorial Imperative*. Animals and their habitation grounds were sacred. He *owned* 99 Sycamore Place and he wasn't about to cede his claim.

He sat down on the piano bench, lifted the gleaming keyboard cover again. It then occurred to him that he hadn't yet asked her to leave, nicely or otherwise. He'd start with an appeal—explain his circumstances with eloquence. But if she refused, he needed a game plan. He was not frightened or disgusted by vermin or rodents after living with them for a dozen years. He'd bring in some big rats. Snakes were a possibility. A lion out of the question, unfortunately; they were, after all, in Beverly Hills.

Oh, and there was her waltz from the Vienna Woods. Nazis on dress parade in BH 90212, chanting Heil Hitler. Crooked, lazy cops, an axiom of life, here and everywhere. But nothing else about her made sense to him. Why had she nested with his aunt? She could undoubtedly afford to rent a place. No, this lady wasn't broke. Bad credit? Deadbeat? Landlord's hit list? What was the angle? There definitely had to be one.

The cat snuggled against his ankle. *"Sprechen zie Deutsche?"* Horne closed the piano cover and found the cat clinging to him like a sloth.

"More pickled herring with our fine Moselle, Herr Glück?"

The cat released his hold on Horne's thigh, sprang on the antique writing table littered with folders, arched his back, and meowed like a castrato. Glück stomped his paw, and Horne bent over to investigate the complaint. Unexpectedly, he felt his pulse spurting. His temples pounded.

Set out were a group of glossy photos of a naked woman with a shaved head, hideously branded with a swastika.

"Oh, shit. Rebecca has a righteous cause. Feed the cat, right? What a move on me. I never could go to my left, and she drove right past me for a slam dunk."

In Africa decisions were simple: people killed or were victims, they starved or survived. Horne had re-entered a complex world of decisions and choices. The first principle of the hunt was to select the quarry and not to break cover. He was becoming involved in something beyond a pretty woman mooching for rent. What exactly did she want from him?

Rebecca had laid out bait, but she didn't know him: He was too sharp to go for it.

8

Rebecca was concluding her afternoon tour of the Holocaust at the Museum of Tolerance. She had joined the docent program shortly after being hired by Rose and worked there several afternoons a week as a volunteer. It was a small, rainy-day adult group, mostly tourists from abroad, who had felt it their duty to visit or were bored in their hotel rooms.

She preferred the mass of teenage androids who knew nothing about World War II. Their principal connection with Jews were TV images of bloody suicide attacks on Israelis, followed by their tanks retaliating and flattening Palestinian buildings in Gaza. The world at large cloaked their anti-Semitism behind the aggression of Israel's troops. The designer abhorrence of Jews had become desirable, not just among their Middle-East antagonists. The Jewish Flu had infected everyone—even in America.

She waited for stragglers and waved them to the final artifacts collection, captured from the Nazis. She nodded to the attentive, bald, gray-bearded, shuffling old Protestant minister who had taken the tour with her. His presence inspired her on this desolate afternoon, with rain pelting the windows and roof. Whenever leaders of other faiths came to visit, she felt it helped strengthen the ties between the Jews and other religions.

"The canisters you see in the display case contain a gas called Zyklon-B. The SS death squads used it in Auschwitz. These monsters had no conscience. They would use knouts to flog Jewish infants, children, pregnant women, crippled old people, and then jam them into concrete chambers. The original manufacturer was I.G. Farben. You might like to know that Farben's shares are still traded on the German stock exchange, and they still haven't paid any reparations to the slave laborers who worked in their factories."

She moved to the last showcase where a faded American flag was on view, its number of states unfilled. "This flag was sewn by the inmates of the Mauthausen camp in Austria as a tribute to their G.I. liberators." She paused. "Ladies and gentlemen, we, at the Wiesenthal Center, would be grateful for any contribution you can make."

The group thanked Rebecca and dispersed, but the minister lingered. He smiled, slouching up to her. She shook hands with him. "I'm

Rebecca Benjamin. I really appreciate clergy from other faiths coming here."

He laughed pleasantly. "I'm just an old dragon with a flock up on the Central Coast," he said in a shrill, unsettling voice.

"It's so important for us to have a man like you spreading the word."

"Yes," Magnus said. "But we do it in our different ways, though, don't we?"

He wanted to observe Rebecca up close. In Vienna, he'd had only fleeting glimpses of her at the concert and in the wine bar with Lilli. He wanted to take in her essence, feel her flesh, savor the real woman before exterminating her. Virgil and Noreen, who had her under surveillance, warned him that she was a rabble-rouser. She had continued to stir up the Jewish community at synagogues and the Museum of Tolerance, dishing out flyers about Miriam's murder and raving about a Nazi plot.

"All this prejudice is poisonous," she stated.

"Not to everyone.... yet," he noted. "By the way, Rebecca, the Farben Company gave up their patent for Zyklon-B at the time of the eradication policy. Tesch, and Degesch, were the firms who had a wider-ranging expertise in handling contamination problems. They specialized in insects and rodents."

"I knew that. But left it out. You can't overwhelm visitors." She might have a messenger to spread the word. "So you're a history enthusiast."

Magnus overcame his inclination to follow her home with Noreen, who was driving him, and take her at once to Winterhaven. He had brought along a hypodermic loaded with cyanide, which he had told the security guard was insulin. It would be fitting to close the book on Rebecca here and now, in this of all places.

Bruno, however, had persuaded him to wait. Magnus continually deferred to his son, but wanted an explanation. Bruno was not a man who vacillated. Yet, to his amazement, Magnus had watched him flounder since their return from Vienna the previous year. It troubled him.

"A history enthusiast.... I certainly made some in my day," Magnus said, smiling. "Thank you for the tour, Rebecca."

The conversation left Rebecca with an acrid taste in her mouth. Apart from Jews and schools touring the Center, a trickle of sinister people sometimes came to gawk at the exhibits, as though taking in a freak show.

After putting on her red slicker and hood in the staff room, she drove her bike from the center's garage into the prickly evening rain, haunting the bleary spires of the Century City skyline. Even after a year, she still felt mystified and lost by Los Angeles's lesion-like neighborhoods that emerged like weeds without any organic design. It reminded her of something she'd once read about ganglia in biology: nerve centers that were housed outside the brain. She felt like an extraterrestrial in this glassy, indefinite city.

Earlier that afternoon she had found an unstamped envelope in her mailbox. To her surprise it contained a money-order for two thousand dollars and also a First Class, one-way ticket to Vienna but no note. She was convinced that it came from Harry. She still didn't know what to do.

His office was nearby in one of the towers on Avenue of the Stars. It was five o'clock and she phoned Summerfield Associates.

"Hi, Rebecca," his assistant said. "I'd put you through but he's in a meeting."

"Could I drop by and wait for him, Betsy?"

"Hang on." She came back in a moment. "He's got someone coming in at six. But come up; he always makes time for you."

Summerfield Associates occupied an entire floor at Fox Plaza. Dozens of employees were building models of projects, drafting blueprints, and devising complex three-dimensional designs on their humming computers in the open-plan space. Rebecca relished her occasional visits to Harry's office.

Harry treated his team, all forty-seven of them—from structural and electrical engineers, architects, interns—as family. But inevitably, this provided the perfect climate for hothouse gossip. A single question emerged: Why hadn't Harry Summerfield ever married?

Now his secret was out. He was besotted by this young Viennese woman. She was said to be a well-known pianist, but nobody had heard of her. She was stunning and had a cosmopolitan manner rarely encountered among young American women. Ever-protective when it came to Harry, no one in the office could find anything to criticize about Rebecca Benjamin. But no one had ever seen Harry so manifestly depressed, moody, unapproachable. His collegial discussions of art and greatness seemed to have faded into a black hole of silence.

A number of the staff greeted Rebecca as she made her way to his assistant, staked out like a bodyguard in front of his office. Betsy, also an architect, was the stylish mother hen of the organization. She had on her headphones; she smiled and waved. When she hung up, she left her L-shaped desk and ushered Rebecca into the private client waiting room, with its soft sofas and plush Oriental carpets. Rebecca took off her slicker, folded it, and pushed it into a side pocket of her large tote bag. The photo montages of Harry's sleek earlier buildings, ranging from art deco hotels to housing developments and skyscrapers, always dazzled her.

"How've you been, Rebecca?" Betsy asked.

"Fine."

"Playing any concerts?"

"Not for a while."

She had lost any possible connections to concerts at the homes of rich people when the Leopolds had flung her out. Having cancelled her debut in Vienna and being still untried in the United States made professional recitals impossible.

Guilt for turning her back on her career continued to upset her. "Besides, I'm not practicing enough."

"Everyone's still talking about your playing at the Christmas party."

Harry held the annual Christmas party at the Beverly Hills Hotel. The buzz regarding Harry's love life had turned to earsplitting volume in the office when this sumptuous redhead had reinstated adolescence into Harry's middle age. Only he seemed blind to his public behavior when she was around.

Rebecca's time passed quickly with the arrival of a genial, impeccably dressed old-school gentleman, with a rich basso profundo voice. Betsy, who hung up his stylish Burberry trench coat inside the closet and also offered him a drink, treated him with great deference. He removed his tweed trilby hat and smoothed down his thick gray hair.

Magnus had not expected to see Rebecca, and resourcefully hid his surprise behind a benevolent smile, sitting close to her on the sofa.

"You're a pleasant relief from this weather. I'll bet you're the pianist Harry's been raving about."

"And famously unknown," she replied, amused and infected by the old man's euphoric mood. Negotiating fees had never been her strong suit. "If you have a large room with decent acoustics and a thousand dollars, I'll play all night for you and your friends."

"Oh, I think I can arrange that. I have a country house. I don't know why Harry hasn't brought you over." Like a conductor, he moved his hand through the air with balletic grace. "There's even a vintage Bechstein concert grand." He touched her hand. "Debussy said, 'One should write music only on a Bechstein.'"

She was filled with admiration for this stranger. "You certainly know your music."

"That I do. Brahms and Chopin played Bechsteins. We'll feed you, too." He pushed back a cowl of hair from his forehead. "But not tonight, unfortunately. Do you have a card?"

"Not with me. Is Harry designing something for you?"

"An extension to my castle. But he keeps putting me off. I hope to live long enough to see it...and him."

"He's totally occupied with his art center in Tampa. A year ago, I saw the models...sheer genius."

"I agree, he's a genius. But from my standpoint, he's wasting his time."

She felt censure creeping into the man's mellifluous voice, which sounded like that of professional lecturer. And yet there was a quality of serene confidence and sophistication about him that charmed her. She had no idea of his age. There was no hint of fragility about him; despite weathered skin, he had very few lines. In his subdued tweed jacket, the bright, chic, viridian tie, he exuded a squire-like wealth. He was a man well-cared for.

"Have you known him very long?"

"Oh, a lifetime. But you interest me more.... Harry claims no one can play Schubert, Mozart, Beethoven like you."

She reflected for a moment about her past concerts and shook off her disappointment.

"It's the old Viennese tradition, and I'm part of it."

"It won't ever go out of style, so stick with it."

"Yes, sir, you're right."

"My name is Martin."

"I'm Rebecca Benjamin and delighted to meet you."

He lowered his head, took her hand, and a crackling sensation of electricity, probably from the carpet, disconcerted him. He kissed her hand. "What hands you have...."

At that moment, Harry came out of his office. Astonished, he gaped at them. Martin bounded up and clapped an arm around his shoulder.

"Hi, Rebecca." Harry salvaged his poise. "I guess you've already met my father, Martin."

She had been too concerned about her own conflicts to notice the resemblance between the two men, the oval shape of their faces, the resolute, self-assured blue eyes and attitude. She looked down, her gaze falling on Martin's handsome, black wingtip brogues.

"I didn't realize....Forgive me, Mr. Summerfield," she said, awkwardly. "I had no idea."

Magnus relished her disquiet. "I think Harry has something that belongs to you," he said with a snicker. "Come over here to us, Rebecca."

"I don't understand," she said. Magnus crooked his finger and she found herself between them, turning from one to the other.

"Harry, what have you got in your breast pocket? Go on, Rebecca, feel it. Take it out."

She was mesmerized by Martin Summerfield. His voice seemed to come from another location in the room.

"I don't know why, but you're making me giddy."

"He has that effect on everyone—not just women," Harry declared.

Magnus cajoled her. "Look in my boy's pocket,"

"I don't believe it. My father's doing his parlor act here," Harry said, removing her wallet from his pocket. "He's a virtuoso performer."

"And still proud of it. I am a conjurer." He pressed close to her. "Rebecca, you shouldn't keep your valuables in the side pocket outside your handbag. Let a thief dig for it. Los Angeles is a very dangerous place for young women. When you visit us in the country and play for us, I'll show you all my tricks. We can afford a thousand dollars, can't we, Harry?"

The embittered, stung expression on Harry's face puzzled Rebecca.

"I can come back another time?" she said.

"No, I won't be long." Harry towed his father into his office. "He always gets rid of me in record time. You must know what a nuisance old people are."

Magnus shoved a drafting board out of his way, ruffled some renderings of the art center, fleetingly glanced at them, and carelessly tossed them on the floor. He sat down at Harry's bowed desk, a rare, curly

Koa wood from Hawaii. Swiveling around, taking in the view of the skyscrapers silhouetted in the mist, he was reminded of the secret Ministry of Identity, which had been under his direction in Berlin. He had watched B-17s and English Wellington bombers demolish the building. In the blaze, records of his activities and all photographs of him had turned to ash. Days later, disguised, he had slipped through Allied lines and back to Vienna. He had to see Lilli and his newborn son.

Magnus cut the tip of a Cohiba Siglo and lit it. "Rebecca won't mind the odor of cigar smoke. I would imagine she's been in enough smoky cafés with Lilli."

Harry ignored the taunt. "If the alarm goes off, I'll disable it."

"Anything to please me," Magnus said, scoffing and at his most perfidious.

Harry waited for the firestorm to take shape; first with dry kindling, twigs in the yard, spreading to overgrown brush before flaring over the desiccated landscape of dead trees. On some levels he could out-think his father, but usually Magnus would win the game because of some unpredictable move he kept up his magician's sleeve.

"Rebecca's hands are astounding." Magnus considered this. "If mine had been that size, I would have been even better at my art. My God, what you could only hide from an audience with them...! As far as her talent is concerned, you'd know more about that. I heard her only that once in Vienna. Never up close like you."

He burrowed through his own memories and was arrested by the unrevealed parallels between their lives. He'd do anything to save his treasured son.

"Rebecca has a great deal in common with your mother, Lilli. They both play with that singing tone. Lilli called it *voicing* the piano. But even at her best in concert, she never had Rebecca's depth, those lyrical gestures to go with it. In Lilli's defense, she detested the people I brought home to the Berggasse."

"Rebecca's playing is unique, and we've seen the best."

"I know what we can do. We'll send Rebecca's hands to Lilli on your birthday—with a card from you in your fine copperplate. A keepsake from the child she wanted to murder."

"That's not funny."

"No?" He puffed away on the cigar. "Well, maybe you're right. You don't have to be defensive with me. Are you sleeping with her yet, Bruno...?"

"*Don't* use that name here."

Magnus nodded. "You're in love...? What? I can't believe you haven't slipped your hand inside her pants yet. Lost your touch with the young ones? It happens after schmoozing all these Jews. Don't you miss your harem in Winterhaven? They're pining for their demon lover—the father of their children who never see you. We've recruited some pretty new ones. All scrubbed down after they did prison time. You never think about the nights we crept in, sent their men out, so that you could fuck their wives and have them breed for us?" He shrugged ironically. "I suppose that's no longer important to you."

Harry was adept at controlling his anger. The implied threats in their games were familiar tactics. He tended to wait for his father to draw him in with a calculating remark before mounting a defense. This time there was too much at stake to allow him to take control.

"I want to let Rebecca go."

"Virgil says she's a threat and too dangerous."

"Virgil, that psychotic moron! If he ever comes near me again, I'll shoot him *and* that demented *nurse*."

"That was last year. How dare you refer to Virgil as 'psychotic'! Damn it, a loyal man who defends our beliefs and puts his life on the line is a *patriot*! He was keeping an eye on Rebecca when he came into your garage...following *my* orders. He still has no idea who you are. No one at Winterhaven does. I lie to them." Magnus was indignant about Bruno's behavior. He was determined to make his case.

"'Bruno's traveling in disguise in Europe and the MiddleEast, recruiting legions to join us.' That's the story I put out. I've invented a heroic god for them. 'Bruno's Chanukah Directive,'" he jeered. "You're my myth. It's preferable to the truth about you: selling your soul to a Jew." Magnus stood up, and his venom filled the office. "Have someone bring me a drink. You've got enough people here slaving for the *Jew* Leopold."

"I have drinks here. Will a twenty-five-year old single malt Ardbeg suit you?"

"Fine. You'll join me. And don't look at your watch when you're with me. Your beautiful Jewish fiancée can be kept waiting...till eternity."

THE WINTERHAVEN SOLUTION

Bruno poured them drinks, and Magnus changed course by appealing to his son's artistic sensibility. This would be a finely tuned composition, a symmetry, if Rebecca were to be removed precisely as Miriam had been. The suspicion might fall on someone in Vienna—a man settling a family grievance—and could not be traced to them.

Eventually men, like Leopold, would be combined with the Jewish Bride program and gassed at Winterhaven. It would seem to be worldwide in scope. He imagined how it would resonate with the Palestinians being slaughtered by Israel.

"I bought Rebecca a ticket back to Vienna."

"Are you mad? Don't you realize what you're doing? You're taking sides—protecting Lilli against me! I've told you time and again she wanted to abort you. *I* saved your life. Look at the love and attention she's given to these girls! Her maternal instincts should've been brought out by you—not them."

The argument raged back and forth.

"Explain why you wanted Miriam killed, and not Rebecca."

"Miriam was a different case entirely. She was one of those self-sacrificing leeches. Her groveling do-gooder act was nauseating. She played her hand like a Vegas hustler—stunningly—with the Leopolds and their sniveling, junky son. I hated her."

Magnus sipped his drink and pretended to be absentminded.

"I forgot. You were going through one of your emotional dips, brooding about Lilli's lack of maternal love. How you were deprived...My sacrifices bringing you up alone weren't nearly enough."

Suddenly furious, Magnus gripped Bruno's arm. "I watched my parents in flames—eaten by *their* lions!"

His father was inexorable when he had his quarry, and bided his time for the kill.

"The Leopolds...I'm so proud of you, surrounding yourself with the most expensive collection of Jewish trash and parasites in Los Angeles," Magnus said in a voice at once intimidating and reproachful. "Let me tell you something that you've never grasped about Jews. If you don't annihilate them, they'll eventually tear you apart, chop you up for soup, and suck the marrow out of your bones."

Bruno realized that Magnus remained out of touch with the reality of his profession.

"Jack Leopold and his people still control my world. Nothing's changed. I assured you in Vienna that after I completed Tampa, I'd quit and go back to Winterhaven again. I loved growing up there with you. We built the castle. I took your ideas and helped design it, for God's sake. When I went off to MIT, I knew I wanted to be an architect, and not a painter. I had to leave you. This job is my professional swan song."

Harry walked to the miniature model and stared at the astonishing structures he had visualized, scrawling down a pad with his pencil over the years. Art.

"You look really worn out, Bruno. With Jews riding on your back like a camel, and one of their women bleeding you dry...it takes a crippling toll. You start to develop humps."

"Let's not play the game again tonight. I'll do whatever I want."

Bruno was not about to let his father undermine his lifetime's work. For Magnus, the primacy of the idea prevailed over the individual—even his own son.

"Let me explain this simply to you—*Harry*. I'm the client, you're the architect. Out of some emotional desperation in Vienna when we were discussing Lilli, *you*—not *I*—suggested we resume my Jewish brides-to-be program. And so I revived it. But, as I said, it will develop into something larger! Virgil and Noreen buried a young rabbi alive and then threw a jeweler out of his office window. But let's get back to Miriam.

"You didn't like her, and so you picked her. As usual, I thought your logic was breathtaking. Brilliant strategy! But when we undertake a campaign like this, personal revenge is infantile...ludicrous...petty...it doesn't matter. I have to convince our men that *der Aktion* is the right means—their destiny. I couldn't explain to them that this was about a son who felt he was victimized—wronged. Miriam was your revenge against Lilli."

Before Hitler's impending annexation of Austria, and weeks after their meeting in Salzburg, Lilli had agreed to Magnus's terms. The contract had been clear on both sides: Magnus would allow her parents and the young baker's apprentice Herta to live. Lilli's stipulation was that they never have children. She would entertain Hitler and all the people he brought to the house.

"I never planned to keep my word." Magnus closed his eyes, and to Harry he was the inspired companion Hitler had adored. "I caught Lilli at the right time of her cycle. I knew the war was lost. Still, I wanted a child more than anything. *Mein Sohn.* You–*you*–I wanted *you.*"

Bruno turned away from the models, capitulating to his father's passionate sincerity.

"But you didn't kill Lilli."

"No, she had delivered you and I chose to let her live."

Magnus had a variety of moves to checkmate his son, but decided against it. He had always succeeded in disputes by grinding down his opposition.

"I would've taken Lilli to Zurich with you."

"Why didn't you? We would have been a family."

"I wanted that for us."

"What stopped you?"

"She would have smothered you in the crib."

"*What!*"

Magnus opened his eyes and distances receded, like smash close-ups on movie screens.

"That's what convinces me Lilli wasn't a real Jew–a true Jew. You see, she *kept* her part of our bargain...her word. Jews never do. In these special circumstances, I was the one who broke the covenant. But for the moment, let's forget whether Lilli was Jewish or not–I fell in love with her.

"She was adopted by the Benjamins when she was three. She'd already demonstrated she was a musical prodigy at an orphans' home. And the Jews are always in the marketplace for talent. Lilli's father, Leon Benjamin, was one of the wealthiest music publishers in Austria. Her mother, Elise, was filled with self-importance. Decked herself out in flowing satin gowns, diamonds larger than walnuts."

Magnus had cut the strings out of their piano, dragged Lilli's father up to the apartment on top of the house. He'd made Leon strip naked, then tied the piano wire around his testicles. As a music lover like Adolf, he had composed a tone poem of torture, music with a theme, a subject.

"That's when I learned that the Benjamins couldn't have children. So if I were you, I wouldn't worry about whether Lilli was Jewish or not. She's like everyone in the world: she does whatever is expedient or profitable. Especially when it's a question of life and death."

Harry was unnerved and his eyes roved, seemed blank. "I met Lilli at the funeral. She calls me collect sometimes to talk about Rebecca."

"You call her, too?"

There was a hesitant knock on the door. The door gradually opened a crack. Rebecca peered in.

The split within Bruno had become so entrenched that he couldn't reconcile the past with the love and adulation he felt for her. She carried the sunlight, and the artistic affinity he experienced produced ecstasy.

"I apologize for interrupting you. But I've got to run or I'll be late for work."

"What a pity," Magnus said, disappointed. "I was hoping you would join us for cocktails and a good steak dinner."

"I wish I could. Thank you. Some other time, maybe."

"I'll look forward to it."

"More magic tricks," she said with naive delight.

"All of them. My disappearing woman is a classic."

She smiled at Harry, waved, and closed the door.

Magnus always knew when to force his enemy to resign.

"Possibly one day, you'll finally appreciate how much I sacrificed for you."

Bruno embraced Magnus and his father kissed him and felt the iron return in his son.

"Years ago we decided to stamp out some Jewish women around the country. Sport to keep our men interested. But now it's become their single most powerful core idea. And now it's yours to fulfill, Bruno!"

9

Once back at Sycamore Place, Rebecca searched for a note from Horne. The photos of Miriam were out of order. He had looked at them and she was afraid of his reaction. Had he been affected by them? And to what degree? Rose Fleming had described her nephew as resolute, worthy of trust and respect. She had to find out.

She wandered into the bathroom, cleaned the cat box; then, as Glück serenaded her and butted her ankles, he nudged her into the kitchen. She mashed up some tuna for his dinner and gave him fresh water. Sitting at her writing table, she fixed her eyes on the coroner's photos of Miriam, head shaved and with a swastika on her forehead. But something else distracted her. During her tour of the museum, the minister's attitude had nettled her.

He had worn black shoes, and Martin Summerfield had on a similar pair of wingtips. No, it couldn't be. Her mind was playing tricks on her. They were so different physically; height, weight, features, all poles apart; their voices were at unconnected pitches, and sound was, after all, her medium.

As she shuffled Miriam's pictures and was about to put them back in her meticulously kept files, her sister reappeared in the photos. She was dressed for the shower with her school friends. She smiled at Rebecca; then a faint echo of her cello stole through the apartment.

Rebecca closed her eyes. When she reopened them, Miriam was gone.

The rain had stopped and she called the Cobra Room where she worked part-time as a parking valet. The drug-lord aristocrats and the rap stars would leave their lairs tonight. They were princely tippers and she might surface from this lowlife Mariana Trench with two hundred on a good night.

The men always propositioned her. The other night a cokehead had taunted her, holding out ten hundred-dollar bills to retain her for a jerk-off. He'd counted out another thousand for a blowjob. She had declined with a gracious smile. When he'd persisted, she had told him her jealous boyfriend had just been released from prison and always watched her.

She stripped off the cleaner's wrapping from her tight black slacks and slid into her Rockports, a black satin blouse, and her short valet jacket. She grabbed her London Fog raincoat and a Yankee baseball cap. As she was double-locking the door, her cell phone rang.

The large party of crackheads they had expected had cancelled. Apparently, the DEA's good-works branch had raided their house. A dozen Bentleys and Ferraris had been seized, their shackled owners presently under lock and key. She trooped downstairs to check on Horne. Six bell rings and she went back upstairs.

She had prepared a welcome-home dinner for him. Uncertain of his arrival date, she had decided on a classic German dish. Tonight with him or not, it would be cooked and she would eat it alone. Time, more time alone and she poured herself the dregs of Trader Joe's thrift Vodka of the gods, made in Greece.

What, she wondered, could Harry want for his two thousand dollars? Why had he given her money with a one-way airline ticket back to Vienna? She had tried sympathetically—as humanely as she could—to put him out of his misery for the past year. Her answer had always been clear. Her regard for his architectural talent was not a signal of arousal. In fact, she couldn't imagine them with their clothes off together.

He'd been accurate about Horne. He was a pig. They all were. But he was her noble pig. Him, she'd spit-roast with her Eve's apple jammed in his mouth.

An hour earlier, Horne had read the local giveaway papers and simmered. Gym freebies held no appeal, or picking up a sweat hog who demanded carrot juice instead of accepting a highball were not the answer to depression. The most disturbing obstruction to his freedom was Rebecca. If she balked, how could he remove her without winding up back in prison?

Horne contemplated his options and picked up the phone. His father's oldest friend lived in the Valley. He dialed the number, surprised by his shakiness. The likely cause, the photos of Rebecca's sister and the slaughters he'd seen. His sympathy for her was tethered by suspicion of his tenant.

"Is this opportunity or trouble? If this is the *Times* again, don't say another word, I've been getting it for a zillion years...."

"...It's Doug."

"*Doug!* Shit, where are you?"

"The other side of Coldwater. At Rose's place."

"You're out of jail!"

"Yeah."

"Booze, steaks, and pussy?"

"I just grew wings."

"I moved to Sherman Oaks on Valley Vista. Here's the address."

Horne picked up the file of Rose's legal papers and carried them out to the car. Compared to the beat-up junky Land Rover he'd been pounding for years in Africa, his aunt's Lexus felt like space travel. It zipped up the canyon. The CD player had an airy Mozart piano chirping. Horne recognized the composer only because he didn't like him or the awful film of his life. But in Arusha, when you caught a movie, you hung in or suffered through TV repeats of *Happy Days* or the adolescent Travolta in *Welcome Back, Kotter.*

Christened Ignatius Liam Arthur Wylie, Butch—if you wanted to see tomorrow—had, through quirks of the universe's string theory, evolved into a respectable citizen. He lived in a brick-faced brute with a circular driveway and hissing fountains. Horne announced himself at the gate phone and was buzzed in by the master of black arts, gun savant, and sometime arsonist.

Wood smoke curled from the chimney in the feathery drizzle. The hulking Irishman, smelling of pipe tobacco and holding a swaggering glass of scotch in his hand, met Horne at the big oak door. He threw his arms around him, and wetly kissed him on the cheek.

They hadn't seen each other for five years. Like Rose's lawyer, Butch had come out to Africa for a rueful farewell to his missing parents and stuck around for a safari and an endless drinking bout. They had kept in touch with a Christmas phone call.

There was a soothing fire in the generously paneled and bricked den, where all things Irish prevailed. The bar was stocked with enough bottles to pacify a wake with a hundred serious mourners. Emerald-green flags and festoons, drinking mugs, a "GUINNESS IS GOOD FOR YOU" sign, golf clubs with green snoods, books and memorabilia, photos of his parents and Horne with Butch from his childhood in Oregon comprised the doctor.

"How are you, babe?"

"Better for seeing you, Butch. How'd you get so prosperous?"

"Opened a weapons discount depot called Guns 'R' Us, and hired a couple of ex-L.A. detectives to manage it for me. I'm an assassin's-assistant-to-gentlemen now. What can I get you?"

"A pro shot of Black Label."

"Yes, sir." Behind the bar, Butch mulled over the events. "I just can't believe what happened to you. Fucking crazy Dutchman."

"Point a gun at me and you're the Headless Horseman."

"Ummm. Shit, when I taught you to shoot in the woods, who'd ever thought it'd be anything but deer and fat-assed wild turkeys fluttering their feathers?"

Butch ran his hand through what had once been a rainforest of shoulder-length blonde Robin Hood ringlets but were now dead souls, plugs taking root, revealing with forensic accuracy the topography of his skull.

"You're my boy. *What* can I do for you, Douglas...?"

"Mean that, Butch?"

"Shit, yeah."

"Haggerty fronted me ten thousand, so I can breathe the local fumes for a while."

"The Hag, really," he sniped.

"I thought you Irishmen hit it off?"

"He's too important for a deadbeat like me."

Butch carted drinks over and sat down on the green leather ottoman, like a courtesan.

"I can give you a job as a firearms instructor, lend you money. Name it, anything."

"Burn my fucking house down!"

10

Butch's lady owned The Viking, a gleaming, blonde-wooded barrel house in North Hollywood. The interior reveled in its Norse heritage: Sköl signs, portraits with horned helmets covering the heads of Eric the Red, his son Leif Erickson, and a convention of Olafs.

For Horne, home from Africa, it was one of those amiable, red-leather-booth Valley lodges—dedicated to steak and more steak, three-ounce drinks in hefty mason jars, barmaids with quivering cleavages, and a freebie hors d'oeuvre table hosting chafing dishes the size of Egyptian tombs.

"I love the place. It's one of the last of the breed," Butch informed him, his face brimming over with leering connivance.

Horne and Butch sat in a cove of the bar away from the good-humored local office coquettes, elderly dentists, chiropractors, and body-shop surgeons who were happy-houring themselves with Buffalo wings and Swedish meatballs.

"Three years ago, Ingrid inherited it from her husband."

"You were a friend of his?"

A sulky hesitation preceded Butch's answer. "Not exactly. She'd been a working girl before she married this Thor. And you know me. Ingrid and I were doing a little body surfing before the cops exhumed him. There were some misty questions about his actual cause of death after Ingrid looted the vault while he was in intensive care, and a nosy nurse claimed some drug scribble on his chart wasn't hers. But I took her under my wing. My darling beat the shit out of two poly-graphs and so fell heiress to The Viking, the house, all free and clear, and more green than Augusta National."

"Your coaching goes a long way, Butch. God must have been impressed with your fine works and Christian virtue. I never thought you were such a romantic."

"Yes, very romantic, passionate, tender-hearted, lovey-dovey."

Horne knew of three ex-wives and a squadron of mistresses who might have dissented.

"My parents would be falling down in a dead faint if they could hear you."

"That's the effect Viagra's had on me. I'm still a softie but my dick's meaner than a Rottweiler."

Horne checked the other end of the bar and noticed that it was filling up with big hair and war paint.

Horne's reappearance into Butch's life opened wounds, chafing old scar tissue that he had sutured. Nothing, however, could put to rest the guilt he felt at his own dishonorable behavior toward Horne's parents. Butch was a man who had avoided soul-searching until now.

"You and my father must've had a trail of weeping women when you were single."

"Your parents.... Do I ever miss Bonnie and Keith...." Butch turned away from Horne. "Hang on...."

Like the mayor of a suburb, Butch high-fived a few regulars and exchanged some mordant hearsay about who was doing what with whom among the rakes.

"Ingrid, I'm crazy about her. And let me tell you, Doug, did I fall in," he clucked. "She's got some knockout friends. A few turn an occasional trick. Makes it interesting when your fifties are just a memory. Live and let live, is Ingrid's rule. Everyone welcome." More salutes to some customers, then he resumed: "Ingrid does a little matchmaking with her pals and select customers."

"Does she get dividends from the girls?"

"You crazy? The Viking is a cash cow and pandering is illegal. So let's not be tactless. This is a kind of mobile chat room. Here and there, some jewelry, a gift. But, no, she's no madam," Butch assured him. "We're law-abiding citizens." He gave a pleasurable sigh. "Why not? I'm into a fantabalous scene. I never really, actually, *lived* until I met the Swede!"

Butch made it sound as though his alliance with a Scandinavian murderess had ushered him into the midst of sophisticated artistic circles.

"I'm very impressed with your sexual connections. But, please, Butch, stop bullshitting me. I asked you about creating one of your Dante's infernos—not fixing me up with hookers. You were a demolitions expert in Vietnam," Horne insisted, recalling conflagrations initiated by Butch during his Picasso pyromania period. A plume of multi colored skywriting smoke had been his signature reception to shark housing developers who had been ravaging Oregon's natural beauty.

"Jesus Christ, Doug, I don't burn people!" With huffy disapproval he assumed the attitude of an Old Testament prophet-peddling doom.

"In any case, what I do now is investigate fire claims, especially arson. That's my profession."

"I remember when I was a kid up in Eugene, your theme song was 'burn, baby, burn.' You were a Friend of the Earth. You had charisma with the commune people."

"Fuck it, that was aimed at the logging companies and the scummy new tract houses developers were building. My Shake 'n' Bakes were never for profit.... "

"Yeah, causes. This may be hard for you to understand, Butch, but my inheritance is a *religious* cause for me."

"Look...I work *with* the police now—not against them."

"Oh, stop, you've always had a passion for the flame. An acetylene torch was your brush."

"*Then*, yes. Now I don't make fires, bombs—anything that fulminates. My clients are insurance companies. In court, I charge three grand a day as an expert witness. You're asking me to give that up?"

"Yes, absolutely, out of friendship for my parents—and me!"

"And kill your tenant after she nursed Rose?"

"No, I—" Horne thought for a moment. "—No, not her."

Butch beckoned the bartender for more fuel and asked when Ingrid was expected so he could dump Horne. Before using this as a gambit, Horne thrust Rose's insurance policy with Home Mutual on the beleaguered ex-incendiary.

"I'd clear two-fifty if it's totaled, like a Serengeti burn. I want your house special—volcanic crater ash. I'll throw in ten percent."

Butch flipped through the pages and growled, low cries of distress, which fraternized with sick, sepulchral laughter. Butch handed the papers back to Horne, belted down his drink, and shook his head.

"Rose was under-insured. For two-fifty in Beverly Hills, you might get yourself a micro one-bedroom condo, Noah's Ark kitchen, and plumbing from Macbeth's castle."

"I don't intend to live in Beverly Hills. I hated it when I was stuck there with Rose and couldn't wait to see you and Haggerty for dinner or a ballgame."

"That's not the point. Rose's place is worth a couple of million. Say you reinsure, then scorch, Mutual will nominate you as prom queen and take you to the dance in chains. They'll know it's arson and do months of forensic testing. Burn patterns, hum-throughs, V-patterns; gas chromatography analysis, which measures accelerant peaks. Then they'll identify every component with mass spectrometry and computer models."

Butch took another slug from his drink. "If the work is done perfectly, you're looking at a couple of years by the time the lawyers stop squabbling and the cops, and the BHFD sign off. For the two-fifty you *might* collect, and the distressed lot you might unload, you'd maybe luck out with another five hundred grand...*provided you got away with it!*"

Horne swallowed his drink, and other solutions occurred to him. "Butch, the furnace is acting up, the hot water heater might also be suspect—the fireplace, maybe the chimney hasn't been swept."

"Keep away from them! They're obvious ignition sources."

"Hey, I'm on roll: Does flammable—acetone, turpentine, gasoline, DIESEL—I'm thinking...have to be used?"

"Shit, no, that's for amateurs who want to torch their schmata factories downtown. Electrical is the only way to go for an ignition source. And for that to really take off, you need a secondary material. It would have to be plastic, and don't think of going out and buying rolls of Cling Wrap. Oh, boy, this is Satan's quilt."

"Why?"

"*Why?* Well, Douglas, aside from having to do a tango with the wires, did you ever hear of fires, like, *spreading*, huh? It would have to be done without a timing device during the day. Kids have to be out in school. Then *you*, my dear, must canvas the neighborhood, find out if there are any shut-ins, invalids—what-have-you. Means you identify yourself as an arsonist right off the bat. This isn't Africa, Doug, where tribes just roast villages and after a campfire singsong, they barbecue their enemies' brains and salsa till dawn."

Horne was not encouraged. "Anything not to help."

"I *am* helping! For someone who cries at football games, this is not moving me. Have you talked to this, Rebecca Darling?"

"Not yet. But I know she won't budge. Her sister was murdered by neo-Nazis."

Butch gave a courtesy bow. "Well, we're sorry for her. But she's standing in your way to wealth and the pursuit of a fishing boat and happiness in squalls."

Butch placed his bucket glass against his broad forehead. "I've got it! You told me she plays the piano. Suppose you go down to an embassy. Pick any one African—Kenya—and tell them you want to

house Masai students gratis. You speak their gibberish. Get yourself
four or five of them, have them wear tribal dress, do spear dances,
and play the talking drums all night long to keep her company."

"For Christ's sake, she's a virtuoso concert pianist."

"Perfect, Ingrid'll book her. Listen up, will you? Bongos don't go
with Beethoven. Rebecca'll hit the road."

Horne was bewildered. When he turned around, his eyes rested on
a hunky blonde smothered in a pink leather suit. Appraising Horne,
she advanced, sensuously puckering her lips. For a moment he thought
she was about to leap on him. Instead she splayed across Butch,
dealing generous kisses.

"Ingrid Anders, meet my best friends' son, Douglas Horne."

"Finally. Butch talked about you for years."

"A great pleasure, ma'am."

Horne had met scores of these unquenchable Swedish smoothies
on safari. They required very little wooing. Her telephoto topaz eyes
moved to wide-angle in a welcome-to-my life examination.

"Please stay for dinner...afterwards I'll ask my girlfriends to stop
by. My special friend, Taylor, needs comforting." Laced with jovial
perversity, she had the slaphappy manner of a pro and the downhill
cleavage of deadman's run. "We've got prime steaks and plenty of
room at my house, if you'd like a sleepover."

Horne avoided an invitation to the post T-bone fireworks. "I have
a date."

"Bring her."

"Come on, Doug, you did bad time, now you deserve to party."

"I have to head off now. Another time, but thank you."

Butch beamed joyously, excused himself, and walked Horne to the
door.

"Dougie, lad, do you think any fucking donkey can get himself a
rifle, go out on the Serengeti—and shoot a lion?"

"No, of course not."

"Same thing with fires. It's a miracle nowadays when you get away
with one. Get those drummers and she'll leave town. Stay in touch."

11

After weaving through Coldwater Canyon at reckless speed, Horne decided on a quiet bachelor self-flagellation drunk at Sycamore Place—a befuddled intoxication that yielded oblivion and dehydrated agony. He'd check on the ten thousand Haggerty had promised would be in the bank tomorrow, then sleep it off and try to locate due north on his mental compass.

As he was surfing the Pay-Per-View channels with commands he couldn't yet decipher, his doorbell chimed three times.

"Yeah, I'm coming." He banged his knee into saintly Aunt Rose's art deco armchairs. Holding his .45 on his hip, he opened the door and stepped back.

"You!"

"Good evening. It's Ms. Sauerbraten and her potato pancakes, and you don't have to shoot them. They're already cooked."

He flipped the .45 like a gunfighter. "Get out of my sight...and the line of fire."

Rebecca ignored him, pressed her chest against his, standing up to a schoolyard bully.

"I have wine with dinner. Aargh, scotch—I bought it as a courtesy. I never thought you'd actually drink it." He brought a clenched fist to her face, which she ignored. "Oh...bring it with you, if you must."

He stood in brief contemplation of his rage and a possible barter: her or a hockey game.

"You're very angry. It's fragmenting your character."

"I have a right to be damn angry. And don't give me any more of your slick Viennese condescension." He trembled with wrath. "You think I'm some demented, harebrained gun freak? Lady, I've read most of the books in your fancy bindings! *You* took advantage of a dying woman. Exploited her! You're a swindler and a fraud."

Rebecca didn't take the bait and bristled. "A fraud? In what way?"

"You've got some kind of agenda."

She raised her head, high and mighty. "People in business organizations have agendas. I have a purpose."

"Cut this out. How much do you want to sign off on this?"

"My honor is not for sale. This is not a question of compensation, but retribution. There was no quid pro quo involved with Rose. She believed in what I'm doing."

"Get out!"

"I'm an artist. Do you think I would waste my time and cheat a dying woman? Do you, *do* you?" she shouted. "For an apartment? Did prison make you totally insane?"

"Will you leave if I pay you...a percentage?"

"No!"

"Yes, I'm the crazy one. Hunting imaginary Nazis who brand girls? While you're at it, find out who killed Kennedy and Martin Luther King!"

"I'll find my sister's murderer, don't worry.... Now let's settle the accusation of fraud. You of all people know what it's like to be falsely accused."

"Damn right I do."

She gathered herself and would not be baited into charges and counter-charges.

"Horne, I'd like you to accept my invitation. We'll see if we can settle this."

Finally, he nodded with a hint of grace: dining and a possible compensation screw afterwards always brought out the best in him. On the other hand, property had imposed its divine right and he had mixed feelings about which came first.

"Yes, Lady Rebecca."

Rebecca had changed clothes the minute she'd heard the car pull in. Her showgirl thighs peeped out from behind her short skirt. Horne slowly trailed her upstairs as though in a surveyor's interval, measuring bottom contours, buoys, channels, and shoals. He developed a quick game plan. He would only show his interest in her as a person—a woman, certainly—but he would leave "sheathed," like a character in a romance novel he'd read on the crapper in his prison cell. Let her beg!

Once inside *her* apartment, an odor of ginger, muddled with piquant beef gravy, floated in from the kitchen's sticky, damp air. Dimmer lights curved inward from her aged porcelain lamps and wall sconces. Glück the cat gave, an endless greeting who taking possession of his inner thigh; Horne tried to unravel the Himalayan without actually snapping his neck. Aware that his mood was homicidal, Rebecca took possession of the cat.

"He likes my cooking."

"Tell him in German: I'm sorry I kept him waiting."

"*Genug*, Glück! Horne, I have Blaukraut and French beans with our dinner."

"What, no smoked eel, herring from the Baltic?"

"I thought about it but wondered. You're not allergic to anything?"

"Just you."

"The feeling is mutual," she said, trying to make light of it. "That's a healthy sign in a tenant-landlord relationship. Would you like a glass of wine?"

"I'll drink my own scotch. In turn, since you're so gracious, may I offer you an eviction notice."

"Oh, serve me later...if you like." She heard a bubbling sound. "The split-pea soup's heating. Would you put the logs on and make a fire? I'm sure you know how."

"I'm taking a course on precise kiln temperatures for pottery turning."

He was about to pour himself another hefty shot when she whisked his glass away. The swish and scent of her got him high.

"Don't drink ice dregs. I have cubes made with Arrowhead Water."

"You're so caring for an enemy."

"Horne, you're a sorry pain in the ass. But we'll cure that. We're not enemies and I'm not your prison cellmate."

On the sideboard, she grasped silver tongs and tinkled in cubes from a blown glass bucket. "Do you take water or siphon?"

"Rocks are fine."

"Debussy, Chopin—Mahler?"

"None of the above."

"Brahms....?"

"If I wanted to listen to music, I'd find someone to do it with."

"All right. You don't have to get so touchy."

She sat down opposite him in a threadbare, tapestried armchair and placed their drinks on porcelain coasters depicting the faces of composers. An ornate wooden coffee table separated them, another heirloom she had probably conned his aunt into shipping over.

"No Beethoven, no bull, Rebecca. But...if you have any Grateful Dead...Sinatra, Tony Bennett, Lady Day....John Coltrane...Neil Young is my hero."

"Unfortunately, we don't play top forties here."

Insulted by her characterization of these artists, he barked, "What will it take to get you to vacate?"

"I must say, I love the openness of the plains—American frankness. I'll think about it."

"How *much* do you want to take a walk?" Horne's temper, usually under control, had become mutinous during his confinement. "I'm talking U.S. dollars."

"I'll let you know—and it won't be easy."

He sipped his drink and fumbled for his cigarettes.

"Is smoking permitted?"

"If I can have one as well. My grandmother, Lilli, would have a fit, but let her...."

"I quit, too, but in prison I needed company. Now, thanks to you, I'm chain-smoking."

"So...cigarettes and drinks." Her sharp eyes skimmed along him. "I'm in the mood for civility. I think I ought to define my position. I have to tell you that your old photos didn't do you justice. You're thinner, but my cooking will help. You clean up well. In German, I would describe you as *stattlich*, stately...the secondary meaning is magnificent."

He was fuming. What was next in this grifter's bag of tricks?

"You're so flattering, fraulein." He clenched his fist. "I want to sell this goddamn place. Poverty doesn't agree with me. I want my money! Do you need a subtitle for that?"

"No-no-no."

She stretched her long legs on the table, inadvertently providing a view of her bare thighs and skimpy cream panties. They wouldn't do for a fast-food napkin. His brain waves developed static, the neurons short-circuiting. Damn, it was all he could do not to dive right in. This insight limped along as tardily as a mule caravan, and he chided himself for missing the signal. Rebecca was waiting for one of his *succès fou* lionesque mating moves! Statistically, they had zero failure rate. Encouraged by her description of him—stately, magnificent—he'd go with the modified Graham Greene approach.

"Would you like to go to bed?" he asked, brimming with confidence.

Her ease and genial sigh encouraged Horne. Paydirt! They both needed to get off; afterwards they'd settle the property matter with no trouble. Never take a lawyer's advice.

"Yes, but not with you." She wrinkled her nose. "I'm curious, Horne. Is this a Masai warrior courtship overture?"

Ignoring her brush-off, he continued, "I'll make sure you enjoy yourself." He had in mind his leisurely stop-and-go milk-train special. "You can count on hours of pleasure."

"I see." She gave him the genetic look of everywoman coming into contact with male weirdness. "Am I giving off some sort of sign of arousal? A scent only an experienced hunter like you could detect?" She stubbed out his cigarette. "Sex with a stranger—especially *you*—is much too risky."

"Some risk. Dinner first. On a full stomach, I'll see if *I'm* interested in a body reading."

Never losing her composure, or raising her voice, she said, as though to an unruly student, "I ought to throw *you* out. First you threaten to evict me...then...have the audacity to ask me go to bed? If this is an example of your strategic planning, I'm glad I never went on safari with you."

Sandbagged again, Horne was bemused. He simply had no idea how to crack this nut. But he did know when to shut up. His run of misfortune loitered like a gin hangover. Cursing himself for dismissing Taylor out of hand, he figured out that he was submitting to a mind-fuck from a specialist.

"I guess I was out of line." He was ready to leave. "I don't know how much more abuse I can take for a bowl of split-pea soup and pot roast."

She stood up, her expression sphinx-like. "I won't be long. Let me check dinner."

"And don't be burning the croutons."

Fuck her. He picked up the kindling and started the fire with tusked old fir logs, disrupting civilizations of spiders. The crackle of flames brought her back.

He would have liked some smoke, killer ganja from the fields, with friends. He could hear echoes of the laughter that ensued before being led into a rondavel by the twittering treasure of the pride of his Kikuyu guides. He had been brought there to shoot a rogue elephant that had destroyed their *shambas* and consumed the crops. To celebrate, after the kill, Horne would be offered the purity of their future. He always declined, knowing that the girl had been pledged, and so he drank their beer, smoked dope, faded into oblivion, and developed a lasting camaraderie.

Smiling inwardly, Rebecca returned.

"What's so funny?"

"Oh, you, men in general."

"We're all idiots, right?"

"You've won that contest hands down."

"So, Rebecca Darling, with the drugs you shot into my aunt, you and Rose had lots of heart-to-heart chats."

"We certainly did. I was with her constantly."

"What a martyr."

The kitchen timer went off and he followed her into the dining room, starved. It had once contained a deal table, unmatched chairs, and a lazy Susan that his parents had spun crazily when they were stoned and his dad started playing guitar. This total rearrangement of his life was getting to be too much for him.

"What, no placecards! I don't know if I'm eating here," he said. "Where's the Krug '61? What do you take me for, some easy pick-up that you can treat this way?"

"Screw you."

"I'm a gentleman and I don't *appreciate* that kind of language."

He had drunk the best wines on safari with the immensely rich. He was delighted at gaining ground, inches, keeping her hopping.

"Oh, sit down and open the wine. I'll bring in your drink."

He yanked the cork, cleaned the lip, and poured a passable Chambertin. Other people's money went a long way for Rebecca. On safari, the megabucks crews brought along Pétrus; Chateau d'Yquem with dessert, before settling into stores of ancient Napoleon.

The adversarial mood vanished when she recited the Mourner's *Kaddish* for her sister Miriam. She raised her glass to his.

"*L'chaim.* To life."

"Yes, of course."

12

There was no doubt about Rebecca's expertise in the kitchen, or that they should have music. Bach was king, not Neil Young. The mistress of the house was in charge, not her guest. She had baked a brown dill bread and toasted croutons for the split-pea soup filled with chunks of ham and kielbasa. Thickly buttering his bread, Horne ate ravenously.

When he complimented her, she said, "I want you to have room for the main course and dessert. The soup will be better tomorrow. I put some aside for you to reheat. So, no seconds."

"Don't be so bossy."

She nodded, somewhat at a loss. "I'm not as a rule. Since someone broke into Rose's apartment, I've had to be on the lookout. I'm nervous—unsure of myself. It's not like me. I'm relieved you're back and ready to take charge."

He liked this declaration of his dominance. If she were telling the truth—and a man never knew until the plunge—he'd crank her up. His mind explored the vector space of such unions, and the intimate landscapes of these expeditions. His companions in Africa, a league of hunters, had all mounted frothing oversexed Barnard sirens, brazen Benningtonites, maidens from Stanford. Nymphs lost in the storm of life, whose moneyed parents hauled them to Africa for a graduation finale and a sweaty dive with Horne or one of his mates. In the bush...with lion prides growling, their panic attacks subsided, yielding to multiple orgasms. From the Serengeti to the Masai Mara, during elephant charges and lion stalkings, he'd weathered their meteorological conditions.

"You'd probably be safer in an apartment house with security guys—video cameras everywhere."

"I don't think so."

Rebecca put on another CD.

"Now, what're we listening to?"

"Brahms' 'Third Symphony,' Bruno Walter conducting. In my opinion, the best interpretation. My grandmother prefers Van Karajan."

"Yes, warden," he replied.

He had no idea where this unforeseen killing-the-enemy-with-kindness was leading, but her approach eased the tension at present.

In different circumstances her screwball behavior, coupled with her physical attributes, might swerve them into a relationship. Horne was a man at home with animals and understood their behavior: scents, sounds, appearances were what counted. He knew this might be construed as superficial on a human level; personality and intelligence had dominions, but ultimately, physical power and primordial instincts ruled, transcending rational behavior.

Casting aside these meditations, right now, he was in the mood for expulsion. But nicely: considerately booting her ass out, shelling out a few bucks for visitation-dating rights when he sold Sycamore Place and became flush. He'd throw in a few thousand for her relocation. With yet another maneuver in place, he permitted himself a moment of serenity. Not many men in Beverly Hills, or for that matter, the rest of the world, were eating this well, with such a beautiful woman waiting on them.

He stood up and settled Rebecca in her chair, then paused, soiled by conflict. In between courses, the wily sneak had pinned up her hair, tempting him to stroke the nape of her neck. His forced abstinence continued to rear its titanic head. But why take a chance, especially after she had said "no"? Ultimately, the sauerbraten won out.

Halfway through his dining assault, he murmured, "Heaven."

"I'm delighted. Your aunt enjoyed my cooking before she became too ill to enjoy anything. And the Brahms hasn't offended you?"

"I love it all."

"I was looking forward to this. Pity you were so boorish...maybe you were just hungry," she mused. "I was forgetting your time in prison."

Horne let that one ride and thought the tide might be turning as he charted his erotic maneuvers. Possibly a fondle in the kitchen while she was doing the dishes. Women felt protected around the fridge and a range. The proximity of ovens brought out the best in them. But because of his size, kitchen-counter romance in the past had always led to bungling—banging against drawers, nasty bruises, crunching an instep.

Ultimately dismissing prospects of a sexual romp, he furiously layered the fire with more logs on blazing red ashes. Rebecca's overbearing Germanic manner was insufferable. He found himself in the position of vassal to the queen's whims and this quashed prospects of any kind of relationship with her.

She reappeared carrying an ornate, Kaiser silver tray, and he bounded to his feet like a steward. She waved him away and set the tray down. It was laden with coffee and another intoxicating concoction, the scents of vanilla, nutmeg, and cinnamon.

"Apple Nut Torte with crème fraîche."

Her conniving behavior with his aunt had been odious. In the flesh, she was a feast. The ambivalence she fostered within him had brought him to a state of passive dejection.

"I think I can live with that. Your dinner was delicious."

"Thank you. Did you notice I didn't touch the bread? If you wake up in the middle of the night, it's because I used an undetectable, slow-acting poison."

"Dry heaves first?"

"Yes." She patted him on the head like a dog. "You like your coffee black."

"Yes, please."

They smoked in silence.

"Cognac?"

"No, thanks. Rebecca, I really appreciate your knocking yourself out this way. I should have brought flowers, wine, chocolates." And served her with a deportation notice.

"Horne, let's make an effort to get along."

"I swear I'm trying. Going out of my way. I'm truly not a bastard."

"I know that. Come into my bedroom. I want to show you something."

He accepted the invitation and didn't know how to trace the effect she was having on him: whether it was the honeyed Brahms symphony, her gingery German pot roast, the shape of her ass, or all of them synchronizing into some form of hallucinatory magic. The public could keep all those scrawny, starved, hollow-cheeked Hollywood actresses and models who looked as if they needed an intravenous feed. This was a mountain of a woman worth climbing. Again he found himself growing mellow, but the urgency of a quitclaim stung him back to reality.

Bowled over, he stared at himself. He hadn't noticed the blown-up photograph of him after his first lion kill, which he had sent to Rose. Drooping from the top of an old mirrored, wooden wardrobe were short uniform jackets that didn't seem to match up with her persona.

"*That's* what I think of you. I borrowed it from Rose's room after she died." She looked at him earnestly. "Horne, I have all of her scrapbooks of your exploits. And your letters to her. I studied them and they *spoke* to me. I don't know how, but I've been tuned into you.

He didn't know what to make of this wacky assertion.

"Do you mind me asking if you're on some kind of medication?"

"We are not amused."

Like a lioness, marking the hunter downwind, she kept him off-balance, wary.

"I just don't get you. One minute you're ready to toss me out, the next you invite me into your bedroom."

"We're both very troubled people." He was reluctant to admit this or reveal any vulnerability. "And that's what's behind this squabble. Not property."

"Then what...what?"

"You! You're the reason I've stayed here. Rose told me you were a good man—a heroic one."

"I'm not," he protested, backing away from her. "I've been through a hellish period, killed a man...."

"Yes, I know. That's why tonight is so important. You see, you have to talk about it, relive it with me."

"No...I can't, Rebecca."

"I want to protect you. Your dreams are horrifying. *I* can free you."

Horne was getting strange vibes and became unnerved. He had never mentioned this to anyone, and broke out in sweat chills. It was as if he'd had a relapse of the Blackwater Fever, which he'd contracted the second year he had been in Africa. He'd been an apprentice hunter and had forgotten to bring along the DEET to repel the mosquitoes at Lake Mayanara.

"I think I better get going."

"Don't turn this chance down," she insisted. "You're still in prison. Sit down on my bed. You'll be safe. Put your hands in mine," she said in a hushed tone. Her voice was hypnotic and now he felt himself drawn into her twilight world. "Close your eyes."

He discovered that he had placed his palms on hers. The vibrancy of the grief within her gained momentum. She was transmitting waves of it to him. His hands trembled and his knees wobbled.

13

Horne had been booked by a group from Arusha for what was for him the usual photo safari during the Serengeti migration of wilde-beests and their escort of predatory lions; the track-star giraffes enabled the group to capture the usual home video to bore relatives and friends. The couples had picked Horne months before, through Leighton and Morgan, the English firm that employed him. Over the years, Horne had built a following.

"I was really looking forward to this because it was early in the season," he told Rebecca. "There are two wealthy couples from New York. And a Dutchman, a single. Hendrik Stovart, in his fifties and very fit. He has one of those chiseled, angular faces engraved with late nights and booze. He's hunted before, but for some reason, there was a screw-up with his license to shoot lion on a private preserve. It didn't come through. The office was trying to cut through the red tape—that's why he came along. I was supposed to drop him off at the company preserve, because my party and I aren't out to shoot lion."

They had camped below the steep face of the southern wall of the Ngorongoro Crater. It had been a good day for the Americans, Horne having spotted shiny ox-peckers on the backs of a family of rhino who cooperated for photo ops, until the bull became jittery, marking lion in the neighborhood.

The couples were close friends and had spent a year planning their trip. The women were attractive, amusing, and had gone to college together. The men were knowledgeable: one of them taught Economics at NYU, the other owned a restaurant. It was a happy, smart quartet. They had photographed a pair of lionesses in pursuit of a zebra and captured the kill.

Stovart, the Dutchman, and the couples got along well. He spoke perfect English and was in the entertainment business in disco-clubs—in Amsterdam. He invited them to visit him. He'd show them around.

"So far, Rebecca, everything is working out just brilliantly. We return to the company camp, comfortable tents, hot showers for everyone. My staff is happy, popping Cristal champagne. Kivo, my camp manager, has organized things perfectly and he's not raiding the *wompo*—whiskey.

"At dinner, I have to perform: tell stories about my travels, the hunting experiences—all the close calls I've had in the twelve years I've been in Africa. My time culling elephants at the Selous Game Preserve, then guarding lion prides in Tsavo for five years. It's part of my routine.

"The highlight is my escape from rhino poachers. It's unspeakable, monstrous. Bastards hack them up, even calves, leave the putrefying carcasses, then head out to Mombassa, sail out on a dhow and peddle the horns to the black market in Yemen. The tribal warlords, *shifta*, ride into Sana, their capital. The traffickers auction the horns off to carve into dagger handles. What doesn't wind up there goes to Hong Kong, where it's ground up into powder and sold as an aphrodisiac throughout mainland China. No Viagra for them."

A charge passed from Rebecca's hands to his. His muscles quivered and he gave an involuntary, convulsive jerk.

"These Somali bandits are barbarians, some of the cruelest people on earth!" Rebecca exclaimed. "I can *see* what happened to you."

Horne's eyes fluttered, and she maintained her grasp on his hands. Waves of current continued to riffle through him, like the crackling shocks walking over new carpet. The sensation alarmed him. His heart was beating rapidly.

"How could you know they were Somalis? I never discussed that with anyone...Rose...even my boss, Jimmy Leighton." Horne's voice emerged from a spatial dimension that was no longer the present. "Where are you taking me?" he asked.

"Don't be afraid. I'm synchronized into what's happened to you and the other dead people."

"How?"

"I can't explain how or why. It has something to do with music...and it's connected to the things that happened in the house I grew up in." His hands relaxed. "We must explore this to find the real you. Before you can help me."

He tried to open his eyes, but they were locked, and he was forced to yield to her. He had begun to trust her and banished thoughts of her schemes.

"The chef on my safari is first class and he's prepared an elaborate dinner—caviar, foie gras, fresh perch, wild game birds, venison, all served with vintage wines.

"At about ten, I suggest we turn in because we are going to be up at daybreak and head down to the waterhole. The Americans particularly wanted photos of a leopard. I'd salted some impala meat to draw out the big cats. The leopards and cheetahs get there first."

Her fingers tightly grasped his. "Horne, there's an urgent message for you on the short-wave set!"

"Yes, yes..." He no longer wondered about her rarefied spiritual connections. "It's one of the park game wardens. He warns me that a rogue lion is near our camp. It's a big male, possibly with dementia from a snake bite. The lion ripped apart a couple of pregnant females in a pride.

"This rogue lion is on a rampage. He's already mauled a Masai herdsman. A second one is missing. It's a very dangerous situation. A murderous lion is reported near us. I can't leave my party unprotected.

"I tell Kivo to close down the camp, keep a watchful eye. Make sure the porters and maids don't smoke any ganja, or wander off into the fields.

"Solomon, my tracker, is ready to move out. But at the last minute, I'm uneasy. He's a fine shot, but Kivo isn't. The safety of the party comes first. I order Solomon to remain at camp.

"The Dutchman volunteers, says he can shoot. He's not afraid. He's brought a .30/'06 caliber Winchester rifle, a Ruger .44 magnum and a big-game skinning knife. I could use another hand to carry my other rifle, watch my ass.

"But I decide to go it alone. I can't take a chance with a stranger. If he gets hurt, sprains an ankle, or he's bitten by a snake, attacked, whatever—I hang for it. And what's more, I deserve it.

"I've had my hunting license for eight years, four years as an apprentice, and I'm not about to forget everything drummed into my head by other hunters, my idols. It's too perilous for someone whose skill and nerve I haven't tested. It's the hunter's canon, his protocol, never to endanger a client.

"At about one, I find the missing Masai—part of him; his stomach has been gouged out. The lion's a man-eater...and not far from his kill.

"I wait it out for a few hours. Sweating it, dying a little, not scared because, Rebecca, when my parents disappeared, I became fatalistic. Living in Africa, you can't help but take a short view. Here today, missing or dead tomorrow. No explanation, never a final answer.

"After years of chasing false leads and searching for them, I live in the here and now. And there's a lion out there that's killed people and is threatening my camp. I could've used Solomon and curse myself for leaving him behind. But I made the right decision.

"I'm hunkered in a riverine bush by a salt lake. The air hisses with bugs, mosquitoes gorging in the bacterial sludge. It's a starry night with a full moon. Nearing two, there's a startling blaze of summer lightning. The chalky layers of salt are actually glowing. The reflection dazzles me. Deep grumbles of thunder follow on.

"I spot the lion—or rather, he sees me. I'm the one being stalked, not him.

"He's moving towards me slowly, deliberately, then waiting. Naturally, he sensed I was there. He can smell for miles. He's caught my scent downwind and he's actually been circling me.

"He's immense, easily over five hundred pounds, with a blood-slick black mane that gleams like satin in the moonlight. I don't use nightscopes for hunting. If you're a true hunter you try to make it as fair as possible. Now I'm sorry about the code we have.

"He's about thirty yards away, growling ferociously. Between him and the thunderclap, it's like nature playing a death counterpoint. I hear an unbroken barrage of roars—not just of rage—but madness. He wants his kill, and I'm it.

"Twenty yards, near enough, and he's closing. I've shouldered my Holland and Holland Royal. It holds two soft-nosed cartridges. They explode inside the target when they hit. I need a clean shot, and can't get one. No pursuing a mad, wounded killer in the bush, while he hides in the high grass, waiting, and attacks anything in his path.

"He's in motion, heading faster towards me. I can smell his acrid breath, the stench of wet blood. He's closing. I have to wait, wait. It feels like the afterlife. But I don't have a choice. If I miss, it's over: *I die*. I'm stranded in impenetrable forest bush. If he mauls me, it would take days for a rescue party to find me.

"This demon lion charges. His roars are deafening. He begins his leap about twenty feet from me. I take him down with a heart shot.

He doesn't know he's dead. His front paws are extended, reaching out, and he's still flying at me like a diver in mid-air.

"The rifle is slippery. My hands are sweating and so slick that I don't know if I can get off another shot. But I fire again. A head shot. I swerve out of the way. Beside an acacia trunk, and he crashes on my legs. His claws and involuntary muscles are caught in the rhythm of dying and he digs into my legs."

Reliving the moment, Horne caught his breath.

Rebecca continued. "You're exhausted, wounded, but you're proud at that moment."

Horne seemed to be floating with her in unexplored space.

"Rebecca, you're there—with me!"

"Yes, I feel I am."

He realized that she was a witness of the landscape of his mind, fusing hers with his.

"When you get your bearings, you realize you're closer to the safari camp than you'd thought. You've walked about a square mile, but you're only a mile away."

Horne was shocked by her clairvoyance. The factuality of her observation made it clear that she could inhabit his time and space. Rebecca had succeeded in absorbing his shadows, his past experience in actual time. She was not merely satisfied with appropriating his property, she had determined she would *occupy him.*

"You're making me as tense as the lion did."

"Accept what I'm offering."

Horne is now back in the jungle, thrashing through the bush with his flashlight, making for camp. He checks the clients' tents. The couples are asleep, but he senses something wrong.

Stovart's tent is empty.

A Coleman lantern is alight, and small haloes of smoke dance. On the camp table is a firestarter and two glass pipes with a sparkling bed of stinking old crack.

Did Stovart come after him?

Is he out there in the crater, lost?

Horne searches for Kivo. Solomon has deserted his sentry post. He has broken a cardinal rule when they are in camp. Horne could lose his hunter's license for such a serious violation.

Furious, he goes to the staff tent. The maids are also missing.

"I'm too confused to bother about my wounds. Did the lion come to the camp after I left, and carry off five people? Are there two lions, three? I'm stunned, overcome by terrible forebodings.

"I stumble over to our Land Rovers. Kivo and Solomon are laid out flat, one body on top of the other—both dead."

Rebecca clasped her arms around Horne and stroked his sweaty forehead and hair.

"The camp girls! They're...." he stammered, shuddering. "Unspeakable."

"It was like when I saw Miriam dead."

He stopped. "The pictures of Miriam."

"Tell me, please."

"I hear an ungodly screech that makes me shiver. It's a sound I've heard often—too often. A human being is being killed, dying. I follow the pitch, hack my way through down to the waterhole...surrounded by a clan of *fisis*—hyenas. The queen is watching, like a music conductor pausing for the choir.

"A lion pride and a family of elephants with big ivory tusks are watching, waiting. It's like the end of the world; the universe is dead, soundless—to me.

She felt as though she were having a seizure. "The Dutchman..."

"—Stovart! He's naked, covered in blood."

Rebecca cried, "Oh, God, no. I can't bear this!"

"I can't stop. You're with me and you brought me back to this hellish place, and you can't leave me now, Rebecca!"

"I won't."

Horne groaned, anguished by the vision. The violation had made him kill-crazy.

"He's *tamed* the hyenas!" Horne cried. "Oh, my God! He's dismembered the camp girls. He's eating their raw flesh—and throwing hunks of it to the hyenas."

Horne was accustomed to lions, the charges of bull elephants, the unpredictability of the rhino—the trade of the hunter—but he'd never witnessed a sight of such bestiality.

He bellowed at Stovart who appeared surprised to hear a human voice in a world in which the language of humans had perished. In this universe of depravity, only the elements prevailed. The sough of wind, the flow of water.

"'Stovart! Stovart!'" Horne was shaking, his shirt sopping wet. "Stovart threw a piece of a woman...I don't know what...at me. I was distracted. When I looked down, he had his rifle aimed at me. Easy shot, maybe thirty feet."

Horrified, Rebecca had imagined the scene and pictured it through Horne's eyes.

"Stovart, the cannibal, has a full belly. He's too slow for you," she said.

"Yes-yes." Reliving the moment, Horne was overcome. "Anyone picks up a weapon and points it at me—

"I whirl, twisting in the mud, rousing the crocodiles, and blast a shot into his head."

"You don't miss, do you?"

"No...."

Horne's eyesight was his gift, a marvel of peripheral magic enhanced by visual perception at great distances. He rubbed his knuckles over his eyes and opened them, finding himself in a loose, fragmented, irrational realm where he was still alone, tormented by the apparition.

He roamed around the room, unsteady, touching Rebecca's prized objects, paperweights emblazoned with delicate portraits, sinuous bronze figurines, crackling, ivory-yellow music scores, his fingers grazing the edge of an ancient wooden table, its bowl duped in hide. He recognized that Rebecca was a woman beyond his comprehension. But the mere suggestion that he could lose his composure to such a degree goaded him.

"No, I don't miss a target when my life is on the line. I blew Stovart's head off with a .500/.465. That would bring down an elephant with tusks of two hundred pounds of ivory."

Rebecca remorselessly drew out the venom inside him, leading him through the shock of approaching the Dutchman, his kill.

"You'd betrayed your code."

"I couldn't stop firing. I'm so fast at this...and speed loaded, my hands danced over the cartridges, the way your fingers do on the piano. I kept reloading. *More-more-more!* I stood over this savage, riddling his body. Gaping holes. I was as barbaric as him."

Horne staggered, corkscrewed, felt as though he were about to faint and smash into the armoire. Rebecca helped him to a chair.

"Later, when your boss arrived with the police, they thought you'd murdered the Dutchman and the others."

Horne felt trapped in the mazes of Rebecca's counterplots. No question, she had done a remarkable investigation of his case. Had she inveigled her way into the raw files of his lawyers in Tanzania, read about the case? Was there a transcript? But where? Haggerty would never sell him out.

"Rebecca, it was self-defense."

"I know it was," she said, consoling him.

"But it didn't look that way to the local *Askari*. They claimed I was a killer—not Stovart." He shook his head remorsefully. "I still can't pardon myself."

"Killing a monster is a divine gesture to God," she proclaimed.

Hendrik Stovart had friends in important government positions throughout Europe, with secrets to bury. Their envoys came from Amsterdam, Brussels, and Hamburg; they coerced the local authorities to keep silent about the Dutchman. Haggerty and his barrister had uncovered the whole story. But Stovart's personal history was judged irrelevant. Horne stood trial for murder.

"Yeah, he was in the 'entertainment business.' He had a string of porn mills, cast with nine-year-olds that he bought from India, Bosnia, Romania—and animals. Children who fell into the hands of slavers and phony orphanages.... A bona-fide entrepreneur. Whatever you need—arms to terrorists, fascists, dope for anybody, homemade pharmaceuticals...give Hendrik a call. He's your guy.

"And I became part of his madness, the degradation. Yeah, I killed a bad guy. But the point is, I'm supposed to be civilized."

"And you are."

Rebecca helped Horne up to his feet.

"Come, come, with me."

14

Horne had returned from his journey. He was in present time. How had Rebecca infiltrated his state of mind with Stovart? Had he imagined this or was he having a nervous breakdown? Leading him back into the living room, she poured two glasses of cognac and handed him one.

"Drink some, please."

The cat sensed something was wrong and flew into her arms; she stroked and soothed him.

"Stovart is like my enemy, Magnus Von Winter. They're evil. I almost think a cosmic influence molds their behavior. They're exiles from other worlds." She had been holding back since Miriam's death, and her words tumbled out. "Everyone is game to them. *Your* Hendrik Stovart, *my* Magnus—and his son Bruno—didn't simply murder my sister and your friends on that safari. They murdered *us* by slaughtering people we cared about."

The phone rang. She stared at it listlessly, then picked it up on the fourth ring.

"I hope I didn't wake you." Harry's voice was muffled by heavy engine noise.

"No, no. Where are you?"

"At Santa Monica Airport. I'm going to leave for Tampa. We're filing a flight report."

"More snags?"

"I can handle them."

"Harry, your father is incredible. He has such character and charm."

"His specialty is bewitching beautiful women."

Harry had persuaded Magnus to relent, and had temporarily rescued Rebecca. But the reprieve could only succeed if she left the country. In America, she was an obstruction that had to be eradicated.

"I've got a silly question. Where did he get those shoes? I've never seen anything like them in the States."

"You won't," Harry said. "They're made for him by Lobb in London."

She had clearly made a mistake about the minister's shoes—the old fellow who had taken the tour.

"Rebecca, how about a change of scenery? Come to Tampa for a few days? You can see the way the art center is taking shape. Then fly back to Vienna." She was perplexed. "Rebecca, are you still there?"

"Yes. I'm not sure about my plans or what to do about the check."

She glanced over at Horne. His eyes were closed but he was listening to her.

"If it makes you feel better, consider it a loan. When you're playing the circuit in Europe, you can pay me back. You know how I feel about you. But I'm not thinking about myself. I'll arrange to have your furniture sent back to Vienna. I'm really worried about you staying in L.A."

"Why?"

"I told my father about what you're doing. We both feel that sooner or later, these people are going to come after you. That's why I sent you the ticket. The important thing is, you have to leave."

Harry's insistence disturbed her. "I've been thinking about it. Maybe in a few weeks at the most. When will you be back?"

"Hard to say at this stage. But I'll probably go to Europe later in the year and see you then. I've got to dash now. Goodbye."

"'Bye, and thank you for everything."

Horne finished the brandy. He stood up, unsteadily—curling low and shaking.

She held his arm. "My friend thinks I'm in trouble."

His defenses kicked in once more. He had no intention of being lured into her personal affairs.

"Rebecca, I wish to hell I could figure out what you're really after."

She flushed with anger. "I don't care about your aunt's apartment! I need your help to find who murdered my sister...and the others. I tried to do it alone. I can't."

She had taken possession of his thoughts and virtual control of his every action, but he now detected a helplessness, hidden by what had been a display of omniscience.

"Be *my* hunter, Horne."

Once again he was left swinging. "I think for once you're the one who's confused. I hunted game—not human beings."

"But you can hunt for me," she insisted.

"How?"

"I know of three people who have information about these murders. But they won't talk to me."

"What makes you think it'd be any different if *I* tried?"

"You're the chosen one. I've waited for you—"

"—Why me?"

"You were a man who had a sacred goal. You went to Africa to search for your parents."

"I failed." He shook his head with frustration. "And right now, I'm the one who's lost."

With eyes closed, she stood so motionless that she seemed in a trance.

"Horne, you're not lost. I'll do everything I can to find your parents."

The offer was quixotically genuine and untainted by desperation. He was unable to dismiss his fascination with Rebecca's mystical perception, or the physical attraction she continued to evoke.

"Rebecca, this isn't going to work. I'm not for hire. And...Jesus, are we bartering for the apartment?"

"No...The day I was interviewed by your aunt and we agreed that I'd be her companion, she showed me pictures of you. Rose told me all about you. A power greater than mine kept me here for *you*."

She grazed his face with her fingertips. "I'm your pathfinder. Horne, be mine."

When he remained silent, her resignation expressed the poignancy of her situation.

As they moved to the door, she pointed at a painting of a woman and man above a tarnished bronze plaque.

"Horne, look at this carefully."

The Jewish Bride
(Isaac & Rebecca) c 1666
REMBRANDT

The woman wore a warm, red-purplish dress, attuned with gold-yellow against a brown background. Isaac had his left arm around his wife Rebecca's shoulder, and his right hand over her left breast. She, in turn, obligingly accepted this intimacy by placing her fingers over his hand, and pressed it more firmly to her breast. The painting was erotic, spiritual, loving, intimate, proprietary, revealing a profound degree of exclusivity.

"Is this related in some way to Miriam?"

Grim-faced, she nodded. "Yes, I have a theory about Magnus. He's obsessed with Jewish brides...and murdering them."

It was two A.M. when Horne left. He stopped for a moment on the balcony, refreshed by the cold night air. He was out of view of two men across the street and smoked a cigarette while she turned off the lights inside and locked up. The men were walking a whining dachshund, sniffing for its territory, and eventually stopping beside a hydrant.

Virgil extended the leash and said, "I don't know what Rebecca's involved in now."

"She's still working at the Museum of Tolerance," Magnus said. "But are you tracking her when she leaves?"

"We keep losing her. She's all over Los Angeles on her motorbike."

"That's very troubling."

"When you ordered me down here, we didn't think she'd stay this long," Virgil replied defensively.

"Yes, I thought she'd've gotten tired of snooping by now."

"I'm puzzled, Magnus. Why hasn't she gone back to Vienna?"

For a moment, Magnus thought about his pact with Bruno. He was by turns disturbed and angry.

With the assassin's missionary fervor, Virgil persisted. "There's a very simple way out. I could go upstairs right now and kill her."

"Wait until you hear from Bruno. She's his personal project."

"Where is Bruno?"

"Syria."

"Everyone up at Winterhaven is so anxious to hear about his heroic work and meet him."

"You will at a grand homecoming I'm planning."

At the corner, a black Mercedes limo waited, and a chauffeur immediately climbed out and held the door for Magnus. In the interior light, Magnus Von Winter's regal face was godlike in its certainty, and his rich voice was compelling and self-possessed. "Virgil, have you and Noreen talked about getting married, a family?"

"Marriage, yes, we have." Virgil twitched. "A family would be a problem."

"How so?"

A Jew bastard she worked for when she was kid knocked her up. She had an abortion and can't have kids."

"Maybe I can do something about that when you're ready. Arrange an adoption."

Virgil was overwhelmed by his generosity. "That would be wonderful."

"I like the way you look after the little dog I gave you, Virgil. Good night."

"Good night, sir. It was an honor to have you visit."

Virgil headed back to the furnished apartment around the corner from Sycamore Place. Despite its prestigious Carlyle Drive address, this Beverly Hills quartet of one-bedroom garden apartments was more or less a shag port for rotating Lolitas and some married skulkers, and at sixteen hundred dollars per month, too!

Thank God for Noreen, or he would have lost it. Along with maternal love for Dort, Noreen convoyed her sewing kit, sprang for an ironing board, and was Joan of Arc with laundry, as well as providing as much untidy sex as he could handle.

He entered with Dort, who was chirpy and already licking Noreen's ankles. She held out her hand with a late snack of some liver chips, and Dort swooned with delight.

"Did he do his business?"

"I should be that regular," Virgil said, shivering from the chill.

"I don't mind taking him."

"Better we take turns."

She handed Virgil a hot rum toddy and he nodded gratefully.

"Is there something fishy with the new guy who moved in below? Hasn't he crawled under Rebecca's covers yet?"

He shook his head. "I couldn't see what was going on upstairs without crossing the street. But I don't think he's up to much. They went to bed separately." He pondered. "Even though he's big and bearded, he could be gay."

"Did you find out his name?"

"Fleming," Virgil said. "He didn't change the name-plate. I'm thinking he could be the dead old lady's son. Maybe Fleming will slap her silly ass back to Vienneski. If she knows what's good for her and enjoys living, she'd better call Cheap Tickets for standby."

"Oh, shit, Virgil, you make me laugh and that makes me horny."

"Noreen, at this rate you'll spoil the rod. More than two fill-ups a night and OPEC will treat me as a hostile nation."

He had decided not to broach the subject of marriage and adoption. He didn't want Noreen to lose her focus.

She was anxious to hear about his meeting with Magnus.

"What's going on with Bruno, the mystery man?"

"The old man told me he was in Syria and heading back to Winter-haven."

"Winterhaven did nothing but train us for war." Noreen spewed out her venom. "We've got a Jew bitch running around L.A. ranting about Nazi plots. Sooner or later, someone's going to take her seriously."

Virgil slipped his hand under her nightdress and she groaned with desire, smiling lasciviously.

"I don't think I'm on empty. Relax, babe. Bruno's going to kill Rebecca himself."

15

For Horne, the days straggled by, lapsing into something makeshift, time itself delinquent, nothing more than the stale interludes of a life on hold. Movies in the afternoons, bars late, were no antidote to his wayward existence. But sometimes an enemy turned out to be valuable as a test of character. Possibly in this property market, Rebecca was doing him a favor. ninety-nine Sycamore Place would be appreciating by the second. He, too, could be patient, wait for the moment, before firing a shot.

He hadn't laid eyes on the enigmatic "channeling" pianist for ten days. All the same, she had left her black mark on his psyche. He was mortified about having confessed such personal details to her. An easy rationalization came to him: she'd helped him terminate his undiagnosed nervous breakdown. But his indebtedness was grudging. From ambivalence towards her, he reverted to nature's laws, which dictated a cobra-mongoose bonding between landlord and tenant. This mistress of male manipulation would now be in for a battle.

To sustain hope, and pull his life together, he made a record number of calls to real estate agents. Nobody was terribly excited about listing a property for sale with only an apartment to rent. In Beverly Hills, no one cared about such small potatoes.

One real estate agent bit, a miracle of high-shiny plastic surgery that mirrored goitrous eyes and cherry-colored lipstick on her fangs. Donna Seymour arrived with the requisite saffron MB 500 convertible. She was a model of flamboyant coarseness and zipped through the apartment like a building inspector who'd inhaled too much old asbestos.

"You really should make your bed and empty the ashtrays."

He was defensive. "I had no idea you'd be here this quick."

"I move fast. Do you want month-to-month, furnished or un-; pets, smoking? Sub or no sub?"

"I was thinking furnished, a year lease. Pets're okay, so're smokers, but no sublet."

"I'd list it at forty-two hundred a month." She fiddled with her Palm Pilot. "Here, you're in luck. Nice couple with four children and two friendly Saint Bernards."

In innocence he asked, "Where're six people going to sleep?"

"Their problem," she snapped.

As she was about to drill her cell phone, he stopped her. "This has nothing to do with renting, but since you're an expert on Beverly Hills, could you help me out?" Her smile was more like a grimace, and stretched the unstretchable fabric of skin on her mouth. "Do you know someone by the name of Jack Leopold?"

"Who doesn't?" She made it sound like an accusation of feeble-mindedness.

"Well, who is he?"

"There's a fifty-story skyscraper on Wilshire with gold initials twelve feet high that says JL. The word "Development" is right underneath. Jack built maybe half the condos on the Wilshire Corridor. Tracts from Vegas to Europe. Roads, dams, hotels, hospitals. Jack and his pals are the most powerful real estate people in L.A. Let me be more accurate: I know *of* Jack Leopold; I haven't actually met him."

"Where does he live?"

"He has a fortress in Beverly Hills." She was astounded by Horne's innocence. "Believe me, he doesn't want you to sign him to rent your apartment."

"This Jack has a son who's a musician...plays with the symphony orchestra."

"So?"

"It's important to me."

She shrugged indifferently. "Maybe he does."

"About a year ago, his son was going to be married. And his fiancée was murdered by neo-Nazis. She was a musician from Vienna, a cellist."

Donna's gold bracelets and chains jangled, accompanying her shudder. "Yeah, I vaguely recall." She scrutinized Horne with something approaching alarm. "Mr. Horne, what has this got to do with renting your apartment?"

"Nothing and everything. You see, I'd really like to sell this duplex."

"Let me view the upstairs unit."

"We're talking five thousand square feet all told. Before I do that, what do you think it might go for?"

"Ballpark, two-million-two, as is. You've got a hundred percent location, walking distance to Beverly High and Rodeo Drive, no arterial traffic."

"My problem, Donna, if I may, is that I've got a sitting tenant."

"There's always a turd in the punchbowl."

"Exactly. Now in your lengthy experience of real estate, how do I get rid of this pest?"

"Honey-money, vermin thrive on it."

"If she refuses?

"You've got a problem. Rental laws are worse than the Constitution in Beverly Hills. No amendments. Lawyers, petitions, hearings before the City Council. Tenants' bill of rights. There is one way only to liberate yourself. If you have a relative, you can force the tenant to vacate so that the relative can move in. But believe me, it has to be a bona fide blood kin. A friendly ex-wife won't do. Get you and the relative DNA tests."

They both pondered the issue, and Donna's scheme machine went into overdrive. "How old is this lady?"

"Twenties."

"And is she employed?"

"She plays the piano, concerts."

"I'll bet. Sounds to me like it's outcalls. She could be a hooker and peddles dope, in which case we're in business. Install a video camera. You catch her sucking on a bong, with a john 'in flagrante,' and she's on the street with yesterday's news. See, especially after Madam Heidi, our local detectives live for these cases. They sell their life stories to some weasel publisher and wind up on *Geraldo*, yapping about dodging bullets and how they had to bring in the SWAT team to recover Trashy Lingerie panties and whips. ninety-nine Sycamore Place acquires cachet, notoriety—and we list at two-point-five mil."

Thank God he hadn't touched Rebecca. He had shown restraint, character...utter panic.

Horne wished that he could get a visa for one of the fierce Giriama hunters who killed their prey with arrows poisoned with *acokanthera*—no antidote—to terminate Rebecca's tenancy. Failing such an ally, the notion of a frame-up held a certain appeal.

"I thought that might hurt the sale."

"Darling, for every ass there's a seat. The buyers can brag to their friends that they bought a whorehouse. Empty lives need a conversation piece."

Under such a tutor, Horne was getting the hang of Beverly Hills, and found himself won over by this sales drummer. Donna Seymour, liquidator, left enough business cards for a Vegas convention.

16

Horne's identity had to be redefined within a divided universe of authorities: from his maxed-out credit cards to his invalid driver's license. In no mood to screw with the law, he sped from one state bureau to the other. Fortunately, the IRS was not on his ass. He had filed his returns annually at what had formerly been the embassy in Dar-es-Salaam.

Passport in hand, he was treated with the deference accorded the rich because of Haggerty's solid-gold endorsement at City National. Horne took out two thousand in cash. Bucks in his kick resulted in a merry mood swing, a Sprint cell phone, and a Dell laptop. After being extinguished by AM-EX earlier that morning, he was desperate for plastic. When the manager presented him with a new VISA with a $10,000 limit, he felt as flighty as a teenager.

A stroll through the clothing shops on Rodeo Drive convinced Horne that his liquidity wouldn't last till sundown if he bought anything there. He had always enjoyed the frenetic outdoor markets in Africa, but at the Beverly Center, he discovered he had a horror of malls. His reaction to crowds infected him with demophobia; people glided by, filling space, and he felt himself a witness to the dissolution of society, its commerce of base materials.

While walking home down Charleville, he asked a Mexican gardener, in reputable Spanish, where he had bought his jeans and work clothes. He was given a drenched map on graph paper directing him downtown.

He was more comfortable amid street stands, pushcarts, and small shops, and imagined he was walking, bargaining in Arusha in the dukas of merchants. Stuffing his big bags in the Lexus trunk, he cruised around.

Los Angeles remained an unrealized world to him, embalmed behind shop-façade coffins, the hidden imagery of addresses. Deprived of blood, long scattered, it possessed only the antagonism of a vampire territory in which modern-day sculptors were the plastic surgeons. Everyone he had encountered on his Rodeo Drive stroll had had something done, fixed, or had been about to, with savings or on credit cards. What had been the outdoors was now in harness, confined to malls.

He stopped at the Music Center, got out of the car, and found it deserted. Across the street, the Disney Concert Hall bloomed under gangs of riveters and metal specialists, giving life to a form that reminded him of something in Africa. Here was the primeval coast around Zanzibar, where the wind played tricks and gouged out the shapeless abnormality of temperamental storms. It was the unfinished genius of the Dark Ages.

Not a bad day. Horne felt like a debutante who had splurged—seven hundred in cash and fourteen on the plastic. He'd bought khakis, jeans, some decent trousers, denim shirts, a blazer—"The sport jacket has been made from the finest Tijuana cashmere"—and enough underwear to sport through decades.

He unloaded in the back driveway, his bags ballooning by the wind. Like a teenager, he couldn't wait to cut off the tags and head out to the Peninsula bar. He'd splurge for a drink in the hope of encountering a horny lady susceptible to safari tales. He'd mastered the technique of sneaking into the hotel's men's room, replenishing his drink from a flask—total cost for cocktails, twelve bucks including tip.

While he fumbled with his key, Rebecca zoomed in on her bike and parked it.

"If you give me the keys, I'll help Madam inside," she said, wearing a tight red valet parking jacket, mashing her jumbo breasts.

"My GYN said I can carry light packages now, but thank you, sir.—Oh, hi, it's you, Rebecca. I thought you were some guy trying to pick me up. I like your ensemble."

"When I'm not playing at a charity event, I work as a valet."

"Yeah, without formerly rich aunts around, we all have problems hacking it."

"It's for our airline tickets," she informed him earnestly. "I've been working twelve-hour shifts. I wouldn't expect you to pay."

She had him on the ropes again. "Airline tickets? Did I miss something? Are they for our honeymoon? I must've forgotten."

"I'm a foreigner, but I don't think Milwaukee is a honeymoon destination."

"Milwaukee. Well, it's German. Home away from home for you."

He was struck by a brilliant idea. Maybe she had overstayed her visa. He'd report her to the INS. She'd be deported, returned in leg irons, or, at the very least, handcuffed.

Seized by pure inspiration, he went with his rush. "As the owner, I don't have to tell you...but I thought I would. Since you have your religious music group, I thought I'd put together a kind of outreach-support group for sex offenders and crack addicts."

"Just try it," she countered, "and you'll be seeing more of Mr. Haggerty than you ever imagined—from your Beverly Hills cell."

She had him by the balls. "It was just a joke."

She ignored him and went inside *his* apartment. She busied herself, laying out his new wardrobe on the kitchen table.

"Ah, the scissors. I know where Rose's sewing basket is—unless you moved it." She glared at the caked plates in the sink. "The dishwasher works. I checked it."

"I don't like the sound it makes."

"You're a man of great sensitivity. Flies don't bother you?"

"I can't sleep without them buzzing." Horne, rabid, dashed into the bedroom and searched through unpacked suitcases, finally plucking his skinning knife from its sheath. He returned to the kitchen, armed. He realized it was a bad move.

BEVERLY HILLS LANDLORD THREATENS TENANT
WITH SKINNING KNIFE AFTER MURDER TRIAL

This would certainly make the TV news.

Rebecca was snipping away plastic tags with diminutive nostril-hair scissors, the dishwasher was churning out its version of rap, and she was as intent as a surgeon. "These work best." She looked up at the knife with interest. "Maybe I can borrow that when I find these Nazis—or they find me."

He could see how serious she was. "Not a good idea."

She held up a shantung, cocoa-colored jacket. "You'll look like our local weather-forecaster with this." She shook her head. "Your clothes are...a retreat from fashion."

"I damn well like them. Nerve you've got—"

"Your doorbell's ringing."

"I'd like you to leave."

"Why? You having a dinner party with cold pastrami, corned beef, salami.... All this smoked meat is death."

"I'll have Glück in for a blind tasting and ask his advice." He was getting more pissed off by the moment. "And by the way, if you haven't had a deli sandwich on rye bread with Gulden's mustard for twelve years, you can lose your sanity. Now please...."—This time the chimes were worthy of a cathedral—"go find a double-parked car and move it."

Having discovered he was living in a lawless enclave, Horne answered the door with a .45 by his side. The most dangerous game around, as far as he was concerned, was in his kitchen. He looked through the spyhole, quickly slipped on the safety, and stashed the gun in the umbrella stand.

As soon as he opened the door, Ingrid's arms swept around his neck and wet kisses depressed his cheeks. The tawny mixture of her suede outfit commingled with the scent of Bandit. The safari guide and expert on scents had last whiffed this on a French divorcée in Arusha who'd spent him four times the night before they'd arrived at a photo op.

Butch's spitfire said, "This is my dear friend, Taylor Anne."

A sapphire-eyed, twentyish blonde with serpentine curves and arches supported by black boots with platformed heels as attenuated as knitting needles smiled at him.

"Hi, darlin'," she said.

"Butch asked me to drop by to check on how you were doing. And look, Horne, I've brought prime steaks."

Ingrid thrust the package on him. His reaction time had slowed to a turtle crawl in this hemisphere. The women were already sitting on the opposing sofas in front of the fireplace, waiting for him.

"You really should make your bed and empty the ashtrays," Rebecca's voice roiled from the kitchen.

"May I use the restroom?" Taylor asked.

"Sure, down the hall." As she tip-tapped down the wooden floors, Horne explained to Ingrid, "My cleaning lady is very bossy."

Ingrid's jaded smile was a welcome relief. "I'll bet." She exuded the warmth of an old hand in gender politics. He could see how Butch had become besotted with this mid-thirties pro. "Look, my friend, Taylor is looking for a special someone. Believe me, she's a treat, and she'll kickstart you."

"That sounds very appealing, Ingrid. I didn't mean to be rude the night we met. Butch got me sore."

"He has that effect on most people. But I love him." Her voice dropped in register. "Invite Taylor to stay for dinner and I'll leave after a while...."

Rebecca, sweater sleeves rolled up, was jamming her insured hands into red-rubber murderer's gloves. She inspected his guest with suspicion.

"Oh, excuse me, I didn't know you had a visitor," she said, taking the steaks from Horne and darting away before he could toss her out.

"The tenant?" Ingrid asked.

"That's her, and I can't get rid of her."

"Wow, she's a beauty. That hair color's natural, too," Ingrid declared. "If you'd like Taylor for another evening or to stay and frolic with you and your tenant, I'm sure she could be persuaded."

Mystified, he tried to read some clue on the restaurateur's face. "Sorry. Oh, I appreciate the steaks and your stopping by. Don't get me wrong."

Ingrid winked, guy-to-guy. "Well, you didn't join us the first night, and Butch feels terrible. He wanted to give you a surprise welcome-home present."

"Forgive me, Ingrid. I've been away in Africa for too long. I don't get it."

As though an accomplice in planning a crime, she whispered, "I had to see my meat wholesaler and hooked up with Taylor, but I called Butch first, naturally. He's worried about you. He thinks you need some friends. Taylor can stay as long as you like. Don't save your bodily fluids for the best."

"That sounds like Butch."

"Yes, thank the Lord."

Warily checking the tongue and grooves of the planked, ancient wooden floor to avoid snapping her ankle off in the spiked boots, Taylor reappeared, beaming at him.

Horne went to the liquor cabinet. His day was wavily improving.

"Get you ladies a drink?"

"Sure," Taylor said, "Vodka on the rocks. Piece of lemon if you've got one."

Rebecca's voice carried from another room. Her hearing would be a welcome addition to CIA snoops. "Ice cubes and lemon coming up."

The thought of steak, sex, and his new wardrobe had a miraculous, almost chemical, effect on his frame of mind. But like one of Hals' tavern wenches, Rebecca, glowering, invaded the cocktail hour, bearing Rose's silver tray laden with a bucket of ice cubes and Schweppes mixes.

"I've left the filets out. They should be cooked at room temperature," Rebecca said.

"Good girl," Ingrid agreed. "Steaks right out of the fridge shrink and get tough."

Taylor turned her lavish smile on Horne. "I'll grill the steaks for *our* dinner if you like."

Horne made grumpy introductions. Rebecca removed her gloves and before he knew it, had insinuated herself into the group. Horne found himself making drinks for the four of them. The women seemed, to his alarm, to be getting along well.

"White wine for me, please, Horne," Rebecca said. "There's a friendly Chablis I bought for your homecoming. Chilled glasses in the freezer."

A bemused, nervous voyeur at his own theoretical orgy, Horne did not know if there were a scientific phrase for his male condition. He simply felt there was no latitude left in the storm center of his lust. The prospect of a ménage with Taylor and Rebecca seemed as likely as life on Mars. Taylor was bagged game, Rebecca still undercover in the veldt.

The pianist was holding forth. He picked up a trail mix of her gabbing. "...I'm doing what I can to help him through a psychologically difficult period of adjustment, Taylor. Being imprisoned on a murder charge in Tanzania took a terrible toll on his nerves...."

"I didn't know that," Taylor responded, on edge.

Horne's .45 fell out of the umbrella furl and clanged ominously on the floor. The three women stared at it. Horne stooped to pick it up, and jammed it into his belt.

"Horne beat the murder charge," Ingrid advised her. "Taylor, he's cool."

Rebecca stood up. "Can I get you ladies anything else before I vacuum?" she graciously inquired.

"No, thanks a lot." Taylor anxiously signaled Ingrid. "We ought to try to beat the rush hour traffic to the Valley." She gave Horne a worried smile. "Lovely meeting you."

"Another time," he said, wallowing in grief.

Considerate in farewell, Rebecca escorted the ladies outside. Horne stood at the doorway, crazed with frustration, watching Ingrid's car pull away.

"Will it bother you if I vacuum?" The fierce look in his eyes made her reconsider. "Maybe you should have a little nap. Shopping can be so exhausting," Rebecca said, her mocking grated on his nerves.

Fists clenched, he bellowed, "Get out!" He slammed the door in her face. His deep bass sounded to him like a male monkey's pre-coital anxiety.

At six o'clock, overwrought, and unable to find the promised land of macho release from the barking announcers on *Monday Night Football*, Horne rushed to the kitchen in a panic. He had microwaved the pastrami to a languishing death.

17

Jack and Paula Leopold were allergic to scandal. It brought them out in social hives. Scott was out of drug rehab, once again healthy, and seriously involved with a Midwestern JC teacher who wore comfy twin sets and Laura Ashley. The last thing Jack needed was the re-entry of Nazis into his life and business.

Miriam was gone. Certainly no one in their rarefied financial circles ever offered a commiserative reminder of her. With a colossal deal tiptoeing in his direction, Jack had cast aside all thoughts of the Benjamin family and their tainted history. It was with reluctance that he had agreed to see Douglas Horne.

Horne trekked through glassed-in bunkers, bulging with secretaries and personal assistants, ultimately arriving in an office containing grotesque wire sculptures. Congeries of priceless, madcap, comic-book compositions layered the vast walls. The lacquered conference table and chairs gleamed so brightly that his eyes smarted.

Horne had played the intrepid younger brother to many men like Leopold, but never in *their* dens. Jack Leopold stopped chewing and arose from behind an antique walnut desk with cabriole legs and lion-paw feet.

"I sneak a hard salami sandwich once a month."

"Everything that tastes any good is forbidden," Horne said.

"With my cholesterol, it is."

"Mr. Leopold, I really appreciate...."

"Let's start with Jack—no sirs, okay, Doug?"

"Fine with me."

"I play poker with the cunning, renowned Tommy Haggerty. Golf sometimes. He gets me into the L.A. Country Club. It's not for Jews. I take him to Hillcrest. So, naturally, when he called me about you and said you didn't want money or a job, I was looking forward to meeting you." He looked longingly at a pickle but decided to push the plate away. "Over the years, he's mentioned you. In fact, I saw the photos of the two of you on safari. Want a drink?"

"No, thanks."

"Now, how can I be of help?"

Horne had reached the top and his view contained feeble spindles of a liverish sun prying through dusky clouds that had the density of coffee-shop gravy slopping over a plate. He missed the African whorls of havoc and the primitive, sincere art of natives.

"I'll get right to the point. Rebecca Benjamin is holding a gun to my head."

Jack Leopold always negotiated his version of the truth. Facts, actuality, were editorial problems that he seldom observed. At his level in society, indiscretion was simply not tolerated.

"That and playing the piano are her God-given skills."

Horne liked his tone of disapproval. "I've met some strange people. But she's the queen."

"Rebecca is what we Jews call a *meshuggunah*...obsessed with her sister's murder. She tried to hire *the* Thomas Haggerty—your friend and mine—to sue *me* for withholding evidence! Can you believe that? After I spent close to half a million dollars to find Miriam's killer! I shut down my office and all my jobs and paid people to fly in to help, until the cops found Miriam's body."

Afterwards, there had been private detectives on call; his specialist, Frank Salica, had employed many others.

"My architect friend, Harry Summerfield...."

"...Yeah, I met him."

"Harry offered to lend Rebecca his Gulfstream to fly anywhere in the country to interview people." Jack Leopold was just limbering up. "Rebecca stole files from my guy Frank. He paid to have them *stolen* from the LAPD. Two cops got busted and work in a gun shop in the Valley now. I paid their legal fees when Internal Affairs investigated them because of the missing files. You have no idea the trouble Rebecca's caused."

Demoralized, Horne made a plea. "Please, please, you're a property authority, or whatever the correct term is for what you do. Tell me how to deal with this?"

Jack Leopold had not acquired his fortune through chance, but by brilliant, imaginative stratagems. The lightbulb in his brain illuminated Horne's predicament.

"She wants you to go with her to Milwaukee. Go, do it. If she doesn't sign off on a quitclaim after that, take her on a tour special in Africa. People die on safari, get attacked by animals, shot accidentally hunting tigers or whatever you shoot there?" Horne was not about to correct the mogul for such an egregious error in the category of animal habitation. "A mysterious disappearance, say. Untraceable pygmy poison. A vine strangulation?"

"Happens all the time," Horne agreed with a faint laugh. "You're a treasury of homicidal ideas." In despair, he went on. "Miriam's murder was brutal."

Confronted by reality, Jack Leopold's bloodthirsty cheerfulness vanished. "Yes. Miriam was a sweetheart and we all loved her."

"What about this Grandma Lilli, and the housekeeper who lived with Rebecca in Vienna?"

Jack Leopold's genius for deception lay in its apparent objectivity, but his anger ruled in this case. "They're wonderful, cultured people. But they have something of a problem."

"Would it help me boot Rebecca out?" Horne asked in a beseeching voice. "Is it serious?"

"If you're a Jew who lost family in the Holocaust—as I am—*yes*! Lilli Benjamin was married to a top-ranking Nazi and used to entertain Hitler and play the piano for him and his animals." Horne was blown away. "To me, that's a little more than an error of omission when the subject of Nazis comes up. Rather than shoot her, my wife Paula and I threw Rebecca out of the house."

"Rebecca forgot to mention that."

"Would you?" Jack snarled. "That's not exactly a merit badge in the Jewish community."

"Or in my circles either, Jack."

"I haven't even told my closest friend about it. I'm too ashamed."

Horne was befuddled. "Then why me?"

"She's a troublemaker, as you now know. We'd like to see the back of her."

"Let's swear eternal friendship."

"Keep it to yourself."

"For sure," Horne promised.

"Anything we can do to help get rid of her, we're for."

"I really appreciate this, Jack."

"Keep in touch and let me know how you make out."

They cordially shook hands.

18

With all avenues of action or reaction hopelessly nebulous, Horne returned to the cul-de-sac of his life in Sycamore Place. He balanced his checkbook: eight thousand dollars at City National; eighty-five hundred gathering moss with VISA. That he was temporarily secure offered little solace. The somber grayness of terminal February in Beverly Hills had its counterpart in the elderly, round-shouldered men, forsaken by children and divorced wives, coaxing their dogs to spend a penny under the great trees while the wind rifled through the playing fields of the nearby Beverly Hills High School.

Chewing a TUMS, Horne found it hard to reconcile the vagaries of diet: he'd eaten monkey stew napped with simmering spiders during a hunt in Gabon. Several weeks back in zip code 90212, and he was choking on tuna salad on whole wheat bread at the Brighton Coffee Shop. Thanks to Rebecca.

He was at a loss as to how to flush her out. He could not move forward; his plans for the future were beached, merely the idle prison dream of owning a fishing charter boat. The scent of waning lavender did not encourage him to make his bed. This was not a consequence of depression, but some inflexible attribute that chained him to adolescence, a defiant sandbag moored against the tidy *hausfrau*'s domination. He found himself in an abyss and wondered if he'd ever see the promised horizon that gave human beings faith. He realized he was not cut out for civilization.

Horne's more tangible crisis appeared in the shower. Once the owner of a redwood, he now suffered from a condition hunters at The Norfolk Hotel bar in Nairobi referred to as Limpus Dictus, when discussing their memorable seductions while lions slept in their dens.

After refilling his bar flask with vodka and preparing for another plate of free nuts and rejections at the Peninsula Hotel—"You're such an angry man!" tolled in his ears from one of these encounters—he found himself toying with an embryonic idea.

Overhead, *The Tenant* pounded away on the piano. With his rage scale increasing and decreasing based on the use of her pedal, the brainchild emerged.

A THIRTY SHRIMP RED LOBSTER TV special was just the ticket to slay the dragon.

Mooches never said no to a free dinner. Carving the menu with a dinner—no sides or salads for two—and he might escape under $40. He would avoid any mention of Nazis and her family's connection to Hitler. He had no interest in yesterday's news, true or false.

Just to be *au courant* with her bizarre mission, he checked the weather reports in Milwaukee on his new laptop. Everyone's asses freezing, their lips falling off in beer steins. Snow plows with salt and gravel hissing would be hoisting berms two stories highs. He knew nothing about the city, except for the fact that Milwaukee happened to be another word for the Arctic.

Naturally, Rebecca accepted his dinner proposal. The Mamba Room wouldn't be busy and she could have a night off parking the crack-fumed Bentleys of gangsta rappers. In absentia, Horne reviled her, but sitting beside him in Rose's Lexus war-horse, Rebecca was a lustrous vision of femininity. She skillfully employed this artifice. Her apparent submissiveness didn't fool him for a minute. She could strike instantly.

They approached the Red Lobster when Horne had another brainstorm! Why pay for dinner when he could be a house guest at The Viking? He'd improve his tipping, having recently learned that 10 percent minus tax was an insult even at Denny's.

"I know you enjoy wine, and they have really rare vintages." He'd let the cowardly Butch settle. "And from what I hear the steaks are the best in L.A."

"So, *auf wiedersehen* to thirty shrimp."

"Don't be too hasty. I'm sure they have jumbos on the menu there."

"I'll be the Judge of that!"

"I know you're not a veggie."

"Correct."

At her direction, as though he were an immigrant, Horne took several brazen shortcuts through Hollywood to the Valley. She put something gabby on the radio called NPR but then switched to K-Mozart, closed her eyes, and suppressed conversation.

At eight-thirty, they rolled onto The Viking lot. Two Turks in slickers and umbrellas grabbed the doors.

"It's three dollars to park!" she exclaimed.

"It's steep. But...I don't think they allow self-parking even for members of the valet union."

"Money's tight with you, and it's my fault."

Horne's downcast eyes seemed to be having an effect on her. Like a running back reversing field, he had come up with a seam in the line and went for a big gain. His tactical vulnerability was getting to her, finally.

"I don't know what to do. Being so broke—a deadbeat—at my age is humiliating."

He took the parking ticket and tucked his arm under hers. Rebecca declared a brief truce and leaned her head on his shoulder. At the appearance of umbrellas, she dismissed the valet.

"Don't bother, we won't melt." When Horne opened the door, she whispered, "That's another tip I saved you."

"Everything helps...Hey, the hell with it. We're having a night out, so let's go for it."

The Viking's pandemonium absorbed them, churning their bodies through a jostling herd of drinkers and tipsy laughter. Approaching them was the sergeant-at-arms whose steroid biceps had the girth of Cape buffalo thighs.

"Do you have a reservation?"

Horne brought out his ace. "Butch Wylie."

"He's at the bar. Come through."

The crowd was swarming, emitting vapors of scented sweat. In a roped-off corner, the fire-insurance investigator was describing to a band of regulars his heroic underwater mine-demolitions at Haiphong Harbor during his Vietnam tour. Most of it true. Butch knew more about guns and munitions than anyone, and could blow up hell.

"Rebecca Benjamin, Butch Wylie."

Eyes lingering on Rebecca's assets, Butch lumbered off his captain's stool.

"Ah, the world-famous tenant."

"Yes, that's me. America's international guest," Rebecca replied.

Horne submitted to Butch's whisky hug, and peered at platters of food being served.

"I'm starved. Do we dance for our dinner? Or get house steaks?"

"Naturally, Doug. At my private table."

"That's very generous of you," Rebecca noted, at her most ingratiating. "I'm eager to see your vintage wine list."

"Order anything," Butch said.

He introduced them to two staff from his gun store—buzz-cut Latinos in their thirties, with cops' treacherous eyes.

"Horne, shall I hang up our coats?" Rebecca asked sweetly.

"Uh, yes, thanks."

Butch gaped at Rebecca when she walked over to the clothes hooks at the end of the bar.

"You were going to harm this woman, Dougie?" he whispered. "She's worth a stroke—a fatal heart attack."

Horne was livid. "What's with you? You've got nothing but pussy on the brain. And what was the idea of sending over this Taylor?"

"Strictly Ingrid's. Taylor was on the recoil. She'd been poking some rich property guy who bounced her, and Ingrid thought she'd play matchmaker with you and her. Forget her and concentrate on Rebecca. She ever walks into the Playboy Mansion, all Hef's girls'd run for cover."

"Look, Haggerty told me to keep my hands off Rebecca."

Butch rolled his eyes. "My sympathies. It's a sad fucking day in a man's life when he has to ask an old lawyer if he can drop his pants."

"She's blackmailing me."

"Poor dear. If she gets tired of blackmailing you, give her my card."

Draping her jacket on her shoulders, Rebecca narrowed her eyes. It had been some time since she had encountered crowds this large.

"The steaks look good" she said, amiably.

"They are. Let me escort you to my table—in the Valhalla Room." As though leading her into the White House dining room, Butch escorted her like royalty and Horne trailed them.

Genuinely pleased to see Rebecca, Ingrid brushed through the mob. She had been told by Butch about the murder of her sister and remembered the media coverage.

"Rebecca, welcome. I'm so glad Horne gave you the evening off."

"I'm very tough on the help," he declared, resigned to his fate as the despicable property owner.

The Valhalla Room was filled with tables and thirty-odd stools. A horseshoe bar displayed "Reserved" plaques for a fifteen-buck minimum.

On a raised platform stood a piano; a buzzing green neon light announced:

SAL ENDURO, PIANO STYLIST

"Mr. Velvet Fingers packs them in," Ingrid said.

Defeated by his estrangement from culture, Horne dug himself a deeper hole. "On Wednesday nights in the rain?"

"Wednesday in the Valley is equivalent to a Saturday night in Paris."

"I can't wait to hear him." He had lost sight of Rebecca for the moment. But then her presence became obvious when a piano test intruded.

"A Yamaha," she burst out, "is so brassy, and the 'E' is a bit flat. But it would work for serial music. Alban Berg would have loved it."

"No one is permitted to touch the maestro's keyboard," Ingrid informed Horne.

"Rebecca!"

"Just checking." She darted off the stage, beaming at Ingrid. "What does Maestro Enduro play on this?"

"Jazz!"

"I love it."

Ingrid signaled a waiter to take their order quickly and rejoined the music lovers getting their wrists stamped outside the chained entry.

19

Nothing went seriously wrong with the whopping shrimp cocktail, sauce on the side, or the eighty-five-dollar-bottle of Meursault, which the waiter couldn't pronounce. As the room filled up with well-dressed diners and piano-bar drifters, Rebecca suggested that the service was too hurried to suit her. As a lady, she naturally advised Horne to inform the waiter before borrowing his flashlight so that Horne could read the files she had brought along. This wasn't a safari where the privileged stretched dinners into a timeless universe of gab.

"How long do you usually spend when someone takes you to dinner in Vienna?"

"It depends on the quality of the conversation. Three, maybe four hours, if Armagnac or digestifs are brought to the table. Sometimes a fine grappa to settle the stomach."

"I see." Aimlessly shuffling through her dossier, Horne decided to assert the bill of dating rights. "Couldn't we just have one easy night—fun—and put the investigation and your tenancy status on hold?"

"You're right. But there's one document at the bottom that's of special interest to you."

He burrowed through the dog-eared pages—then emitted a sound that resonated with some familiarity. Specifically, it was the noise he had made in the distant past when he'd reached orgasm. The probability of improved financial conditions inspired a certain fondness for this lost soul.

"A quitclaim!" This document he scrutinized with pleasure. It even had Haggerty's firm's name on it. "Forget the red wine. Let's go for champagne. I really misjudged you. I hope you won't hold it against me."

"No, naturally not. We'll do this another time?"

"Is later tonight...tomorrow, too soon?"

"We'll have to go through the itinerary first, make airline reservations, you know...sort things out."

"What do I have to look forward to after Milwaukee, or is that the high point?"

"Borough Park, Palm Beach, after that."

"Borough Park? Where's *that*?"

World traveler that he was, he was embarrassed to admit that his excursions in America had excluded New York. She continued like an eager travel agent hitting the high spots. "Borough Park is a Hasidic community in Brooklyn."

He was unsure of the meaning, "My excitement is mounting. Sounds great! I could use some sun."

"You won't find it in New York in February. But you'll fit in fine with your beard."

"Is there a special dress code?"

She ignored his scoffing. But there was a melancholy conviction about her that emerged as domineering. He was briefly reassured when she notified him that after their tri-city excursion she would sign the quitclaim. He ordered the champagne and picked a two-hundred-and-fifty-dollar '90 Krug. Screw it; he wouldn't pay even if Ingrid held a gun to his head. Butch had offered to pick up the tab, let him eat it, Horne thought.

"If you're not working tomorrow, suppose we spend the day working this out. I have a few travel suggestions."

"We're on a budget, Horne."

"It doesn't concern that. We have to plan this carefully. Kind of like you were in my care in Africa and I was leading a party into the bush."

She kissed his hand, and he again wondered how he could survive her impulsive advances, the mixed signals of approach-avoidance.

"I knew I could count on you."

They drank the Krug in leisurely fashion. And when the trencherman platters arrived, she matched him bite for bite, with a perfectly charred sixteen-ounce New York strip. Dessert had to wait; Ingrid took the stage to inform the patrons there would be no service during the performance.

"The Viking takes great pleasure in welcoming back 'The Merlin of the Keyboards,' Maestro Sal Enduro."

Salvos of applause broke out. A plump, elderly man took the stage. When he smiled, his halogen-bright caps were about the size of the ivories he was about to tinkle.

Butch slid in next to them and provided the minstrel's pedigree. "Twelve years at Skinny D'Amato's famous old 500 Club in Atlantic City. From here he goes to Vegas. Plays here a few times a year. The other people Ingrid books aren't in his class."

It seemed Sal had been assigned to accompany Ol' Blue's Eyes when his regular pianist had forgotten the music to "Nancy With the Laughing Eyes." Butch elaborated, "Sal will join us after the first set. You'll hear unprintable stuff about Sinatra's fabled sex life."

In a guttural drone over the piano mike, Sal claimed the spotlight. "Pleasure to back here...at...? Only kidding.... The unforgettable Viking. Best steak and drinks in town. I'm starting off with my Lady Ingrid's favorite song: 'Autumn in New York.' What else would anyone living in North Hollywood want, huh?"

Right hand rising up through air with the grandiose flair of an impending crescendo, the pianist crawled through the standard banalities of the jazz repertoire, from a lisping "Laura" to a mawkish "The Shadow of Your Smile." After some violence committed against Gershwin, a half-hour became an eternity for Rebecca before he concluded with "My Foolish Heart." All of these chummy tunes were creatively distorted by his ponderous improvisation and unremitting humming.

Ingrid gleefully joined the table with a bottle of Jack Daniel's, Sinatra's preferred booze, and also Sal's.

"Now that's a pianist," Ingrid observed, daring Rebecca to challenge her.

"Considering all the painful bad notes, he managed to carry a melody line without any inflection or tone color, but it's too late for him to learn anything about technique no matter how long he studies," the music critic remarked. "He may have arthritis in his right hand."

Butch was mute. Horne closed his eyes but was too big to duck under the table. Ingrid's hand roved over to a massive, serrated steak knife, but Butch beat her to it.

"Be sure to tell him, honey," Ingrid said, her sympathy for Rebecca waning.

Violence was only averted by Sal's eagerness to reach the Jack Daniel's at the table. He was upon them, Ingrid pouring four fingers neat for him.

"Nice to meet you people," Sal said with professional affability. He winked at Rebecca. "Hey, there, Big Red—Butch mentioned you play a little piano yourself."

"Yes," Rebecca replied. "Would you like me to show you how it's supposed to be done?"

No sorehead, he belted back his drink and nodded with a sagacious smirk. "Oh, sure, please, coach."

Service was in full, rapid progress, names and phone numbers busily being scribbled on damp cocktail napkins, sexual pairings and drug bartering in progress in various nooks and crannies. Rebecca observed the motley congregation, limbered her hands, stretched, rotated her shoulders, and drew some interest from the bar outlaws homing in on her while she adjusted the bench to accommodate her height.

With serenity, she began to play *exactly* the tunes that Sal had rendered. All at once, the Yamaha gave birth to lungs and the wooing activities hushed. The room fell silent as she brought a deep color and vibrating power to these standards, with such flawless technique that the audience was soon gasping. The same music they had heard before now had a voice.

When she finished, even Ingrid sat humbled. Rebecca came through the crowd, courteous but aloof. At the table, she wiped her forehead with a napkin and nodded graciously at the owner.

Sal perked up, "I could listen to you for the rest of my life."

"Thank you. You're very kind. I didn't mean to be rude to you. But, you see, the world I came from was so intensely competitive that no one ever had a generous thing to say about performance."

"I understand," he said. "I was never in that loop. But tell me, young lady, how did you learn all the songs I played?"

"You played them, I heard them, the rest is magic."

"You have absolute pitch." He filled his glass. "I'm up." With reverence, he added, "You're a helluva act to follow."

Ingrid reassured him. "Oh, Sal, you're a legend, they love you here."

The moment Sal reached the stage, Ingrid, the shrewd business-woman, got down the nitty-gritty. "Rebecca, how many nights a week are you free?"

Rebecca laid her head on Horne's shoulder. "You can talk to my manager. We're going on a short trip, right, Horne?"

Glumly, he said, "A week—no longer."

Ingrid at her most obsequious made a further inquiry. "Do you also sing a little?"

Rebecca's eyebrows arched in supercilious astonishment. "Does Pavarotti dance?" the diva thundered in return.

Horne felt no guilt dodging the check, and tipped the waiter twenty-five dollars without a twinge in his bones. He had brought a solid act for his beef and booze. His new client had performed.

"Thanks. A free dinner and a new job. How much did Ingrid finally say she'd pay?"

"Two hundred a night plus tips."

"That's real music. The big glass bowl on the piano fills up" faster than valet parking."

"You bring me luck," she said, hugging him.

"I have expensive habits. You can keep me."

"I intend to. Oh, by the way, how much do I pay in commission?"

Horne would quibble with the sentiment that virtue was its own reward. In the darkness, he stood cloistered with Rebecca in the doorway of Sycamore Place to avoid the burrs of the wind beating against the leafless branches. From the street, they were out of view. A hefty woman was walking the bleating dachshund for its nightly, timid shit. A bit late, he thought.

"How about an Irish coffee?" she asked.

He had seldom refused such invitations. "I've got a lot to do tomorrow." This, between a doorway hug. "I want to be alert. Even more important, you have to be on point."

"I suppose you're right." She dropped her arms from his neck. "Oh, I better call the Python Room back. I'm supposed to interview there, and they have colossal tippers."

"Are all your dives named after vipers?"

"That's the way they attract their clientele." She handed him the thick accordion file. "Your bedtime reading."

She nestled close and forced a kiss on him. He pulled away before anything got started. He had been warned by two of the smartest men in Los Angeles to keep her at a distance, and he hadn't forgotten his stay in prison.

"Please, Ms. Benjamin, what will the neighbors think? My reputation...."

His reaction amazed her. It had never happened to her before.

"Bastard. Good night."

He waited for her to lock the door, then peered across the street as the woman with the dach headed off.

Once in her nightgown and about to brush her teeth, Rebecca stared at herself in the mirror, then smiled at her own reflection. She had been deeply aroused, and the sensation had a raw urgency. Her sexual desire, quiescent for such a long period, had swooped down like a bird of prey and seized her. There would be no sidestepping this and flitting away—her usual policy. Previous affairs had been nothing more than satisfying her appetite, a convenience, rash self-indulgence. They had never led to a genuine emotional involvement. As her eyes closed, Horne's face skittered through her imagination.

"Horne, I'm ready," she murmured to herself.

20

At noon the next day, Horne knocked on the French windows, since the doorbell he'd repeatedly pressed was drowned out by the piano. He took out his key and unlocked the door. Rebecca's eyes were closed. She tilted her head back without turning from her practice session. He and the cat arched their backs at each other. He leaned over behind her and glanced at her music score. She was limbering up with a rash called Scriabin, which he didn't like and thought, what else could this be called?

"That should pack them in at The Viking."

"Go!" she commanded. "There's coffee in the kitchen."

Shortly after, the music stopped. Rebecca came in, startled, and sprang back.

"Oh, what happened? My God, is this you?"

He had shaved his beard and moustache and sprung for a non-90210 haircut. "Yeah, the new, old me."

She touched his cheeks without familiarity and he was uncertain if her attitude contained scorn or approval. Possibly both. And in a way it would be better for both of them, he reflected, if she kept her distance.

"You're so much *younger*."

"I'll carry ID in case I get carded."

Her eyes bulged with gloom. "That haircut.... Did you find a pet shop?"

"You're so rude. It was a place called Fantastic Sam's in Culver City. It cost twelve ninety-five dollars. My tracker used to do it for a buck."

She smirked. "If it ever grows back, I'll do it free."

"Thanks, but no. Now look, I've got a lot to talk to you about, Rebecca. I was up very early and I did my homework. I'm treating this as if it were a big-game safari. I've tried to prepare for reasonable problems. But there's always the unknown."

Rebecca was surprised by his resolve. "Ah, I love my tour guide. Horne, will you bring your guns?"

"What? My *guns*? No! Now, listen to me for once."

In the living room, Horne sat at her Hapsburg desk reviewing three unsolved murder cases and her summaries.

He sipped his coffee. "You think someone's following you?"

"Yes."

"Well, Rebecca, you're not one of those silent complainers. I've read your files and you've stirred the pot. These Nazi groups are fanatical."

She nodded. "They're all around us in Europe...and now you know they're here."

"They certainly are." After the evening during which she had forced him to reconstruct the killing of Hendrik Stovart, he expected her to have visions about everything. "Do you imagine or see anyone threatening you in your...your...states?"

"These aren't *states*," she said, honestly. "I have *events*. Sometimes the longer ones are actual *visitations*. They never involve living people." Her eyes roved around the room. "I'm an intruder in their darkness."

He did not want to alarm her. In Rose's living room, he had found a hole drilled in the corner of the ceiling where it joined the molding. It was directly under Rebecca's quaint telephone table, which had a seat, and he guessed Europeans usually possessed a single phone and indulged in long conversations. He had decided not to fill the hole below. He guessed that the burglar Rebecca had mentioned when he had first arrived had done this. There hadn't been a robbery; a voyeur would have selected her bedroom and probably have known that the bathroom upstairs had a tile floor.

"Who was this Magnus Von Winter?" he asked

"A Nazi mass murderer who escaped from Germany."

Horne shook his head. "I never heard of him."

"Nor has anyone else."

"You claim he was Hitler's friend?"

"Von Winter was more than that. He was Hitler's shadow...his guide, actually."

"He must be ancient—if he's still alive."

"He's eternal, the embodiment of evil. He's passed on his hatred to his son Bruno."

"So Magnus has a son. You actually believe this old man is still alive?"

"I'm sure he is."

Horne was puzzled by her conviction. "How you can be?"

She refused to betray Lilli's relationship. "Herta saw him in Vienna."

"What's her connection?"

A vague tremble told him Rebecca was at the site of a lie. "Herta—she's more an aunt than an employee—knew him."

"And Lilli recognized him? Sorry, I meant Herta."

Rebecca's silence was an obvious clue to sidestep this. She had revealed compassion when he had relived his own nightmare, and he didn't want to rattle her about her grandmother's connections to Nazis or, as Leopold had told him, her marriage to one.

"The point of our trip is to meet the relatives who've had women family members murdered. The murders of these people corresponded with Miriam's. They won't talk to me. When I called last year they were unnerved."

"You can't blame them."

He knew she was withholding information. Horne always carefully checked his party's kit—their guns, first aid—before going out with them in Africa. An unknown territory required even more preparation and vigilance.

"Okay, so we have a former fiancé in Milwaukee; the mother of a woman in Borough Park; and a couple in Palm Beach who also lost their daughter. The victims were all about to get married."

"Yes, Horne. They were about to become Jewish brides."

"Maybe it's a coincidence."

"It's not. Your aunt said to me, 'Doug never gives up. He's the most relentless man on the face of the earth.' I'm like you."

"You don't have to stroke me, Rebecca. Just be truthful. Look, after the local homicide and FBI quit on Miriam, the private detective Leopold used seems to have been thorough."

She was infuriated. "All Frank Salica did was bribe computer clerks at Parker Center and screw the yoga freak at the Leopold house."

"How'd you get your hands on these files?"

"Frank gave them to me."

"This is sensitive stuff. Didn't he and the cops want them back?"

"I'd rather not to go into this. Jack and I are not friends."

She returned to the kitchen and brought in a fresh pot of Viennese coffee. She also laid down a stack of bills. "I have thirty-eight hundred dollars for our trip."

"I'll pay my own way."

"No, Horne, that's not right. I've pressured you into this and I have to pay."

"Suppose we table the financial arrangements for the moment, Rebecca."

She yielded with reluctance. He had delicate matters to raise and there was no way of avoiding them.

"Miriam and the three other women weren't raped. Isn't that odd?"

"That's a *crucial* clue. The murders of these women echo my sister's. The killer was obeying the Nuremberg Laws."

He was lost again and searched her face for some explanation. "What are they?"

"No Aryan could have sexual relations with anyone who was Jewish. The Nazis executed people who were guilty of this...*crime*. But of course there were those, like Von Winter, who were above the law. They believed they were acting on some higher authority. They and their *Einsatzgruppen*—action-death squads—were dedicated to Hitler's plan to exterminate the Jews. That—" her eyes filled with anguish—"became the Holocaust."

"I don't know much about this." His ignorance frustrated him. He had avidly read books all of his life, but little about Germany and World War II. Vietnam had been his parents' war, and ultimately his. "So a good Nazi wouldn't have sex with these—" he looked at the photos on the files— "women?"

"Absolutely not. Maybe Von Winter was testing his killers."

"You think there're more than one?"

"I'm convinced there are. You see, Horne, these aren't anything like the serial killings Americans are so enthralled with. The Nazis were organized. They had journeymen death squads who gassed Jews in trucks. There were battalions of men who weren't called up for army service for one reason or another: lame bank clerks, asthmatic salesmen, overweight office workers, unskilled men. They were given several weeks of training and they'd march into a *shtetl*—some little town—in Poland, Hungary, Bulgaria, Lithuania, Czechoslovakia—wherever there were Jews."

Horne had never considered the possibility that a coordinated group might be responsible for the fate of these women. Miriam's cause of death was yet another challenge in the chain Rebecca had linked together.

"I think it's reasonable to ask why Miriam had a swastika brand and the other women didn't."

"A new man performing a ceremony? An initiation? It's a statement for a cause. The police used this excuse and told me that a killer up in Seattle has this signature. It's a game the Von Winters play to throw the police off. It has everything to do with the fact that Miriam was about to be a bride and that she was Jewish."

She had made a vague link into an obsession.

21

After Rebecca had cooked a breakfast of Viennese apple pancakes, Horne continued to study the files with her. He had never before been so well looked after—certainly not by his mother, always busy baking for others and gone in the middle of the night to open her coffeehouse and begin preparing for the morning rush.

"The three women died of gas inhalation."

She loftily waved her hand, brushing science away like a housefly. "Does that sound logical to you?"

"Two of the reports suggest that they were suicides. Who knows, maybe these women couldn't go through with the marriage and got depressed. It happens." There was no sign of agreement. "Why is Miriam's actual cause of death whited out?"

Rebecca gave him a distressed and bitter smile. "When this was the police's 'hot case,' they decided to withhold it so the media wouldn't sensationalize it and the killers would assume that some other cause of death had been determined."

Rebecca handed him an undoctored Xerox of the post mortem. He read it carefully, gradually disavowing his reservations. Miriam had been gassed with Zyklon-B, hydrogen cyanide. It had been specifically designed to eradicate Jews and tested in Auschwitz-Birkenau before coming into use at the other death camps. In some states today with the death penalty, a variation of it was administered to murderers. In Africa, annihilation was much simpler: if AIDS, TB, malaria—hosts of other diseases—didn't devastate the populace, machetes settled feuds.

"If it's the same gas stock the Nazis used, it must have been what...fifty-sixty years old?"

"Magnus found a way to manufacture it."

As she continued with this portentous recitation of the horrors, he discovered that in spite of struggling against it, he had become emotionally engaged in what he had thought was her personal, neurotic crusade.

Horne looked up when Glück butted his ankles, and he invited the cat to sit on his lap. The silky white hairball rolled over on his back and raised all of his paws for a massage. Horne lightly rubbed the cat's belly. Damn, Rebecca had even enlisted her house cat to charm him. The Himalayan had led him to Miriam's photographs. Maybe he also communicated with the dead, like his mistress.

"Me, you push away," she said fractiously.

"Him! I like."

Rebecca busied herself with endless refills of black coffee, scanned a music score to avoid staring at Horne, ever conscious of her expectations. She was nervous, afraid of distracting him, and couldn't resume practicing.

Horne put down the documents, offered her a cigarette and lit both of theirs, then paced through the rooms. In her bedroom, the fragrant scent of her body oils drew him into yet another ambush. A bulky suitcase lay on a red velvet bench at the foot of the bed. On it, a mink coat was spread with a muff and mink-lined gloves. He hated furs, particularly mink, cannibal animals who, when they were hungry, ate their mates and their young. He strode around the apartment, ultimately halting at the portrait of "The Jewish Bride" and studied the adoring expression on the face of the expectant husband.

"You have a cell phone?"

"Yes."

"With roaming?"

"No."

"We'll get you another one. It's a free month from Sprint for me delivering a new customer. But never mind." He continued his wandering, touching old inherited objects in the apartment. "Your laptop works?"

"It was your aunt's." He was about to lose his temper again about her grand heist, but desisted. "I'm online and it's reliable...so far." She switched it on. "I did some research. There's a boutique hotel called—"

"We're staying at a commercial old beer-brewers' palace called The Pfister in the center of Milwaukee."

"I checked and it's expensive."

"Easy to get lost in. We travel together but separately. We never give each other any sign of recognition. Do you understand? Whatever happens, don't talk to me in public."

She gasped, thrilled. "Yes."

"Order a taxi to take you to the airport—tomorrow at three P.M., non-stop. American Airlines."

"Will you be on the same flight?"

"Rebecca, I'll be there, just don't look for me. We arrive at Mitchell Field about nine—in theory. One carry-on bag, put your hair up, wear a baseball cap or something, no make-up, sunglasses. What I'm trying to say is, please—if it's humanly possible—look, act, low-key. Don't mention where you're going to anyone. And that includes the snake joints you work for or the people at the Museum of Tolerance. Take a cab to the Holiday Inn in Milwaukee."

"Yes, fine."

"Check in! I've made a reservation in your name. Go to the room and wait for me to call on the cell."

"Horne, you're going too fast."

"So did Rachmaninoff, didn't he? And no mink coat!"

"It's freezing in Milwaukee. It's my grandmother's coat, not mine."

"I don't care if it belonged to Queen Victoria. Layer yourself. Look, why don't you run downtown to Little Tijuana for a coat. You'll find an Armani for sixty bucks."

"Lilli's muff to keep my hands warm?"

"Look great with jeans and nobody'll notice you. Try gloves, and not lined with mink or chinchilla."

She was amused. "Herta packed them. Will I need thermal underwear?"

"I'll leave that to you."

"Do I bring...buy clothes for Florida? Palm Beach is eighty degrees!"

He too had lightened up. "If we stay more than a day, I'll spring for one of those Rio jobs and take you Salsa dancing in it."

"I think I'd like that." She swung her hips as though to a Latin beat. "Can you dance?"

He sniggered. "My father was a musician, lady. When I was three, maybe four, we'd dance together. He'd put me on top of his shoes. I can dance, and shoot—not much else. Actually...I forgot....There's another thing I do well."

As he loped downstairs, she wanted to leap on his back, attack him, and claw him like a lioness and take him. But he had already eluded her.

She shouted, "Where does Glück stay?"

"I'll drop him at an animal shelter."

"The lion killer has no heart and is a monster!"

"Yours for hire." Horne bounced down the steps, but flipped around. "Ingrid loves cats. I'll see if I can get him laid."

"You're disgusting."

"An animal—like you."

He had reversed everything in her plans. She was the one now in pursuit, the endangered species.

"Horne, I left you an urgent note. Check your mailbox."

He burst into his apartment, churned his computer to work out the rest of their schedule, send emails, confirm hotel and car reservations. About to head downtown in search of a sheepskin jacket, he flipped the mail slot. In a rush, he tore open the envelope.

Trust

R

He unfolded the attached document on which it had been clipped and found the signed quitclaim. He was stunned. Apparently, Rebecca had no devious scheme to steal his property. She had been honest all along. He could toss her out at once. She remained at Sycamore Place at his pleasure. For some reason, this leverage tipped the balance again in her favor. He marveled at her smarts.

Since arriving in California, his character had been reshaped, warped by pettiness in conflict with a woman who had abandoned her career, nursed his aunt until her dying moment, all the while suffering through a heartbreaking tragedy. It was time for him to conduct himself like the man he knew himself to be. He was disgusted and contrite about his own behavior. He'd always been considered a decent human being, someone people respected and could depend on. Had prison changed him so profoundly, coarsened him beyond recognition? On the other hand, despite the gruesome circumstances, Rebecca had handled herself with grace.

If her course of action in the past had been unfathomable, it now became clear. She had released him of all responsibility. He could call the real estate agent, tell her to peddle the house, and go through the motions of helping Rebecca investigate her sister's murder. He'd return to Beverly Hills and find a check for a deposit. Haggerty already had power-of-attorney. He'd trade Rose's Lexus shopping cart for a Land Cruiser free and clear. He could say he'd had changed his mind about accompanying her to Milwaukee or anywhere else.

What held him back was her faith in him. *Trust.* This made him abandon all thoughts of dumping her. She might have relinquished her legal rights to an apartment, signed a quitclaim, but now she owned him.

He phoned Haggerty, who arranged for a messenger to pick up the document; then he would contact Donna Seymour and give her an exclusive on the property. She had been the only soul to drop by.

"Well, Dougie, your wizardry prevailed. Frankly, I never believed you could move Rebecca an inch."

"Looks like you'll get your ten grand back, Tommy."

"I wasn't worried. When Rose died, and Rebecca turned your assets into ash, I knew you might be indigent. I increased your share of my estate. Made sure when I croaked, you wouldn't be left needy. As a new man of property, that doesn't have quite the urgency. Let's think about more pressing issues." Haggerty's cackle was a preamble: "You can now bang Milady Rebecca to your heart's content—without any legal fallout. Just be careful of depositing bodily fluids in fertile eggs. Proving paternity—"

"—No, no, you're wrong. I'm not going to screw her. It's not like that anymore...."

"I'm sure. Another call, must take. Good luck. Ass up to the office when you're back."

22

Mustard! Horne had forgotten how delicious it tasted. It was also so hot that floaters paddled through his eyes, but even so he lashed it on the crisp roll of his second pork French Dip at Philippe's. Sitting on a bench at the trestle table opposite Butch, he smiled happily.

"You never learn, Dougie. You burned your tongue the first time I took you here."

"It was before a Raiders game when they were in L.A."

"Food in Africa wasn't so terrific, huh?"

"On safari, it was great. But after a while anyone would get tired of fish and curry."

He had phoned Butch on his cell and caught up with the "expert arson investigator" at the law courts after he had given testimony in a case.

"I got to give it to you, Doug. Triple double, hat trick, grand slam."

"I'm traveling with her."

"A life of atonement for your sins," he said with a knowing cackle. "Where to?"

"Milwaukee."

Butch gave him a look of incredulity. "This time of year? What's there, for chrissake?"

"It was a trade-off. Well, she let me off the hook, and I can sell Sycamore Place. But I have to help her with the investigation."

"*What?* You're kidding."

"Nope."

"Has this got to do with the sister?"

"She's convinced it is. There's a guy living there whose fiancée was murdered some years back. Rebecca believes he's holding out. She claims there's some similarity with her sister's murder."

Butch swigged his beer. "You got yourself a head case. A beautiful, talented one, I admit—but still, a dingbat."

Horne nodded. "Maybe she *has* found something. You see, someone went to a lot of trouble to murder her sister."

"I'm listening...and?"

"It's like all this is part of a mission—an initiation of some kind. Miriam was branded with a swastika, so obviously this guy had access to a blacksmith's forge. Maybe on some ranch with horses and cattle, where it'd be easy."

Butch agreed that a truck interior could hardly be the place to carry this out.

"That's the least of it. You see, the cause of death was a type of cyanide gas that was only used by the Nazis at their death camps. But the wise men at Parker Center decided to withhold that bit of info. Because Jews all over the world would have freaked, and the pressure on the cops would've had their asses in a sling again."

Listening intently, Butch gauged the circumstances.

"Butch, they were licking their wounds after they'd just blown the O.J. case. There's another part of this that makes me think Rebecca may be onto something. Miriam *wasn't* sexually molested."

"Really? This is getting stranger by the moment, Douglas."

"Damn right it is. A true, diehard Nazi wasn't allowed to have sexual relations with a Jew. Hitler passed some kind of law that made it a hanging offense."

Butch cast aside his beer and leaned forward, now deeply engaged.

"I didn't really follow her sister's case. But it does sound like there's a crew of very sophisticated, insane people out there." He paused and took Horne's arm. "Doug, things are finally working out for you. You sure you want to get involved?"

"Do I? No." Horne carefully considered his answer. His blue eyes were unwavering. "But I gave her my word." Horne struggled. "I can't dump her. Now do me a favor, Butch. You're connected everywhere."

"What do you need?"

"A sharp limo driver—non-stretch—who can handle himself and his cargo."

"Milwaukee, huh?" Ruefully, Butch wrapped a bulky arm around Horne. "Okay, I'll make a few calls."

At noon, Noreen quickly crossed the street to Sycamore Place, tugging Dort along on the leash. Something wasn't right at Rebecca's place. A taxi belched exhaust fumes in front of the house. The driver was at the curb, puffing on a cigar.

"Hello, where're we headed?" she asked with an easygoing smile.

"Ms. Benjamin, didn't you call us for American Airlines at LAX?" he replied, without suspicion. "Need a hand with your bags?"

Noreen picked up the dog and sprinted around the corner, already on the cell to Virgil.

"My bag in the car?"

"Always is. What's happening?"

"That bitch is flying someplace."

"Want me to go?"

"No, it's better if I do and you can meet me—wherever. Bring my black wig."

"Got it. I'll pick you right up."

Enroute to LAX, Noreen fumbled with the cap in the passenger mirror, then fitted the wig.

In pursuit, Virgil's excitement alarmed Noreen. He was a daredevil driver, and she reckoned, one of the few men who could watch hours of mind-numbing NASCAR on TV. She could barely maintain her equilibrium during these Formula One prison terms. He was also afflicted with a passion for hockey, bowling, and pool tournaments. Thank God for Nora Roberts and Mary Higgins Clark.

"No parking" threats boomed from the airport loudspeakers, preventing Virgil from a romantic farewell. He opened the trunk, handed her an overnight carry-on, and drove off.

Once in the American Airlines terminal, Noreen was rattled by the constant garbled announcements and had no way of knowing which flight Rebecca would be taking. She parked herself in front of a departures monitor and watched the doors as passengers swooped in.

In about twenty minutes, she spotted Rebecca paying the cab driver. She had a hanging bag, a shoulder tote, and a heavy black wool overcoat with a velvet collar slung over her arm. The pockets were stuffed with a scarf and leather gloves. She had on what looked like ski pants, a thick ribbed red turtleneck sweater, and a beret. Noreen studied the flights leaving for New York, Chicago, and other snow-packed cities. She immediately got in line behind Rebecca and whipped out her driver's license and Visa.

When Rebecca reached the counter attendant and handed her ticket over, Noreen overheard her—"Milwaukee. New York, Miami, return L.A. are all open. Do you want to make reservations now for any of them?"

Rebecca said, "I'm not sure when I'm returning."

She handed Rebecca her boarding pass. "That's to your left, up the escalator, Gate Twelve. Thank you for flying American."

Noreen had no problem buying a ticket and getting on the same flight. It was fourteen hundred dollars because she hadn't pre-booked. She was outraged by the price and wanted to strangle the attendant. No point in causing a fuss.

Several minutes later, she galloped away from security, then stopped short. Rebecca had stopped at a Starbucks. Noreen could use some coffee. It had been a frantic rush and she hadn't had lunch yet.

While Rebecca was producing a dust storm topping her coffee with powdered cinnamon and chocolate flakes at the counter, Noreen said, "Just black," and pointed at a muffin the size of horned toad.

Grumbling to herself about the trouble this bitch was causing in everyone's life, she awkwardly lurched onto the gangway trying not to burn herself. Hardly anyone was traveling to Milwaukee. She dropped into her seat and grabbed a *USA Today*. She discovered that the high in Milwaukee was 9 degrees; the low horrifying, and snow expected. Lord, how she hated cold weather. She had on jeans, a short-sleeved sweater, a thin windbreaker, and her Reeboks.

Rebecca sat three rows in front of her on the other side of the aisle. She did not look around for anyone. It was evident she was traveling alone. Noreen hit Virgil's pre-set number on her cell and whined:

"Milwaukee, can you believe it? What's there?"

"No idea. Maybe she's going to play a concert or something."

"I'll freeze to death."

"Look, soon as I drop Dort off at the vet, I'll fly out with some warm clothes for you."

"She's heading for New York, and Miami after that."

"Definitely a concert tour. Now, Noreen, no matter what it costs, don't lose her. I'll check with Winterhaven HQ. We've got an organization in Milwaukee. Somebody'll meet you. I'll be in touch when I have word."

"I'd like to bury her in the snow there!"

He laughed. "If Lake Michigan hasn't frozen over, I'll ask Magnus if he'd like us to take her for a swim."

23

Horne had been tracking Rebecca from the moment she had arrived at the American Airlines terminal, and she hadn't noticed him. To avoid her, he had spent the night at a motel near LAX and booked himself in Business Class. He waited on the perimeter of the gate, drinking a beer at the dismal bar, half-watching a college basketball game on TV, and surveyed the thin flock moping in the waiting area.

Horne couldn't recall when he'd been this uncomfortable. He had endured torrid temperatures, Serengeti burns, dust storms, freezing temperatures on the ice-capped Kilimanjaro, but now, attired in a charcoal-gray flannel suit, tie, khaki raincoat with a zip-in lining, and snap-brim hat on, he felt like an alien. He'd almost forgotten how to tie a half-Windsor knot.

When the boarding call came for Business Class, he carried his bag quickly to the entrance. He jammed it in the overhead compartment, grabbed a pillow, and curled up with *Sports Illustrated*, but he kept an eye on the line of passengers. No one caught his attention.

He had years of experience doing headcounts of groups in Africa and came up with fifty-eight passengers once they were at cruising altitude. Many of them were already dozing. Rebecca was at the midway point of Coach with an aisle seat. She kept her head down when he walked by.

Nothing unusual occurred during the flight, but he reckoned he had a sense of everyone aboard. When they arrived, he reset his watch an hour ahead, strode swiftly to the exit marked "transportation/baggage." He reached the carousel while it was still empty. A burly, red-faced man, in a green duffel coat and plaid cap, edgily peered around.

"Were you on the Los Angeles flight?" he asked.

"Yeah," Horne replied. "Meeting someone?"

"Yes."

The man drifted over to the escalator. Rebecca passed him, as did other passengers, and the man seemed confused until spotting a hefty woman with long black hair in jeans and sneakers. She had been several seats away from Rebecca and inconspicuous. Sniffing around each other with indecision, they finally shook hands. The woman was not prepared for the change in climate. Already shivering, she aroused

Horne's suspicion. He waved to a limo driver holding out a card with the name Butch.

Bundled up in her coat and gloves, Rebecca got into a taxi. Horne flagged the limo driver. "I'm Butch. Run me over to the Holiday Inn on Sixth and Wisconsin."

"Yes, sir. Did you have a good flight?"

"Fine, thanks. Now let's roll."

As they pulled away, the man who had spoken to him inside furiously peeled a parking ticket off his Lincoln Town Car while the woman got into the passenger side. Rebecca's cab was ahead.

It was a twenty-minute drive downtown, and Horne had the driver wait in the valet entrance to the Holiday Inn.

"Can I have your cell-phone number?" Horne asked the driver.

"Sure."

"What's the area code?"

"Four-one-four."

"Thanks. I won't be staying here. I have to pick up my friend and we'll be checking into The Pfister."

"That's fine, sir."

"Is there another exit besides this one in front?"

"Yeah, Fitzgerald's Cocktail Lounge takes you out."

As Horne left the car, he was hit by quills of wind roaring off the lake.

"One other thing: Let me know if you spot a dark-blue, four-door Lincoln Town car hanging around." He handed the driver a twenty. "Guy at the wheel has on a plaid cap and a hefty woman beside him."

"Will do."

Ten minutes later, Rebecca signed in at the front desk. Horne had parked himself beside the elevator. When she had her room card, he got into the elevator with her. They were alone. For a moment, she didn't speak.

"No safari suit? I hardly recognize you in a suit and tie."

"I'm a master of disguises."

"Which Mexican designer did your clothes this time?"

"Emilio Zapata."

"Well, you look pretty good in clothes that almost fit."

The elevator stopped at the fourth floor and Horne took her bag. They walked to a room beside the ice machine.

"When did you get here?"

"Just before you."

"How long are we staying?"

"I'm waiting to see how soon you get a phone call."

In the room, paradise after his cell in Dar, he removed his flask and took a swig, then offered it to her.

"I'm *hungry*." She was like a kid grumbling after a long car trip. "Isn't there an all-night Bratwurst stand?"

"Will the *Gnadige Fraulein* have it with our wine-soaked sauerkraut or chili and onions?"

"You speak German!" she asked, surprised.

"No, of course I don't. Who would want to? It's the name of a lousy play my aunt dragged me to by Tennessee Williams."

He brought out her violence. She wanted to smack him, but the phone rang twice. Horne motioned her to pick up.

"Good evening, Ms. Benjamin?"

"Yes. Hi, who's this?"

"Front desk. We're just checking to see if your room is all right, or if you need anything."

"No, it's perfect, thank you."

After she hung up, Horne said, "A woman."

"Yes. Look, how'd you know I'd be getting a call?"

"Call the front desk and ask if *they* just phoned you."

She dialed and a man's voice responded. "No, ma'am, no one from the hotel called you. I'll connect you with the operator." The operator confirmed that there had been an outside call to her room.

Horne dialed the limo driver. "Lincoln Town car waiting?"

"Yeah. I got the license number."

"Right down. Pull up close as you can to the guest elevator in the underground lot."

Rebecca was worn out and surly. "There *are* people following me." Horne nodded. "Do you know who they are?"

"Not as well-dressed as me."

She grabbed his flask and gulped vodka. "You're fantastic. You *did* bring your guns?"

"Damn, I knew there was something I forgot to pack."

24

Chilled to the bone, Noreen sat alongside Arthur Kress in his car outside the Holiday Inn. He had loaned her his cap and brought along one of his overcoats. He had an angular face, wiry hair, jug ears, a granite jaw, and a tendency to laugh without reason.

"Heater high enough for you now?"

"Yes, thanks. Arthur," she said, "I really appreciate you picking me up."

Kress was the *Gauleiter* of the Midwest heartland, one of the main Nazi encampments in America. His barony stretched from Wisconsin to the Dakotas; the malcontents, anti-government forces, and militia were all under his stick.

"After you buried that rabbi alive last year, you became the heroine of our movement. Magnus himself called me." He found Noreen Porter fiercely attractive. "I simply had to meet you."

"The rabbi was Virgil's idea. We were going after a Yid jeweler."

"And you killed him too."

Reliving the scene, she gloated, "*I* heaved him out of the window."

"That's what I heard."

"Do I check into the Holiday Inn, or what?"

A car's brights flashed and Kress flashed his. "The convoy is right behind us. As long as we know where this woman is, she'll have my wolf pack around day and night. I have a house on the lake with staff. I'll try to make your stay very comfortable."

Another car pulled up across the street and a man trotted over. Kress lowered the window.

"Her name is Rebecca Benjamin. She's in three-one-eight. Don't let her out of your sight. I'll be at home."

"Yes, sir." The man lingered. "Is this Fraulein Porter?"

"It's her," Kress said proudly.

He bowed his head. "You're a very courageous woman. Just what Winterhaven needs."

Unlike the prison rabble in Winterhaven, Kress was successful and had grown wealthy in the plumbing and heating trade. He drove through the electric gates of a monumental Gothic stone house. Floodlights illuminated a citadel of wealth. After the cramped apartment, and the never-ending routine, Noreen got her second wind. She felt like a queen, tingling with warmth toward her host.

"This was one of the mansions built in the 'twenties. The beer barons, meat packers, and industrialists wanted a view of Lake Michigan. If I'd had any warning of your coming I would have arranged a reception and introduced you to our group."

When Noreen entered the great hall, she was struck by the collection of swords and armor, the wall tapestries, the buffed wooden floors, covered in areas by Persian carpets. She felt as though she had stepped into fantasyland.

"I'm...knocked out."

"This is the way a Nazi is *meant* to live." In the salon, an immense photograph of the youthful Magnus, embraced by the idolatrous figure of Hitler, hung over a fireplace. Noreen peered at the gold commemorative inscription.

BERCHTESGASDEN 1937

She dropped to her knees and raised her hand in a worshipful salute:
"Heil!"

Kress laughed eerily. "Don't worry, we'll deal with this problem. I'm used to situations like this. For your information, Bruno and I exterminated a Jewish woman here."

Noreen's mind raced. She was suddenly wary. "In Milwaukee? Maybe that's why Rebecca came here. Could there be a connection?"

"I doubt it," Kress said, guiding her into the living room where a welcoming fire and a housekeeper greeted her. A butler brought in a platter of cold German delicacies. Kress fixed her a Sapphire martini.

"Why is this Benjamin woman here?"

"She's a concert pianist. Virgil thinks she might be performing."

"Unlikely. I'm a patron of the symphony and would've gotten a notice."

Kress had received a hurried briefing from Winterhaven, but wanted further clarification.

"This would be a perfect place to pair up the sisters. We could tattoo her entire body and put her severed head in a synagogue arc. That would be a statement."

"We can't." Noreen was well aware that all the key groups wanted to outdo Virgil. "Bruno has a special plan for her."

Kress roared with laughter, and his luminous new caps flashed.

"Oh, yes, yes, *Bruno*. She must be a beauty."

Noreen fixed herself a plate of headcheese and smoked ham on warm pumpernickel.

"You actually know Bruno?"

"Yes. He's an amazing, mysterious man. You know about the work he's doing in the Middle East?"

"Everyone at Winterhaven talks about it. I can't wait to meet him."

"I hope Virgil's not jealous."

"What...are you serious?"

Kress pursed his lips, and eyed her covetously as a fellow connoisseur. "Bruno loves women."

According to Kress, eleven years ago, Bruno had passed through the city for a confidential meeting with the museum curator. Something to do with architecture. It had been a privilege entertaining Magnus's son.

"Talk about an adventure...Bruno showed me how an utterly fearless Nazi conducts himself. You see, Noreen, I'd been at the mercy of an overbearing Jewess, the top real estate producer in the city. In all the years I'd been in business as a plumbing and heating contractor, her company never gave us a job. Even when we were the low bidders, they froze us out."

Bruno had told him about Magnus's theories about eliminating Jewish women, which Hitler, in his all-out Holocaust purge, had irresponsibly ignored.

"It just so happened that this organism was about to get married in the largest synagogue in Milwaukee. It would be a *luxe* affair. Her father was rich Zionist."

Bruno had called the woman at her office and made an appointment to see a listing she happened to have. Kress and he had driven out late one winter afternoon. Bruno had charmed her, as he did all females. Then the conversation had taken a more serious, ominous turn.

Noreen listened, enthralled.

Bruno had looked over the house very carefully. He'd found a list of substandard code violations and calmly pointed them out to her.

"Bruno's a true expert about building. Knew more about it even than me. The woman became very angry and told him to get out. He asked her why her company never offered my firm work on their properties. She was flustered. Then it came out. She and her father thought we were anti-Semitic."

Kress was laughing so hard that he had to steady his drink before it spilled. "We were now in the kitchen. Bruno said something to the effect that we had every right to our views. They were justified! Here, this kike operator was trying to sell a jerrybuilt fire trap to an apparently ignorant man with a family."

"Bruno dragged her into the kitchen. I switched on the oven, and the rest is history."

With the prospect of a two-million-dollar-plus deposit in his bank account shortly, Horne upgraded for a suite with two bedrooms at the Pfister and was gratified by Rebecca's reaction. She looked up at the vaulted ceiling, the finely wrought-iron balustrades him through and the undulating staircase, the swooping ferns and the Old World gentility. He had checked in as Mr. & Mrs. Douglas Horne to avoid having Rebecca's name on the registration.

"I feel like I'm back in Europe," she whispered as they followed the grand lobby.

The bellhop led them to a tower apartment that had been stylishly decorated with what appeared to be authentic Victorian furniture, and all mod cons, including a Jacuzzi.

"Horne, you're a marvel."

He was tempted to kiss her. Her eyes were willing, but the situation made him cautious. He had also decided that a more decorous approach suited him. He had begun to uncover her deep layers of character. She embodied a fine and rare cultural tradition quickly fading.

He knew for certain now that her obsession with Nazis was well-founded. He admired the casual fearlessness she continued to display and thought that if they were ever in trouble on a hunt in Africa, he could depend on her.

"How do we make contact with the man we want to interview?" she asked.

"I will." He handed her the room-service menu. "Still hungry?"

"No, just bed—and—" her eyes flickered—"never mind."

Horne shied away. "Immoral thoughts?"

"It's unbelievable, how you've manipulated everything."

"That's the art of hunting."

"People."

"Especially people."

"In that case, you'd better lock your door."

"Since I didn't bring my rifle, I'll stack phone books against it to keep you at bay." He raised his head smugly. "And don't be peeping when I'm undressing."

She flashed a smile. "You want to play chess with me. We'll see who resigns."

There had been no sightings of Rebecca at the Holiday Inn. By ten-thirty the following morning, Kress was enraged and ordered his men on duty to change shifts. He assigned another team to drag Rebecca out of her room if necessary.

Noreen got up from the table in his resplendent dining room, which had a view of Lake Michigan. The sun had made a curtsy, and the steel-gray shimmering light revealed freighters and tugs on the water. Short of a Las Vegas buffet, she couldn't remember eating such a lavish breakfast: courses of smoked fish, followed by omelets, and French toast served by two people, in uniform.

"Arthur, let me call the hotel."

"Yes, go ahead."

She waited impatiently while the phone in Rebecca's rang endlessly. Noreen was finally switched to a message machine. She called the operator back.

"Look, my daughter is a very sick woman. Please have the maid check on her. I'll hold on..." She listened. "*What!* What do you mean by 'a while?'"

Kress seized the phone. "Give me the manager immediately!" As soon as Kress heard a voice, he boomed. "This is an emergency! I'm the father of—" Noreen mouthed her name—"Rebecca...Benjamin. My daughter checked in last night and suffers from epilepsy. It's manage-able if she takes her medication. You send a security man up right now and check to see that she didn't have a seizure!...Yes, I'll wait....Pardon? I'm an attorney."

Kress cupped his hand over the mouthpiece. "He's got Security on it."

Noreen beamed her appreciation. "You're amazing, Arthur."

"This is nothing. Wait till you see me in action. Believe me, if I had been Hitler's general at Stalingrad, they'd be speaking German now." Noreen handed him a fresh cup of coffee, and he was back barking on the phone. "Yes, this is he. You're Security? Are you absolutely sure that's the right room? The bed hasn't been slept in? The bathroom...? No clothes left. And she didn't check out?...Yes, I can hear you." He cupped the phone, turning quizzically to Noreen. "What address would she have used?"

Noreen seized the phone. "99 Sycamore Place, Beverly Hills, 90212. Yes, yes, thank you."

She slammed down the phone. "That slut skipped out!"

Fuming, he said, "No one skips fast enough for Kress."

25

Sy Hoffman, chairman and CEO of Hoffman Properties, was one of those local, perpetual boosters who owned a small-time local realty operation. His "Sell, Sell, Sell" gift had not, however, been passed onto the drones at his company.

"Turnover is dead—beyond tragic," he drilled the nine members of his flu-ridden sales staff. "You're all too passive." He had fifty-one listings and they hadn't moved a one for two weeks. "Zero in escrow, mortgage rates never lower. I want explanations."

The stoical group sipped their coffees and chomped on their donuts.

"Come spring, it'll pick up," someone remarked.

"What? I pay rent, taxes, and your draw every week, no matter what the season. You're all slacking off because of a little chill in the air."

It had been four degrees below zero at seven when Sy had dropped off his wife at the Miller Brewing Company, where she was an executive. Still Sy, the physical fitness buff, had on his spiked running shoes and sheepskin-lined track suit and jogged around the park. He was determined to keep in shape. Rather than face an operation at Duke, he'd lost sixty pounds and sprung for a nose bob which an Irishman would've been proud of. Propecia had increased his hair count by a good third and he was thinking of blond streaks come spring. He was five seven but walked tall.

Sy's secretary, coughing her lungs out, signaled him.

"Mr. Hoffman, there's a live one staying at the Pfister. Says he's looking for an estate on the lake."

Sy was no longer a practicing Jew, certainly not with Milly, a wife he worshipped. God is good, he thought, and was about to recite the *Sh'Ma* when he remembered he had converted to Catholicism to get into Milly Cork's pants.

"Really." He surprised himself with a sudden erection. "Did he talk price?"

"A million plus."

It was a dirge of a day. The ice storm had stalled in Lake Superior and chosen its favorite child, Duluth, sparing its influence on Lake Michigan's tribal-shoreline cities. For Sy, this was comfort weather. The wind was possessed of chorale of howling ghosts, rocking Sy's

Mercedes SUV like a butterfly, and sending his cell phone to hell. Eternal optimism made Sy giddy when he picked up the dazzling couple at the hotel. He eased their bags into the back. Mr. Horne was considering a move of his financial empire to Milwaukee. His breathtaking, redheaded wife was a musician.

He deluged the couple with his hyperbolic drivel—schools, gold coast society, hogwash low-crime stats. He drove them to a twenty-five room "Prohibition-Baron" on the market for two years that needed martyrdom and twice the asking price to fix up.

"A simple refurbishment and it's ready for mixing and mingling, dinner parties, fundraisers," he droned. "It's my wife Milly's favorite house. If we could afford it, I'd snap it up."

It would be a soup-to-nuts job, years of contractor torment, to make it habitable just for swineherds, which he'd listed at a million-seven for the widow's half-witted heirs.

"Arthur Kress, the plumbing king, lives down the street. He has every builder in his pocket and I'll introduce you."

In the driveway, set back half a city block from the street, Horne and Rebecca encountered a gray fieldstone deformity, choked by denuded vines, with rotting vertical sheaves of timber that resembled a bad case of psoriasis. Leaded windows would defeat any source of light and reminded Horne of his prison cell.

Sy waved at the towering oaks. "Plenty of shade in the summer from these beauties."

"They'd block out a nuclear explosion," Rebecca said cheerfully.

"And that's a fact," Sy agreed. "By the way, Mr. Horne, what line of work are you in?"

"I was a hunter in Africa."

"Fascinating. Big money there, huh, I'll bet. King Solomon's mines sort of thing." Sy was back to business. "History has it that Al Capone used to party here and have meetings with the mob."

"And carry out murders," Horne said.

"Really," Rebecca said, "like the Nazis?"

Sy was unprepared, shaken by the lurid turn the conversation was taking and lofted them into the great hall, a desiccated wood-paneled affair, the only piece of furniture a mildewed sofa. They entered a fog of dry rot in the entry, their hosts an armored division of rodents who appeared indignant that non-members had interrupted their gym routine.

He waved his arm with a flourish. "There's an elevated loggia...Sunday brunches and picnics. Your Missus is a musician. Perfect for outdoor concerts."

"I want to see the grounds and the dock. You stay here," Horne told Rebecca.

There were grounds indeed, just over three acres, and a forsaken swimming pool veined with seismic cracks and large enough for training gladiators. When they passed a crumbling gazebo, the sun slunk out again. The lake, leaden all morning, refracted stings of light that glinted off the crackling, icy shores. The wind's punctuated eruptions swayed the crippled dock.

"I was always curious about Atlantis, and now I've seen it."

Hoffman's horse laugh echoed. "Joe Kennedy unloaded plenty of scotch here. All those 'twenties' flappers waiting for a chug-a-lug with the crafty Irishman."

"Spare me the bullshit." Horne seized Hoffman's arm. "Come on, Sy, let's check out the dock and see how sturdy the robber barons built it."

Hoffman demurred. "Look, Mr. Horne, I wouldn't swear for it.... I don't think we ought to walk out. The client's safety is my—"

"—Oh, come on, don't be afraid," Horne said gently, pushing him ahead. "I'm a good swimmer."

"My liability umbrella has a 'due care' clause."

Huffing with anxiety, Sy tiptoed out, rammed by Horne, who had seen that the timber supports were solid enough, better than most bridges he'd crossed in Africa. When they reached the end, he handed Hoffman a news clipping with a bold headline from *Tanzania Today*. It featured a large photograph of Horne, bearded, fierce, and in chains.

DOUGLAS HORNE NOTED WHITE HUNTER ARRESTED FOR MURDER DUTCHMAN SHOT MULTIPLE TIMES IN THE HEAD

"That's me, last year," Horne said. "I beat the case. I did some awful stuff to this guy, but I had a good reason. Like I do now."

Terror seized Sy Hoffman. He felt himself lose contact with reality, about to black out.

"Really," he murmured.

"I'm ready to toss you right into the lake."

Hoffman's apprehension was palpable. "What have I done? Why *me*?"

"I want you to answer some questions about your fiancée's murder. And if you fucking lie to me, I swear I'll chop you into pieces."

Hoffman swayed. "My *fiancée*? You're talking to the wrong man. I've been married for five years to Milly—maiden name—Cork."

"I want to hear about Judith."

Hoffman's leather gloves covered his face, dislodging his hat, which plopped into the frozen lake and skated in the wind.

"The lady I'm with tried to contact you last year. You kept hanging up on her. Remember?" Horne seized hold of the trembling real estate agent. "That was rude."

"I'm sorry, I'll apologize to her."

"We want to hear what you didn't tell the police about Judith Rosen."

Hoffman was aghast. "You think *I* did it?"

"I didn't say that. But the reports I read in the newspaper and from the detectives bear a similarity to the murder of Rebecca Benjamin's sister."

"Judie was killed eleven years ago! It's buried."

"It's just been resurrected."

He cowered. "Oh, shit, this could ruin my business. My wife hates scandal—my past."

"Look, Sy, I'm no one to have as an enemy. But the lady inside is worse than me. Just be straight with her and we'll be on our way."

26

They found some rickety chairs around a scarred table in the huge, moldy kitchen. Behind them, pulleys from a cranky dumbwaiter writhed in a wind tunnel that shot down from the upstairs rooms. Sy Hoffman was unnerved and averted his eyes from Rebecca's. She seemed to become more furious by the moment as he recounted the events of Judith Rosen's murder.

He had met Judith twelve years ago at a Jewish singles dance. Having failed his CPA exam for a third time, he had found employment as a spy for a bankruptcy liquidator and was hunting for an heiress.

"Judie's father was Morris Rosen. He was loaded and had a big real estate operation, residential and commercial. Judie worked there. She was an econ major at the University of Wisconsin and had whipped through her broker's exam—no easy matter."

Sy halted abruptly, then, staring at the couple, came to a decision.

"To be honest, I wasn't in love with her. In six months, we were engaged and I had a manager's job at the company, and Judie was coaching me for the broker's test. Morris was a big wheel at the Beth Jehudah synagogue and was planning a lavish wedding."

"Was there publicity?" Rebecca asked.

"Was there ever. Announcements in the local Jewish press and photos of us in the *Journal*. Morris invited family from Israel and was about to give the *shul* a million dollars for a building addition to be named after his dead wife."

A week before the wedding, Judie had taken a call from a builder who had completed a spec house in West Allis, a neighboring town.

"Judie went to meet him there."

"Was that usual?" Horne asked.

"Sure. The boss's daughter always wanted a new listing. She'd get a piece of the pie on a sale, whether it was sold by someone in the office, or another broker if it went multiple. In a case like this, everyone asks for an exclusive for as long as they can get it so there's no split commission."

"Why didn't you go with her?" Rebecca demanded.

"Ms. Benjamin, with all due respect, that isn't the way it's done in a real estate office. Someone gets a call—the listing—it's theirs. And the man called Judie directly, asked for her by name. She was hot stuff. No one could close like Judie—not even her father."

He shook his head in wonderment. "Her pitch was fantastic. She claimed to have a child with MS and a dying mother she nursed at home. If a client was on the fence, or about to walk, she'd start with the waterworks. She'd lose her job, and—with the husband who'd battered her coming out of prison—she needed a lawyer to get a restraining order. In the six months we were together, she taught me every angle."

"What made *you* go to the spec house?" Rebecca, now calmer, asked.

"Everyone at the office regularly checked in for calls and information. I was going to meet Judie for lunch."

Rebecca waved her hand in his face. "Tell me about her murder."

Sy Hoffman sensed there was something maniacal about Horne and Rebecca.

"This was before cell phones. So everyone has to call in...and I hadn't heard from Judie by four o'clock. A first. She'd usually call every five minutes to check her messages. She and her father had car phones even then."

"Rebecca, this a waste of our time. This guy's lying. His wife works at the Miller Brewing Company. Let's go to her office and ask her to tell us what happened."

Hoffman yelped. "Please, no!"

The situation he recounted was grisly and painful for Rebecca. As was customary with a new property-viewing, Judie had left the address of the house.

By four-thirty, unable to contact her car phone, Sy had driven out to West Allis. He suspected that she might have gone for coffee with the builder and was pitching him hard and giving him area comp prices.

"The house was in a good upper middle-class area on Portage Road. There was a sign outside giving the builder's name and phone number. I wasn't really uptight about anything. Judie's Volvo was outside the garage and a light was on in the house. I'm thinking: 'That's my girl, relentlessly closing.'

"I thought we'd head over to the Pfister for cocktails. Go for dinner at Polonez. Judie enjoyed her food. She loved their pierogi and stuffed cabbage. I was starting to feel good about us getting married that week. Until the honeymoon in Bermuda, we wouldn't have any time on our own."

Hoffman took a deep breath. "I ring the doorbell. No one answers. I knock on the living-room window. Finally, I try the door, and it's open. I call out, 'Judie.... '"

Rebecca's intensity at this moment overpowered the two men. "Was there a smell of gas?"

Sy's face turned ashen. "Yeah, very strong—emergency-strong. With new houses, sometimes the utility people mess things up, or the contractor's plumber."

Sy had walked from the living room through to the dining room and into the kitchen. Judie was on her knees and her head was in the oven. She was fully clothed...and dead. In his panic, he thought he might be blamed for her death.

"I open the window, turn off the gas, pull her head out of the oven. She's on the floor. Her face is blue." Sy's voice shook. "It's a suicide. Her father is sure to blame me. He never really liked me. Always said, if not for Judie, I'd be slicing salami in a deli."

Rebecca urged him on. "You gave her the kiss of life?"

"No, I felt for a pulse. She was gone."

"Then what?" Horne demanded. Hoffman hesitated sheepishly. "Come on, give it up, I'm the last man to call the police."

"Judie had a swastika drawn in ink on her forehead."

"So you knew she was murdered!" Rebecca burst out.

Sy Hoffman's head slumped on the table, and he whimpered. "I don't know what I thought. The sight of a swastika on her head was so repugnant that I took out my handkerchief, ran it under some water and wiped it off. I was in shock."

He searched Horne's face for a sign of compassion. "You know all about finding dead bodies and killing people. I don't, Mr. Horne."

Horne seized Hoffman by the throat and thrust him back, finally releasing him. "Why, *why*, did you rub off the swastika? There was nothing in any police report about this being a neo-Nazi murder."

"I was afraid," he responded. "Look, let's assume it was a Nazi clan of some kind—maybe a lone wacko. He might come after me."

"It's a pity he didn't," Rebecca said.

"Rebecca, I think that's enough," Horne said, apparently rebuking her.

BETH ASHER

Despite Hoffman's protests that there was nothing more to disclose, Horne was not satisfied. He found a length of electrical cord. With a penknife, he scraped it until the copper wire was exposed. Sy Hoffman watched him fearfully.

"What are you going to do with that?"

He ignored Hoffman and turned to Rebecca. "You'll see. This always worked in Rwanda when the Hutu death squads wanted information." She nodded with approval. "I'll just wet it..."

"No, no!" Hoffman yelped.

"What else did you steal or cover up?" Rebecca demanded.

Hoffman's shoulders hunched and he lurched out of the chair, struggled to get past Horne, and was thrust against the wall. Horne's hands were around his throat.

"Please! There was a picture."

Rebecca, sitting on the edge of the table, leaped up. "What kind of picture?"

"An oil painting. I returned all the wedding presents but one. It was delivered about a week later with no return address. I didn't open it for months."

"Was there a note?" Horne asked.

"Yes."

"Do you remember the name of the person who sent it?"

"No, but I have it at home. It looked old and valuable. It's of a couple from the middle ages or thereabouts—"

—"The woman is wearing a red-purplish dress, the man is wearing a courtier's outfit and black, brimmed hat harmonized with gold-yellow against a deep brown background. His name is Isaac and he has his left arm around the woman's shoulder and his right hand over her left breast. She tenderly accepts this moment of intimacy by placing her fingers over his hand and presses it more firmly to her breast."

Sy wanted to jump out of his skin. "I have a masterpiece and you want to steal it! My God, that's what this is all about!"

Horne shouted, "It's a reproduction of Rembrandt's 'The Jewish Bride.' That's why the killers sent it to you!"

"It's their signature, or was in this case," Rebecca mused.

"We want to see it, Sy."

With counterplots of paranoia weaving through his mind, Virgil had been roaming the icy city searching for Noreen. He had given up on Rebecca. She might be anywhere. Finally, after repeatedly contacting Winterhaven, he was given Arthur Kress's home address, where he ultimately decamped. He could not reach Noreen on her cell.

As a Mercedes SUV drove past him, he glimpsed a woman with a beret and two men in the front. His cell suddenly came to life. His hands were so cold that he almost lost the call.

"Where the hell are you, Noreen?" he shouted.

"With Arthur looking everywhere for that bitch."

"How come?"

"She lost us coming out from the airport last night. I've barely slept. I've been chasing around with Mr. K's people all night." There was a pause. "Virgil, this is life and death. We've got to find her."

"Go back to the airport. American Airlines terminal. I'll try to meet up with you there. She's on her way to New York next. We can't lose her again!"

The 'For Sale' sign outside of a commodious two-story cream-brick house in the Third Ward had historic value, according to Hoffman.

"...I realize you're not considering relocation, but have a look around. It's become an artist's colony—"

"—Horne, if he doesn't stop, take out your hunting knife."

"Just trying to show you what real Milwaukee hospitality is like. This is a friendly city."

Finally, they were ushered into the den. Sy lifted the painting off the wall and removed the card taped to the back. He handed it to Rebecca, who read it aloud.

YOU CAN NOW HAVE A HAPPY LIFE.

BRUNO VON WINTER

The picture was enormously convincing as an original Rembrandt, apart from the signature of Bruno Von Winter and the lines beside it.

"Wonderful," she said, "especially the words in German Gothic and the musical notation."

"Doesn't that make it even more valuable?" Sy asked.

Rebecca glared at Hoffman. "If you're a Nazi, the answer is yes." She now read the German: "'Bald flattern Hitler-fahnen über allen Strassen.'"

"The translation is, 'Soon Hitler's flags will fly over every street.' This is from the 'Horst Wessel Lied.' It was a popular music-hall song which Wessel copied."

"I don't get it, Rebecca," Horne said.

"It's the 'Nazi Anthem,' named for some nobody who died for Hitler in a beer hall fight. Horst Wessel became a Party hero. And Von Winter's son painted this obscene tribute."

Rebecca was racing through the LaGuardia airport concourse after the flight had been delayed for three hours. When Virgil attempted to follow her through its maze, he had a vision of what life must have been like in a concentration camp. He had never been involved in such an unpredictable situation.

This time, he had a friendly squad of people on time, in place, with cars and connections, who had driven down from upstate New York and Pennsylvania. True rank-and-file diehards. As the head of the largest SS group in California, Virgil was treated with the respect of a visiting dignitary. He was in charge. Noreen had either missed her flight or gotten lost. Someone in the group would meet her when she arrived.

As instructed by Horne, Rebecca made no effort this time to lose anyone who might be pursuing her. Since the dark-haired woman who had trailed her to Milwaukee was not on their plane, it was crucial for Horne to pinpoint the identity of whoever had taken her place.

To his surprise, the man following Rebecca from LaGuardia Airport looked familiar to him. Maybe his mind was playing tricks. Horne couldn't be sure where he had seen this man and it intensified an already explosive situation. Horne watched him join a pack of middle-aged men in black leather jackets, hissing on their cell phones.

He concluded that the Von Winter organization had branches everywhere. There was nothing the police could do about this. No laws had been broken. Suspicions didn't interest cops, and the less Horne had to do with the police, the better.

Rebecca and Horne had shared a room at the convention-ridden Marriott near Times Square and the following morning, ordered room service and retailored their plans. No adjoining room for Rebecca and her protector, thanks to an Adult Film Society Seminar.

Rebecca knew that nothing—certainly no barrier she had erected—prevented them from making love. Was Horne waiting for the ideal moment? It had become intolerable for her. There was no doubt in her mind that she was falling in love with him.

27

The following morning they took the subway together from 42nd Street to Brooklyn. Horne vanished amid the shift of graveyard-shift-workers returning home.

By eight, Rebecca climbed up the slippery steps out of the subway on Church Avenue, walked several blocks to the bus and eventually got off on 13th Avenue.

She had arrived in a foreign land, the heart of Borough Park's Bobover Hasidic establishment. Bearded men were bundled in long black coats and upturned, wide-brimmed beaver hats, others in Old-Country fur helmets; the women, all bewigged, wheeled their baby carriages and marched legions of older children to school.

In store windows and house fronts were photographs of a young bearded man. Some kind of messiah, she thought. She stopped to look at the picture.

OUR MARTYR RABBI LABEL FRIEDMAN
MURDERED BY NAZIS
THURSDAY, DECEMBER, 1999
FOR INFORMATION OR THE CAPTURE OF HIS KILLERS
$250,000 REWARD

A rabbi! Rebecca wondered if the neo-Nazi groups had some depraved vision, larger in scope than the murder of her sister and Judith Rosen. Had these madmen conceived of some master plan? Shuddering, she brushed away an enraged tear. There was no longer a reward for Miriam's killers. Jack Leopold had withdrawn it.

She wiggled through squads of Yeshiva boys with *payess*, curled sideburn locks of hair, under the yarmulkes, walking separately from the girls, chivvied along by their mothers. They, too, were wrapped from head to toe in dark sheepskin-lined mackinaws, heads covered with leather-ear-lapped flaps.

Rebecca vigilantly walked to 44th Street, trying to avoid the thin, ice-masked puddles. She checked addresses before halting in front of a small shingled house. She had no idea what had happened to Horne. He had vanished.

Before leaving the hotel, he had phoned the Maimonides Medical Center, posing as a FedEx supervisor. Esther Klein worked there as a nurse, and he wanted to confirm that she still lived at the address Rebecca had taken from the private detectives' files.

Rebecca sat on the stoop post, thumbing through the *Times*. Along the way, she had picked up a bag of warm bagels at a bakery and now nibbled on one. Across the street on the corner, she finally spied Horne coming out of a store.

She read the sign above: her first encounter with a "Kosher" car-hire driving service. Apparently, taxis were taboo in this area. On the opposite corner, a man waited. She had spotted him at the airport. She became furious with Horne, and frightened. Why hadn't he taken his guns, or shipped them? Why hadn't he given her one of his revolvers to protect herself?

In about fifteen minutes, a fatigued, gaunt woman with deep brown pouches gouged under her eyes, wearing a nurse's uniform, cap, and navy-blue cape, reached the house.

Rebecca smiled at her. The woman was perplexed. She had just come off an exhausting shift. But ultimately, she returned her smile.

"Good morning, Mrs. Klein. I've spoken to you on the phone."

"Really?" she asked suspiciously. "Do I know you?"

"My name is Rebecca Benjamin, and I've flown in from California to talk to you. It's about your daughter."

Esther Klein's momentary affability was displaced by agitation.

"You're not from some news program?" She had been curt and angry when Rebecca had called her the previous year. Rebecca expected to be rebuffed again.

"No. I'm from Vienna. I'm a musician, like my sister. She was murdered over a year ago. The police haven't done anything in Los Angeles to solve the case."

"They haven't here, either, for my daughter," Esther said gloomily.

"Please, Mrs. Klein, I beg you, let me talk to you with my friend."

"Your friend?"

"Yes, he's across the street. I'm in serious trouble."

"Why?"

"People from a Nazi group have been following me across the country. This gentleman has been traveling with me as protection."

Esther nervously peered over Rebecca's shoulder and took her arm. They walked up half a dozen steps. She paused before unlocking the front door. She pressed her fingers to her lips and touched the *mezuzah*, fixed to the right of the door jamb, and Rebecca did as well.

"I'm not a Hasid or even that religious," Esther said, "but I keep the faith. You never know."

"No, we don't...."

"Come in, take off your coat, and I'll put up coffee."

"You're probably hungry after your shift. I picked up some bagels."

"That was thoughtful...You're such a *schöne Mädel*, with beautiful hair, like my Helen."

Like a sunken vessel laden with old cargo, the house was heavy, weighted with photos of Esther's dead husband and daughter; keepsakes, old heirloom furniture, and gold velvet drapes. There was a good-sized garden and storage shed in the rear.

Rebecca's cell beeped, and, after getting Esther's permission, she instructed Horne to come in through the alley entry in the garden. She tinkled on an out-of-tune small Steinway while Esther brought cups and plates into the dining room.

"My friend is here."

"I'll go out and undo the latch."

In a few moments, Horne bounded in. His determination and physical presence filled the room.

"Mrs. Klein, you're very gracious and brave to see us."

Rebecca realized that Horne's charm to strangers, particularly women, was inescapable. In Africa, he must have had a harem on call, as desperately in love with him as she now was.

She opened her file to an autopsy report on Helen Klein. Apart from the suspicious cause of death by gas, there was little of use and virtually no connection to Miriam's murder that they could discern. Yet Rebecca was convinced that Helen Klein's murder was not coincidental.

"Whom did the police suspect?" she asked.

"Oh, they wanted to say it was suicide for a few days. It was ridiculous. Suicides are depressed, give off signals, leave a note. Helen was going to be married the following week—she was on top of the world! She and her fiancé were deeply in love—just like you two."

Neither Horne nor Rebecca demurred; besides, they wanted to keep Esther on track. The coffee was perking and Esther went back into the kitchen and returned with an old-fashioned pot, placed it on a trivet, made another trip for butter and cheese. She sat down and poured the coffee, appearing distracted.

"After the police decided it looked fishy, they turned on her fiancé, Lewis, for about ten minutes. He was a resident at the hospital and the pediatric OD when Helen was murdered."

Something elusive disturbed Rebecca and she thought aloud.

"This young doctor, Lewis...was there any problem *he* had?" she asked.

Esther had a moment's hesitation. "You know, there had been. Earlier that year, a baby was brought to the ER. He was having convulsions, and Lewis tried to save him. I don't recall what the diagnosis was. But the child died. The parents went crazy and blamed him. This happens often when parents are bereaved. The hospital investigated the case. Lewis was very upset. But his conduct and treatment were faultless."

Horne pondered this new information.

"Did the police question this couple?"

"Not that I know of...." she stopped, suddenly wary. "The father called Lewis a kike bastard. But, no, Lewis didn't mention that to anyone but me—years later."

"Did Lewis find your daughter?" Horne asked.

The moment of this tragedy assumed a tactile presence and immediacy despite the passage of seven years. Esther struggled to maintain her professional demeanor.

"No, *I* found Helen. She was studying to be a nurse and in the program at Maimonides. When I was on the day shift, sometimes we'd have breakfast here or at her apartment, and go to the hospital together." Rebecca held Esther's hand, and her eyes clouded. "She'd get up early and wait outside the Shalom Bakery and go next door for Farmer cheese and lox."

Rebecca began to feel the strain of these disclosures.

"Helen was running late and hadn't answered the phone when I buzzed her to say I was on my way. I had a key."

Horne, with his hunter's instinct, rushed to the front window. A Ford Explorer with Pennsylvania plates waited at the curb.

"What's wrong?" Esther asked in alarm.

"Nothing. I just like to watch the traffic."

"I'm sad but relieved my husband had already died before this happened. He couldn't have dealt with it. Helen was an only child and very close with her dad."

The strain of listening to this courageous woman harboring tears and emotional insolvency had struck a chord with Horne. "I lived in Africa for twelve years and witnessed some hideous acts, and the families' reaction to them. They get revenge...eventually."

Esther grasped his hand and nodded. "Will you kill them?"

"Only if I have to." Rebecca saw Horne standing over the dead lion. "Now can I ask you something: When you found your daughter and called the police did you or the detectives notice anything unusual—odd—about the circumstances?"

Esther stared at him, distracted and puzzled. "I'm not sure. Wait...."

She left the room and returned with a tawny piece of poster paper, held in place by rusted clips. She unrolled it, the curled edges snapping and flapping back and forth. Horne placed the cups at the top and Rebecca held the bottom down with a dish.

A charcoal drawing of a naked woman, lying back in the classic posture of Manet's *Olympia*. But her eyes were closed, rather than daring the viewer to meet her arrogant gaze. The woman's pubic hair was starkly electric, vitally drawn by a masterly artist, but with contempt, like torn wires.

"Meet Helen Klein...murdered," her mother said, choking. "Mr. Horne, you know about death in Africa."

"It's the same everywhere."

"Death this way? This monster murdered my daughter and afterwards was so brazen that he took the time to *draw* her."

Horne brought out a pen and pad. "Would you send this to me?"

"Yes, yes, if it'll help. I think the reason the detectives were so lax was because they thought my Helen had posed for this."

Rebecca overcame her repugnance for the work and studied it for several minutes. If Bruno hadn't murdered her himself, the killer must have taken photos, sent it to him so that he could copy it. The complications of this Nazi group grew, changing like a virus.

"This is a trashy imitation of a great Viennese artist, Egon Schiele," Rebecca said. "He's in every major museum. His work was considered pornographic." She pondered over the work. "This is so strange, Horne. Hitler was a *secret* admirer of Schiele's."

She turned it so that Horne and Esther could have a better view.

"Here, across her stomach—this isn't a shadow or a spontaneous squiggle. It's a musical notation from the Nazi 'Horst Wessel song.'" Rebecca gasped. "Look! You can make out initials...BVW, Bruno Von Winter.

"Even if you'd given it to the detectives, they wouldn't have understood the Nazi myth involved. It's the hallmark of these killers."

"Maybe it'll be evidence you and Mr. Horne can use."

Horne checked the street again. "Possibly. Thank you for everything, Mrs. Klein. "We're going to have to leave now. Preferably through the back garden."

"Are they here—outside?" Esther asked, trembling.

Horne did not respond. He dialed the number of the car hire across the street and instructed the driver to make sure a Ford Explorer wasn't following him and to pick them up in the alley. He had given the manager a hundred dollars in good faith and was assured that his instructions would be followed.

"Could you possibly lend Rebecca a dark shawl? I want her to cover her head. And is there a chance you have a cane and one of those skullcaps?"

"Yes. My husband had a walking stick."

In five minutes, he and Rebecca were in the backseat of the Star of David Car Hire, a Buick with religion, living through its winter years.

"LaGuardia airport," he told the bearded driver.

"What about our bags in the hotel?" Rebecca asked.

"We'll have them shipped. I might buy you a new concert wardrobe after I sell Sycamore."

"Does that mean I'm a keeper?" she asked, pleading.

He stroked her face. "You know that the most basic thing about dating is not to rush the other person. I like to get to know a person. I wish you didn't come on so strong."

"Go to hell."

28

Horne had maintained contact with Butch during the trip. It came as a relief to him to rediscover how razor-sharp the man who'd taught him to shoot actually was—when it suited him. In some respects, Butch's help baffled him. Playing the guilt game with Butch hadn't worked; maybe a taste of action had brought out his warrior skills.

At Miami International Airport, a nifty Hertz Solara waited at the curb for Horne. He shook hands with Luke Montgomery, a long-haired, scrawny, fiftyish ex-cop-turned-limo-driver. He was going to pick up Rebecca. Horne wanted to make it easy for the couple pursuing her. Give them enough time to meet their people.

He was not disappointed. Three men in their late twenties with buzzcuts, piercings, Marlin baseball caps, gaudy flowered shirts, and lightning-bolt tattoos on their iron-pumped arms, showed up for the man and woman trailing them. Horne made a note of the license of their Expedition van. When the five neo-Nazis were behind the limo, he crawled through the airport and phoned Luke.

"Take Rebecca to The Breakers in Palm Beach. Don't stop for any-thing."

"You got it. Butch said you were an African hunter."

"A lifetime ago. Luke, I may need some heavy equipment."

"Rifles, shotguns....I've got everything."

"Get it ready."

Horne had picked the hotel because he was curious about how he would feel, revisiting a place where his parents had worked when he was five: Bonnie in the kitchen kneading dough as a baker's assistant; his father as a guitarist during cocktail hour, well before retro Man-hattans and martinis had made a recovery in today's bars.

Hours later he showed up in their suite, laden with Polo shopping bags from the hotel store. The bathroom door was ajar, water running and Rebecca bent over, squeezing a tube of bath foam, its piney scent wafting pleasantly through the air. The mini-bar had been under siege. A pair of vodkas had been tackled. He rapped on the door to avoid frightening her.

"Hello, Daddy's home."

"It took two hours to get here. I was so worried about you."

"Don't. Smells good in here."

I had Vita-Bath sent up," she said.

"You don't give a damn about how you spend someone else's money."

"I'll make it worth your while, believe me."

Horne's reawakening of her sensuality amplified into a maddening fever. Her nipples hardened, and she wasn't surprised by her excitement.

"The tub will take two. Shall we try?"

"My legs are too long and I'm a shower man. You go on."

His newly acquired restraint exasperated her. She rose from the side of the tub, a little tipsy, preparing to undo her belt for full exposure, but he turned his back.

"Horne...aren't you going to make a move? Or do we become enemies again? That seems to be the way you're most comfortable in relationships with women."

She grabbed him and brushed her lips against his, but he craned his neck away.

"I feel like a big brother about you."

Her feminine radar exploded. "No! You're not—no—it's impossible—not really gay?"

"Nothing wrong with being gay. Happens I'm not." He smiled coldly. "We have killers out there. Let's put this on hold."

In humiliation and fear, she asked, "Aren't we're safe here?"

"As long as *I've* got my panties on, we are."

"I'm in heat."

"I'll phone it in to an outcall."

She wanted to weep, throw herself at his feet, but restrained herself.

"You are a tyrant."

"I guess I am," he said gravely. "When you kill a human being, something inside you changes."

He handed her a large blue bag from the hotel's Polo shop. "I've just had my first experience shopping for lingerie and ladies' wear. Did I tell you, I do a little cross-dressing? If you want to exchange anything, they're open till eight."

"How would you know my sizes?"

"I copped a look the other night when your stuff was drying. Soiled underwear doesn't offend me."

"Animal."

"Hunt long enough, you become what you are—them."

He smiled insidiously at her. The unadulterated joy of bagging this trophy in his own good time was certainly a mood elevator. That, and the intoxicating prospect of future millions in his bank account had bought him a pair of aces on the deal. From cutting corners at Tijuana's finest in Downtown L.A. to retail prices at The Breakers. He was $1,200 lighter, but this investment seemed to him a change of luck at the table.

"Oh, *darling*, I picked up toothbrushes and other stuff."

"Toothbrushes," she said with a scowl.

"Hygiene's important to me."

She pulled a white linen blouse and skirt out of the bag.

"Wow, you're a real spendthrift."

"You'll find a bill at the end of this safari. When you start working at Ingrid's place, I'll put a lien on your salary. You'll make plenty of money for me when you're hitting the concert track in Europe."

She rooted through the bag, and raised her fist at him. "Where's the Rio bikini you promised me?"

"What do you do, record voices, write down things people casually say?" He loved needling her. "I'm not going to make it easy on you. You'll have to model the whole collection for me tomorrow."

"Not now?"

"*Nein.*"

He whipped out baseball caps and a man's extra large T-shirt from his bag, which he tossed to her. "You can wear this to bed."

She held it against her breasts, then glanced at the logo: THE BREAKERS.

"The humor of American males. God, give me strength."

"It's just the name of the hotel. Take your bath, princess."

His cell phone rang, sparing him another of her temper flares. He picked it up immediately. She raised her palms, alarmed and mystified.

"How we doing, Luke?...Really. Have they spotted me?" He paused. "That's good. Yeah, I think that would be best." He scrutinized Rebecca. "It would be a problem disguising her. I agree—the Statue of Liberty. I'll have a drink at the bar, then head over to her table." He smirked at her. "What...? She looks like a pick-up, trying to mooch a dinner." She raised a fist in his face and he batted it down. "Yeah, the rich ones would eat dinner with a gorilla rather than grab a check." He nodded reassuringly to Rebecca. "Okay, Luke, thanks. Butch said you were more than reliable."

"What's this about?" she asked when he had clicked off.

"Your driver is a friend of Butch's. Former undercover detective. He owns a limo service. Feel secure, now?"

She nodded in amazement. "You're so devious, Horne."

"Can't take people out into the bush and let harm come to them—especially a woman who's seriously interested in me. I think I'd like a friendship ring or something before I go any further. They have a jewelry shop here. I'll pick out something tasteful, not too gaudy."

She retreated and solemnly asked, "Do you really care about me?"

He nodded. "Ummm, a little, I think. Now use plenty of that bath stuff, I paid for it."

She became unexpectedly emotional. "It's an abominable thought...but something good has come out of Miriam's death. You're her gift to me."

"You mean that?" he asked, touched.

"Yes."

When she was in the bath, Horne moved out to the terrace with the remainder of the vodkas. Luke Montgomery had left a package for him at the concierge's desk and he unwrapped it to find a snub-nosed .32 pea-shooter with a holster. He checked it, then snuggled it into the blazer he had just bought. He'd take his new clothes into the bathroom in case she started snooping or clipping tags with nostril scissors.

Alone on the terrace overlooking the ocean, he poured himself three midget vodkas on some ice and tried to collect his thoughts. How could they see the couple they had come to question without exposing themselves to the Nazis?

Horne was an old hand at watching women blow-drying their hair, fixing themselves, but this was a new and tender experience for him. Rebecca gazed at him in the mirror with such desire that he was dumbfounded by the emotion she projected. Her luminous, gray-green eyes lingered on him. He welcomed the new ease of their relationship, its evolution into friendship, the growing affection. He had spent years observing the behavior of animals in the wild and their mating rituals. On a human level, he had ignored this process. In the past, his connection with women had not possessed this fertile, rounded shape. It had been linear: they needed protection and were to be snared to satisfy his needs.

"I have no make-up."

"That'd be pushing me a bit after the undies scandal at the hotel shop."

"You didn't check through my former make-up case in Milwaukee?"

"You don't need anything, Rebecca."

She rose from the vanity stool and her head reached his chin. He was invariably a foot taller than most women. Not her. He kissed her on the forehead. Behind her imperial exterior, he had discovered just how delicate she was. Despite her habitual autocratic manner, Rebecca Benjamin was an apprehensive woman who wanted to perform the most intimate recital of her life for his pleasure.

He enjoyed ragging her. "I'd like a little privacy."

"Oh, yes, of course, after the grasslands of Africa, you're used to it."

"This is not the bush. I'll shave and shower and be ready in fifteen minutes. No more drinks for you until dinner."

"Privacy," she grumbled, "you've probably populated half of Africa on your *safaris*."

"Not enough. They're losing millions every year to AIDS. Now get lost."

Personality conflicts occurred at Charlie's Crab restaurant in Palm Beach. Noreen and Virgil had settled in for a big dinner. But the three local Nazi Low Riders assigned to them by Winterhaven ordered more rounds of drinks. Two of them had recently been furloughed from Florida State Prison and were doing riffs on their time, rather than concentrating on the danger that Rebecca presented.

"We have complaints," the local assistant *Gauleiter*, who called himself Captain Polk, said, "and all the big shots at Winterhaven never listen to us. No decent legal aid, visits, canteen money, like my boys were promised. Now you come marching into our sector ordering us around."

Polk was in his early thirties with close-set, feral eyes, and, except for the lightning-bolt tattoo on his mahogany caveman arms, might have passed for a citizen; the other two menaces were young skanks with dyed-blonde hair and calamitous attitudes.

THE WINTERHAVEN SOLUTION

"Tell them about the green bologna and raw chicken they forced us to eat," Art Spindler said, spraying out some loose tobacco from the end of a busted Lucky Strike. He was a pasty-faced musclehead whose face was so heavily rigged with metal rings and spikes, it would be impossible to accurately identify his features in a line-up.

"Don't forget 'management loaf,'" squawked Joey Hinson, slugging down his fourth heavy-metal rum concoction, then grabbing for Virgil's beer.

Noreen had left behind this world of rebellious misfits in various mental wards, and she was not prepared to tolerate insolence. "This is not what we're used to as dinner table conversation."

"Well, fuck conversation, lady," Hinson barked.

"That's enough," Virgil said, slamming down his fist.

Blood boiling, she said, "I know what management loaf is. I used to feed it to rowdy patients. If you two were under my care, I'd've laced the dog shit with arsenic, since you're never going to learn manners this side of hell."

"Hate is survival," observed Polk philosophically in an effort to quell a revolt and calm down the party.

Spindler immediately came to his cellmate's defense. "You know who you're talking to? I did seven hard for—"

Noreen fired back furiously, "—What, molesting sheep?"

"Listen to me," Virgil said, "we're all in danger because a Yid bitch is investigating *us*! Now, what happened down here some years ago? Who would she contact? Winterhaven is having a problem locating this record."

The waiter served the drinks and with a sunshine smile flapped the menus. "You folks ready to feast?"

"One more time you ask and I'll grab a lobster cracker and split your balls," Spindler informed him.

He sprinted away, and Virgil could see him complaining to a manager. He had to settle them down. "Look, gentlemen, we're all on the same side. We'll convey your complaints to Magnus when we get back."

Polk nodded. "Just tell us who this bitch is and we'll drain her blood."

Virgil agreed. "Let me check with Winterhaven. I'd like to put an end to her now myself."

"We dry-cleaned our SS dress blacks," Spindler said. "Be nice to get her back to the house and go to work on her."

Virgil fluttered a twenty-dollar bill at the waiter. "We're ready now."

He approached cautiously. "I won't take any more abuse."

Noreen stroked his hand. "Don't worry, Mama's bad boys will behave or I'll shove their heads in the lobster tank and hold them down until bubbles squirt up."

29

The change of scenery in Tampa, lulling bay winds and sunshine, exerted a calming influence on Harry; work diffused his passion for Rebecca. The mystical grandeur of the sinuous, triangular structures he had created enthralled him. He thought of them as Bruno's Pyramids. They would evolve over time into an architectural masterpiece. Working on site with the earthmovers and foundation team had bonded his relations with the contractor's men. He loved to wear a hardhat and drive a CAT himself, unusual for a lead architect. But even as a boy at Winterhaven, Harry had skillfully handled heavy machinery and had never outgrown his affection.

It had been a long day on site. Battling with Jack Leopold, Harry had insisted on reinforced concrete, rather than steel framing, which would have been cheaper and faster. But in the event of fire, it would buckle. Harry was a concrete, classical-column man. Uninterrupted adaptable space had to be sacrificed for endurance and safety. At the top of the structure, a circular glass restaurant would sit poised, seemingly precarious, on a hidden support.

His private cell phone rang while he was riding down the shaft elevator with his team from the fortieth story. Only his father and Rebecca had this number. His phone was out of satellite range. Let it be Rebecca, he thought. The gleaming bay illuminated the verdant tapestry of his embryonic park frontage. Here, he planned a serene Japanese bonsai garden with waterfalls and imported rocks.

At ground level, he and his team, exuberant with bonhomie, strolled to the office trailer. After they cleaned up at their rented apartments, he would take them to dinner at Don Shula's Steakhouse.

"I'll catch up with you guys in a minute," he said as they filed into the trailer for the first ritual drink of the night.

"Martini, Harry?"

"Make it a vodka on the rocks."

Eyes sullen, he glared at the number and hit the callback.

"I thought you'd like to know that your angel is in the neighborhood," Magnus informed him in a sneering voice.

"What are you talking about? Listen, you can't keep breaking our protocol."

"Rebecca is at The Breakers—in *Palm Beach*. Doesn't that ring a bell?"

For an instant he was too shocked to speak. "Are you serious?"

"I think you better meet Virgil and Noreen. They're waiting to hear from you."

"I just can't—"

"—Can't *what*?"

He recognized the danger now. "Okay, give me their number."

Canceling his dinner plans, he calculated that if he drove to his jet, parked, filed a flight plan to West Palm Beach, rented a car or was picked up, it would take more time than speeding the two hundred miles in his leased Toyota Land Cruiser.

Horne spent half an hour at the hotel's Flagler steakhouse bar drinking big Grey Goose martinis. He had a childhood glimmer of the past, the early seventies: his parents smoking joints and drinking wine; his father strumming his guitar like Neil Young. He must've been five, hanging out at the beach, carefully watching Man-of-War jellyfish, their dark blue cords flowing in on the crest of waves after storms. On the family break, they had driven to Vero Beach to see the Dodgers in spring training and later to Tarpon Springs to fish snook and pompano.

As an adult he had craved their company with a yearning that might have seemed callow to others. Apart from shared love, the creamy essence of what his parents offered was a good time. The three of them had become one another's treasures. He had never tired of them.

"Refill?" the bartender inquired.

"Maybe a few." Horne inclined his head toward Rebecca, seated at a table by the window. "Hey, is that redhead babe in the alcove alone?" He felt reasonably sure that the couple pursuing Rebecca still didn't actually know his real identity.

"I'm sorry, sir, I wouldn't know."

"Do me a favor and send someone over to ask if I can buy her a drink.—Never mind, I'll do it myself."

Weaving through tables larded with men in raucous plaids regaling tales of the links to stultified women in chessboard blouses and pastel pantsuits, Horne pressed through to the unaccompanied beauty at the alcove window table, carefully observed by the dining room.

"You're very beautiful in white. Another schnapps, Fraulein?"

Quick as a mongoose, the station captain appeared and viewed the landscape of another pick-up.

"Will you be joining the lady?"

"Yes, I believe he will," she said, extending her hand to Horne.

30

Virgil and Noreen refused to stay with Polk at his beach enclave. They had a crucial meeting. In any case, the place was a virtual arsenal, and, in the night humidity, reeked of sweating oils and metal.

"No way we can meet Bruno in this shit-hole," Noreen whispered to Virgil when Polk was fiddling with the tumblers on his safe.

"All we know, DEA and ATF are doing a surveillance on these lunatics."

Polk laid a tightly packed kilo of coke on the table.

"You could make hospital beds with those tight corners," Noreen declared.

"Southern hospitality," Polk said, "after the ruckus at dinner."

Virgil stood up. "Another time. Actually we've got to check on the bitch at the hotel."

"I'll drop you off."

"We'd appreciate the loan of one of your cars," Noreen asked.

"Sure, take my Bronco."

Virgil and Polk shook hands. "See you tomorrow, and thanks."

They drove past Spindler and Hinson, who had been dropped off at one of the trailers on the property to sample the fresh batch of meth brew and await a crack delivery.

"Imagine taking a bust here and doing time with these crawlers," Noreen said.

"I'd shoot myself first."

Noreen peered at her watch. "It's just after ten." She evaluated the situation. "We've got to lose these people. When we report back to Winterhaven, we tell Magnus this chapter needs to have him send in the Orkin crew."

The call from Bruno came at ten-thirty and he arranged to meet them at the Hilton parking lot. He would see only Noreen. Virgil was still complaining about being given short shrift and the insult to his dignity. Fluttering with nerves, she got out of the Bronco and gave him Bruno's license tag.

"Hon, he's got to have his reasons."

Barely a minute after they arrived, bright lights flashed behind them twice. Noreen hurriedly kissed Virgil, then walked to the passenger side of the Land Cruiser. The window zipped down and the door was unlocked. She climbed in.

A man with tinted glasses and a Buccaneers cap, pulled low, put the car in gear. As he pulled into a spot, she was overcome by a stirring of recognition. She was astounded and audibly gasped.

"You're—"

"Yes, Noreen, you and Virgil have seen me before."

She recalled that he'd had a gun in his hand when he'd come up to Virgil in the garage the day they were following Rebecca.

When he removed his glasses, she was overcome by panic. "My God!—you're the *architect*!" There was a familiar, terrifying quality about him.

"I am. You almost caused serious trouble for all of us last year."

"We were acting on your father's orders."

For a moment, he did not respond and she, too, remained taciturn. She didn't dare ask why he called himself Harry Summerfield. In the interstices of Magnus's mind a mystical, grand design dwelled, far beyond the knowledge of his disciples. She thought: The Son has descended and is in my presence with a message.

"Explain to Virgil that it's safer to have a man and woman talking in a parked car, rather than two men with a woman."

"You're right, of course. It's an honor to meet you at last."

"That goes both ways. I'm very proud of both of you. Your commitment and bravery are models for everyone."

"It's our cause," she said with conviction. "Your father saved us, and we're true believers in the total extermination of all Jews."

During Bruno's high-speed drive from Tampa, the soaring mission to which he had been born and bred had reasserted itself. He had wanted to live in the real world of choices to see for himself if he enjoyed its irregularities, and had found only a lack of symmetry within himself. But more than anything, he'd had to find out if, as an artist, he could quell all doubts about his talent.

Magnus had reclaimed another lost, wandering soul. Of all people, his own son. His father had always been right about everything. The year of chaos—the year of attempting to forge a hellish alliance with his dragon, Rebecca—had at last dissipated, and he saw a clear link and purpose to his future at Winterhaven.

"What's going on with Rebecca—this trip of hers?"

Noreen provided a nurselike crisp summary of the situation. It became unmistakable to Bruno that Rebecca had pieced together incongruent strings, and developed a geometric form. He couldn't help but admire her ingenuity.

"She won't be a danger to us much longer," he said at the end. "Is she alone or traveling with someone?"

"On her own. But she's running us ragged. One minute she's in limos and staying in the best hotels, the next, she disappears."

His money had gone a long way, he thought.

"We want her badly, and this place—Palm Beach, wherever—would get us headlines, just like when we buried that rabbi alive. We could do her as a sand sculpture. In pieces...."

"I'm the architect, Noreen. Rebecca came here to go to an antique shop off Worth Avenue called Cognoscente."

"What? You're going too fast. Please spell it," she asked, furiously writing on her palm. "Okay, got it. What do you want us to do?"

"Keep on her. Not so she'd notice. Rebecca's eventually heading back to L.A."

"You're so sure. How?"

He gave her a sour, knowledgeable smile. "She'd never leave her piano."

"You know everything."

His heritage, ignored for years, returned, and he felt the supremacy instilled in him. "I'm the heir to a kingdom of magicians."

"We know that....Can I mention something personal?" Caught in the current of her adulation, Bruno waved his hand. "The women at Winterhaven are going crazy. They miss you...your visits...."

"They want to see more of me?" he asked, with a tinny laugh.

"They sure do. They love what you do...the way you and Magnus blindfold them...they can't imagine what you look like. But the children are beautiful. Images of *you*! You've got a crowd of worshippers at Winterhaven. They're waiting...waiting."

The information pleased him, soothing his battered self-esteem.

"I'm glad they enjoy themselves. Hitler once told my father that women fake their orgasms because they think men actually care."

Noreen's rowdy laughter filled the car. "You're the exception to Hitler's rule." She had never been so intrigued and intimidated of anyone before. "They don't know how you manage to just fade away afterwards."

"Do they? That's a secret."

"I promise not to say a word."

"When I was helping to build the castle at Winterhaven, my father wanted underground passages. I thought it was unreasonable. But he was my first client. And you do what the client wants." Bruno found himself totally seduced by Noreen, without the crawl of desire. "I designed a maze for him."

She was thrilled to become his confidante. "I'll never tell a soul."

"Good night." He took his cap off and kissed her forehead. "You were worth the ride, Noreen."

Hyperventilating, she slowly walked back to the Bronco, trying to bring down her blood pressure. An insight of magnitude churned through her mind. She could detect the modes of insanity as only an expert could. The aura Bruno radiated had frightened her.

Virgil grabbed hold of her, close to hysteria.

"What's he like?"

"He's the son of our God. Charming...and stark, raving mad."

As after-dinner Irish Coffees were being served to Horne and Rebecca, a loud party of blitzed golf groupies meandered toward the golf-course exit to the pro shop.

"Stop eating. Get up and wiggle into this crowd. Wait outside the pro shop."

"Is this another of your tactics—taking me on some manicured fairway so that you can imagine you're on the Serengeti?"

"Don't look up. Our friends are at the bar and they haven't seen us."

Rebecca's watchdogs had moved to a corner table, calmly observing the scene. They probably had spotted him in Beverly Hills with his beard and moustache. He doubted if they'd recognize him. He ordered a grappa and joined a chattering foursome, shook hands and discussed handicaps. Edging away from his new bar buddies, he dialed the hotel's operator and asked if there were any calls or messages. He was reassured to learn no one had phoned. He lingered on the far side of the couple's table. He punched in Rebecca's cell number. She picked up at once.

"You okay?...Good, I'll be right out."

Drink in hand, he scanned their faces and slipped by them. They hadn't been suspicious. He hesitated, tempted to yank out the .32 and march these people outside, but sanity prevailed. He was at The Breakers in Palm Beach, not in Africa drinking cold beer in a corrugated iron-roof sinkhole with highway whores cackling with truck drivers.

He circled the pro shop, now closed, but people were looking in the window admiring new Callaway clubs. Coming from behind, he took Rebecca's arm, startling her.

"If only I knew their names," he said. "Doesn't matter. I'll fix 'em good."

"What about me?"

In the darkness of the dewy course, he paused beside an undulating sand trap and kissed her. Moments later, he ignored her in the elevator, escorted her to the suite, checked it, and said: "Back soon."

"Where are you going now?"

"I'd like to make sure we have an undisturbed night."

"That's reassuring," she said, smiling.

He returned to the lobby, cut through to the golf course, and stood outside the bar for some time, where he had a view of the couple. He dialed Luke Montgomery's number.

"Hi, the bastards who've been on our asses since L.A. are in the Flagler bar. Do you know anyone in security here?" Horne laughed. "An ex-con, that's good. My guy's got a clothespin nose; he's well built; shaved head; wearing a starched white shirt; rep tie and khakis. She's a short-haired battleship blonde in one of those Mahjong red-print tops and black pants—both wearing running shoes. Can you get 'em rousted the fuck out of here?...Yeah, and thanks for the piece. It should take down a mosquito. I need some serious weapons for tomorrow." He waited. "Okay. Yep, we'll sneak out with some bikes near the spa. Pick us up at the staff entrance at seven."

31

Before returning to her, Horne checked the grounds for the three men at the airport. At the front, near the fountains, he spotted them. He did another survey of the lobby, took the elevator up to the suite and monitored the entire floor.

As he slid the card into the door, he caught a few bars of a once-familiar melody and a voice that sounded like his father's.

Keith was playing guitar and singing Neil Young's "Heart of Gold." His father had a deeper voice than Young's and his own style, but the recurrent melancholy of the original had never been quite there. Still, it was enough to get Keith sizable tips, keep his car tuned, the bong filled and new clothes for Bonnie when they had worked at the hotel.

The music faded. Horne was still unnerved by the unexpected impact. When he was inside the suite, Rebecca was standing on the terrace.

A spectral, lambent glow danced over her head, illuminating her with sparks. Were kids on the beach, letting off fireworks?

He called out, "I'm back."

Radiating gaiety, she smiled mysteriously at him. He wrapped his arms around her. Holding her tightly, he found himself in a state of rapturous love. Yet Rebecca's ethereal quality inhibited him. Unlike his nights at Lake Mayanara, when he would swim naked with a woman, and afterwards plunge into a mindless merger in the dark, waking to the flapping flight of the flamingoes before they went on their way, this moment would endure.

He herded her to the bed, dislodging gold-wrapped chocolates on the pillows. With willowlike grace, she curled into him. Her attire was, at best, scanty: The Breakers T-shirt fully inflated now, baseball cap and silk panties.

"Did I buy this stuff for you?"

"Yes. Isn't it athletic enough? I can get a lot of wear out of it as a running outfit in Beverly Hills. I've heard about wealthy women having personal shoppers. I think I'll give you a trial." He rolled away. "Horne, relax. You're in the hands of an expert. I just watched twenty minutes of the adult channel...."

"Part of your duties of running up my bill." He brushed the hair off her face and kissed her nose. "I hope you learned something useful."

"I'm not sure. You'll have to decide that."

She unzipped his trousers slowly, then gulped, like someone attending the unveiling of Cleopatra's obelisk during a fertility rite. Her baseball cap flopped off. She had always been the quarry and hadn't undressed a man before. He was amused by her ineptness.

"I'm not squandering your money. That was a tutorial. I'm ready for higher learning. Damn, we have no baby oil." They both laughed. "Are you an ice-cube man?"

Seized by a mating hunger, a condition of desire-anxiety throbbing for her, his frisky mood became less playful.

As he slipped his hand under her T-shirt, she smiled enigmatically. His fingers glided over her breast. She seemed to be drifting to another plane. In a silky voice she began to sing the opening of Neil Young's "Heart of Gold."

Horne suddenly pulled away, stared at her, and froze.

"What's wrong? Excessive modesty doesn't become you, Horne."

"That song...!"

She was puzzled. "I don't know what you mean."

He assumed the role of interrogator. "I'd like an explanation, right now."

She was taking too long to reply, shrinking away, her easy smile vanishing into a mask of gloom. "Don't go on with this, please."

"You heard—my father's voice. *You saw him?*"

He became angry when she tried to divert him.

"I don't want to talk about it, please."

"Rebecca, tell me the truth."

"I don't want to spoil this moment with you."

"Tell me what happened!"

She edged away from the bed and he followed her out to the terrace. He turned her around. Her eyes were closed. Rebecca had often wondered if she possessed a gift or whether she were cursed by this access into the cosmic collective unconscious. Were these images merely delusions, and would she always think of herself, as others did, as the girl who imagined she saw ghosts and communicated with them? At heart, she knew she had been forced to inhabit a rarefied sphere and could not find her way out. Since her childhood visions of her parents trapped under the ice, this burden had darkened her moods.

"I saw specters of Miriam again. Then, all at once, she came back to me. I can't begin to explain in a logical way how or why these visitations take place. There is *another* world. It surrounds us. It's veiled, and sometimes I catch glimpses of it. When this happens, I feel I'm with many people...I don't know, wandering in some strange country."

He was again stunned by Rebecca's powers.

"Tonight, Miriam introduced me to Keith and Bonnie. Musicians seem to find each other *there*. It must be some affinity. Music is the connection to other dimensions. It's a ghostlike communion."

Horne had tears in his eyes. He rubbed them away with his knuckles and struggled to recover his composure.

"They're dead?" Horne's voice had a submissiveness.

Rebecca, somber, nodded.

"Jesus. I knew, yet I didn't. About four years ago, when I'd just about given up hope, I ran into an Arab trader who thought I'd throw some safari trade his way. He owned a roadside *duka*, a kind of truckstop, and he said they might have drifted into Rwanda. Over the years, I traveled there three times during their endless civil wars."

Rebecca clamped her fingers around his hands with such force that his pulse throbbed.

"What? Is there more?"

"Yes. They met some musicians—nomadic Tutsis." Her eyes became distended, unfocused. "These people were very striking, tall and graceful, with elegant, carved features. Your father was fascinated by their music. He and Bonnie traveled with them for a few days."

Horne could not stop shivering, and she held him tightly.

"When they were making camp, a heavily armed gang of men—their mortal enemies—much smaller and shorter men than the Tutsis...stormed the village."

"Hutus," he said, "they've been at war with the Tutsis for centuries, and still are—all through Central Africa. Both sides have lost millions in a genocide."

"I know about things like that."

"You do, don't you." His attitude, even his voice, had a muted timbre. He kissed her and she ran her hand through his hair. "You're a brave woman and I'm hopelessly in love with you. I never imagined I was capable of feeling this way."

"And I love you too, Horne. You're my searcher, and I've become your guide. I want us to be together as long as always is for us."

She released him and her eyes closed again, the lids pulsating. When they opened, they were filled with a vista of dazzling spaciousness, as though encompassing the world in her view. Rebecca was still trapped in a waking trance and he became alarmed.

He shook her. "Are you okay?"

"I think so."

"Is there anything more you remember about my parents?"

"At the end...fire...I saw a devastating fire in the sky. Like films of Hiroshima."

Horne's quest had ended. He sank into a depressed and futile rage. His parents were dead. He had twisted his life, changed his destiny, but at last he knew the truth.

They returned to the bedroom, undressing in private, silently. The prospect of making love surrendered now to consolation. She held him tightly as he drifted off to sleep. Miriam had brought her this love.

By six-thirty the next morning, Horne had already paid the bill and arranged for Hertz to send over a driver to pick up his rental. He pedaled a bike and rode around the fountains in the driveway of the hotel. He spied the bald, wiry man sitting at the wheel of a gray Ford Taurus, reading a *Miami Herald*. Horne whipped by him. Off to the side, the woman—Rebecca's constant shadow—was talking to a couple of sleepy bellhops. Horne slipped into high gear and rode down the bike path as though it were a practice run for the Tour de France.

Rebecca sat inside Luke Montgomery's Cadillac limo, listening to local news, a round-up of robberies, murders, woundings, and weather. Horne slid the bike into a stand and got into the back seat, now loaded with their clothes. Luke pulled out to South Ocean Boulevard into a hornet's nest of traffic and headed for a local place called Testa's.

On the terrace over breakfast and coffee, the languid sea breeze rustling the tapered palm trees, a lazy belch of thunder vibrated from the south, they might have been in paradise instead of being pursued like game.

Luke hadn't heard of Cognoscente or the Edelsteins, who owned this exclusive shop off Worth Avenue. "How would I know a place like that? I'm working on my third divorce and fourth mortgage," he said with cynical self-deprecation. "Now, take Butch: He owns a house free and clear, and always finds a rich girlfriend. That Ingrid's a gem."

When they nodded, he continued, "Butch collects astronomical fees for investigating fires. He made fifty big ones on a motel arson job down here and he gave me ten. He didn't have to do that because I was still on the force, and we've been friends ever since."

Rebecca flipped her files open and handed them to Luke. "Did you know or hear anything about this young woman's murder when you were on the police force?"

Luke scanned the police report. "Cynthia Edelstein. No, it was a Palm Beach case. Unless it was drugs or serious narcotics, it would just evaporate. Someone would've had to confess for something like this to have been solved. It's a bleep, and nobody has the time to listen. The caseloads homicide has are staggering."

"Are there neo-Nazi crimes down here?" Horne asked.

Luke reflected for a moment. "Not much reported in this part of Florida. There're some groups and action in the northern counties of the state—on the borders between Georgia and Alabama—where you've got the backwoods white supremacists." He flipped over pages of the report. "This seems to have been a suicide."

Rebecca protested. "It was murder!"

32

Cognoscente, the Edelstein shop, led a covert existence in a dark, tree-lined fork off Worth Avenue. A quixotic two-tiered sign in the window greeted clientele.

"NOWADAYS PEOPLE KNOW THE PRICE OF EVERYTHING AND THE VALUE OF NOTHING."
—OSCAR WILDE

When the shop door creaked open, a woman in green velvet pajamas, a tortoiseshell comb jammed into dyed black hair, confronted Rebecca and Horne. She was as sour as the grapefruit she was scooping out with a plastic knife and fork. Her husband teetered on a wobbly ladder, trying to balance a figured vase on a dusty shelf, staving off spiders, and sneezing into the cuff of his denim shirt.

"Good morning. That's a very fine Biedermeier ice pail—probably early nineteenth century," Rebecca remarked.

Milton Edelstein clambered down the steps. "You don't have an appointment."

"You one of those phonies from the 'Antique Roadshow' trying to hustle us?" his wife Denise demanded, spitting out a pip.

"No. We had a collection at home in Vienna," Rebecca replied. She peered up at the sullen man. "May I have a look at this cavalier wooing his princess? I'll tell you if it's real."

"Sure, you seem to know what you're talking about."

Horne was at his most affable and reassuring. "Hello, there. We've made a long trip to meet you. I think it'll be worthwhile for all of us."

The couple were perplexed and looked at Rebecca and Horne, who were smiling warmly at them.

"I'm Rebecca Benjamin, and this is Douglas Horne. To be honest, we're not really interested in antiques. We've traveled across the country to discuss Cynthia's murder and see if we can shed some light on it. We *know* it wasn't a suicide or an accident."

Milton stared at them for a moment through the bulging red pillows hanging under his somber brown eyes. He was over six feet tall, but stooped.

"So someone still does care," he ventured, nodding to his wife.

"We prayed for something like this," Denise said.

"My friend's sister was murdered last year in Los Angeles," Horne informed them. "We believe there's a link to the people who killed your daughter." Horne's attitude and demeanor were once again those of the hunter challenging the forces of nature to defy him. "I think we can help each other."

Rebecca eyes pleaded. "We're not the kind of people who would hurt you."

The shock of this statement burst through the couple's armor and long pent-up hopes. Denise curled into Milton's arms and as he held her, he soothed her.

"Milton, you stopped believing." She began to weep. "The Messiah sent these people."

Milton led Rebecca and Horne through a door at the back of the rabbit warren up a flight of stairs. They beheld a bright, open loft, with a monumental retractable skylight; exploding orange and purple bougainvillea trained on trellises set beside a greenhouse filled with lady's slipper orchids. An entire wall was given to oversized art and antique books.

After the griminess of the shop below, the couple's hidden life seemed magical. Rebecca wandered through the massive space, peering with an artist's eye at walls with paintings by Klee, Picabia, Breton, and Giacometti; alongside these were sets of original Bauhaus drawings by Gropius, and others by Mies van der Rohe and Le Corbusier.

In a corner, Rebecca arrived at a gleaming black Ritmüller grand. Her eyed roved over the piano and her fingers brushed the closed hood. She had abandoned her career and Horne realized how despondent and lost this made her feel.

"Rebecca's a concert pianist. She was going to have her debut with the Vienna Philharmonic."

Milton bowed his head. "Really?"

"Oh, nobody cares about last year. I'll never play with them." She tested the piano, listening acutely to the notes and studying the hammers striking. "A soloist's death is the only reason the orchestra accepts for a cancellation. Maybe it was *barschert*."

The Edelsteins listened, intrigued.

She gave them a tight smile. "Let's forget it, Mr. Edelstein. If we find the people who murdered my sister—and your daughter—maybe one day, I'll go back to my music."

Denise directed Horne and Rebecca to a long, multicolored Murano glass shelf below the skylight, which illuminated photographs of a vivacious, suntanned girl with long, black curled hair and fine features. The light filtered in and the photographs of Cynthia glimmered.

Rebecca picked up a chased silver frame off the shelf, a collage of Cynthia's photographs. Low string vibrations emanated from the images. She clutched one to her breast, then kissed it.

Denise was alarmed by Rebecca's behavior. "What are you doing?"

Milton began to shiver. "Cynthia's...*here*! I can smell her perfume."

Rebecca's voice seemed to emerge from another dimension.

"Cynthia has contacted me. She wants you to talk to us."

A vortex of sun rays swirled through the room from the photograph in Rebecca's hand. The three onlookers became transfixed by a scent of gardenias and the ballet of light crisscrossing the tables and the walls.

Rebecca explained what she had extracted from old detective reports. The Edelsteins had not discussed Cynthia's case for years and it was grueling for them to go back to it now.

They had traveled to Europe for a vacation and left Cynthia to look after the shop. She was doing research and writing articles for magazines as well as doing appraisals. She had met Julian Marks, an English scholar and photographer who had come to Miami Beach to make a study of the art deco hotels on Ocean Drive.

"In those days it was a retirement community for old Jewish people," Milton said. "Ocean Drive always had something charming, though, its architecture and the beach across the street from the hotels. It was in transition. A few years later, the college kids discovered it, because the hotel rates were cheap. The developers moved in to restore the hotels and now it's the world-famous South Beach."

"Julian did a shoot of our loft for *Arts and Antiques*."

Denise said, "I can find the article."

When the photos appeared in the magazine, the highlight was the collection of architectural drawings.

"I bought them from a dealer in Zurich. Pure serendipity. I saw a massive Rococo vase in his window. I knew I could move it immediately in Palm Beach. I also wound up with some drawings."

"Milton and I became very attached to them. We had a lot of interest from museums, but decided not to sell them."

A collector had come to Cognoscente and asked Cynthia if he could see them. They were hanging in a special section. Cynthia tracked down her parents in Europe.

"She said this man was charming and very knowledgeable. She asked what Milton had paid for the drawings."

"I guessed it must've been about sixty thousand dollars. Cynthia told me this guy made an offer."

"I grabbed the phone from Milton. For once, he was speechless. This character was ready to pay half a million dollars."

"I was bowled over!" Milton continued, "If you're in the trade and someone comes in out of the blue and makes such an outrageous offer, you suspect he's acting for a very wealthy collector. It just struck me that these drawings should be kept in the family for Cynthia. Julian also loved them."

Cynthia agreed, and turned down his offer. Since Julian was in New York, she told her parents this gentleman was despondent. She agreed to go out to dinner with him to console him. He admitted that he was acquiring things for his father, who was from Vienna, such as Biedermeier, objects d'art, books.

Horne was tantalized and tried to be piece these facts together. "Vienna?"

Rebecca nodded, convinced that Magnus had orchestrated this. "Please go on," she said.

"Two days later, we flew back. We were surprised Cynthia didn't meet us at the airport with the station wagon. We had tons of stuff and had to hire a limo to take us to Palm Beach. We called the store, then her place, from the limo. We thought maybe she'd gone to New York. It was very disturbing because Cynthia would've left word."

"Julian flew in the same night from New York, a few hours after us," Milton recalled. "We tried to reach Cynthia again. He hadn't heard from her, either."

They had a key to the townhouse. The moment they entered, gas fumes overcame them. They covered their faces and opened all the windows. When they eventually reached the kitchen, they discovered Cynthia, naked, with her head in the oven. They eased her body out. It was evident that she had been dead for some time. Their exhaustion was compounded by hysteria, but they managed to contact the police, who sent over investigators and a forensic team.

"We were asked these ridiculous questions about Cynthia's emotional state." Milton extended his arms, imploring God for a reason. "Had Cynthia attempted suicide *before*, and were we covering up? What was the name of Cynthia's psychiatrist? I thought, my God, what the hell's going on? A beautiful young woman has been murdered! Her parents, her fiancé, don't count, even though their world is over!"

Denise stared into space for a moment. Years after their tragedy, it still retained the brutal reality of its horror. Bereavement had been displaced by imperishable anger.

Horne knew that the trail was steaming. "Did you ever find anything in the townhouse that might have struck you as odd?" he asked.

Denise was thinking, then leapt up and rushed to the back of the room; she searched through a vintage steamer trunk, producing a small painting.

Rebecca said, "It's signed Bruno Von Winter."

Shock played across the Edelstein's ashen faces. "How could you know that?" Denise asked. "Unless he's the killer?"

"We believe he is," Horne stated. "Bruno is the son of a man who was Hitler's closest friend. Magnus Von Winter and his followers are neo-Nazis. They've been killing Jewish women, even a rabbi, for years. After they murdered Miriam, Rebecca found a bizarre link."

"We were told this is repro of Vermeer's 'The Procuress,'" Milton said.

Rebecca placed the copy on a table and the four of them scrutinized it under a crazy quilt of sunshine beaming in from the skylight.

"I saw it in the Dresden Museum when I performed there," Rebecca explained. "Rembrandt painted 'The Jewish Bride' about ten years after the Vermeer," she noted. "It's possible that he met Vermeer, who was also an art dealer, some time earlier in Amsterdam, and saw the painting. Even though the circumstances are different, in both pictures, a man's hand is on a woman's right breast.

"Since my sister was murdered, I've given a lot of thought to Rembrandt's painting. For reasons I can't fathom, Bruno identifies with the world's greatest painters. In Borough Park, we talked to a woman whose daughter was also a victim, we believe. She found a drawing in *her* daughter's place. It was a remarkable copy of Egon Schiele's style with nudes."

"We know his work well," Milton said. "He was a famous Viennese Expressionist. But his work was scandalous in his day."

Rebecca sprang up, beaming. "That's it! I think I understand! Somehow or other Bruno gave up on his mission to become another Vermeer or Rembrandt, and turned to Schiele. His work is a corruption, a pastiche of great art. There's really nothing odd about your finding this. It's Bruno's calling card."

"It's obvious when you put it that way," Horne said excitedly. He had noticed something that Rebecca had missed. Picking up a large, bone-handled magnifying glass, he held it over the brilliant, patterned tapestry in the foreground of the painting."

Rebecca and the Edelsteins shrank away, appalled.

"I'm no expert on paintings, for sure. But I don't think Vermeer painted swastikas. See the way Bruno interwove them into the table-cloth's pattern and along the borders?"

"How did I miss this?" Milton chastised himself.

"You and Denise didn't know what to look for. Neither did the cops," Horne said. "When Rebecca called you last year, she was trying to find some evidence that this was murder and not a suicide."

"Thank God you came into lives," Denise said tearfully.

"And you into ours," Rebecca murmured.

33

A nimbus of black clouds raced through the sky, followed by a sudden burst of rain.

When the Edelsteins embraced Rebecca, Horne slipped down the stairs and searched for a back entrance. It was a reinforced steel door with a spyhole. He phoned Luke and asked him drive into the lane behind the store.

"Doug, I've got a Bronco with three guys and a Ford with the couple on my back."

"Can we fly out of Lauderdale?"

"Hang on, let me check the airlines' schedule." In a moment, he muttered, "I'll see if I can get you on."

"Luke, it's important. I'll let you have the .32 back. I need something big right now."

"A twelve gauge and a couple of other items."

"Does the rifle take four .375s or three .416 Rigbys?"

"Four H&H."

"I can live with it. Get them loaded and in the passenger seat. I'll have your pea-shooter and be out with Rebecca in five minutes. Is that enough time?"

"Make it ten so I can check the airlines. I'll call soon as I'm outside and cover you. Have Rebecca wear a hat and coat."

Horne turned to Milton. "I need a scarf or something to cover my face."

Rebecca slipped into Denise's raincoat and quickly pinned up her hair under a peaked cap. She kissed Milton and Denise.

"I'll keep in touch," she said, joining Horne at the steel door.

It was now fifteen minutes since he had spoken to Luke, and he was worried.

"Milton, if our friend isn't here in five more minutes, I'm going to have to borrow your car and leave it at the Lauderdale airport."

"We'll drive you," Denise said.

"Thanks, but no."

Horne pressed his eye to the spy hole. A UPS truck was making a delivery next door. He went outside in a low crouch, the .32 revolver concealed at his side. The alley was blocked with trucks. Through the foggy rain, he spotted Luke leaning out the window, arguing with a driver. Car horns blared and angry voices echoed.

Denise tried to hold Rebecca back. "Don't go!"

"What's wrong?" Milton asked.

"We have to leave now. Thanks for your help," Horne said to the Edelsteins, then took Rebecca's hand.

They dashed to Luke's car. It was now crawling behind trucks but closer to the outlet. Horne opened the rear door and Rebecca climbed in. The rain had eased, but the visibility was still poor.

"We loaded, Luke?"

"Yeah."

"Can we get out of Lauderdale?"

"American non-stop four forty-five P.M. it'll get you into LAX at seven ten P.M."

Rebecca was plainly frightened. "What's going on?"

Horne slid into the front seat, and she craned her head forward.

"Rebecca, I don't have plugs." He took out some Kleenex from Luke's box. "Do exactly what I tell you! Wad these tissues up; stuff them deep in your ears. Do it now! Then lie face down on the floor of the backseat."

"There's a blanket, Rebecca, cover yourself with it," Luke said tersely.

She was confused. With the balled tissue in her ears, she couldn't hear the men.

Horne picked up the Ruger shotgun and ammo.

"These fuckers just walked into the lion's den. I'll give them a little SS field training."

"What do you want me to do?" Luke asked.

"Just carry the ammo."

Horne pulled the visor down on his baseball cap and tied the black scarf over his face. He and Luke scrambled out of the car, wove low past a truck, and reached Virgil's Ford. In a crouch, he slipped by. He was now in front of the Bronco carrying the three men.

Horne fired the shotgun through the grill of the car. The explosive sound echoed. When smoke appeared, the men tried to get out. He quickly took the rifle from Luke, smashed the passenger window, and held the muzzle against one of the men's heads.

"Now, you scumbags get the fuck out of the van—very fast. Don't get cute or look back. Start running in the other direction or I'll blow you to pieces."

Gone was the aplomb and boldness of the neo-Nazi trio. In abject fear, they hustled out and sprinted away. Horne fired two shots over their heads and another into the van's gas tank.

He reloaded the shotgun and rushed to the Ford with the couple inside. He swiveled around on his knees and unloaded into their transmission. In a panic, Noreen was about to get out on the passenger side.

"Stay in the car, lady!"

Petrified, she screamed. Horne leaned into the car, shoving his elbow into her throat. Behind the wheel, Virgil, boggle-eyed, quaked. Horne stuck the scalding shotgun muzzle close to his forehead.

"Next time you and your sweetheart show up, bring coffins."

Flames and dense smoke spiraled through the air from the van in front of Virgil. In a moment the alleyway became an exploding inferno. Veiled in a stench of cordite, Luke, puffing, ran ahead of Horne, and jumped behind the wheel of his limo. A second detonation from the Ford thundered through the alleyway.

Horne climbed in next to him. "The closest airport, please, driver." He leaned over the seat, touched the backside of the human bundle lying on the floor.

"You okay, Rebecca?"

Luke slammed down on the accelerator and swerved out of the alley onto Worth Avenue, barreling past Gucci, Neiman's, and Saks.

Rebecca peeked out, tore out the Kleenex from her ears. She was still shuddering from the explosions. She leaned over to the front seat.

"Horne, are you all right? Did you have to shoot someone?"

Horne's expression portrayed innocence. "Oh, come on, Rebecca. I wouldn't do a thing like that. It was a gas main."

She was relieved to discover that Luke was as nervous as she. "Horne has his own way of getting out of traffic."

34

Back in L.A. and on the run like fugitives, Horne and Rebecca were forced to take refuge in Butch's guesthouse. The living room had a TV, a well-stocked bar, easy chairs, a plaid sofa; a small kitchen and fridge were filled with beer, soft drinks, and coffee. Butch's new golf clubs were still wrapped. Horne recalled the loop of his corkscrew swing. French doors from the emerald-green bedroom opened to a flagstone terrace and spa; Horne turned it on as Rebecca hung their clothes. He found a blender, a bottle of Patrón, Margarita mix, and fixed them drinks.

Rebecca sat down between his legs on a chaise. "Jacuzzi should be ready in about fifteen minutes," he said, handing her a drink.

"This is wonderland."

"Good friends make for easy living."

"Butch really loves you."

"He and Keith served in Vietnam together. He was like my dad's brother."

Rebecca underwent one of her mercurial mood changes.

Confused, he asked, "What's wrong? You're so sad, like the life's been knocked out of you."

She turned away from him, grimacing, and stared into the darkness. "I have a serious problem. You're going to despise me."

"Well, if you've got a husband and two kids in Vienna, you'll just have to leave them," he said, amused.

"It's a lot worse...and so humiliating and dishonest that I don't know where to begin."

He was disturbed by her tone. "Okay, you've got my attention."

She found confession painful, but she had an obligation to Horne and the future of their relationship to expose her surreptitious omission of Magnus's connection to Lilli. Eyes averted, she recounted how Lilli had shared Magnus Von Winter's letter with her after Miriam's death, and how appalled she had been by the discovery.

"I confided in Jack Leopold and showed him the letter. He and Paula went berserk and threw me out of the house. They believed Miriam and I knew all about it...."

She was tearful and humbled, and he hated to see her agonizing over someone else's conduct.

"I should've told you the truth from the outset."

He held her close. "Rebecca, Lilli was trapped...prisoners don't have choices. It's a miracle she survived. My God, she was forced to marry Magnus and bear his child! It has to be every woman's worst nightmare."

"It still is. Especially when this son turns out to be as perverted as Bruno. Thank God she doesn't know! Those pictures he planted at the murders. That's his idea of art." She was distraught. "And he's actually related to me." She lashed out at herself. "I also lied to everyone at the Museum of Tolerance—and you. You deserve someone better. I've put your life at risk....I've been utterly sick about my dishonesty," she said, thrashing at the demons haunting her.

"Rebecca, to me, you're perfect."

To ease his own conscience, he related the details of his visit to Jack Leopold.

"So, you knew all along."

"Yes. I had my own self-interest, and its name was money. I had to get rid of you, even though I didn't really want to," he admitted.

"Mine was the greater sin."

He laughed. "Well, there's no question that you're holier than me."

"Don't make a joke out of it." She nudged him with her forehead like a cat. "Do you forgive me?"

"Get your clothes off and I'll let you know...or do you need my help?"

When they left the hot tub, his Viennese goddess insisted on a proper bath. He had glimpsed her partially naked during their trip, but forced himself to look away. It had struck him as gross adolescent voyeurism. In the hot tub, he'd tried to preserve a semblance of detachment and kept his hands off her.

He found a jazz station playing a tribute to Miles Davis. When Rebecca came into the bedroom, her sweeping, coppery hair pinned up, the air redolent of Vitabath, she and her flimsy yellow paisley robe were greeted by the seductive poetry of Miles playing "The Maids of Cádiz."

"I hope you don't hate this."

"I love Miles Davis."

"That's a good start."

Jazz greats served as innocuous foreplay. Rebecca lay beside him, her powerful fingers clasping his. Her gaze underwent a passage from friendliness to confusion and ultimately passionate arousal when he undid the tie of her robe and kissed her buttery nipples.

"Afraid?"

"No," she said, stemming tears with the back of her hand, "it's just that I never want this moment to end. This discovery of myself. It's such a crucial event in a woman's life."

She rubbed her fingers through his damp hair, and he cradled her glowing face.

"I dreamed of a lover, and you arrived. I was going to use you to help me, but you know that. I hadn't imagined this rush of feeling, emotion. I've never experienced such love."

He kissed her fingers, one by one. "Do you ever go into the sun?"

"I can't get my hands sunburned," she said, extending them and cupping his cheeks. "I'm afraid you'll have to live with a woman who doesn't tan."

"I'm glad you told me the truth, for once."

"You're such a bastard. I suppose all your tribal brides went into mourning when you left Dar-es-Salaam."

"It was national. Thousands of them at the airport in black. Throwing themselves on the Tarmac and fainting dead away. A horrible sight for me."

"How could I fall in love with someone so unscrupulous?"

"I beg your pardon, Ms Benjamin. 'I was the more deceived....' That's from *Hamlet*."

This echo of her remark to Miriam startled her then dissipated.

"Don't be so smug. Show me—no sonatas or concertos—just play the notes, will you?"

With a playfulness that titillated her, he said, "I'll tune you first."

It took a few moments to absorb the prosperity of her naked body, its volume. Like the figures in the Rembrandt painting, Horne delicately rested his left hand on Rebecca's shoulder and flexed the fingers of his right hand over her left breast. Dotingly, she pressed her fingers over his.

"My Jewish bride-to-be."

"Do you mean that?"

"I always mean what I say. Now don't be afraid."

"I never was...until this minute."

His eyes roved over her, and second by second the touch of her intoxicated him, the wonder of Rebecca Benjamin, his monumental prize. She had a supple figure, a litheness, and, throughout its grammar of silky-pale, blushing-pink skin, he came upon random plots of contrasting freckles and savored the perfumes that she exuded.

"All this for me?"

"Is it too much? Why don't you ask the waiter to take it back?"

"I don't think so," he said, regarding this feast of a woman. "You're my whipped cream."

She laughed. "Actually, I think you're mine."

To touch a woman he *loved* contradicted his study of animal behavior. This emotion had nothing to do with mating but possessed a spiritual harmony. It existed in an entirely different sphere. The look—the touch of the loved one.

His head descended to the valley below her navel, his fingers exploring her secrets, and he thought of the eons that had passed before such a lavish human being had evolved. The connoisseur of lovemaking experienced a degree of helplessness that left him unstable, as he moistened her and slipped inside her in a spirit of communion.

He had known the moment he'd seen Rebecca that she was unique. Two lost, defeated people had come together. Unlike her, he had no visions. Just instinct, and he trusted it. But he hadn't worked it out; nor had Rebecca. Why, how does this happen? Why love at this moment from that distance? The animals he had hunted and followed on the Serengeti were not the model, nor the embodiment of humans. God had created this chaos, and blessed it as such. Now, Horne, the hunter, knew it for certain.

In the distance, he heard the collision of their bodies and thought of the turbulent winds he had encountered at the peak of Mount Kilimanjaro, a confrontation of forces of nature. Then sound lost its composition. Eventually it was reclaimed in her gasps, twists and shouts, diminishing to a whisper:

"Come inside me, my darling."

But Horne was too connected to pleasure and delayed, galvanized by the impact, climbing, meshing unhindered within her and beyond to new levels of firepower.

She thought of the moment in musical terms, as a mortal fermata, a composition prolonging a moment in infinite time.

When they tried to break apart, gagging for breath, a level of tenderness swept over them. But neither of them would admit to the loneliness that now took its place.

Horne kissed the small of her back, then whirled her around. Her palpitating breasts, pebbled with sweat, the tides of her rising and falling, the fan of her pubic hair weeping from the storm and glued to his. Desire swept over them and became so overpowering that they couldn't unlock their bodies, and this binding carried a degree of unfathomable jeopardy.

"How often can this happen?" Rebecca asked, with stormy fervor.

"I was worried...about hurting you."

Giddy with desire, she sniggered. She wore the afterglow of love like a halo. "Next time, don't be so considerate."

"You're such an opportunist."

"Never mind. How soon will you be ready for my return engagement?"

She stroked his back, gliding her fingers from his neck down broad, sinewy shoulders. "This is certainly preferred for pianists, not stupid gyms." She coiled into his arms in the darkness.

"Jesus Christ, Rebecca"—he squinted at the mess—"this is a 'Flash Flood Zone.' I can't take you anywhere. Especially to a friend's house. What's Butch gonna think?"

"You're good at explaining. I'm off to the bathroom." She kissed him extravagantly, over and over again. "I assume I'm booked for the season."

Horne raised his head and held his lips to her drenched breast.

"I love you beyond—"

"—Shush."

"Take your time. I'm ornery when animals prowl around me."

She hastily improvised, cupping her robe awkwardly around herself to dam the stream laminating her thighs.

"I knew something was always missing from my playing. Something I couldn't quite capture."

"Huh? Like what?" he asked, drowsily, starting to nod off.

"Fucking a man I loved."

35

Nearing nine the following morning, parked outside the Santa Monica Dog & Cat Kennel, Virgil, sullen and furious after the near-death experience in Palm Beach, tried to remain awake while Noreen snorted through a nightmare in the back seat.

Apart from a few hours on the plane back from Miami, they had not slept for almost two days. At last an attendant opened the door, and Virgil roused himself.

"We're here to pick up our dog...Dortmunder. You've been boarding him."

"Oh, the dachs. He's the same color as my favorite handbag."

Virgil snarled, paid the bill in cash, and after a series of hugs, wet kisses, words of endearment, he packed the diminutive hound inside his bag. At the high-pitch squealing yaps, Noreen awoke, beaming, and cuddled the animal.

Bleary-eyed, Virgil drove east down Olympic Boulevard to their miserable one-bedroom in Beverly Hills.

At home, Noreen put on coffee and nuked some blue-veined bread that smelled like one of those French cheeses. Virgil unpacked the dregs of their clothing. Then he took Dort out for his nature hike.

The morning had a peevish chill, the sky overcast, as gardeners and their infernal leaf blowers roved up and down Sycamore Place, unnerving Dort who simply wanted to have a quiet dump under his favorite tree across the street from Rebecca's apartment.

When Virgil got back, the toast tasted like wood pulp, the butter rancid; with this diet, he might just as well have been back in prison. Noreen always did the marketing, but this time, he'd tag along and pick out something substantial: bacon, liver, lamb chops—anything to prevent her from stewing beef, then coagulating its juices into a meat pie, or baking the dreaded rubbery ham loaf which she served with green Jell-O.

As chief officer in the field, Virgil was required to contact Winterhaven. Stripped to his Jockeys, he lit a cigarillo, and reluctantly checked his service, which played a venomous string of messages from Winterhaven.

The ashen light filtering through the leaded windows of Magnus Von Winter's baronial study silhouetted his graven features. From the front angle, he appeared to be an eyeless skull. Running his fingers along the carved relief of the god Wotan, he sat stolidly at a replication of Hitler's ornate desk in Berchtesgaden. The thick gray stone fortress walls were armored with Nazi memorabilia and early beer-hall photographs of the Leadership, the martial motif flanked by a series of Bruno's early masterpieces.

Magnus switched on Strauss's "Salomé" to calm his nerves, poured himself another cup of coffee from the heated carafe, and stared into fire. The phone rang. An aide screened all of his calls.

Felix knocked on the door. "They've returned, Herr Von Winter."

Magnus nodded. He picked up the phone and his voice held a deadly bite. "I thought you'd be back in prison by now," he said by way of greeting Virgil.

Virgil had expected a degree of concern. "Noreen and I were almost killed by those animals! Our people in Florida said it was a grudge attack by a prison crew called the Texas Syndicate. Very hostile to us. Far as I'm concerned, every...district–" Virgil was about to say *gauen*, but caught himself–"needs to be re-evaluated by you."

"What did you tell the police?"

"Nothing."

He and Noreen had professed to be tourists who'd taken a wrong turn and wound up in the midst of a firefight. They had never met the neo-Nazi outlaws in the van.

"Never mind. Where is Rebecca?"

Virgil faltered. "I...I'm not sure. But she'll be back."

"How do you know?"

"I walked by the apartment and saw her piano still there. Bruno told Noreen she'd never leave it."

Magnus was not to be placated. "How did you keep losing her–even with Kress helping you?"

"We had no idea she had friends in these cities. She was very organized."

"Obviously better than you. I want you up here to make a full report."

"May I please have a few days, sir, to locate her?"

"All right. But make sure you do," Magnus replied harshly.

The phone went dead.

Virgil wondered if his meter had expired at Winterhaven. Magnus did not tolerate failure. He also had to consider Noreen's conclusions about his son, Bruno. The image of the Winterhaven lions gorging on Corley was never far from his mind.

Outside the guesthouse, Rebecca clung to Horne; he was carrying a golf bag. Gardeners were busily trimming Butch's trees and watering the flowerbeds already layered with new mulch. The pool man was lazily fishing out leaves with a net and testing the pH levels. Calamity overshadowed Rebecca's face. She turned when Butch honked in the driveway.

"Horne, why're you leaving now?" Rebecca asked, the sound of bliss noticeably absent. "I don't believe you're really going to play *golf!*"

"Yeah, Butch got us a tee time at his club. Can't be late."

Rebecca's fingers tightened and lodged around Horne's brawny forearm until the pressure hurt her, not him. All she could think about was his thrusting himself inside her, the accumulation of pleasure during the frantic rhythms, the unbroken arpeggios, the block chords of their lovemaking.

For Horne, desire denied in her eyes conspired with her natural ripeness to make her more alluring than ever. Her hair cast a ginger stream over the collar of a long green suede coat. How could anyone want to harm a woman like her? In her mossy cords and turtleneck, she resembled one of those unobtainable figures shading a fashion magazine.

"Is this your usual one-night safari honeymoon?" Earlier that morning she had waited in vain for him to propose. Her antagonism had the spirit of aristocracy, someone for whom favors and demands were legitimate rights. "Don't you know that I love you? Haven't I performed well enough? Is that it?"

"I'll send you your grade."

She flushed and fumed. "I should belt you."

His offhand behavior now made her edgy. This abrupt departure and the rigidity of his expression were telltale signs of something menacing.

"Don't you want to find the people who murdered Miriam and the other women?"

"You know where these people are?"

"I will eventually."

"Butch—" she began and faltered—"he'll be with you?"

"Yeah, sure." Horne stared unflinchingly at her. "Look, Ingrid's going to take you to a place to buy music.... Butch's partner Ricardo from the gun shop will tag along."

Her apprehension grew. "I need a bodyguard?"

"After Palm Beach, I'd say so."

Butch was outside the car, shouting for Horne. Rebecca trailed after him, speed walking to keep up with him. At last they paused. Butch was dangerously swinging a Callaway driver with a head the size of a George Foreman grill. Horne wrapped Rebecca tightly against him.

"I could be gone for a few days."

She was lost and not aware of the tears trickling down her cheeks.

"Hey, come on. I'll be okay, so stop worrying."

"You're everything...."

"And you are for me, Rebecca. The jungle is a dangerous place; this is going to be easy."

Butch waggled the golf club and pointed it at them. "Let's go, guys. Ingrid's here for you, Rebecca."

Horne cinched his arm around Rebecca's waist as they headed to the cars.

"Promise me one thing."

"Anything," she said.

"Don't wander off on your own. Make sure Ricardo is with you and don't give him any heat."

"Horne, you didn't actually propose last night," she said with earnestness.

"Oh, I never do the first time."

PART IV
BRUNO

1

A combination of factors compelled Harry to return to Los Angeles. On the return flight from Tampa, the staff aboard was troubled by his state of mind. No one had ever seen him so depressed and moody. To everyone's relief, he was not piloting the plane. He sat alone, sleepless, on the five-hour flight. Although the work at Tampa was proceeding well after the initial delays, and Harry should have been part of the collegial discussions about the work, a black hole of silence enclosed him.

In disbelief, Harry had watched the TV coverage of the inexplicable shootings and explosions in Palm Beach behind Cognoscente. He had seen Virgil and Noreen on screen, posing as innocent tourists. They'd claimed they were lost and had turned into the alley to check the map.

For the time being, he would keep them at a distance—as well as his father. It had been a serious, perhaps fatal, blunder to have broken cover and exposed himself to Noreen. The men in the SUV, part of the Florida cadre, were missing; the police still had no idea who owned the charred vehicle and were attempting to trace the owner through the VIN.

Harry tried to analyze the situation by using probability factors. Did Rebecca figure into this scenario? Where had she been during the firefight? He had been certain that she was going to see the dead girl's parents. He had forgotten her name—not that it mattered to him.

His first responsibility, however, was to meet Jack Leopold, who had returned from a European trip the previous day and insisted on seeing him in Los Angeles. There was nothing threatening about the request: another update. Harry had taken digital photos of the project from every angle; his assistant had downloaded them on the office computers. Yet Harry had a premonition that something was amiss. He had the ability to anticipate people's actions, where their behavior would lead, and now he found himself in the unmanageable position of waiting to discover if the switching tracks of his dual existence might at long last have intersected.

Jack was already waiting impatiently in Harry's office. For a short, pudgy man, his nemesis had a misguided sartorial sense. He looked ridiculous in a loud Savile Row tweed squire's jacket; a mottled-green silk tie, bold, striped shirt, and charcoal trousers completed the ensemble. He had the effrontery to enlighten Harry about how bespoke Lobb shoes "made the man." He was wearing their mildly tanned four-thousand-dollar Mambo classic loafers and was discussing the company's elaborate fittings and fussiness.

Harry restrained his laughter: Magnus, without telling Hitler or the shoemaker, had had a pair of them made for his benefactor's birthday in nineteen eighty-nine. Magnus, of course, wore nothing but Lobb's.

Unshaven, in dire need of a shower, and still in his Tampa Bay Arts Center sweatshirt, Harry pulled up on his wide-screen plasma monitor the digitized photographs he had taken of his progress on the art center. He superimposed them on the computer graphic mock-up of the site.

From Jack's mood, Harry assumed that he was delighted. "Gorgeous!" Jack said. "To celebrate, I bought you a case of Pétrus 1989."

"Must have cost a fortune."

"Harry, you're worth it."

After their quarrels during the year, Harry had every right to be distrustful of Jack. "Now what I've done?" Harry asked. "You're firing me?"

"You kidding? You smoking grass in Tampa?" Jack hugged him.

"We've had World War II over my design."

"It's a triumph, and it'll be a classic for future generations."

Harry knew immediately that he was going under.

"Fact is, I defended you."

"I'm a little confused. Against who? Do I still have to fence for my dinner?—Come on, Jack, don't bullshit *me*."

Jack rose from the swivel chair beside the computer. He walked to the window, sat on the ledge, end took in the misty silhouettes of the skyscrapers that he had foreseen would eventually become a commercial center. Years ago, he had been part of the consortium that had persuaded the cash-poor Twentieth-Century Fox to sell off the land to Alcoa. For years the area had been a graveyard, and Alcoa had had a windfall of tax losses. Through his maneuvering, Jack had made his early millions catching buyer and seller "coming and going."

But his creative financial coup in London made the Century City deal blanch by comparison.

"Do I get us a drink or cut my wrists? Which would you prefer?" Harry asked.

Jack giggled roguishly. "No-no-no. I made *you* some important money in London."

"Oh, so now I'm a partner to your gambling." He relaxed for the first time since Jack's arrival. "Crockford's is bleeding?"

"No, The City. Banks." Jack gleefully wove his fingers together. "I love and adore European bankers. I just eat 'em up. They're delicious."

"I can't wait...."

Jack looked at his watch. He had to meet Paula for a cocktail-party fundraiser for the Shoah Foundation.

"On second thought, a short malt and I've got to run."

With Byzantine cunning, Jack had sucked in a syndicate of European banks and laid off his entire billion-dollar investment in Tampa Bay, while retaining a ten percent equity position and the title of managing partner. He quickly sipped his drink. Harry listened to the details with dread.

"Go on."

"There was a small trade-off. They want a pair of hundred-story office towers."

"*What!*" Harry felt as though he had suddenly been struck with food poisoning.

"I let them twist my arm and—you know me—I agreed."

Harry could not believe that trashy office towers would ravage his years of work!

"Why didn't you put in a trailer park while you were at it?" In a fury, Harry continued, "The whole idea destroys the scale, the definition of art...what we were trying to achieve. It's a desecration...complete barbarism! You'll bastardize the entire project. It'll look like a fucking dog's dinner."

"I don't think so. You've got your twenty acres," Jack countered. "Nobody's going to mess with your plans. Listen, Harry, this'll work."

Harry's saliva dried and he could barely swallow. "You chipped away at the site from the start. I only had five acres for the waterfront parks."

"Parks, parks, sounds like farts. These bankers don't want morons picnicking, schlepping cases of beer, and playing their boom boxes. *We* need the public strolling slowly, bug-eyed, through the malls. Shopping. Buying. Workers taking elevators to their offices. Think of the views corporations can have, and the high retail density."

Jack was in his salesman mode and never gave anyone air.

"You, my dear friend, come out with five percent of my original investment. That's fifty million dollars—in *addition* to your fees. Plus, our piece of the rental money is financial heaven." Jack laughed, amused. "I did a fucking job on them...forget heaven, we'll lease space to God!" He smirked and decided on another tot of the single malt. "The only battle I had to fight for three days was for the parking concession. We have it for the first ten years and then we become fifty-fifty partners. We'll have space for fifteen thousand cars. With the office towers, there'll be even more—underground. It's a license to steal!"

In this hawker role, Jack Leopold was a force of nature, a tornado that arrived so suddenly that it was impossible to track before cities were completely razed. Ringing in Harry's ears was proof of Magnus's dictum: "When you do business with Jews, it's always seller beware!"

"I know you must be thinking permits, land use, coastal commission. The banks already have contacted the city and state. It was painless. We were welcomed with open arms. It increases the tax base for them. Jobs for locals, state and city. Inspectors, security, stores, more and more restaurants. Love at first sight."

Harry's heart pumped erratically. "I don't want the money."

"Harry, it's done—the contracts are signed. You have first dibs on the towers. I said, we'll see how Harry feels. Everyone thinks you're fantastic and holds your work in the highest regard. This isn't going to be some schlock job." Jack sipped his drink. "If you decide to pass, the bankers mentioned some other architects they'd approach. Renzo Piano's name came up; Norman Foster, Rem Kollhaas."

"Why don't you have Santiago Calatrava build one of his fucking flying vampire bridges while you're at it!"

Harry was wobbly. He had perfected the art of concealing his actual feelings. Only Rebecca had pierced the chainmail of his deceptions. In the midst of this unbearable moment, he conjured up her face and felt a harmony, a stillness within himself. This brought his murderous rage under control.

"Do I have a choice?"

"The choice is 'yes.' It's still my candy store. Now I really have to leave."

"Jack, drink the wine yourself."

"Cut it out. Hey, it was five thousand dollars a bottle—not a case price—either!"

"I'll just pour it down the sink and piss in the bottles."

"You'll change your mind." Jack hugged him and kissed him on the cheek. "I'll call you." He stopped. "I forgot. If you're free tonight, we're playing poker at the house."

2

Horne had spent two hours shooting at the Guns 'R' Us range outside. He tested several new handguns: Smith & Wessons, Brownings, Glock automatics, rifle scopes for the weekend hunter. None of the season's latest equipment pleased him.

Of a new Remington shotgun, he said, "You need to romance it. Not for me. I need mobility. It's all style and the kick's too heavy."

He also caught a glimpse of Butch's arsenal of heavy combat weapons and armaments in the steel-gated warehouse behind the shop. Horne was astonished that a civilian could possess such a cache of illegal munitions. Butch didn't want to discuss this and Horne understood. Or thought he did.

Butch had agreed to accompany him back to Sycamore Place. Horne was intent on discovering if Rebecca's pursuers were back in the neighborhood. Spring had arrived with an aimless, windy band of blood-orange sunshine that ruffled the unkempt grape ivy, needing a trim, but the husky trees were thriving with buds. Horne went into his apartment and brought out a couple of Beck's beers. Butch had lined up a bunch of wiffle balls on the front lawn and the two of them took turns refining perfectly horrible swings. They spent about a half hour and four beers in this futile exercise when they were interrupted by a warbling bark. Horne paid no attention and chipped some real golf balls.

Across the street, in a black windbreaker and narrow-legged jeans, Virgil emerged with his dog.

"Don't look, but guess who's come for happy hour?"

"Who?"

"My guy."

"No!"

"Yep. Animals are curious."

Horne squirted a ball into the narrow road and disgustedly watched it slalom crazily around. He chased it until it dribbled into a sewer.

"Good thing I used a water ball," he said with an abashed smile to Virgil.

Rebecca's enemy had a military posture, long legs, and a splotchy complexion, with dried crumbs of redness. Fluttering tusks of hair extruded from his thin nose, and the barren gray eyes held a waxy menace. He sported a dirty-blonde wig, cupped unevenly over the whimsy of his former hairline.

"It's a tough game," Virgil replied affably.

Horne stooped and stroked his pooch, the dog lover oily as an aunt. "Love these little guys."

"They're smart and loyal."

"What's his name?"

"Dort, that's short for Dortmunder. You live near here?"

"Yeah, at ninety-nine...you?"

"Around the corner."

"Want a beer?"

Virgil extended Dort's territory with the leash. "Little early for me, but thanks."

Butch continued chipping, occasionally looking up and sighing at his own ineptness.

Horne extended his hand. "I'm Doug Horne."

Virgil regarded him with a flicker of suspicion. "I thought the name was Fleming there. I looked over the place for a rental after the old lady passed away."

Horne now seemed puzzled. "Oh, did she? I'm just a month-to-month squatter, myself. Sub-letting from a friend. It came furnished and it's comfortable, Mr.—"

"Virgil Hoyt."

"Good to meet you. Come on over with Dort. We'll get *him* a cocktail."

They crossed the road and stood below Rebecca's porch.

"Want another beer, Doug?" Butch called.

"Sure. Hey, Virgil, this is my golf buddy, Butch."

"Should I get three brews?"

Dort was already lolling on the luxuriant grass. "Okay, then, thank you, I'll join you," Virgil said, not to be prissy.

This big, lumbering tenant, who lived below the kike reptile, might inadvertently provide information. He was friendly enough and with that slaphappy oafishness Virgil had encountered among inmates during his prison years. You could piss on them as long as you didn't change the channel when they were watching wrestling or *Baywatch*.

"Bring some Arrowhead water for the dog. And use the Wedgwood china," Horne added with a welcoming smile.

"Thanks very much." Virgil studied the innocuous giant and decided to prod him. "This is the prettiest street in Beverly Hills. I'm thinking of moving. Problem is, the good places don't advertise." He glanced up at Rebecca's apartment. "Do you know if there are vacancies on Sycamore Place?"

Horne juggled some golf balls. "There might be."

"Is the tenant upstairs thinking of moving?"

"I sure as hell hope so."

"Really? I miss hearing her play the piano. She's something else. Is she traveling on...a concert tour?"

"I wouldn't know," Horne replied, aggrieved. "She hasn't been around for a while and I don't miss her. I probably haven't spoken to her twice since I moved in—and that's fine with me. I can't stand her. She's one of those bitches with attitude."

"Bad, huh?"

"Superior. I'm a human being, too." Horne glowered. "Either she's practicing all night long or revving her bike at six in the morning."

Butch brought out the beers and also introduced himself to the guest. He lugged his clubs back to the car, nodded, went back inside, and switched on ESPN.

"She's a knock-out, though," Virgil said.

"I just got divorced. None of them are that stunning anymore."

Virgil slugged his beer, Dort lapped up the water, and Horne had an ally.

"Nice meeting you, Doug."

"Same here. I'm a dog lover. If you ever need a sleepover for Dort, let me know. I'm cat-free."

"That's very kind of you."

As they shook hands in a neighborly way, Horne took out his cell phone. "Hey, Virgil, give me your number and I'll give you a buzz if anything happens with the cow upstairs."

Virgil searched the pockets of his jacket. "Uh, I'm not sure of it now. We had it changed. Calls in the middle of the night from a wacko...and my wife would have to see the apartment."

"They call the shots, don't they?"

Dort yanked the leash a good six inches and whimpered. "Yes, yes, chicken liver for dinner," Virgil advised.

Horne clapped his new friend on the back. "Special of the day. We're slaves to the ladies and their pets." The new mates ambled together down Sycamore Place and reached its outlet on Carlyle Drive. The terminus was the Friars Club, before the street formed a right angle with Little Santa Monica.

"I was a park ranger till the fucking government cut the budgets and laid me off. Know of a job?"

Virgil considered himself an unparalleled judge of character and warmed to this openhearted, naïve man. "Are you political?"

"I'm for guns, dogs, and booze.... And more guns. And I'm no lover of minorities who seem to be running the country. Switch on the TV and these mongrels are in your face. Blacks, Mexicans, Yids."

"Amen. How right you are. The thing is, when you find a faith you believe in, *you* can change the system—over time. If you've got the balls."

Horne assumed the dullard role. "I can shoot, so count me in. Anytime you want to talk, I'm available."

Virgil's mood was airy; a leisurely stroll with Dort, information culled, and even a possible recruit. Virgil was tickled with himself. The risk he had taken had been worth the exposure. Only Rebecca Benjamin remained in their path.

Moments later, Horne and Butch were in the car outside of Virgil's nest on Carlyle Drive. The small flaking block was set back from the street, and was divided from the next building by a scruffy patch of grass, with rusted night lanterns over the doorways and mailboxes the color of collectible old pennies. It struck Horne as an anomaly, set amidst the luxury of Beverly Hills.

A strapping woman, wearing a T-shirt with a lightning bolt, came out of an apartment. She took the leash off the dog, picked him up, and smothered him in her muscular arms. When she and Virgil went inside, Butch inched the car up.

"You always pick charismatic neighbors. You can become barbecue buddies."

"Big Mama traveled with him," Horne said. "She's always wearing wigs, but I'd know that brick shithouse anywhere." He was awed by their audacity and the danger they presented to Rebecca. "They've been spying on Rebecca way before I got back." Then it dawned on him. "My God, they must've broken in after Rose died and drilled the hole in the ceiling. If they didn't murder her sister, they damn well know who did."

Visions of the hunt in Africa spilled through Horne's mind. "On the Serengeti, I discovered the truth of warfare and survival, like you did in Vietnam with my dad. Whenever three lions surrounded me and two were moving, I had to watch the one who remained stationary. Because he was the one who didn't know what he was he going to do. The uncommitted enemy is the most dangerous."

3

Harry returned to his apartment and listlessly flopped down on a leather chair in his studio, a cool, uncluttered room, all of the furnishings spare. He never tired of the Raphael and Rubens drawings; they reflected draftsmanship and not the insincere glamour of oils, and he was a draftsman. After a few minutes he roused himself, fixed himself a vodka, and sipped it.

The light blinked on his telephone. He half-listened to the scat-wails of women, their invitations—Taylor's voice gurgling sexual specials of the day—and erased them. He craved the sound of Rebecca's husky voice, the way she invariably ended with a deep laugh. She had not called and his bleak mood turned vindictive. Where was she?

Often, when he was in town, he would leave the office early, only to catch Rebecca in a last-minute dash for a chamber concert as a fill-in pianist. At those moments, the architect studied the masterly curvatures and angles of Rebecca's figure, the heft and clash of her braless breasts. His desire for her transcended the physical. He recognized genius. Jewish or not, he yearned for her to be part of his life, assimilate her sensibility.

Of course Rebecca had lied to him. She was parking cars to hack it. At the same time, he understood her. She was not for sale and had to maintain her independence.

To escape from himself and the horrors of professional and personal failure, he rooted through his mail, dumping the junk. Then something caught his eye; he picked a crumpled piece of slick, white paper from the pile in the basket. His hand was shaking.

APPEARING ONLY AT THE VIKING
REBECCA BENJAMIN
THE CELEBRATED VIENNESE PIANIST
MAKES HER AMERICAN DEBUT
CALL FOR DATES AND RESERVATIONS

How could his angelic, innocent Rebecca have descended into his own hunting grounds...? *TheViking?* He visualized her surrounded by the mass of rutting male bodies that converged there. He was sweating, and the acrid taste in his mouth forced him to rush to the bathroom. Racked by dry heaves, he couldn't bring up anything. He stripped off his clothes, barely making it to the shower.

Did Rebecca know that Taylor had been his pick of The Viking's litter? Ingrid was a den mother to these girls. They were good for business. Ingrid cultivated them, and men like him found an oasis in a city devoted to the social interests of teenagers and designer drugs.

Harry discarded a variety of probabilities. No one in his circles knew about Taylor. How could Rebecca have met Ingrid? Who was the link between them?

Ricardo Rivera stood guard over Rebecca. She had met him at The Viking along with a gaggle of people during her first jazz performance. He was in his intensely virile shaved-headed forties and had been an LAPD detective.

"This is Peet's version of Viennese coffee," he said, helping her into Ingrid's house.

"Thank you for being so thoughtful."

With the cat in her arms along with an overnight bag, Rebecca resumed her fugitive life in Ingrid's rambling mock-château, another pale-ochre stone tribute to the San Fernando Valley contractors' enduring love affair with France. The entourage now included the moping, lovelorn Taylor, apparently a permanent houseguest. The blonde seductress was in deep mourning: The man with whom she had fallen in love had dumped her.

Rebecca was installed in the adjoining bedroom, a fussy pink chamber with an assortment of dolls residing on the window seat.

Half-listening to sob-sister tales of the outcall life from the front lines, Rebecca nonetheless found herself engaged by Taylor. "I made the fatal mistake," Taylor informed Rebecca, busily unpacking yet again.

"Yes?"

"I fell in love with a client."

Vienna had a centuries' long tradition of *das Strichmädchen*, the red-light window, less obtrusive than Amsterdam's, but nevertheless a vital, legal sector of commerce. Before Rebecca had had any glimmering of what her grandmother had endured under the Nazis as Von Winter's mistress, she had been brought up to dismiss bourgeois sanctimony.

"Sometimes you can't help yourself," she said, thinking of how much she missed Horne. "What's your friend like?"

"Fifties, but he looks a lot younger," she was quick to add. "Very good-looking and elegant. He's so classy and well educated. I don't know exactly how he made his fortune. He's some kind of builder. He never discusses money."

"Maybe he was married and it didn't work out."

"That's just the point, Rebecca, he's never been married."

To cheer her up, Rebecca said, "Come on down to The Viking. Keep me company while I rehearse."

"I'm a mess."

"You'll be my sound expert."

Taylor ran a brush through her tangled blonde hair, swept it back, and fixed it with a comb. In Olympic time, she applied her make-up.

"In my line, we're not supposed to ask questions. But I can't resist."

She amused Rebecca. "It's quite all right, I'm not a client."

"Why are you staying here, Rebecca? Didn't it work out with you and Horne?"

"It's worked out better than I'd hoped. It's just that someone's stalking me. Horne wanted me to stay away for a while, until he finds him."

"That's really creepy."

"This man's murdered a number of women."

Taylor's glazed eyes regained focus. "Christ, so that's why Ricardo is here!"

"Yes, he works with Butch."

"Damn right he does—as the firearms instructor."

4

In spite of Horne's aversion to Beverly Hills, he had to admit that it offered certain conveniences not available in Africa. Outside of Virgil's apartment in the chill of early darkness, a Nate 's deli truck arrived. Butch signaled the driver, and an exchange was made. Butch paid him cash for two brisket sandwiches and a Coke.

"First time I've ever witnessed a takeout to an SUV," Horne remarked, amazed.

"We're very sophisticated here. I'll call you on the cell if Virgil or Big Bertha makes a move."

Horne had contacted Jack Leopold and whetted his appetite about his trip with Rebecca. He also intended to burrow through any ideas Jack and his wife might have about the deadly conspiracy Rebecca had uncovered. He was rewarded with an invitation for cocktails at the baron's palace. He hopped on Rebecca's ancient Harley. If he and Butch had to follow Virgil it would seem less suspicious than having two cars alternating behind him.

Wearing Rebecca's crash helmet, strands of her hair still clinging to it, he eased along Lexington where global mansions were being built, rebuilt, and demolished, and thriving contractors drove Mercedeses with license plates that read "Teardown."

Once through the robotic surveillance of the Leopold compound, staffed with silent security men, he realized how widely paranoia had spread. He was ushered into a garden room stuffed with large chairs and sofas; the interior had been lit so that the dancing fountains, modern statuary, and illuminated pool, would awe him. For a moment he stood alone, watched by unseen cameras and guards, before a woman's hospitable voice intruded on the light show:

"I'm Paula Leopold, Mr. Horne. Welcome to our home."

"It's a pleasure to meet you, ma'am."

"Paula."

"Just Horne."

He regarded a svelte blonde, with an oval face and guarded emerald eyes that disowned her relaxed manner. Her sleek Italian pantsuit dabbled in green or gray. But something else caught his attention. Her minimal pearls were matched South Sea nuggets, of higher quality than any he'd unclasped among some very rich lionesses on safari.

She led him to the sofa and motioned for him to sit. "Are there any lions in Beverly Hills?" she asked. "I'm kidding, of course."

"The only one I know of is your husband."

"Jack mentioned that you and Rebecca had some problems over your aunt's house."

"We've since settled, and the fact is, she didn't do anything wrong. I did. My aunt bequeathed the apartment to her."

"I see." Paula felt secure with Horne. "After Miriam was murdered, Rebecca stayed here." She glanced at the doorway waiting for Jack. "I'm afraid it ended rather badly."

"I can assure you Rebecca's not in the blame business." Horne's warmth and sympathy reassured her. "She never said a word against you."

"I'm relieved to hear that. Because, well, what happened is nothing we're proud of." Paula's frankness was tantalizing and disarming. "When Jack comes down, he'll tell you our version." Then, artfully slipping into the role of smiling-hostess-intrigued-by-a-guest, she turned the subject to Horne. "Actually, before you got involved in this Rebecca mess, we'd thought of contacting you for a safari."

He frowned. "I'm no longer running them."

Cell phone pressed to his ear, Jack waved at Horne and proceeded to bellow at an underling, then clicked off. A white-coated servant emerged from another door.

"My apologies. It's good seeing you again." He pecked Paula on the cheek. "What can we get you?"

A shelf of tequilas was displayed at the bottom of the liquor cart. "A Chinaco shooter will be fine."

"Leave the bottles, Brad, a dish of limes, and check on the canapés, please," Paula instructed the houseman.

"Wish we'd been out with you on the Serengeti," Jack said. "After you came up to my office, Tommy Haggerty sent over the video of his trip with you. It was incredible." Jack threw up his hands in wonderment and awe. "Paula, this man shot a lion that was practically on top of him."

Horne laughed. "Trick photography."

"I know what enhanced computer graphics look like."

"He was at least fifteen yards away. Charged us out of nowhere or I wouldn't have killed him. He was a wounded nomad and probably lost a fight with another male." Horne totaled his shooter and the houseman was there with the bottle, refilling it. "I'd be happy to recommend my old firm when you're ready for a safari."

An aura of boon companionship reigned. Without enthusiasm, and despising himself for his sanctimony, Horne inquired about their son who had run for cover.

"He's finally out of his shell. He's living in Minneapolis now." Paula was aglow. "The Symphony signed him up as third cello. And he's got a new fiancée," she added proudly. "Cathy teaches at a college, and she's one of those lovable, Midwest girls. Big on family."

How easily Miriam had been replaced, Horne thought. Rebecca had been right about the Leopold heir.

Jack set his feet on a bulky ottoman. "My wife and I behaved disgracefully to Rebecca."

Paula's face became solemn. "We've regretted it ever since. At the time of Miriam's murder, our son collapsed...and went on a drug binge. He'd been clean with Miriam."

"What set us off was that Rebecca told us her grandmother had been involved with a high-ranking Nazi. Imagine, a friend of Hitler's! And I just went bonkers and blamed Rebecca. Because she was there. And because it was convenient. Sometimes you just lose it and can't control yourself."

"In retrospect, we realized that she'd been straight about everything."

"I can understand that," Horne said. "I'm as guilty as you are. I thought she'd conned my aunt, too." He had shared in their attack on Rebecca's character. "I spent twelve years in Africa and hadn't been back to the States in all that time. I was blindsided. I guess life's changed so drastically here that we just don't believe anyone's actually telling the truth. But Rebecca was absolutely up-front with me. She nursed Rose till the end."

An air of contrition hung over them.

"I thought about trying to contact her," Paula said.

"For the time being, I think it's better if you don't," Horne advised them.

"It's a pity she gave up her career. We've never heard anyone play like her." Jack nodded to Horne. "You wanted to bring us up to date on your trip with her."

"Actually, your detective, Frank Whatever, did find something. But no one but Rebecca had the motivation or the guts to put it all together."

Horne recounted the salient points of the trip and the evidence they had uncovered about the three other murdered women. He decided, however, to avoid specifics concerning his relationship with Rebecca. His disclosure of a murderous underground neo-Nazi movement thundered through the room and shocked the Leopolds. But after a while, he realized that the Leopolds had moved on, and had sheered off from the troubled past.

"You have no idea how well these Nazis are organized. They had a couple following us, and they met teams of guys in every city."

"Have you contacted the FBI?" Paula asked nervously.

Horne laughed cynically. "Their top terrorist threat is animal rights activists."

Sulky with remorse, Jack guided Horne through acres of marble and his art galleries. At the temple's figured brass entry doors, he directed Horne into a small room and switched on the lights. Horne saw walls of architectural drawings.

"These are mind-blowing," he commented. "Even I know who they are."

"I thought you might. I have Bauhaus, Gropius, Breuer, Mies, Le Corbusier, Saarinen, Böhm, Sullivan, Frank Lloyd Wright, and other master drawings." For a moment he was in a child's wonderland. He pointed to another wall. "These are Harry Summerfield's final renderings for the Tampa Bay Arts Center. He's up with these greats."

Horne looked closely at graceful pyramid-like structures, with intricate walkways and swirling webs of geometric designs. They were astonishing, beautiful, works of art.

"People like Harry are creating our future. I'm just the money."

"I never would've guessed. Hey, how'd you guys hook up?"

"Some time back, I was in Miami for some land deals, and as I was walking down Ocean Drive, I decided to buy as many hotels as I could. They were rundown—filled with old people from New York and the Midwest, living on social security, who'd come there to die." Jack winked. "I took a flyer. These joints were falling apart. But they were located across from the ocean. And had unbelievable views. I thought—no one likes to walk to the beach, carrying kids and picnics. It's obvious now."

"Is that how South Beach started?" Horne asked.

"Some people say so. I'd met Harry at various functions. I desperately wanted to be in business with him. But he was the high-art end. I asked his advice. The next thing I knew, he signed on as consultant in between his other projects. Harry loved art deco. He brought me into the mainstream of developers."

Horne had gone around the room several times, pausing before other drawings, admiring the ideas that created modernity.

"Harry and I collect these drawings. When we were redoing the Miami Beach hotels, Paula's decorator spotted an article in a magazine about a shop in Florida that had architectural drawings like mine, and I went after them."

Horne spun away from the drawings of Louis Kahn's Kimbell Museum in Fort Worth. He put an arm around Jack Leopold, his new buddy.

"I try to keep up with art. That shop is Cognoscente in Palm Beach."

Leopold was enjoying the company, and was impressed.

"How the hell would you know....?"

"My dark African juju training. The owners have a collection of architectural drawings." There was a nebulous evasiveness about Jack. "I wonder if you or Harry made an offer for these drawings?"

"Uh-huh. They weren't for sale. You're extremely well informed. We should have hired *you* after Miriam was murdered."

"Cynthia Edelstein, the daughter of the people who own Cognoscente, showed the drawings to a man who offered her a half a million dollars for them. Her father bought them for sixty thousand in Zurich. He was in Europe when she contacted him and turned down the offer. The buyer was very persistent and sweet-talked Cynthia into dinner."

Jack dimmed the lights and he and Horne walked down the corridor to the door, cobbling over ancient tiles—shipped, stolen, from god knows where.

"You're starting to confuse me, and that's troubling," Jack said.

"I'm also troubled. We have an equation that doesn't balance. This is like elephants killing lions for *their* meat. Do you remember the detective reports about Miriam when you launched your private investigation?"

"I never even saw them."

"Cynthia Edelstein was also about to be married." Horne's cell phone vibrated in his pocket. "Excuse me a second, Jack." He listened to Butch

"Your favorite travel partners are on the move. Packed the dog in his carrier. She's carrying a suitcase." Horne stared at Jack—"I'm on my way—" and quickly hung up.

"I'll walk you out. Get some air."

"Did Harry have any interest in Miriam?"

"What! Absolutely not. He only met her a few times and was redesigning a house for my son and her. He was working flat out on Tampa.... If anything, maybe the bride-to-be was busting his balls a little. But he never complained."

Horne hopped on Rebecca's bike. Jack stood in front of it as Horne revved the engine.

"Horne, we're worn out with this. I'm trying to put my family back together, and it hasn't been easy."

"I'm very sympathetic. You better move, Jack."

In a moment, Horne was flying out on the bike, like a Hell's Angel fulminating vengeance.

Paula stood at the entryway, distraught by the visit. She clung to Jack.

"When is this hell going to end?" she asked, imploring him to alter fate.

With a voice filled with lament, he said, "I don't know—maybe never."

5

In The Viking's banquet room, Rebecca completed hours practicing jazz standards. She had listened to Bud Powell, Errol Garner, The Monk, Dave Brubeck, and other great pianists to get a sense of how this music should be played. The cast of her face intimated emotional loss; her mind darkened with visions of the dead women whose spirits had revealed themselves to her and brought out a heartrending interpretation.

She concluded her rendition of Joe Sample's "Invitation," with an expressive depth to it.

Taylor comprised her audience and had been deeply moved by the romanticism of her playing.

"Maybe by Saturday I'll get it right," Rebecca, fatigued, sighed.

"You're wonderful. This is just a new experience for you."

She thought of Miriam and the early promise they'd revealed as children. "I've become old with new experiences."

Ricardo knocked on the door, and Taylor unlocked it.

"Ladies, would you like a drink and some dinner?"

"Yes, thanks," Rebecca said.

He led them to a table in the busy main room of the restaurant. Ingrid broke away from some customers. She gave Rebecca a hug, then Taylor.

"How's my star doing?"

"She's unbelievable," Taylor said. "She hears a song once and plays it better than the original recording."

Only a short time ago, Rebecca had been alone and in a desperate situation, parking cars and scrounging to stay alive. With all of these benevolent people worrying about her every whim, she had come to like these women. It made her reflect on the miserable period she had endured without female companionship. She owed it all, of course, to Horne. It seemed clear that people would lie down in the road for him and, for that matter, so would she. And yet, he didn't work at ingratiating himself, but stood aloof, watching, ever-aware.

At last, her cell phone rang. She rose from the table, slapping a palm against her left ear to blot the bar noise. Whatever leads Horne was following infused her with panic.

"Are you all right?"

"Yeah. I'm going down Coldwater on your Harley."

She couldn't hear clearly. "Where's Butch?"

"I'm on my way to meet him."

"What? You're breaking up."

"Hang on. I'm out of the canyon. I've just had drinks with your favorite couple on Tower Way."

"The Leopolds!"

"They send their love."

"I'll trust anything you say, but not that. Are you coming to The Viking? And what's wrong with your car?"

She waited for one of his tales to spring forth. "The battery died and I didn't want to wait for a tow truck."

"I see." Pressing him would be futile.

"The bike sounds good," he said.

"I still owe the mechanic four hundred dollars."

He chortled. "Only you could get away owing a mechanic that much."

"I promised to pose naked for his Internet porn chat room."

"I figured as much."

She roamed into a more subdued area near the bathroom. Mistake—a ladies' bowling society had booked their coke shower there and regarded her with suspicion.

"Horne, come back, please!" She had a premonition that he was in a dangerous situation.

"...Let's talk business: How many miles per gallon do you get on this old crank?"

"I think about forty—more on the road." A sense of disquiet overcame her. "What's this all about?" she insisted.

"I'm making progress."

The prospect daunted her. "Horne, don't—I'm afraid—" but the phone went dead.

She went into the ladies' room, which was now empty. Staring into the mirror, she witnessed Horne speeding along the unlit black curves of Coldwater. Without warning, the image of Horne dissipated.

Images of flames and smoke appeared to her; a brilliant conflagration discharged by a huge furnace, where a savage blacksmith in an apron of black skins worked at a forge with thick gloves up to his raw forearms. As he wrenched a branding iron from the inferno, the aura around him filled with indecipherable symbols and lines, which appeared in the mirror. They fused into a message from Magnus.

The Hoyts were also winding down Coldwater Canyon; at the intersection of Ventura Boulevard, they pulled into a 76 Station. Behind them, Butch passed the light and waited at the curb, across the street. Virgil was filling up and could head in any direction, but Butch suspected he'd head for the 101 Freeway. Hoyt's wife carried out a shopping bag and balanced coffees in a carton. She had a donut stuck in her mouth. Butch's cell rang.

"I'm just behind you, beside the Ralph's supermarket," Horne said.

"They're across the street at a 76 station. Driving a dark blue Lincoln Town Car, license 'Bmac4.'"

"Stay in close and I'll buzz past them from time to time."

"Are you armed?"

"Yeah, I'm packing."

Butch was uneasy and knew Horne had no firearms license. "Don't speed and get stopped by the CHP. Be sure to wear Rebecca's helmet or they'll pull you over."

"Will do."

On the Ventura Freeway, Virgil kept to sixty-five and, by ten, had covered ninety miles and was threading through the wide looped bay of Seacliff outside of Santa Barbara. On the beach below, music floated up through the thrush of easy waves from camper vans parked on the dirt road. As soon as they passed the exit turn-offs to Santa Barbara, Virgil heavy-footed it to eighty.

Butch increased his speed and Horne whipped past both cars, a bike renegade in the night. When fog drifted over the road, they slowed through a canyon. Horne had a sensation of giddy pleasure. He was on a California freeway road, not some rutted trail in the jungle where viscous hazes from Mount Meru mixed when seasonal burns rose and made visibility and breathing difficult. Luminous signs floated like cadavers in the mist, and yellow road guards prevented the driver from diving off a cliff or churning into a rockslide.

Close to midnight up on the Central Coast, Virgil pulled into the lot of a sleek, silver all-night Airstream diner outside of Shell Beach. Horne circled the lot behind Butch, switched off the bike, and stretched as he walked to Butch's SUV.

"I'm too fucking old to be following people," Butch groaned. "I should be home waiting to see who Ingrid's brought in for a sleep-over."

"You're a pervert."

"And grateful to be one."

Virgil and his wife sat at a window booth, menus in hand, while a waitress hovered.

The men gassed up next door at a full serve. Horne went into the market side and bought twenty dollars' worth of beef jerky, which he stuffed into his backpack.

Waiting in the lot, Butch became edgy. "I really think we ought to head home."

Horne was amused. "Don't be an old lady. Now stop worrying, dear. I'm used to tracking wild animals. Consider this a safari."

6

Harry sat in his Eames chair in the living room, leafing through a book of Pierre Koenig's architectural drawings. He admired his sinuous lines, the use of light and shade in *Case Study No. 22*, the cantilevered house with its legendary view of Los Angeles. Koenig's drawings by hand were peerless. Now everything was pumped into computers for instant three-dimensional renderings.

The phone rang. Maybe this time it would be Rebecca. "I hope I'm not disturbing you," Jack said.

"No, I'm was reading. What's up?"

Jack cleared his voice. "I hope you're not still pissed off with me."

"Well, I understand how important money is."

"I'd be lying if I said there wasn't some profit motive behind selling off Tampa. But the fact is, we have more projects to do together. And for us to go to banks for financing at the start means that we'd have a bunch of asshole committees telling *you*—at this stage of your career—and me what to do."

He still marveled at Jack's gift for rationalizing, a skill doubtlessly honed through centuries of Jewish tribal dishonesty and conniving. The Jew's hand was first outstretched, and then, soon enough, into everyone's pocket.

"I'm with you—go on."

"Harry..." Jack hesitated uncharacteristically. "I had a very disturbing visit a few hours ago. You're the only one I can talk to about it."

Harry's interest was piqued. "Shoot."

"Do you still see much of Rebecca?"

"Not lately." Harry's throat tightened. "Has something happened to her? Is she okay?"

"Far as I know. Remember meeting a guy by the name of Douglas Horne, her landlord, a big guy, who was a hunter in Africa? He's very sharp."

"Yes, once, the night he arrived...in February, I think. What does he have to do with Rebecca?" The moment Harry asked the question, he felt his body go rigid.

"This Horne came to see me then—through a lawyer pal we have in common. He was trying to figure out some way of evicting Rebecca.

Did you know she was left the Sycamore Place apartment by Horne's aunt?"

"No, she never mentioned it," Harry replied, feeling the tension ease. "I've tried to help her out from time to time."

"Oh, Horne's doing that. Head first. She got her hooks into him real good." The silence at Harry's end was prolonged and developed an unnerving oddity. "You there, Harry?"

"Is this call a good-deed notification of who she's fucking?"

"Not at all. I assumed she was on your list at one time or another."

Harry tried to salvage his poise in the face of this tumultuous emotional disaster. In a moment, fury begot clarity. "So Rebecca's got a guy. Where do you come in?"

"I got sidetracked, Harry. I'm actually calling about Miriam. This character Horne has been tracking a well-organized crew of neo-Nazis across the country. It's like a replay of Hitler's death camps. Horne thinks that's why Miriam was put in a gas chamber."

Harry was jolted by Jack's detailed account.

"I just got off the phone with Tommy Haggerty. He's the lawyer who fixed the meeting with Horne and me. You know Haggerty?"

"Irish con-man attorney."

"Aren't they all? But he's very influential and powerful. He's also Horne's godfather. Knew the family way back. It seems Horne was involved in a murder in Africa—Tanzania. He beat it and got booted home. The government there wanted him out and revoked his hunter's license. This Horne is one smart, very tough guy. For crissake, the guy used to shoot lions for a living."

"Jack, give me a minute to switch off my computer and save some notes."

Rebecca was more brilliant than he had even imagined. She had cunningly sold herself to an assassin. He was astounded by her patience and mode of planning. At the time, it had struck him as inconceivable that a woman of such talent and beauty would take a hospice job with a dying woman. She had stayed because she'd known Horne would return. By then, she would have finagled a claim on *his* property and could blackmail him. Money and sex were her weapons of war. He had underestimated the backstabbing duplicity of *this* Jewess.

His mind now had Magnus's clarity. He reclaimed his Nazi heritage, salvaging the unity within himself. *Rule or be conquered.*

"I'm back. Jack, what's this all got to do with *us*?"

"Nothing, Harry. Except for one puzzling thing that Horne dropped on me. Remember when we first started to work together in Miami Beach?"

"Sure...the art deco restorations on Ocean Drive. It was very exciting, and they turned out well, didn't they?"

"Thanks to you. I think they've been flipped five or six times since."

"You didn't leave poor."

"Am I supposed to? You're still sore about me selling off Tampa. But leave it, please. During the Florida jobs, I mentioned something about a shop in Palm Beach. They had a slew of original Bauhaus drawings. Some other great ones too—Mies, Le Corbusier...."

"I have no recollection of this."

"I never made it to the shop, or maybe I had someone call to ask if they were for sale."

"Jack, I honestly don't remember. I was so busy. We were gutting four-six hotels then."

"The shop owners had a daughter who was going to be married, and she was murdered. Gassed! Horne and Rebecca went to see them. Horne's convinced that this murder and others around the country are connected to Miriam's."

Harry grew cautious and solicitous. "My God that's hideous."

This explained what had happened in Palm Beach to the local group as well as Virgil and Noreen. Rebecca seemed to have outfoxed him all along. Poison had been injected into his passion and he recognized what a formidable enemy she had turned out to be.

"Frightening, isn't it?"

"That it is." Harry worked best under pressure and swiftly regrouped. "What do you intend to do about it?"

"I don't know what I *can* do. I'm just numb. Scott's found his feet and has a new girl that he's serious about.... I hate to drag him through this ugly mess again."

Harry had to set his mind at rest. "I'm a believer in Zen philosophy: when you're unsure, wait—do nothing."

Jack sighed with relief. "Harry, I knew I'd get the right answer from you."

Like a problem he might grapple with in architecture, eventually only one solution could overcome the obstacle.

"Jack, I'm not pissed off anymore about the towers. You and your bankers hire whoever you want for them. But I'll give you a running start. I've got two brilliant unknowns for you. You can't imagine the plan they've come up with."

"Really? Who are they?"

"My protégés: Noreen Porter and Virgil Hoyt. They won't be expensive. I'll work with them pro bono."

"Great, I can't wait to meet them. Get them to call me. And thanks."

Rebecca returned to Ingrid's house with her entourage. Ever since Horne's call, she'd had a growing consciousness of the danger into which she had drawn him. As she headed upstairs, Ricardo stopped her. The shotgun cradled under his arm was ominous.

"Are you expecting trouble?"

"No, not unless it comes from you. My partner Menudo's coming to relieve me, Rebecca. Please don't sleepwalk or get any ideas about leaving."

Upstairs, she flopped on the bed, and checked her messages on the answering machine at Sycamore Place. Perhaps one of the people she and Horne had visited in their investigation had tried to contact her and had remembered something valuable.

There were two messages, both from Harry Summerfield. She had no idea when he had called and she felt rueful and guilty that she hadn't been forthright with him before she'd left on the trip with Horne. He'd been the one person she could trust and had supported her before Horne had arrived on the scene.

She dialed his home number. "I hope I haven't caught you at a bad moment."

Harry rounded into his usual bonhomie. "I've been worried about you."

"I'm apologize, Harry. I should have explained what was going on."

"And what's that?" he asked, enraged.

"I...I went away with someone—a man."

"Really?" he replied, concealing his anguish. "I hope he's been treating you well."

"It's not like that, Harry. He's been helping me. We're close to finding out who killed Miriam."

"I admire you for being so single-minded, Rebecca."

"Harry...you don't know anything about my family involvement with the Nazis. I couldn't let it rest. It became a fixation."

"You never discussed your family. And Lilli never mentioned it either when we spoke."

"She wouldn't."

"Is this connected to the Holocaust?"

Rebecca caught her breath. "In some ways."

"We need to talk this through. I'm still dressed. Let me drive over, or do you want to come to my place? It won't take long."

She faltered, uncertain about what or how much to disclose. In some way, she longed to be with Harry and embrace the security he always offered. "Thanks, Harry. But I'm staying with a girlfriend."

"I want to see you."

"It's not a good time."

"Why?"

"My girlfriend's lover broke up with her. She's a wreck."

"These things happen. Rebecca, I'm confused about your behavior. I got a flyer from a joint in the Valley that claims you're performing. At first I thought it was a joke."

"No, it's me."

"Why there?" He sounded offended.

"It's better than parking cars."

His outrage turned into disdain. "Why would you of all people do this?"

"I need to play before a live audience."

"You've got a point...you always do."

He wanted to keep her on the line forever. The tonality of her voice, especially in grief, and the subtlety of her deception had become thrilling. She was a game-player and strategist on the highest level, even more persuasive and ingenious than the developers he had dealt with over the years—including Jack. She was Eve, a match for God, not Adam.

"But they have Jazz," he said. "Do you know anything about it?"

"Not much. I can do passable imitations of Brubeck, Sample, and Bud Powell. I'll hide behind my classical technique. Thunderbolts for the bar drunks." She laughed, hesitantly. "I'm an actress."

For once she had given him a truthful description of herself. "The Viking...?"

"Yes."

His attraction to her continued to decline. "I've been there," he admitted.

She finally relaxed, happy to be in tune with him again. He had been so benevolent, not really questioning her relationship with Horne, and his tact deepened her guilt.

"Come on, let's get together. It's not too late. I'll send a car to pick you up."

She remembered Menudo downstairs; he'd taken Ricardo's place as her bodyguard. The sound of her voice altered and she roved around the room indecisively. Through the common door to their bedrooms, Taylor slunk through.

"Give me the address," Harry insisted.

"I can't. But I want you to know that I do care deeply about you. I'm in a precarious situation. I don't want you to get involved and hurt."

When she hung up, Taylor said knowingly, "The woman's always the sinner when there are two guys."

7

The traffic was light on the coastal road. Horne and Butch stayed well back when Virgil passed Morro Bay's monolithic volcanic rock, which loomed up like a sea monster veiled by crashing waves. On the ocean side, craggy inlets and bays fumed with turbulent blowholes. Through rolling, dark fields, surrounded by hovering mountains, the peaks were silhouetted as they snaked around looping curves on the broad highway. From the crest of a hill they drove parallel for a few moments and spotted Virgil turning off. Horne sped past Butch and stopped. Virgil's taillights and the splay of his brights illuminated a farm or ranch, laced with high-security fences, steel posts, and double-curled razor wire.

Butch pulled alongside Horne.

"They're going inland," Horne said, pulling on a dark khaki water-proof jacket over his buffalo-hide sheepskin vest filled with cartridge pockets. He slipped on his .45 holster belt and attached his sheathed knife, then lifted his safari backpack off the bike. Butch opened the rear, and Horne unzipped the bag holding his Sako. He loaded the drop-box magazine with 4.375 H&H cartridges, and jammed two boxes of fifty into his backpack.

In the distance, they made out the specter of Virgil's brake lights.

"I'm too old for a nature hike," Butch complained. "We'd be better off coming back in the morning."

"No, wait off to the side on the verge. I don't know if the cell phones will work up here. If I have any trouble, I'll fire off a flare."

"Doug, I don't like this. It's too risky. You don't know what you're going to run into. Your ass is bare."

"Hey, I'm just a hunter out camping who got lost."

"I don't think Virgil will buy that." The car lights faded, and Butch was fettered with thoughts of what might lie ahead. "Why take a chance and go in now?"

"I have to."

"It's one o'clock. If you're not in contact or back by light, I'll drive in."

"Don't, it'll blow everything. I'll manage."

There was a manned guard post. Horne turned south about a hundred yards away. He cut through the razor wires, climbed the eight-foot fence, and hoisted himself over, then vaulted to the ground. He trotted uphill, cutting through a maze of gnarled oak and manzanitas drooping with panicles. The land smelled of lush grass, perfumed by the sea, mixed with bracken and coastal dune scrub. In the copse a malignant coyote working party eyed a family of black-tailed deer. Jackrabbits vaulted through the velvety mists of the dew-laden woods. For the first time since he'd come back from Africa, he was in his natural habitat. He felt a unity with the country and dreaded a return to the cage of a city.

He walked about a half-mile before finding a huge meadow. He followed a horse trail and reached a straightaway. He beheld a complex of outbuildings and a small, well-built bungalow colony; a fleet of pick-ups and Humvees with gun turrets was parked outside. The lowing of cattle in barns and pens, the distant bark of dogs, impinged on the night's silence. After being encircled by starved packs of wild dogs in Africa, he didn't fear domestic varieties. He'd brought along mace and jerky.

Moving soundlessly past various workshops, he stopped at a stable and peered inside. Six pampered Arabians were stalled: four stallions, two mares, all silvery-white with dapples of gray. He slipped into the tack room. He was surprised not to see a Western saddle among the array of equipment. Everything was English: handcrafted saddles, raised snaffle bridles, running martingales, girths, reins, stirrups. Rows of handmade boots mirror-polished, made by Lobb, stood in neat rows.

He opened a large cedar-lined wardrobe, home to black breeches with a red military stripe down the leg and the jackets embroidered with swastikas. Affixed on a Field Marshal's tunic was a gleaming Iron Cross First Class for valor. Creeping into the adjoining room, he shone his flashlight around pool and billiard tables. He gaped at the walls. His fury swelled into the lethal violence that had led to his killing Hendrik Stovart.

Photo collages of heaped bodies—bones, limbs, and the severed heads of men, women, and children—from the Nazi death camps had been made into dartboards. These mementos had a visceral life; even more gruesome than those he'd seen at the Center in Los Angeles. He had reached Magnus Von Winter's death fortress.

Two dogs stealthily approached him, both German Shepherds, or in Von Winter's domain, Alsatians. He wondered if they'd had their vocal chords removed so that they could soundlessly advance on an intruder. He stared the dogs down, stood motionless, let them sniff, and heard some yelps. The dogs immediately sensed he was not afraid of them. He decided not to stroke them; guard dogs were frequently trained to attack when strangers tried to befriend them. The dogs seemed calm but curious and he slipped a hand into his pack, pulled out the jerky, and tossed it to them.

"Friends," he whispered.

They trailed after him outside, where he opened a broad-beamed wooden door and found himself in a blacksmith's shop. The forge was cold. He observed a neatly arrayed group of horseshoes, tools, and branding irons hanging from the wall, many with standard cattle marks others with arcane symbols. Nothing indicated the Von Winter name, which did not surprise Horne.

Was this where Rebecca's sister had been brought after she had been kidnapped?

The dogs had finished the jerky and lost interest in his exploration. They scampered off, howling at some night animals scurrying away. He clung to the sides of work buildings and slipped into a large structure filled with vats and skins; the powerful odor of benzene from aniline dye baths and drums of chromium salts permeated the air. Large worktables were spread out, on which soft, mellow hides lay stretched in the process of being cut. He saw molds for briefcases and handbags. A tannery was innocent enough for a multipurpose ranch.

Crouching from one building to another, Horne closed in on a firing range and cupped his flashlight to the ground. Permanent targets were at ranges from fifty yards to what he guessed as far as two hundred. He scooped up a variety of spent shell casings. They were 7.62 Hollow Points used for banned automatic AK-47 assault rifles. He had seen the wounds inflicted on natives by warring tribes. Once the round hit flesh, it mushroomed and tore right through it.

In another area, there were camouflaged hillocks where tripods had been set into the ground with reinforced concrete. Batches of .50 caliber shells used by M.2 machine guns as anti-personnel weapons lay scattered around. He collected a few to show Butch. Von Winter was training a militia group. This evidence might persuade federal authorities—the ATF for sure—to investigate.

Winding around the perimeter of the range, he encountered a gleaming steel, oddly geometric structure with industrial chimneys. Barring entry were electrified, high-spiked gates with skull and crossbones. Huge signs painted red warned:

NICHT OFFEENEN (DO NOT OPEN)
LEBENSGEFAHR (DANGER TO LIFE)

For an instant he wondered if this were the ranch's slaughterhouse and packing assembly line, but the air carried the sour precipitation of corrosive acid. The particles that still lingered burned his nostrils, and he put a leather glove to his mouth.

He had found the gas chamber.

Miriam Benjamin had been murdered here!

He imagined he could behold the grotesque visions of the tortured, emaciated Jews hurled into boxcars who had been brought to hellhouses like this.

It was now 3 A.M. and Horne judged that he had walked about two miles on the reconnaissance. He had never imagined that Von Winter would control such a vast amount of land in secrecy. He skirted through more woods, passing giant firs, cypresses, heavy boscage, and scaly lichen.

Through a clearing, he beheld the strangest sight of all: an ornate, torch-lit Teutonic stone castle, the kind he had once glimpsed on a boat trip up the Rhine, half-amused by these Gothic follies of mad German princes and kings. It must have been four stories high, designed with Saracen windows and flanking towers. It could only be approached over a metal drawbridge; a moat, and large lake below had a dock where several motor launches were anchored. Hunched low, Horne crept forward.

He heard boot steps and dropped down behind a column. Two men in Nazi uniforms, rifles shouldered, had stopped for a smoke, then strode away. Out of the darkness a whelping choir of herded animals joined a truck engine, grinding in low gear. Floodlights on timers came on and he took deep cover in the grass. He made out deer, lambs, and some cows enclosed behind the wooden slats of the truck.

An anachronistic impression of Africa took hold of Horne so suddenly that he thought he was hallucinating: He smelled lion in the wind! This was followed by the distinct vocalizations of a pride roaring, gathering to assign hunting assignments.

"*Lions?*" he whispered to himself, straining to identify the distinct sounds of the members of the pride.

He snaked through the pastures behind the slow-moving truck; until it reached another razor-wired preserve, park like, with symmetrical groves of trees. A man came out of a lighted stucco guardhouse and released a metal gate.

Amid the hoarse, strident growls and snarls, Horne made out two meowing cubs, three lionesses, and a large, black-maned male strutting on a rocky outcrop, reminding him of the *kopjes* in Africa. The truck driver released the wooden slats and began striking the disoriented and panicky animals with a metal pole to get them moving. The lions grunted and hummed a signal, before bolting directly into the open field. A guard with a poised machine gun stood watching.

With his rifle crooked over his arm, Horne ran about a mile, zigzagging through the woodlands. The only consolation was that a lion was not pursuing him.

At ground level he tried Butch on the cell and got static, their voices breaking up.

"I'm...trying to get out!"

"—I'll leave your bike and...drive along the perimeter with my brights on."

Horne rushed to the southern point, flashing his light along the razor wire. He couldn't locate the opening he had made earlier. He strapped the rifle to his shoulder, climbed slowly, looking back; he missed a section, and the razor wire slashed through his gloves, gouging his forearm.

Once on top of the fence, he shone his light on the road but couldn't find Butch. Suddenly out of the mountain mist, a car U-turned and gradually crept toward him. Horne jumped off, rolled to the ground, and tumbled to his side. He lay prone for a moment, rotated his .45, and had the car in his sights. The car stopped, its flashers on. Butch's voice rang through the silence.

"Doug, where are you? *Doug?*"

"Here. I'm coming."

Horne rose awkwardly to his feet. He'd almost wrecked his knee breaking the fall coming over.

Butch helped him over to the car. "You hurt?"

"Cut my arm on the fucking razor wire. I thought I tore my knee, but it's okay. I haven't got enough gas to make it back on the bike."

"I didn't bring a tow or fill my gas can."

"You're really out of practice, Butch."

"True, these days my night crawling is on top of Ingrid."

"Let's strip the license and heave the bike over the embankment."

Butch took a pair of pliers from his toolbox, yanked the tinny plate off, started the ignition, and revved it down a steep incline. They heard a thud when it smashed into a rock pile. In a moment, he was back behind the wheel. Horne had his thin gloves off and had Butch's first-aid kit open on his lap. He splashed iodine over his arm and gritted his teeth. Finally, he stanched the bleeding with a piece of gauze.

"Need stitches?"

"No, it's not deep, just ugly." He laughed. "Lucky it wasn't my trigger finger."

"I was scared shitless about you. What happened?"

"Hitler's friends are alive and well and training militia troops for Armageddon. I saw a building that's probably a gas chamber."

Butch was speechless. "Incredible...Rebecca was on the right track all along. Anything else?"

"Yeah. They've also got a pride of lions."

8

At seven in the morning, with the sun flirting through a slashing cloud cover, they arrived at Ingrid's house. Menudo was in the kitchen making coffee. He had his Glock holstered and his Remington shotgun resting beside the toaster oven. The TV was on to a tape of two Mexican flyweights, both with nasty eye cuts, flailing away at each other.

"'Morning, Butch."

"Everything quiet?"

"Yeah, I watched movies with Ingrid till three, and the ladies are upstairs sleeping."

"Have you checked on them?" Horne asked.

"I didn't think they wanted me coming into their rooms."

Horne crept into the spare bedroom upstairs, which Butch had indicated while he slipped into Ingrid's mirrored pleasure dome.

Rebecca lay on her side, auburn hair rumpled against a bright pink pillow, the covers cast off to her thigh, where a short yellow nightgown rose up, her bare arm curled in an imaginary embrace. He stared lovingly at her.

In sleep, her face had the artlessness of a submissive child, the sharp perceptions blunted, his lioness de-clawed. He tiptoed into the bathroom and closed the partially opened door connecting to Taylor's room, where she also was asleep. He turned the lock.

He stripped the makeshift dressing, cleaned up the gash, heaped his grimy clothes on the floor, and ran the shower. He found an assortment of shampoos and body gels. He stuck his head under the stream of water. The shower door opened. A hand reached in.

"Gott im Himmel."

"I smell like dead buffalo."

"Not to me."

Rebecca clasped his penis.

"Hey, if you don't stop that, I'm calling the manager."

Smiling greedily, she said, "Is this the size of it at rest?"

"Is that the way you were taught to say '*guten Tag*' in Vienna?"

With the showerhead redirected, Rebecca slipped off her rumpled nightgown and propelled herself inside. "Only to you—for the rest of your life."

"Excuse me, are you proposing? No ring, nothing?"

"The shampoo girl's here. Would you like Frederic Fekkai or L'Occitane lavender?"

"No Prell, Lifebuoy. I think I'm checking out."

"I'll get your bags, sir."

She pressed her firm, colossal breasts against his back and massaged his scalp with deft strokes.

"My premiums on the million-buck fingers finally paid off."

While he rinsed his hair, she stood on her toes, kissing him, nipping at his earlobes and inspecting him for signs of wounds.

Discovering that he was intact, she said, "Thank heavens, you're all right. Your arm?"

"Car door. Butch only helps ladies and didn't hold my hand."

"Stop ragging me. You found *them*?"

"Not exactly, but we're getting closer."

"Did you see Von Winter?"

"No. This was only a probe."

Rebecca's attitude was compromised by fear and elation. "It's real, then?"

"Could be." He had decided to withhold the specifics. Rebecca was too unpredictable.

She pressed tightly against him. "Are you going to make love to me?"

He lifted her up, pressing her back against the tiles, thrusting sweetly, then with immense power and swiftness. She clung to him.

"I never thought, believed, I could fall so completely in love with anyone. You're my life, Rebecca."

She became solemn and regarded him with reverence. "And you're God's apology to me. I've forgiven Him because of you."

A squad of young lawyers—property mercenaries and criminal defense Turks—had been assembled in Tommy Haggerty's conference room, which smelled of dead cigars and sausage heroes. The master sat at the head of the table talking on the phone to an official in the state land registry office in Sacramento. He squiggled notes on a yellow legal pad.

Horne and Rebecca sat to his left, Butch to his right. Horne noticed the two men were uncomfortable and sharp-tongued with each other.

Horne wondered what had caused the bad blood between the former friends.

"In 1951 a company based in Zurich purchased sixty thousand acres of land, almost a hundred square miles, between Morro Bay and Cambria," Haggerty declared. "The Feld Hafen Corporation pays its taxes promptly, and it's in an unincorporated area. Its spread's in the vicinity of Hearst Castle in San Simeon. The following year the company bought an additional waterfront parcel out at Point Estero as a wildlife preserve. There's never been any problem with the Coastal Commission."

Another Hugo Boss–dressed lawyer went through a stack of faxes. "The company has state licenses to raise cattle, and all of its livestock is USDA-approved. I'm not a cattle expert, and I can hardly pronounce its breeds: Pinzgau, Braunvieh, Gelbvieh. I know from Prime New York at the Palm and not much else."

"What does *Feld Hafen* mean?" Butch asked Rebecca.

She had been listening carefully and making notes.

"Field Haven. The Pinzgau is a dairy cow. They're raised in Salzburg and their milk makes the best butter and cheese. Every Austrian loves the mountain cheese."

Horne struggled with the pronunciation. "And *Gelbvieh*?"

"It's another breed of cattle; its classic color is yellow. It has a special flavor and we love it when it's made into *geräuchert Fleisch*. That's a mountain dried beef, sliced thin like carpaccio."

"How about Braunvieh?" Haggerty asked.

She was unexpectedly amused by these solemn, well-educated men.

"Brown cow is the meaning. The meat of Braunvieh calves makes the best veal schnitzels. Butchers in Vienna put out a sign when it's available and sell it at a premium." She sneakily laid her hand on Horne's thigh and whispered, "See, I am useful."

Horne nodded, then dumped the shells from the firing range on the table and tried to make a case for a federal investigation. He was quick to learn that none of the *evidence* he had collected at Field Haven had any legal validity. A young criminal attorney, a recent acquisition from the D.A.'s office, shook his head with consternation.

"Mr. Horne, *you broke* into the ranch. At the very least, you're guilty of trespassing."

"Guys in Nazi uniforms with automatic rifles were patrolling.... And that's okay?"

"They have a constitutional right to dress any way they like and even to bear arms."

"Automatic weapons?"

"That's a violation," Butch said. "Doug, sit down, and let this lawyer talk."

"You need legally acquired evidence, Doug," Haggerty explained.

Yet another attorney joined in the case against Horne.

"Mr. Horne, if someone says he's a Nazi, he's exercising his freedom of speech. And he has a constitutional right to protect his property against an intruder. *You* carried a weapon onto private property. Maybe you were going to steal something, rustle cattle, commit a crime, break into the house. You were armed. In this situation, *you're* the criminal."

Rebecca had patiently listened and found the pettifogging legalese insufferable.

"Horne found these people! Tommy, doesn't the law leave any room for common sense?"

"In forty years of practice, I've yet to discover any."

Haggerty's recently acquired deputy D.A. still had a prosecutor's zeal.

"Ms. Benjamin, the D.A. would have him arrested if he admitted this—in *any* jurisdiction. No judge—certainly not a federal one—would grant a search warrant. You see, Field Haven and its owners—whoever they are—have never had a criminal complaint filed against them."

She and Horne were stalemated. Rebecca cited the links between the murder of Miriam and the three other women.

"Tenuous at best," said the former prosecutor.

"The victims' relatives were ridiculed and dismissed—as my claims were—and still are," she persisted.

"You have nothing but a theory, Rebecca," Haggerty said patiently. "Where are the police reports, the Grand Jury proceedings, the documented forensic exhibits, and untainted chain of evidence for these cases?"

Horne was incensed.

"Goddamn it, listen to me, you guys! Von Winter and his crew have been gassing young women! They're connected to the murders of a rabbi in New York as well as jeweler there and other Jews around the country."

"Prove it. And don't go storming into their property again carrying a gun, Boyo, because you're the one who's going to wind up in prison again. They'll drag out your murder case records from Dar-es-Salaam." Tommy rose from the table. In a corner, he picked up a Callaway driver and fondled the grip. "Robbery-Homicide—they'll be on your ass and won't let it rest."

Rather than accept this counsel, Rebecca's could not contain her bitterness. "The law has to bend; I won't."

Tommy replaced the golf club. "Come on, it's late. I'm going to take you both out."

"I accept," Horne said, my VISA's on deathwatch."

"Don't worry." Haggerty held Rebecca's arm and smiled warmly. "When are you guys getting married?"

She looked quizzically at Horne. "These old bachelors have trouble making up their minds. All I can assume is that I'm too much trouble and not rich enough."

"Right on both counts, Fraulein."

"Drive out to Santa Monica and meet me at Shutters. I've got some calls to return. See you there in a bit."

Rebecca grimly went out to the office terrace; the outcast lit a cigarette.

Horne noticed that neither Haggerty nor Butch had exchanged a word or shaken hands, merely nodding icily to each other when the meeting had ended.

"You going to join us, Butch? Tommy's buying dinner."

Something was noticeably ruffling Butch. "No, thanks, Ingrid's got something on."

Rebecca stubbed out her cigarette and returned to the office. Butch kissed her and looked uneasily at Horne.

"Call me, Doug—if you decide to stay in touch," Butch said without explanation, as though this were an irrevocable farewell.

9

At Shutters, they crossed the threshold into the snug world of the rich, plumped on easy-living sofas, absorbed by cocktails and the diversion of an ocean view. Nothing evil could intrude on these lives.

Rebecca was at home here, gilding this well-heeled set, as Horne had been leading safaris. The memory of his evenings at the Mount Kenya Club, with a stylish troop of recruits in tow, and a bottle of vintage Krug to offer hunter friends, rematerialized. He tried to imagine the two of them there together. Yet somehow, Rebecca stubbornly resisted his daydream, leaping out of the idyllic tableaux. Could she ever fit in living in Africa...or as the wife of someone who had a fishing boat in the Northwest?

At the forefront of his mind, visions of Winterhaven's lions and the Nazi sport of throwing darts at photos of tortured Jews played havoc with the hotel ambiance. Rebecca had passed on the virus to him.

"Let's spend a night here," she suggested.

She was at her most seductive, the fox-like female, exploiting the male. Reckless in her passion, she leaned into him and stroked his cock under the table.

"You're an animal."

"You've made me into one. Here's the plan, Horne: We'll have our babies in five years." He raised his hands defensively. "Relax, they'll look like you."

"You're very well organized, Fraulein. Is this like one of Stalin's Five-Year Plans?

"Be quiet and listen. I've thought this out."

"You really want kids—in five years.... Why?"

She pressed her lips against his. "By then, I'll be *famous*. I'll have played with every orchestra that counts. At twenty-nine, I'll be ripe and ready to stay home with our children. I'll record...Play concerts three or four times a year. Horne, you've given me back my life."

She sprang up from the sofa.

Sullenly, he wiggled out his credit card. "I'm not sure it's got any juice left."

"I have a thousand on mine. Or would you like me to see if I can pick up a big spender for an outcall?"

"Jesus, you are a ballbreaker."

"Aren't you used it yet?" She ran her tongue over his lips. "I'll see if I can negotiate a 'cancellation' suite. Then I'd like a look around. I'm in the mood for a good rack of lamb."

"Lowball reservations and check the restaurant prices while you're at it. If Tommy doesn't show, it's Jody Maroni's sausages on the Venice Boardwalk. All you can eat for six bucks."

When Rebecca walked toward the check-in desk, men yammering on cell phones followed her with covetous eyes.

Haggerty appeared, sinking into the folds of a deep chair, and a waiter immediately delivered an arsenal of martinis to the regular.

"So you made it. I thought I'd get stuck with this check."

"I'm a man of my word. I fixed your credit for another ten thousand. Cheers."

"Thank you, Tommy," Horne said with relief. "Hey, what's going on with you and Butch? You act like you hate each other." What have I missed?"

Haggerty ignored the question with lawyerly artistry and diverted him; he sauntered into Horne's affair with Rebecca.

"Well, yeah, I do want to marry her."

"I detect a certain ambivalence. Were you involved with someone in Arusha before the shit hit the fan?"

"No."

Horne was no one to accept advice with grace, and resented meddling. "Let's get off the subject of my life decisions. Something doesn't smell right with you and Butch. What's the big secret?"

Haggerty's narrow shoulders hunched up and he sipped his drink. "It's a case of rotting old twigs in a dead fire."

"What is this bullshit? Is that the way you talk in court—in metaphors, counselor?"

"No, I have a guilty conscience. And Rose did as well."

While keeping an eye on Rebecca at the front desk, he persisted. "Tommy, you've known me most of my life. We're family, for crissake. And your evasiveness really bothers me."

"I don't like to be put in the position of ratting out someone when it won't do any good."

"Enough lawyer talk. Lay it on me."

Haggerty toyed with his foulard bowtie. "Oh, God...Rose...Rose and I pressured Bonnie to go on the trip to Africa with your father."

Horne's bewilderment grew. "My mother didn't want to go?"

"No, not at all. Bonnie was going to stay in L.A. and let Keith go to Africa alone."

"I don't understand. Then why did she go?"

"Rose and I had a long talk with Bonnie. We told her that...that it would save her marriage if she went."

Horne's face froze. "What the hell do you mean? My parents were in love!"

"I think in the early days. With women, we never know. At any given moment, they're susceptible to the right man, or the man they believe is the one for them."

"Whom are we talking about?"

"Butch." Haggerty's discomfort grew under Horne's intent gaze. "I feel like shit telling you this. But if you didn't hear it from me, it would come out and you'd hate *me*."

Horne was flabbergasted. For a moment, Haggerty's face blurred.

"I don't believe this."

"Well, it's true. Keith had settled down teaching in Eugene. He finally had a profession, aside from his passion for Africa and playing the guitar. You grew up there. You know in those days, Butch was the local hero, the revolutionary, ex-Green Beret, wounded in Vietnam and leading protests against everything. He was the big gun in Eugene...and Bonnie fell in love with him."

"What? He was my dad's friend!"

"*And* Bonnie's lover."

"—Shit, how *could* he?"

"Doug-Doug, for a man of the world how can you be so naive?"

Horne snarled at this herald of family betrayal, but he had sought him out.

"I guess I'll never go along with screwing your best friend's wife. I want to puke. It's...sickening...."

The inglorious nature of the human mating instinct was like snakebite when it paid a house call, bedecked with lies, shattering loyalty, and channeling false perceptions into the once-safe harbors of the heart.

"Rose blamed Bonnie," Tommy resumed, now informing a client of everything he didn't wish to hear. "Even today when there's nothing as grand as morality, it was Rose's conviction that it's always the woman who has the option. She can say 'no,' and there's nothing the guy can do about it. Rose was hardly a standard-bearer for traditional virtue—as you know. She had lots of men—including me. And she knew herself so well that she never married."

Haggerty drifted into the reverie of his own affair with Rose and his unrequited love.

"You were sixteen, Doug. The adored boy of five people—I include Butch and myself. That's why he spent so much time with you. But it also gave him access to Bonnie. When Rose and I confronted Butch, he claimed he hadn't forced anything with Bonnie. She'd wanted him as much as he'd wanted her."

The lawyer shored up his position as family savior.

"Rose and I did everything we could to break up this nasty triangle. *We* pressured Bonnie to take the Africa trip. It was a battle. She finally gave in and went with Keith. You lost your parents...and Rose and I spent years mourning our decision...meddling in their lives." He steepled his fingers, sighing deeply. "You try to help people avoid making a disastrous choice. When it doesn't work out, sometimes your own tragedy becomes the greater one."

Horne swigged back his drink, signaled for another, and Haggerty slumped in the chair.

"We had what seemed to be a normal family life in Eugene."

"And Rose wanted it to stay that way. You have to remember that your mother was gorgeous and pretty wild when she was young. Rose always got her out of trouble—emotionally and financially. She put up the money for her bakery—coffeehouse, whatever. She paid Keith's tuition when he decided to become a teacher. It was all intended to give you stability. She loved you above everyone. And there you were rumbling around the country, sleeping in cars, while two hippies spent their time smoking dope and partying."

Horne was repelled by Tommy's revelations.

"Ever wonder why Butch didn't come to Dar when you were charged. Or never visited you in prison?"

"I sure as hell did."

"I'm capable of petty revenge. I knew how badly he wanted to see you. Do something to help you. I made it clear that either I went and tried to get you off, or he could go and fuck things up again. I'd stay here. I wanted him to suffer."

Rebecca, smiling broadly, was approaching, and Tommy rose and bowed.

"You're one lucky bastard, Douglas. Don't fuck this up. Forget the past. We can't reinvent it. The thing with Butch—there's nothing to be gained by rehashing it. He loves you and would put his life on the line for you."

A bit tiddly, Tommy enveloped Rebecca in his arms and kissed her. "Are you checking in with me, I hope?" he asked. "Or this drifter?"

"You're a darling, Tommy." She shook Horne. "Hey, snap out it. Tommy booked us a suite. Pre-paid! That should brighten you up."

Hollowed by memories of a once-happy family, Horne grew distant once he and Rebecca were alone in their suite facing the ocean. Below them, the sour milky lights of the Venice Boardwalk in the gloomy night were hazy. In the last hours of darkness, the elite relics of the Los Angeles Empire were out in full force. Screeching skateboard charioteers ground their wheels on the concrete path to impress a posse of drugged young girls, flaunting their tattoos and body piercings. Their racket drowned out the sluggish waves on the beach.

Rebecca snuggled beside him. "We've been to so many hotels together, it'll be a relief to have our real honeymoon at Sycamore Place."

"We can't go back for some time."

She tucked her ankles behind her on the sofa, stroked his hair, and leaned her head on his shoulder. "You look so unhappy. What is it?"

"I feel kind of lost, and I'm not used to it. It's a very odd sensation. Like being at sea and not knowing where landfall is."

"Is it me?"

He embraced her and kissed her. "No, not you, Rebecca, never."

"Do you want to talk?"

He was uncertain, silent, then yielded to the impulse of unburdening himself to the woman he loved. He felt himself regressing into the role of a teenaged boy, for whom there was something unclean, unforgivable about the man who had slept with his mother.

"Haggerty told me some very shady things about my mother and Butch."

She moved away, tensely. "*That!* I guess it had to come out eventually."

"...You knew?"

Her eyes were doleful. "Family secrets always corrupt our dreamy illusions." Angrily, she added, "Believe me, I know all about that."

"Rose talked to *you* about my mother and Butch?"

"Rarely, and only at the end. Butch phoned a number of times, asking to see Rose, and she'd hang up on him. Sometimes when I answered, he'd question me about you. Was there any news? Did Rose need anything—things like that? But I never met him until I was with you at The Viking. Since there were undercurrents, I felt it was better to pretend we didn't know each other. I didn't want you to blame me for being part of a conspiracy. I was an outsider. It wasn't my place to carry tales. I loathe gossips."

The knowing innocence in her face affected him deeply. He rubbed her cheek with the back of his hand, and she kissed it.

"Rebecca, would you have ever told me?"

"—Hurt you? Never."

Behind his swashbuckling behavior, her big-game hunter revealed a level of emotional fragility that constantly surprised her. His mother had had an affair. Although he'd only learned about it after her death, Horne had taken it to heart.

Rebecca waited for a moment. "Shall we go to bed?" she asked by way of solace.

"Yes...I think so," he said.

Their lovemaking resumed amid a dirge of voices from Horne's past, fleeting mental fragments of childhood, the company of his parents and Butch at barbecues and ballgames, before he had learned that everything had been overshadowed by the lethal weakness of human desire.

He and Rebecca lay naked, not ambitious, but sharing the discreet tenderness of the wounded. She tenderly rested his head on her breast and tried to assuage his pain and disappointment. Without taking sides, she implored him to absolve the lovers' betrayal. There might have been a moral relativism that Horne had not understood. She was careful to avoid the suggestion of an arrangement; standard practice among European couples but considered deviant behavior in the United States, which held fast to a puritanical tradition that could never be sustained and fell under the umbrella of sanctimony. Horne, she had discovered, was mature in some respects, but less worldly than she herself.

"I won't be unfaithful to you," he said softly, caressing her hair.

"You don't have to make promises, Horne," she whispered back. "I know what you are."

10

Harry rolled into The Viking's frenzied parking lot by eight. Despite the Valley's thrashing in a windstorm, the place was invulnerable to weather conditions. With easy sex on the menu, the migrating herd would be thundering through another weekend.

The regular valet took his car, swooning over a twenty-dollar tip.

"Don't bury it."

"Out front, Mr. Summerfield."

"Leave it at the rear exit, please."

"You've got it, sir."

Harry lifted out a florist's box.

He squirmed through the bouncers at the entrance, a known face, slapping them with crisp green. The bar throbbed with a quick-witted clutter of men drumming their patter to tribes of women out for an epic night of boozing and hell-raising. The bartender waved to Harry, and a martini was flying on its way to him in Ingrid's reserved nook.

"Hi, Greg."

"Haven't seen you for the follies for some time, Mr. Summerfield."

Harry gestured toward the women. "Looks like you've restocked."

"Well, this is shag city, Mr. Summerfield. A new troupe...*relocating*...chased out by parents and husbands," the bartender, informed him. "Some farm-fresh sensations from the South at the far end." Greg swatted his hand at cocktail servers, ignoring their orders. "Simi Valley in the mid-section; plus the usual hostile divorcées; yeah, the lethal bowling group trying to score steaks and ecstasy."

Harry had dressed stylishly casual: gray cashmere pleated trousers, a navy-blue turtleneck, and one of his subdued Savile Row tweed jackets. Just another middle-aged man anxious to gorge on prime beef. He still found it unbelievable that the patrician Rebecca would play here.

"I'm on my way...." Greg bellowed to irate waitresses calling orders for...Grasshoppers and Scotch Sours. Bartenders didn't desert fifty-dollar tippers; they listened. "Ingrid found a very hot new lady pianist."

"Where is she? And Ingrid?"

"Ingrid's on her way. The piano lady is in back—the Valhalla Room."

This was Horne's *element*. He had surely been the link to this underworld and *invaded* Harry's anti-establishment domain. Sulking through his martini, the thought of the two of them belly to belly sickened Harry Summerfield. Rebecca would have been attracted by his coarse good looks and the compatibility of their ages. Rebecca had wanted a younger man, all along—a hunter, a puffed-up thug.

In the persona of Bruno Von Winter, he took in the scene before him. He felt he had at last dislodged his vulnerable double; that man tiptoed through a forged life which had about the same substance as the copies of masterworks Bruno had duplicated, which were deposited at murder scenes of Jewish women.

Harry Summerfield had bowed on his knee to Jews.

Bruno killed them.

What mystified him was that nothing in Rebecca's behavior had hinted at premeditation. Yet he was now convinced that she had meticulously planned it all: toying with him, pretending to care; then nursing Rose, all the while waiting to manipulate and seduce Horne to her own ends.

Bruno, the lady-killer, had complacently gone into battle with Rebecca Benjamin—the pure man-killer—without considering his enemy's strategy.

As an architect with thirty years of experience behind him, Harry appreciated the value of painstaking attention to detail that Rebecca had demonstrated. Chord by chord, she had composed a masterly composition to entrap him. He found himself laughing—a dry, mirthless snigger. Lilli's blood ran through them both. There was genius and craft in Rebecca's genes, and sheer ruthlessness; the same implacable coolness that had allowed his mother Lilli to go head-to-head with Magnus Von Winter, and emerge alive. It was essential for Bruno to remember just how much he and Rebecca had in common.

With the box of flowers under his arm, Harry glided through the bar. He smiled at predatory gangs of women, some familiar, hoisting newly plugged breasts, marking him for a get-together later. The men, always poor souls at any-age bars, drowned in musky colognes, and waited for the broken promises of hair transplants to take root and spout. They swarmed around these women like infuriated horseflies.

Next to the empty Valhalla Room were the bathrooms and phones. Harry had a good idea of the layout, having once had a drink with

Ingrid in her office at the rear of the rabbit warren. He reached the windowed freezers where frosted sides of beef swirled off hooks in a mystical solo dance.

"Hi! You're here!" The twangy voice startled Harry. "You were looking for me." Taylor insisted. She flung her arms around him, until he was impaled on thorns by this shrike.

Ever charming and composed, he said, "I must've been guided by a divine spirit. How've you been?"

"Harry—since you asked—downright Prozac-miserable without you." She patted her black mini leather skirt, and moved her long booted legs into the ballerina first position.

"Taylor, I've been working in Tampa for weeks."

"But not too busy to come here. Jesus, you never return my calls...." She licked her lips. "Remember that big redhead I tossed in for a threesome?" He leisurely nodded. "She's got a sister who's a ringer for Julia Roberts...loves leather collars...."

He feigned indifference. "I flew in yesterday night and found out a *family* friend is performing here."

She tossed her head theatrically. "You know *Rebecca*?"

"Very well. I picked up some flowers and wanted to deliver them."

"I'll give them to her."

"I'd rather do it myself."

"Not possible. I gave my word."

At a complete loss, he said, "I don't understand...."

"Her fiancé had to go and change at Ingrid's house." She flaunted the key. "Ingrid's old man Butch gave me the key to her office and said, *no one but me*" —Taylor's detestable self-importance resurfaced—"could go in."

Harry smiled through indecision while an improvised scheme took shape. He put down the box, pulled Taylor close, and kissed her neck, running his tongue over her earlobes. She immediately reached down and fondled his cock through his trousers.

"That's what I love about you, the way you get hard so fast—and *linger*."

"You've been reading Oprah novels. I only linger with you...it's your technique," he crooned. "We've got to work out something—permanent. I can't tell you how often I've thought about you. I haven't been with anyone since you."

"Mean that?"

"Naturally."

"Yes, you do."

Taylor went into overdrive. Harry raised her skirt and with the heel of his palm massaged her soft winter hairdo, probably styled with conditioner to avoid broken ends.

"I'm like a wild man with you," he moaned.

"Come on, the flowers'll keep. Let me teach this evil boy some manners. He needs a private lesson."

"What about Rebecca?" Harry asked.

"She can unlock the door. Only Chubb and me can get in from the outside."

"What's going on—the jealous boyfriend?"

"No way. Horne's anything but that. He and Butch think the psycho who murdered her sister is after her."

Taylor tugged him into a utility room used for floor waxers, vacuums, and handyman tools. The royal-blue carpet remnant had been stained by a toilet with acid reflux. The sink had bluish veins with rust engravings and a towel roll above. Beside it, a clothes rail hung with barmaid outfits, embalmed in plastic.

Taylor slid her panties down and kneeled in front of a full-length tarnished mirror angled on the floor for disposal.

"Let me get behind you. I want you to watch *you*."

"You're so depraved, she said, with a leering giggle. "Never have to get you up...." She pulled up her V-cut top, rescued her well-rounded breasts from captivity, and steered them out. "I love your touch...."

"Can't get any better—"

Taylor was the perfect Midwestern android and fell back against his chest, faint with the mirage of the destiny she had believed in with religious fervor. Here was her ideal—a rich older man she could cherish and worship. Her mother would have a block party when she brought him home.

With his left arm torqued around Taylor's chin, Harry wedged his right forearm forcefully against her windpipe. The pressure forced her to thrust her tongue out. At first with surprise. He seemed to want to take his time and she thrived on roughhouse. Let him build into some pain. They both loved that. She wondered if he was wearing a belt. On their first date, she had cheerfully told him that pain was painstaking. After that, he had given her a thousand dollars to shop for toys.

His grip on her throat tightened. Suddenly, she tried to turn but couldn't. She wanted to protest but her voice was gone. Something was going wrong with her throat. Her tongue choked her and her neck became rubbery before yielding, wobbling.

Her brain had stopped functioning and she fell into a struggle with blackness. She tumbled on her side and descended into a void.

With a closing rapid, expert wrench, Bruno snapped her cervical vertebra.

The bone crunched like a dry twig.

He watched with pleasure as a woman, who had once told him she'd die for him, actually kept her word.

Rebecca made up at a dressing table Ingrid had brought into her office for her. There was a good light, a comfortable sofa, and a meticulously laid-out desk. Before performing, Rebecca always needed some time alone to compose herself. Taylor was outside, solicitous, and mercifully quiet for a spell.

Apart from playing for guests in the apartment, and filling in at pick-up chamber concerts where she wasn't the soloist, Rebecca had not played for a paying audience in almost two years. That she had dazzled a drunken audience after the jazz pianist some weeks before, and beat him at his game, was an exercise any twelve-year-old at a conservatory could have done without practice.

She put on hose, black velvet pants, a loose Titian-red blouse with a scalloped neckline and wide sleeves that were just a bit short, so that they wouldn't interfere with the movement of her hands. She slipped on an old pair of Tod's black loafers.

As she completed her make-up, nothing too dramatic, and coiled her hair into a neat French roll, she found her hands shaking with nerves when she flexed them to warm up. She needed to concentrate and find her way through an unfamiliar repertoire. She decided to take the sheet music with her, unprofessional as it might appear.

She flinched at a knock on the door.

"Delivery."

She wasn't quite sure whose voice it was, then recognized it. She unlocked the door.

"What a marvelous, fantastic surprise!" She hugged Harry and pulled him inside.

He closed the door. He had just committed a murder, but his blithe self-possession belied this. He exuded the relaxed mood of a man looking forward to night music.

"I never imagined you'd come...*here.*"

"Didn't I tell you I'm a jazz lover?"

"I don't recall," she said, elated by the visit of close friend.

He handed her the box and her skin brightened when she saw red peonies. She kissed him on both cheeks. "I love them! Damn, there's no vase. I'll call Taylor."

"Ingrid needed her for something. They'll keep. They're just out. A new season for everything." A silence, loud as the scrape of a rusty hinge, enveloped them. "Rebecca, can I talk to you for a moment later?"

"Of course. Now, if you like."

"No, you've got to go on....Look, it won't upset you, I assure you." He put a hand on her shoulder. "Well, enchant us. You always do."

She rolled her eyes. "I'll try."

"Just trust yourself." With the pleasure of an absent-minded family member celebrating good fortune, he added, "Oh, by the way, congratulations."

"For what?"

"On your engagement to Mr. Horne."

She was on the defensive and looked at him with embarrassment, a wrench of culpability.

"We're not officially engaged."

His attitude was benevolent. "Well, I'm happy that you found the right man. I'll see you later."

11

Minutes later, there was another knock on the door.

"Rebecca, it's Ingrid. Ready?"

Rebecca opened the door and hugged Ingrid.

"Don't mess your face. You look smashing."

"Ingrid, I can't tell you how much—"

"—Oh, cut it out. I should thank you." She peered into her office. "Hey, where's Taylor?"

"She went looking for you."

"I must've missed her. It's a madhouse."

"Is Horne here?"

"Banging 'em back at the bar with Butch. Guy talk. They seem very serious."

She followed Ingrid through the hallway winding around the banqueting rooms and the restaurant. Once Rebecca took the stage alongside a beaming Ingrid, the crowd hushed for the mistress of the castle, who took the mike.

"From the concert halls of Vienna, in her American debut, The Viking is proud to present Rebecca Benjamin, the new queen of the piano."

Rebecca bowed her head to the audience in the scattering applause and adjusted the bench, then lowered the microphone. Accustomed to the mellow and deep color of her Bösendorfer, she had driven the piano tuner to distraction earlier in the day; the Yamaha grand had a metallic vibrato.

"Good evening, everyone. This is an experiment for all of us. I'm a classical pianist, but tonight, I'm going to explore new territory and play some jazz for you."

Chants of "yeah-yeah" greeted her, and she quickly laid the scores on the rest and began. She made a seasonal adjustment because of Harry's peonies with "I'll Remember April," then glided into "Bewitched." As she gained confidence, her momentum improved and she was able to lyrically phrase "Stella by Starlight," occasionally weaving in a Bach fugue and improvising until she returned to the main theme. Concluding the first set, Rebecca mesmerized the audience. Sipping some water, she searched the room for Horne and let her eyes rest on his face for an instant. He was at the bar angrily gesturing at Butch.

Ignoring them, she concentrated on her performance, and moved imperceptibly from "Lush Life," interweaving it with a section of a Rachmaninoff concerto, before a honeyed glide into a medley of romantic Sondheim songs that she had heard Cleo Laine sing. The audience was enthralled by her artistry.

Her blouse was wringing wet. When she reached for a handkerchief to dry her brow, she looked at her watch and realized she had been playing for an hour. She took the mike, stood up, smiled with gratitude, and bowed. The audience broke into riotous applause.

"Thank you for your warm welcome. Please stay. I'll be back for a midnight show."

She stepped off the stage into Horne's arms. In an instant, she was swallowed up by Butch, his cronies, Ingrid, and hundreds of strange faces. People were asking for autographs, and she was overwhelmed by the reception.

"I need a few minutes to cool down," she said, shaking, still tense. "I'll change and see you back out here."

Horne kissed her sweaty brow. "Rebecca, you were out of this world. I just—" his eyes brimmed with adoration—"worship you...."

"And don't you forget it," she said merrily.

Breathing deeply, she returned alone to Ingrid's office. Images of Miriam, smiling, Lilli's embrace, the chatter, and Herta, kissing her, swamped Rebecca's mind. Floating in this new world, she was oblivious of her surroundings until she saw Harry.

He handed her a towel. "What a performance! You weren't good, you were astounding."

"Harry, I was thrilled to have you here." Regarding his dejected face, she gave in to her emotional state. "I'm so sorry about this not working out. I really wish it could have been different for us."

"It never could, Rebecca."

"I'm on fire."

"Let's get some air."

"Oh, yes, yes." He slipped his jacket over her shoulders before opening the rear exit. The wind had subsided to a rasp and collars of fog had settled over the Valley. They walked slowly until they were beside his Jag.

"I'd kill for a cigarette. But I quit for good this time."

She broke off, felt her body twitch with fright when she saw the couple that had followed her and Horne on their travels. They now drew near Harry and her. She felt suspended in space; her world came to a standstill.

"Harry, Harry, my God, it's *them!*" she said in an undertone, shuddering.

"Who?"

"They're the ones who've been after me!"

Harry found his key, pressed the button, and automatically unlocked the car.

"Quick, get in the back." He opened the door and propelled her inside. "Don't worry, I'll take care of them!" He flicked out a gun from a holster behind his back. She recalled that he had an automatic in his Land Rover and was grateful for his quick reflexes. Now she felt protected.

The couple passed by Rebecca who was crouched on the cold leather seat. When she dared to look up, she found herself staring into the woman's face pressing up against the window. The glass distorted her features. She appeared to be puckering her lips in a repugnant kiss. She tapped the window and audaciously flashed Miriam's solitaire engagement ring on her own left hand.

Rebecca's throat closed.

She gasped when the driver's door burst open. The gaunt man, wearing a blond wig, slid behind the wheel.

"*Harry!*" she screamed. "*Harry—*"

Instantly, Harry hurled into the backseat, beside her, slamming the door. The car sped away. The woman, now in the passenger seat, pointed a long-barreled pistol at her. The door locks snapped automatically. The driver rocketed out of the lot and slewed into a darkened street. He double-parked and seized the pistol from the woman.

"Stick out your hands, girl," Noreen growled.

Rebecca could hardly breathe. A veil of fear suffocated her. Numb from shock, she did as she was ordered. The woman handcuffed her.

"Harry...Harry," she cried.

She reached for his hand. By degrees, he turned his head. His eyes had changed, frostbound, devoid of emotion. Could they have injected him with a drug? The car raced onto a freeway. She was too shaken to speak again.

As she caught a glance of the woman's profile, the jumbled maze of memory carried Rebecca back to her first walk on Sycamore Place more than a year ago. Harry had dropped her off after their lunch. She'd been early for her appointment with Rose Fleming. This woman in the front seat—this woman who had handcuffed her—had been walking a toy dachshund and had angrily snarled at her when she'd asked about the dog's name. A German name—a German beer.

Rebecca's eyes closed involuntarily, and she drifted into an isolated twilight world.

A man's voice roused her, but she had difficulty recognizing it as Harry's.

"My father keeps his piano perfectly tuned," he said coolly. You'll play again tonight at Winterhaven. Even better than when we first heard you in Vienna." Harry yanked her arm. "That's when I saw *my* mother for the first time."

She could make no sense of his statement. It spun through the blankness of her mind. She was incapable of assimilating the words. The meanings themselves entered a region that had closed to her.

"Rebecca, you do remember meeting my father at the office? He did one of his old magic tricks with your wallet. You were captivated by him. He didn't like you. But he always puts on a good show." Harry shook her. "You asked about his shoes."

"...Lobb shoes...."

"Yes, you're coming back."

"Not for much longer," Virgil growled.

"Shut up, Virgil! Just drive. Find a classical station on the radio. That should improve Rebecca's memory." He turned his attention back to her and took pleasure in her distress.

"I must admit, Magnus is a better judge of people than I am. I don't know what I expected...history to change? He thought you were a classic kike whore."

"These Jewish sluts screw their landlords. They're all the same, Bruno," Noreen observed.

Eyes agape, she cried, "You...you're *Bruno Von Winter*—not Harry Summerfield!"

"Yes, I am. For years I hid my identity. I had my reasons. But now they don't matter. Harry Summerfield will die. In a few days the police are going to find a decapitated, armless torso, with swastikas tattooed on him. Another victim...lots of ghoulish articles and TV babble. In a week, he'll be another old story. A mystery with no solution. Just like Miriam."

Having emerged from the shade of his former identity, Bruno embraced the harmony within himself. He could now be whole, at peace. He relished his true identity.

"The public needs garden-fresh entertainment," he told Rebecca. "It's Rome at the end of the empire. Eventually the country's going to collapse. We at Winterhaven will be ready to reestablish order. And this time, we'll have a perfect structure for survival... Islam by our side. We'll end these insane wars with allies like Israel. America's a dying, half-breed society of fragmented minorities, ruled by corrupt, self-serving Jews like Jack."

An unbearable silence ensued that petrified Rebecca. Her disbelief assumed a horrifying reality when she studied Harry's face. There was a distinct resemblance to Lilli that she might have noticed, rejected, suppressed, all within the blink of an eye—too quickly to assimilate on a rational level. It became clear that she had subconsciously sensed this connection and repulsed his advances.

He was Lilli's son, without a doubt, bearing the marks she'd overlooked: the well-defined bone structure that could not be hidden behind Lilli's parchment wrinkles; the nib of her nose and its arch that were almost identical to his; their coloring had an impeccable finish.

She tried to fathom the undercurrents of madness. Paintings began with a line, books opened with a word; a solitary symbol of musical notation originated the inscrutability of a symphony. The disastrous events that lay at the heart of the tragedy that had befallen Miriam and now her had evolved because a son had wished to wound his own mother. Could this explain his peculiar calls to Lilli?

It was almost too much to comprehend for her. This man sitting beside her was insane—the monstrous spawn of Magnus Von Winter and her grandmother. Rebecca had been at a loss to recognize the evidence? What frightened her even more was the realization that Bruno had known all along who *she* was, yet had perversely fallen in love with her.

She was to be his "Jewish Bride," as Lilli had been his father's. It was haunting, pathological...a man following in his father's footsteps, wishing to capture his mother through her own granddaughter...keeping it all in the family in an incestuous cycle bound to resurrect the same tragedy. Feeding on hatred through love, and on love through hatred.

To maintain her reason, she had to speak.

"How could you be *this* person? Your friends are Jews, like Jack Leopold!"

"Architects need financing," he responded furiously. "He had the money. I've always *hated* him. I was doing small, artsy commissions—nothing on the scale of Tampa Bay. Whoever he hires to complete the project won't be able to change my work. It'll be too costly. They'll have a competition to design office towers. But Jack won't be around much longer, either. My partners up front are going to pay him a house call."

Bruno had orchestrated Miriam's murder as well as that of the other women. Of all the living relatives of the dead women she had met with Horne, one stood out. She and Cynthia Edelstein had an affinity. Harry had been the mysterious visitor who had wanted to buy the architectural drawings from Cynthia at her parents' shop.

"You met Cynthia at Cognoscente in Palm Beach," Rebecca said, measuring her words so that they were not accusatory.

An expression of scorn anchored Bruno's features. "Cynthia and I...we had a very pleasant dinner. I suppose I was attracted to her."

"Why didn't you take the Bauhaus drawings you wanted?"

"I'm not a thief!" His voice had a vitriolic indignation.

The confusion distilled on Rebecca's face brought with it a degree of sexual kindling that made her even more alluring to him. He imagined her as one of the women in the paintings he had copied and searched his mind for an image. She could have been the beautifully jaded nude in Manet's "Olympia."

He was well aware that behind his bleak fetish for a Jewess lay a residue of unreciprocated love. Bruno fantasized that he was undressing her: the muffled swish of silk, a quick metallic snap, her bra hurriedly dropped on the carpet, the rasp of curtains sliding down the rod, the squish of linen on the bed as their bodies meshed.

The texture of this obsession with Rebecca was a case in which the high treason of his self-discovery had been guided by Magnus's own inclinations. The copper-haired enchantress, her hands sweeping confidently over the keyboard, had excited the desire for custody as Magnus had felt before him with Lilli.

Bruno would have her at last, and the prospect of her unwillingness was thrilling. He laid out a program of festivities for her, its theme degradation. Only then could he turn his love into a weapon for emotional survival. Rebecca would become theater.

The rank odor of poisons within Bruno emerged with psychotic ferocity.

"My father had an fanatical idea for years. It had to do with Jewish women breeding more Jews—the brides to be. Until I saw Lilli in Vienna, and he explained the circumstances—the level of her betrayal, her depraved plan to abort me...smother me after I was born, I realized how malevolent my *mother* actually was.

Rebecca couldn't contain her revulsion. "You're the worst of them, Bruno." She knew that she was dangerously goading him. "You of all people, an educated man who wanted to be an artist and became a brilliant architect. *You* should have known better. But you became an artist of death. I saw the gruesome paintings you left behind, with their Nazi mazes."

He laughed mirthlessly. "They were the movement's calling cards. My attitude toward Jews was bred in the bone. Hitler was only a symbol of something deeper, more permanent, a universal feeling ingrained in all people. But it's a reality that's dominated the world since Eden was corrupted. Eve was the first Jewess...."

Bruno was wild, wound up, and continued to spew out abominable distortions.

"I'm not a Christian. But like my father, a student of history. Just think about what the Jews did to one of their own. Jesus Christ. *They* conspired against Him. They bought the Romans off and He was crucified. Why, why didn't the Vatican do anything to stop the extermination program our Nazis had formulated during World War II? Well, it's clear to everyone: The Pope and his Cardinals weren't deranged. Jews had *murdered* their God."

It was impossible for Rebecca to think of this psychopath as Harry Summerfield. Bruno had lifted the screen behind which he'd lain in wait. He was an artist whose macabre canvases mutated into aberrations, loathsome, sham corruptions of masterworks.

Hidden behind the enlightened façade of a master builder, he was a man with a warped vision of life flourishing within him, confusing beauty with conquest and art with murder. Bruno was the mutant heir to civilization's nightmare. Rebecca's fears evolved into depression. She was a blood relative of Lilli's monstrous son.

Her investigation into her sister's murder had delivered her into the axis of Satan's circle.

She glimpsed freeway signs. They were close to Santa Barbara. Virgil pulled off on a dirt road at the rear of a nursery with a large field behind it. He parked the Jag in a garage beside it. Piercing winds on the open acreage thrashed against the seedlings.

Noreen herded her into the back of an SUV. Bruno sat close beside her and smugly grazed her breasts with the back of his hand. She had expected it, and made up her mind to ignore it and him. Even Nazis tired of indifference.

She would not protest, cry, or show any emotion. She thought of Horne. He would be frantic, slowly dying, as she was at this moment.

12

After finding the peonies and Rebecca's change of clothes in Ingrid's office at ten-thirty, Horne and Butch continued searching for Rebecca. There had been no note, and her cell phone had been left on Ingrid's desk. Just as they were about to rush out to the parking lot, Ingrid's shrieks froze them.

A cold sweat streamed down Horne's face: Rebecca had been found dead. In a panic, they stormed into the storage section. Amid mops and industrial odors of disinfectant, Ingrid knelt on the floor.

Ingrid cradled Taylor's head. The girl's body was rigid, her legs extended from inside the closet. Her sweater had been yanked up and her bare breasts drooped over the bra's cups.

Butch carefully lowered her head to the floor, then helped Ingrid to her feet.

"You shouldn't have touched her."

"I couldn't help it!" She was sobbing. "When I opened the door, she fell out and I caught her before her head hit the floor."

Butch felt for a pulse, pressed Taylor's carotid artery; her neck wobbled, and her skin had already turned ivory.

"Christ, she was strangled. Neck's been broken. Body's still luke-warm."

Butch supported Ingrid. Puddled by tears, her make-up blotted her cheeks.

"Come on now, honey, don't faint on me. Want me to carry you?"

"No, no, I can make it. Get me into my office. I'll have the bar-tenders make an announcement that we're closing."

"No, *don't* do that," Horne commanded her. "The killer might still be here—getting a rush. Butch, I'm going out to talk to the valets. Maybe they've seen Rebecca."

"Yeah, that's possible. I know the local guys at Homicide. I'll call them."

Horne tried to stem his fears, battling to maintain his self-control. His experience in Africa had taught him that the moment he gave into doubt or lost his nerve, he would be swallowed up in an emotional cauldron. He couldn't allow anything dull his mind.

Aided by a group of Viking employees and the valets, he roved through the lot, checking every car. None of the parking attendants had seen the couple. He had no illusions about Virgil or his wife. They'd been relentless in their pursuit. But never once had he sensed that Rebecca was in imminent physical danger. Someone was holding them in check. Horne came to the conclusion that they hadn't killed Rebecca...yet. She had unquestionably been taken against her will. Virgil and the woman had found a way in, and he hadn't seen them.

Under the canopy, customers were lined up, knowing something was wrong, grouching about their cars. Horne was still holding back the valets. In the distance, sirens whined

Leading Ingrid, Butch burrowed through the mob.

One of the valets, trotting toward them, shouted, "I'm missing a dark green Jag. I've got the key."

"The guy left his key?" Butch snapped.

"Yeah."

"Any idea whose car it might be?" Horne asked.

"Yes. It's Harry Summerfield's Jag."

Horne was at a complete loss, then he remembered the architect.

In a rush he asked, "Did you write the tag down?"

"Yeah, here: it's HS 111340. He duked me a twenty to leave it at the back exit."

"He's been a customer for ages," Ingrid said, bewildered. "I didn't see him inside...." The realization struck her like a blow to the face and she fell back against Butch. "Jesus, he was Taylor's steady guy."

"I know him. He was a friend of Rebecca's. He was crawling all over her."

Ingrid, with a bartender in tow, returned. Unnerved, the man asked Butch, "What's going on?"

"Did you see Summerfield tonight, Greg?"

"I made him a martini and shot the shit for a minute."

"Did he ask you anything about Rebecca?"

"No-no. Did I do something wrong?"

"It's okay, Greg. Go back inside," Ingrid said.

Horne whipped out his cell phone. "Harry is Jack Leopold's friend. He'll have his number."

In a moment, he had Paula Leopold on the line.

"This is Doug Horne, Mrs. Leopold. Can I speak to Jack, please?"

"He took a sleeping pill. Can I help?"

"I need to get in touch with your friend Harry Summerfield. May I have his number?"

"What's going on, Doug?"

"I need the number right now. It's urgent! He and Rebecca are missing and she didn't leave willingly."

"You don't think Harry—" the phone clattered—"Sorry. It's 310-555-1765." Her voice was shaking. "What's—"

"Thanks, 'bye." Horne dialed the number and listened to the message service.

"Mr. Summerfield, this is Doug Horne. I'm at The Viking. When you check your messages, call me. Taylor and Rebecca are very worried about you. They think you might have been carjacked, so let us know if you're okay."

"Very cute," Butch said.

With the arrival of black and whites, paramedics, parking attendants rushing through the lot, with car alarms set off, horns blowing, The Viking descended into bedlam. Horne yanked Butch off to the side.

"Let Ingrid handle the cops. If I don't move now, I'm going to lose Rebecca. You coming?"

"You sure you want me around?"

"Yeah."

"You going to take a swing at me."

"Not tonight," Horne replied, his face grim.

13

As Butch drove the Cruiser to his large gun warehouse, Horne knew that he had never encountered anything of this personal magnitude. He loved Rebecca, and to lose her was unimaginable. Right now, he needed Butch and would settle with him about Bonnie at the right time. In Africa, before killing the Dutchman, he had been used to constant adversities. Someone, native or tourist, would sometimes be trapped, alone, frightened, in danger. As the man in charge, he'd remained unflustered; he was responsible for their lives.

"What do you want to do, Doug?"

Horne tried to be logical. "I don't like the idea of Summerfield missing with his car. I can't believe he's actually involved." He shook his head. "But I'm convinced Von Winter's people somehow managed to kidnap Rebecca."

"Maybe she was with Summerfield, like you said, and they were both grabbed," Butch suggested.

"Yeah, carjackers don't bother taking the key."

Horne made an effort to stifle his anxiety, which wove intricate patterns in his mind.

"I believe in bad luck, bad timing, stupid choices, accidents—but *not* coincidences."

In fifteen minutes they were at Guns 'R' Us. Butch had turned cautious with Horne and was not ready to commit himself.

"Exactly why'd you want to come here?"

"You've got a shitload of munitions. I'd like to borrow some stuff."

"Borrow? This isn't a fucking library where you check out books."

"And this isn't the time to bullshit me."

"Everything in here, it's all accounted for."

"By who?"

"Friendly people."

Swaying with anger, Horne clenched his fists. "Is that all you're going to tell me?"

"I have a dark side."

Horne moved closer to him. "Do you? That's a big surprise. You going to take me inside this arsenal?"

"Look, the government doesn't give a rat's ass about neo-Nazis painting graffiti on temples. Even if a few Jews get murdered, it's not a serious threat. The Jews kick up a fuss and the media blows smoke. It's turned over to the FBI and local cops who stash the complaints in their junk files."

"I know that no one gives a fuck about them."

"You're entirely right. As far as these neo-Nazi scumbags are concerned, who've been to prison, organize White Supremacist gangs, and hassle a few U.S. Jews, nobody in power cares. It's nothing to them. National security isn't involved. It's not as if these morons are a danger to *Israel*. Now Israel we care about very, very deeply. They're our gas station attendants. They watch our asses and our oil. And if the Palestinians ever get a state, there goes the station." He shook his head. "Jews here, forget it."

"I don't exactly feel that way about Rebecca's life. Now what is this stockpile of weapons for? And spare me all this double-talk. Are you dealing arms?"

"No...no way. I just don't want you getting hurt."

"I appreciate your concern. I'll go up to that ranch alone with my guns and no real firepower. Just drop me back at Ingrid's and I'll get my own car."

"Hang on."

"For what? You know, Butch, I wish I'd actually looked at you before.... People are always out there with smiling faces, like you...hiding something. You bastard, taking shots at my mother."

Horne's rage wounded Butch. An anguished expression crossed his face. He trembled, trying to suppress his own sorrow, which gave way to his pent-up aggression.

"Listen, I don't owe you or anybody any fucking apologies for what happened with us. I loved Bonnie and she loved me."

"What about all your other women?"

"Strictly window dressing. There was only your mother!"

Butch pressed in the code, which opened the steel doors. Horne glimpsed a computer and monitor. Butch typed in an access password.

He took Horne's arm. "Now do exactly what I say: Walk in backwards, and if you turn, keep your head down, stay low, in profile."

Horne murmured "video cameras," then "microphone" and Butch nodded; with his back to the camera, he in turn mouthed, "Langley."

The air was thick with machine oil, cordite, and the gases emitted by explosives.

They stepped back outside, in a no-man's land beyond the cameras.

"They send me special tourists who *vacation* in unfriendly countries. They don't want any weapons traced back to them."

Horne mocked him. "Ah, you're a patriot."

"I'm paid handsomely for my good citizenship."

"Tax exempt."

"Something like that. Now if you want my advice, travel light, don't overload."

"I can carry eighty pounds in a hundred degrees—uphill."

Butch went back inside alone. Horne kept thinking of a plan, but the name Summerfield intruded and struck him as part of some elaborate puzzle.

Butch brought out a loaded ammo belt and a machine gun with clips. Horne would bear less weight: six TH3 incendiary grenades, which burned to 4,000 degrees and weighed two pounds each; six MK offensive grenades, which could crater The Viking when it was full; for dessert, an M60 machine gun that fired two hundred rounds per minute. It weighed twenty-three pounds, the spare barrel, eight.

"You forgot something."

"What now?"

"A gas mask for me."

He returned with three sets of Israeli Defense Forces 4A1 masks.

"Thank you. And goodbye."

Desperate to reason with Horne, Butch tried to restrain him.

"Doug, this is insane."

"I know the layout."

"Maybe she's back in Beverly Hills with Virgil and his old lady."

"No. They're just the household help for the Von Winters. They've taken her up there to gas her like her sister."

"Please, try to think this out. That ranch is four-five hours, doing seventy without the CHP on your ass."

"I don't have wings."

After some thought, Butch reluctantly said, "I have a helicopter at Van Nuys airport."

"What do you do with it, go on missions for Ingrid to recruit on nudist beaches?"

"I never thought of that. I'll suggest it to her."

They both laughed, nervously, and their camaraderie returned for a moment, until the ghosts of lies dispossessed it.

When they reached the quiet Van Nuys Airport, Horne forced himself to clear his mind of Butch's deceptions. They headed to a hangar where a dark blue Bell Jet Ranger gleamed under the lights. They loaded the weapons aboard.

"You own this?"

"Uh-huh. Pilot's license, too."

"Must've set you back a few bucks."

"They gave me a senior discount. We'll set down in Oceano. It's up the Central Coast, a couple of miles outside of Pismo Beach. Take us a good hour from there by car to...what's the name of Von Winter's place again?"

The tantalizing relationship between the title of the Swiss corporation and Harry's name continued to intertwine oddly in Horne's mind.

"*Feld Hafen*...? Rebecca said it was called 'Field Haven.' Harry *Summerfield*...Magnus Von Winter...Winter Haven...?"

"That's a slick match."

"I was the Muhammad Ali of crossword puzzles in prison. I can give you ten synonyms for 'mitigate.'"

"I'm impressed.... But what are you actually implying, Doug?"

Horne was pensive. "I'm not sure. But something's bugging me about this whole thing."

"Is it Summerfield?"

"Maybe. I can't put my finger on it."

After clearance from the control tower, Butch smoothly took the bird up. "They have a lot of stupid blowhards working in intelligence. Good pay. Think about it."

"What about medical coverage?"

"Excellent. You can pick your own doctor, and deadly prescription drugs are free."

Once they had cleared Santa Monica, and were undulating down the coastline at the maximum cruise speed of 200 knots per hour, Butch lit a cigarette and switched down the air traffic squawk.

"Why do you think they took Rebecca?"

"They want attention—Jewish trophies. But my guess is Rebecca told Harry about us. He had a hard-on for me. It didn't hurt that she was very convenient and she never would have suspected him."

14

Rebecca was alert when the SUV jostled her, grumbling its way up a dirt road to the torch-lit grand stone castle on the hill. She peered at her watch. It was past one in the morning. Bruno had changed places with Noreen. He rode in the front and ignored her. She might have been in the Bavarian Alps, where a feeble-minded relative of the Hapsburgs had tried to reconstruct the grandeur of the past. The Von Winter colony and its shrine had imported these grotesqueries of the vanished Old World into the tamed wilderness and beauty of the California coast.

They pulled up at a large porte-cochère. Bruno came around and grasped the chain of her cuffs, unlocked them, and jerked her out of the backseat.

"Welcome to my home, Rebecca."

"It's a pity you ever left."

He sniggered. "My father would agree. I see I've got the old Rebecca back, as if you were dealing with obsessed fans. Like the way you and Lilli treated us at the wine bar in Vienna."

She had no recollection of this incident, another slight that had frothed to the top.

"I was with *friends* then."

Her brave front wavered when she heard the echoes of roars. Was this what actual lions sounded like? Could it be some audio trick to frighten her even more?

"Lions...?" she said to herself, but Bruno was close and heard her.

"Four generations of them. Monarch, the Fourth, is king of the pride. Our people in South Africa sent them when I was growing up here. Magnus had to have his lions. My grandparents were trainers in a circus owned by a Jew. They were actually eaten by lions. Jews invented mass entertainment to make money, didn't they?"

Rising above the shock wave of her kidnapping, Rebecca now grasped the fact that she had been taken in by an outwardly normal man. Harry-Bruno—whomever he decided to be—was so cunningly insane that no one could have unearthed the truth.

Men in black full-dress SS uniforms, boots gleaming, clicking in unison, joined them. Excitedly, they raised their right hands high, but respectfully kept their distance.

Virgil took the lead. "My friends, this is Bruno Von Winter. He's come back to us."

"*Heil, Bruno!*"

"*Heil, meiner Kamaraden.*"

Bruno went around, shaking hands with everyone. Their warmth and enthusiasm became evident to him. They acted like friends at a football game, arranging a tailgate barbecue. He met the blacksmith, some tanners, and ranch hands. They all bowed to him.

Noreen shoved Rebecca ahead to the entrance. Rebecca banged against the concrete wall and fell to her knees. With the group chattering, she was ignored for the moment. She looked around, frantically searching for a way out.

Suddenly Rebecca was trapped by a pack of fanatical Nazi women wearing gray overcoats. The began singing the "Horst Wessel Lied." As though joined in a playground game, they enclosed Bruno in a moving circle. Their blonde hair in buns, this thrilled cluster of young women flung off their coats. Naked, they stampeded, trampling over Rebecca. Wild as starved animals, they knelt before Bruno, flashing hideous piercings and lightning-bolt tattoos.

A chorus of screeching voices called: "Bruno! Bruno! Me! Me! *Me!*"

Rebecca had never dreamed a collection of women like these existed. This perversion was beyond anything she could have imagined. During his covert visits to Winterhaven, Bruno had slept with all of them. Now he haughtily waved them away.

At the immense, weathered wooden doors, he wrenched Rebecca to her feet and nudged her inside. She crossed a threshold into a hallway, freighted with armor, and found herself in a dimly lighted ballroom.

Falling again, she was pulled up by the naked women and shoved inexorably to the axis.

Magnus Von Winter glanced at the entertainment. But his universe centered on Bruno. His son advanced, haltingly, as though to a throne. Magnus sprang up from his tapestried armchair, with the ardent thrill of a lover hungering for a reunion. He tenderly wrapped his arms around Bruno.

"*Willkommen zu Hause!*"

"*Prasens von Be, Vater,*" Bruno replied.

Magnus kissed his son's lips; he lingered, displaying a craving Rebecca had never before witnessed between a father and son.

Straining to cling to her sanity to stave off a plunge into unconscious-
ness, she called up Horne's face and imagined him smiling. In a danse
macabre, the circle of women unlocked and thrust her at Magnus. He
caught her and held the small of her back like a ballerina at the end
of a pas de deux. His mouth had a painted smirk. He studied Rebecca
like a statue, before helping her into his chair.

She gazed up at him. His face mirrored a fantastic series of visitations luring her into a trance-like web of ghostly figures. Deathmasks
of women floated above the circle of Nazi maidens.

"Rebecca, you're daydreaming!"

Her arm was shaken by the elderly squire in tweeds, wearing high
boots as though out for a country birdshoot. Her gaze was transfixed
by a gold swastika set in a rose petal pinned to his lapel.

"You must remember me.... I was the pastor in your tour group at
the Museum of Tolerance."

She nodded, hesitant, searching to regain the currency of time.

"...We talked afterwards...your shoes.... The magic tricks...."

"I was in such a hurry to see our favorite architect that I forgot to
change them."

Magnus stroked her cheek. "You're a very observant woman. Lilli
was as well," he informed Bruno.

"I am Magnus Von Winter, Bruno's father, my dear. Consider this
a family reunion. We often go to them protesting, but then enjoy
them."

"–*Magnus!*" Rebecca said, horror-stricken by the sound of the
name.

"Lobb shoes and boots. Disguises, disappearances to order," he said
with genial laughter.

"*He is the Magie,*" Bruno proclaimed with reverence. He took
Magnus's arm, intoxicated by the spell of his father's supremacy.

"We've been waiting for you at Winterhaven, Rebecca. We saw you
play at the Bösendorfersaal. The Schumann entranced us; your entire
program was thrilling. I know something about technique. You play
with more color than Lilli. I marveled at the way you carve and shape
the notes. You were like a wood nymph on stage."

Rebecca drifted in and out of a murky consciousness. She sensed
that her torture was beginning with an overture of praise.

"Here, have some Cristal. Lilli always enjoyed a good glass before and after *performing*. Actually, I'm in your debt. You brought my son home for good. He's kept his distance for too many years now."

Everywhere she looked, her eyes fell on bronzes of swooping eagles, tapestries mounted on the wall and swastika flags. The tables held red-and-black, leather-framed photographs of the young Magnus, endearingly signed.

There, he was being embraced by Hitler; with Himmler, sleeves rolled up, cheerfully pointing to a large map of Dachau; Goebbels, a woman, and Magnus in evening dress at a theater entrance; Göring and Magnus in a forest, rifles raised at a shoot; the camera-shy Martin Bormann caught with him, laughing; Heydrich, the designer of the "Final Solution," bowing to him; Albert Speer, proudly showing him model buildings of the chancellery.

Not once in any of the photos was Magnus in uniform. He favored well-cut, double-breasted suits. Pictures in color revealed his vanity with ties and matching handkerchiefs. In all of them his expression was one of gaiety and vitality. On the faces caught in these candid moments, their demeanor—especially Hitler's—conveyed respect and exultation that Magnus was in their company.

This elderly vulture before her had somewhat different features engineered by plastic surgery.

Rebecca, at last, accepted a glass of champagne but could not avoid touching glasses with Magnus and Bruno.

"I warned you in Bruno's office. But you wouldn't listen." Magnus's voice had the caustic tone of rebuke. "Bruno even bought you a ticket back to Vienna." He shook his head with the disapproval of a headmaster reprimanding a defiant student. "You've been a very careless girl, Rebecca."

At last she found her voice. "Oma Lilli and Herta would agree."

Beyond her, dusky green club lamps cast shadows over the people sitting in the huge room. Whorls of cigarette and cigar smoke formed a filmy haze. She was shocked to discover an audience.

"I wrote Lilli a letter from Vienna, partly about you."

"I read it," Rebecca said.

"It's all true. She *is* Bruno's mother and was my wife. I never divorced her, so by law, she's *still* my wife. His smile was triumphant, and utterly chilling. "And Bruno is her only legitimate offspring."

"She had no choice." Rebecca was livid. "You threatened to kill her, and held my grandparents and Herta hostage. What kind of a man would do that? Only someone like you, a man who had no confidence in himself with women," she said with disdain. "What was she?...Sixteen-seventeen? And after the War, she was sure you were dead. She certainly hoped so." She pointed at Bruno—"Both of you! Even I wondered how she could have denied her own son...but now it all makes sense."

Magnus was unprepared for accusations from someone in her circumstances, and this drew out the poisonous defenses of the fanged viper.

"You Jewish women are unbearably arrogant. I *saved* Lilli, the family, and yet she hated me." Magnus appeared bewildered. "You aren't fit to breed—not then, not now, not ever."

"You act as though you were God," she said with contempt.

"My dear young woman, in his absence, *I am*! He was defeated and exiled long ago. Prayer won't save you now. You may as well adjust to this fact and smile for our guests."

More uniformed men, reeking of cologne, had joined the women and fanned out. They sidled up to a bar beside tables set with champagne buckets.

"Our *Einsatzgruppen* all agree, Magnus," Arthur Kress, his *gauleiter* in Milwaukee, declared. He appraised Rebecca like a prize pig at a fair. "She was worth the hunt."

The three men chatted for a moment out of range of her hearing. Then they returned.

"Let me go back to your amateurish, uninformed talk at the museum," Magnus began. "A friend and colleague of Einstein's invented Zyklon-B gas for pesticide control and weaponized it for war. Not even Jews can live with their own."

Virgil reappeared in SS uniform. "We owe *that* Yid, Fritz Haber, an Iron Cross, First Class."

"He'll get it tonight." Noreen's voice resounded impatiently. She was in a starched nurse's uniform. Her hands, encased in red rubber gloves, tightened around Rebecca's face. She pulled her up.

"Wakey, wakey. Washey, washey. We want you to smell good."

For Rebecca, the perception of time again vanished.

"Rebecca, you'll go with Noreen and change. I want to hear you perform," Magnus said as though she'd been hired help at his weekend party.

Noreen again shook her.

"What?" Rebecca asked. "I don't understand."

"Your debut in Winterhaven. I promised my father a concert!" Bruno said.

"I won't play for you," she replied.

Magnus was enthralled by her impudence, but before long his laughter came, shading his surprise. The sound possessed a hyena-like, gloating trill, which intimidated her.

"Then, my dear lady, *our* Lilli, and Herta, won't have an easy time," Magnus said. "The Mauthausen Camp would have been paradise for them. We have close friends, allies, in Vienna. If you like, I'll make a call and those two will vanish."

She was elbowed forward by Noreen and surrounded by several other sniping women. Rebecca was now convinced that her unquiet destiny, the visitations, had been guiding her to this underworld since childhood.

15

Butch had expertly piloted the Jet Ranger and came in for a landing over the Pacific's high, churning swells. Oceano was a small, well-maintained airport with a string of Coast Guard birds and R 22s on the ground. Butch had radioed ahead, and they managed to rent a Dodge Durango. They unloaded the arms into the backseat.

Horne sped along the mountainous highway. What if she had been taken someplace else? What would happen if he never found her? People disappeared constantly and left grieving, tortured lovers and family. Had she already been murdered?

Butch broke the silence. "I'll go with you, Doug."

"You feeling guilty?"

"No, it's one of the few weaknesses I was born without." Butch detected a perilous violence in Horne that could not be contained. "Just don't start shooting anyone."

Grimly Horne said, "Not unless I have to."

Noreen and three other women stripped Rebecca and compelled her to shower. A white silk dress had been laid out for her and she was told to change into it. They even found lingerie and shoes in her size. Had Miriam also endured this depraved ritual before being sacrificed? A performance before dying to please Magnus and the troops?

Noreen nipped at her like a sheep dog. "Move it, Rebecca. The gentlemen are getting impatient."

"I won't play!"

They dragged her back to the ballroom. On a platform, a colossus of a piano was illuminated. Magnus took her hand with excessive gallantry. His touch chilled her. She didn't attempt to shake him off or even hint at her repulsion. She had a sudden change of heart. The longer she performed, the longer she would live.

"Is the gas quick or slow...?"

"Rebecca, don't be so melodramatic. Sit down and adjust the bench. I want you to be comfortable."

Magnus turned away and addressed the room, filling with more people.

"Ladies and gentlemen, to celebrate Bruno's return, we're fortunate enough to have a piano virtuoso as our honored guest. Rebecca Benjamin will be playing on a 1901 Model I Bechstein. Frau Betsy Bechstein gave it to Hitler because of his profound love of music. Fraulein Benjamin will play from Hitler's annotated score of Wagner's *Tristan und Isuelt*. Winifred Wagner, the composer's daughter-in-law, presented it to Adolf in Bayreuth at the festival celebrating a performance of this great opera."

Rebecca broke out in a sweat, her flesh inflamed by the proximity of these jackals thriving on the heinous crimes of the past.

Unprepared and frightened, she shifted the lamplight over the music. Her position—what there was of it—was already compromised. Although Lilli had forbidden the sisters to play Wagner, Rebecca appreciated his artistry. *How could music, especially anything so sublime, be political and represent the views of demonic madmen*, she had asked herself. But to keep the peace they had respected this ban on Wagner's music at home.

Horne, where was he? If only she had had the time...or had thought about leaving him some clue, a track, any hint of what had occurred, she might have....

She imagined his touch, his bare chest against her breasts. He was waving from The Viking bar. He and Butch were drinking, patching up the wrong side of the past. Taylor and she were talking about the client she had fallen in love with. Ingrid, glowing with pleasure, was introducing her to an audience.

Leaning her ear over the Bechstein soundboard, she tested the keys, listening for anything flat or atonal; she pressed the pedals for resistance; she found nothing wrong. She played some chords: there was an unmistakable purity of tone with resonant, mellow harmonic equilibrium that rendered Lilli's prejudices against the maker trivial. Despite its history, this was an instrument of superb character.

Her fingers were stiff; her wrists ached from the handcuffs. To play for these executioners was loathsome, squandering her years of study, and would mirror the unconditional destruction of her soul.

She slowly turned the pages, peering with incredulity at the marked score, each page contaminated with the initials "AH." She came to the end, slapped the leather folder closed. Glaring at Bruno, sitting beside his father only a few feet away, she waved it at him. He came to her.

"Rebecca, you must play," he whispered. In the background were the nervous, pre-performance coughs of this psychotic audience. "Do you want me to turn the pages?"

"I know it."

"Do you?" he asked tenderly. "I thought you would, even though you said you didn't."

"Sit down, like a good boy, *Bru-no*," she pronounced his name harshly, her face tightly drawn with abhorrence.

Her wrists loose now, she closed her eyes. Her fingers swirled into the intangible "Tristan Chord," four notes craving resolution, a melodic vaulting forth that thwarts its own outcome in a mystical unity.

She played with passion, as though holding Horne in her arms and making love. Fondling him, stroking him, with pulsating intensity, she felt her body surging to the tempo of something lost, aching to regain it, like the chord itself.

Butch was at the wheel of the Durango and slowed up when they approached the guard's gatehouse at Winterhaven. Horne was loading clips into the machine gun and his weapons in the backseat.

"This is too heavy for you to carry up a hill through woods," Horne said, wiping the sweat off his face with his gloves.

"What do you want to do?"

"We have to go for it. At least we've got cover in the car."

"The guard's coming out. He's got a sidearm."

"Is he alone?" Horne climbed back into the front seat.

"Can't tell." Butch pulled alongside. "Doug, we don't know for sure she's here."

"I'll ask."

"What...?

"I'll sweet-talk him."

A muscular young thug with long sideburns came out of the booth. He wore a black leather jacket with a lightning bolt and a baseball cap with **WINTERHAVEN** written across the bill.

"You guys lost?" he asked Butch.

"We're on our way to Hearst Castle."

"You made a wrong turn."

Horne came out of the passenger side and whipped around the back of the car. Before the guard could react, Horne jammed his .45 against the guard's mouth.

"We need some directions. Maybe you can help us. For starters, hit the switch for the barrier."

"You're making the mistake of your life, pal."

Horne hauled him inside to an electronic wonderland of monitors, colored buttons, and switches.

"Pick the right one first time. No alarms. I don't give second chances."

"Who are you guys? Cops? Feds?"

"Outlaws."

The guard flicked a switch and the steel barrier rose. Butch drove in a few feet. Horne came out with the guard and propelled him forward.

"We need a tour guide. You get in the back and show us around."

"Fuck you!"

Horne seized him by the throat, lifted his knee, and slammed it into his groin. The guard wailed in agony.

"Can I help you in now?" he said, seizing the groaning, doubled-up man and heaving him into the backseat.

"And don't be puking, kid, this is a Hertz rental," Butch said.

"Right," Horne agreed, "we don't want to be losing our deposit."

The guard's groans and whimpers continued like an aria. Horne was inside beside him. Slipping his Hattori skinning knife from its sheath, he knocked the guard's cap off and grabbed him by the hair.

"Come on, boy, get your pants down. I'm going to start cutting you and skin you bit by bit."

The young guard began to snivel. Horne chopped him hard across the bridge of the nose.

"You better talk to him, kid. He's a fucking nut case. He'll make you chew your balls."

"What do you want from me?" the guard yelped.

"Did Virgil come in tonight with a young woman?"

"Yeah, about one, he drove in with a man in the passenger seat. Noreen had a woman in the backseat. That's all I know."

"Where are they now?"

"They just left the castle. The woman was playing the piano for all of them."

"You saw them on the monitors?"

"Yeah."

"How many people are here?"

"Around a hundred live here permanently and some visitors came from out of town."

"Where would they be going?"

"They're taking the girl to the gas chamber."

16

Encore followed encore, demanded by the audience. Nearing five, her hands limp, Rebecca succumbed to exhaustion and felt faint. She closed the keyboard and stood up, her body unspooling like thread from a spindle. Bruno caught her. Magnus took her other arm.

"Come on, you need some fresh air," Bruno said for the second time that night.

"I have to sleep."

She was guided outside, supported by both men. The others, led by Virgil and Noreen, all in black SS dress uniforms, formed ranks, encircling her and the Von Winters.

Enormous spotlights illuminated the grounds; loudspeakers came on and the group's voices joined the recording of the Nazi marching song to arms:

Die Fahne hoch
Die Reihen fest geschlossen
S.A. marschiert
Mit ruhig festem Schritt...

In the background the eerie, violent growls of aroused lions played a counterpoint to Rebecca's journey in hell.

The procession marched with military precision. Rebecca was towed along, past stables, to a gleaming steel building, a dazzling modern architectural structure.

The towering, spiked gates were open. Machinery buzzed, engines churned.

"It's time, Rebecca," Magnus informed her softly.

Two opposing polar forces were at work: Magnus was pulling her forward, Bruno holding her in place. Eventually, it was the son who surrendered, as she'd known he would.

Stepping inside, Rebecca's mind splintered. Leaping thoughts of her life ending assailed her like a swarm of screeching bats. The audience from the concert confronted her. They sat in rows of numbered seats in a theater, one that she might have attended for a school recital.

The center of the stage held a glass cubicle. Inside it, a high-backed red metal seat had been riveted to the black floor. Color-coded red, blue, yellow, and green tubes and pipes snaked from above and below.

Three people operating video cameras moved toward her, already recording the event.

Rebecca had traveled beyond the logic of fear and maintained an impassive serenity.

Eyes cast down and stooped, Bruno shuffled to the rear. A man on the aisle moved over to make room for him.

Magnus nodded to Rebecca, "You're in good hands. Virgil is the state commander of our *Einsatzgruppen*."

Unlike his behavior in the car, Virgil was now civil, guiding her into the chamber. He strapped her hands and ankles into metal restraints. The door was still open. Rebecca heard Virgil's voice carry over a microphone.

"Rebecca, we're no longer using the Farben Zyklon-B pellets like we did with Miriam. They were too old and took a long time. This is special, hermetically sealed glass," he droned on, a doctor advising a patient of test results. "I'll close the door, open a valve, and you'll hear liquid running into the container beside you—" he pointed to a flat steel pan—"and *smell* the odor. It's hydrochloric acid flowing. When Magnus raises his arm, I'll release ten ounces of potassium cyanide. That produces hydrocyanic gas.

"Now, Rebecca, follow my instructions.... Your sister made it very ugly and hard on herself. She disobeyed. Take a deep breath. You'll be unconscious in ten, fifteen seconds at the most. After that, judging from your weight, five minutes at the most...and it'll be over."

Frozen and floating, Rebecca smiled at Virgil. She had a vision of Miriam, the two of them children, playing with Lilli in the music room in the house on the Berggasse, the garden alive with roses, spring vegetables, and herbs that Herta was gathering in a basket.

She heard a voice from another cycle of time, somewhere in Vienna, and attempted to identify it. It was the professor's at an early meeting at the Café Sperl. They had finished coffee and were sipping cognac when the subject turned to the meaning of Hitler's purpose.

"It's beyond human understanding," the professor had suggested. "Only the Hindu god Vishnu had an inkling when he said: 'I am become death, the destroyer of worlds...' That was Hitler, Rebecca."

A whirling string of hallucinations of liquid, disconnected faces appeared to Rebecca: the mad Dutchman in Africa; Miriam's haunted eyes; Horne's parents, Bonnie and Keith, singing in a bar; the three women, Helen, Judith, and Cynthia, all of them merging into a massive, hydra-headed creature. Horne materialized, raising his arms to embrace her.

Rebecca heard her own voice now, clear and firm, intoning the *Kaddish*.

"*'Yisgahdal, v'yiskahdash, sh'may ray-boh dee-v'roh heer-oo-say...'*"

Virgil was affronted.

"Your Jew spells won't work here. You better pay attention to me."

She became lucid and grasped the situation.

"Maybe this isn't the day of reckoning, but there *will* be one for all of you," she shouted.

Driving past a row of unmanned Humvees with mounted turret guns, Butch said, "Shit, they're armed for a fucking war. I'm calling the cops and ATF."

"There's no time," Horne snapped.

He had suppressed all thought of losing Rebecca. Now the unendurable prospect crystallized as they neared the gleaming trapezoid building. There were sounds of an engine; smoke vented from the chimneys of the steel building. Red lights were flashing.

"Jesus, Almighty Christ," Butch exclaimed, gaping at the floodlit Gothic mansion and the gas chamber. The "Horst Wessel Lied" boomed from speakers. "There's a fucking moat...with a drawbridge."

Lying on the floor, the guard whimpered and trembled in panic. Horne pulled him up by the scruff of the neck.

"Where are the guards, and how many?"

"Two sentries outside the gas chamber. I was supposed to be one of them, but pulled the gatehouse."

The Durango was still out of sight. Butch crawled forward. Horne hefted the machine gun to the front seat and Butch lowered the windows.

"I'm stopping," Butch said.

"Do you want to watch our asses or die now?" Horne asked the guard.

"Anything you say," he pleaded. "When I got out of the joint, I had no idea what I was getting into."

"Slide over into the driver's seat when we move out and stay behind the wheel."

"I swear I will."

"Is the gas chamber locked from the inside?"

"No, it's a precaution and the only escape exit."

"Any rifles inside?"

"Don't think so. The men were on Full Dress with sidearms."

Under the bright halogen beams, the sentries had spotted the unfamiliar vehicle. Immediately, they knelt in combat readiness and pointed the weapons at the Durango. A clack of rifle bullets smashed into the door.

The infernal German music covered the gunfire.

"I like the lighting," Horne said, balancing his Sako on the edge of the metal sill. Using the huge 4.375 cartridges that could fell a bull elephant, he fired twice, hitting both men. They lurched backward and into the air like divers on a high board going for gainers.

Horne speed-loaded the Sako and slung the Benelli shotgun over his shoulder. Butch carried the machine gun and trotted with him to the fallen guards.

Inching stealthily to the entrance, Horne silently slid the heavy door a crack.

In an instant he beheld the backs of the audience's heads.

No one moved.

They were intent on Rebecca. She was strapped in a chair in a sealed glass cage.

He couldn't use the incendiary grenade for fear that she would be trapped inside the building. Horne and Butch slipped on their gas masks.

Horne fired rapidly into the booth, blowing the glass apart.

Smoky acid fumes immediately escaped and whorled into the air. The panicked crowd, many gasping, began to scream. As they tried to leave, Butch released the fuse cord on an MK grenade and pitched it into the center of the group. It would explode in seconds and he retreated, dragging Horne with him.

The blast went through the steel roof. In the gas fumes and smoke, Horne sprinted through the fallen bodies of the dead. Choking, writhing wounded, with twisted hunks of shrapnel gutting them, survivors shrieked. The toxic vapor of the cratered building hung like a lethal cloud over them.

Noreen was headless and dead at Virgil's feet. With one arm severed, and an eye gone, Virgil staggered; he corkscrewed, and pointed a pistol into Horne's line of sight. Horne took him down with a shotgun blast. He ran forward, stumbling over more and more bodies.

An old man lay writhing on the floor with massive chest and head wounds. His fingers curled through the air. Butch, charging in from the rear, automatically fired at the movement, blowing off Magnus's hand.

Horne rushed to free Rebecca. Opening the door of the execution chamber, he swiftly undid her restraints and fireman-carried her outside.

Rebecca was white, her lips blue; she had been hit badly, slashed by glass and was not breathing.

He ripped off his gas mask, laid her on the ground, pounded her chest, pleading, giving her the kiss of life. He lifted his mouth and frantically cried: "Rebecca, Rebecca, don't, don't, *don't* leave me!"

The sky itself shuddered under the yellow-blue halo of fiery death. With his machine gun, Butch covered the wounded people reeling out.

"If any of you have weapons, drop them now or I'll mow you down!"

His warning was unnecessary. Those still alive fell of their own accord. He backed up to Horne and Rebecca. Yanking out his short-wave, he called in a Mayday and an SOS.

The gate guard slinked toward them and stood over Horne and Rebecca. The marching music stopped. "Let me help?"

Out of the blue, a man bolted away from the staggering line of screaming people.

Horne spied Harry Summerfield racing in the direction of the staff housing. With tears in his eyes, Horne kissed Rebecca. He stood up.

"Please, Butch, don't leave her. I'm going after him."

"You'll never find him," the guard said. "He'll take the tunnels. They're underneath the houses."

"Where's the outlet?"

"By the castle-side of the moat."

"You just saved your ass, kid," Butch said.

Horne gazed down at Rebecca. In despair, he turned away.

In the distance, flecks of flashing lights were followed by the violent clamor of sirens.

Reloading, Horne ran across the moat bridge and crouched low in the sodden grass. He took cover in a grove of towering cypresses and had a panoramic view of the entry lawn. Through dark gray coastal clouds, a somber intimation of daybreak emerged. The muffled bleating of penned animals was drowned out by the hunting roars of lions in the preserve behind the castle.

Horne made a sweeping, circular motion with his rifle. He watched the lawn closely for the slightest movement. His eyes closed in on a patch of grass that seemed to be shifting. A tottering figure surfaced. Horne held him in his sights, but waited.

It was a man. Horne left the tree shelter and advanced, proceeding carefully on open ground. Harry spotted him and raised his hands.

"Don't shoot!" he called out.

Horne approached gradually, each step an effort to control his rage.

Filthy and ragged, his hair charred, Harry put his hands down. A rictus of a smile formed on his lips. He opened his arms to Horne.

"Doug Horne, I've never been happier to see anyone...."

The statement astonished Horne. He crooked the rifle in his arm. The hunter knew he had captured his prey.

"Are you serious, *Bruno*?"

Harry shook his head. "*Bruno*?" What're you talking about? You met me at Rebecca's. I'm Harry Summerfield," he protested. "Rebecca's friend. Jack Leopold's architect. You know that."

The grandiosity of his fabrication infuriated Horne to the point of madness.

"Before you die, say your prayers, you fucking Nazi scum."

"No! No! You're wrong!" Harry trembled with indignation.

"How'd you know about the underground passages?"

"Von Winter and his men took me and Rebecca there from this castle—whatever it is."

The ingenuity of this master liar was not wasted on Horne.

"Let's take a walk," Horne said, directing him past the battlement of the fortress, then along the courtyard to the animal preserve.

"I flew in from Tampa to see Jack...heard that Rebecca was performing, and went to The Viking to hear her. She told me about the two of you. I also love her. And I'm her friend. When she finished, I went backstage. She wanted some fresh air and I walked outside with her." He nervously rabbited on. "She told me she'd quit smoking, but was dying for a cigarette. I had a pack someone left in my car.

"When I unlocked the door with the master key—I never give it to the valet—a man and woman with pistols carjacked us." He ran his hand through his charred hair, becoming more and more agitated. "I had no idea who they were."

Horne icily stared at him.

Struggling to catch his breath, he resumed. "We drove for hours until we got up here. This is an entire camp of neo-Nazi fanatics. They forced Rebecca to play German music for hours—ask her."

Horne could not utter the word *dead*. "That's not possible."

"No!...No."

Overcome by the horror of Rebecca's death, Horne nodded bleakly.

"Finally, when she finished playing, they dragged us through an underground passageway into a gas chamber. They put her in—oh, God, I was next! Just as they started the gas, there was an explosion...."

They had reached the deserted entry post of the lion preserve. Except for the rasp of the wind channeling through the trees, it was silent.

"Why would they want to gas *you*?" Horne asked calmly, giving him a measured look.

"I'm *Jewish*," Harry said. "You know how it is: Jewish mother, Jewish blood. Or maybe you didn't know that...? After all, you're not a Jew."

Horne pulled the shotgun from his shoulder sling and blasted the locks off the gate, then shunted Bruno forward, pressing the scorching nozzle against his neck.

"What're you doing?"

"Get your clothes off."

"Why, it's freezing! I need a doctor!" Harry shook his head with incomprehension before surrendering to a sudden panic. "What's the matter with you?"

"Bruno, you're everybody's good friend."

"I try," he pleaded. "And *I'm not Bruno*—whoever he is!"

"Rebecca's, the Leopolds'...a pretty girl named Taylor's, too...."

"Yes, we used to see each other."

Horne slipped the shotgun sling back on his shoulder and now held his big Sako rifle with one hand. He yanked out his skinning knife and ran the side of the blade across Harry's groin.

"Want *me* to *cut* them off?"

"You're insane!"

"I'm certifiable...like Virgil, his old lady, Magnus, and *you*.... Now strip down, or would you like me to slash off your nose first. It's an African tradition."

The wind now carried a growling chorus of snarls, unmistakably roused lions. But they were still hidden in the brush. Harry took off his shoes, pants, shredded jacket, and shirt.

"Drop your panties too. Don't be modest. Taylor wasn't, was she?"

Harry lowered his briefs and stepped out of them. He hunched up, chilled by the wind. Overcome by frantic dread, he gaped into the wasteland of Horne's frozen eyes.

"Move."

"Where?" he howled. "Why're you doing this?"

"Like a good Jew, your Mama should've had the rabbi circumcise you, Bruno."

Horne butted Bruno's bare back with the heavy stock of his rifle and pressured him forward into the field. In the high grass there was the hush of death.

"You can't do this!" he keened.

"Walk ten paces. Turn and face me."

Tears streamed down Horne's face. The venom of revenge raged through his bloodstream.

"Why? *Why?*" he screeched, swerving in terror, as walked, before slowly, unwillingly, turning.

"You fucking, gutless dog. I'll bet Rebecca showed more heart than you."

The moment Bruno was facing him, Horne fired a round and blew off his ear. Blood jetted from the wound. Bruno fell to his knees. Screeching, but still alert, he was aware of another danger. He looked behind him.

The master of the pride roared. He had taken his stand on a rocky hillock, and his ravening, feral bellows echoed, inciting his pride to hunt. The lions had captured their scent at the castle, but with the gunshot wound, the sharp odor of blood engulfed their senses.

"Shoot me! Kill me! You can't leave me like this."

"Ever see a man-eating lion? They work fast in a team. Just smile Bruno, and think of murdering Rebecca and the other Jews you've killed. That should make you feel better."

His rifle primed for the possibility of a lion charge in his direction, Horne vigilantly backed away to the entrance. He closed the gates, making a wedge with a block of wood. He watched Bruno through the barbed wire.

Squealing, Bruno frantically rushed around in circles. He was cut off by three female hunters and trapped on all sides within their triangle. The closest huntress leapt on him, locked his head in a deadly embrace, then clawed out his throat. The two other females, jaws working like machines, began to grind apart his arms and legs. The ravenous cubs joined in.

As they were about to cleave open his stomach and split him, the black-maned king vaulted down from the hill and sped for the downed kill. The wary, intimidated cubs retreated from his fury.

When he arrived, his rumbling snarls and savage bulling warned the pride of his dominance, and forced away the females. His ferocious jaws and massive teeth gouged at the prey's stomach, leaving the females to break apart the skull and gluttonously feed on the brains of the carcass.

PART V
99 SYCAMORE PLACE

Horne had never experienced a more grueling period in his life, beyond his imprisonment in Dar-es-Salaam and subsequent murder trial. He was haunted by the entire incident at Winterhaven. Twenty-three people had been killed by the grenade, some shot; others injured in varying degrees; some handicapped for whatever remained of their lives.

He'd moved into Butch's guesthouse, finding a temporary solace and renewed affection for the man who had betrayed his father and been his mother's lover. It all seemed meaningless now—an affair that assumed the banality of all such suburban affairs. Night after night, he and Butch sat up drinking, until Horne either passed out or slammed the door in Butch's face, only to be confronted by him entering from the back door.

The previous night, Butch had laid it all out for the final time.

"I want another drink," Horne, surly, said with drunken menace.

"No! You're going to listen. Shrinks and medics have all sorts of names for your condition. Stress-this, stress-that. Doug, you were in a war! The fact that you had a good cause doesn't make it go away."

"Damn right, it doesn't."

"When I was in Nam, I watched boats filled with people—strangers—go up in ash, flesh burning. And *I* was the one who'd laid the mines in the harbor. I was personally responsible for villages vanishing in toxic flames. I'd set the explosive devices."

"And how'd you feel about it?"

"Relief that they wouldn't be around to kill my people—torture my boys—fellow soldiers—Americans. There was something greater at stake than me as an individual."

Horne put down his drink and tried to shake off his mood of penitence.

"I'm getting there, Butch."

"I understand. Try harder. It's psychic damage. But look-it, Doug, would you have it any other way than feeding Bruno to the lions? Or not shooting that Dutchman who skinned your friends? Want them back? On trial? You have to look at the nature of evil. Are you here now with me safe, or would you rather have these people alive? Going after Rebecca—bless her...her sister...murdering all the other Jews for no reason? Burying a young rabbi alive? Tell me!"

"No," he said with a shiver. The booze and the night of June gloom in the Valley had dropped the temperature to the fifties. "Thanks. I'll finish packing and see you in the morning."

"Think of the future. You damn well have one."

"Will do."

The following day Horne returned to Sycamore Place. He'd sweated out the booze in Butch's sauna and was starting to feel human again. From the living room window of Rebecca's vacant apartment, Glück bitterly complained about his confinement in his Sherpa carry bag and his mistress's desertion. Horne lifted the cat out.

"I thought after I brought you back Nate 'n' Al's sturgeon, you'd be purring and kissing me." He seemed to want to spew out something. Horne held him away in mid-air. "Don't even think of it...no fur-balls on my new clothes, Herr Glück."

Clearing whatever had caused the congestion, Horne perched him on his shoulder, where the cat established a surveillance post. Together they studied the grotesque, rusted two-ton wrecking ball shackled on a crane arm. It rested at eye-level, threatening, depressing.

Horne and his alter ego went out to the bare, empty patio, trying to ignore it and the chainlink fence below, segregating the street from the impending demolition of 99 Sycamore Place. They watched the comings and goings of neighbors, shaking their heads; the Beverly Hills traffic warden was not the least bit curious at the sight of such equipment and cheerfully ticketed a visitor's car. At least Horne and the cat had the summery full leaves crowding the twisted sycamore branches on the once-quiet street.

It was the time of migration in the Serengeti, another one Horne would miss. No more safaris for Douglas Horne. He had hoped that one day he could take Rebecca to Africa. He'd hold her in his arms, listen to the music of mating lions; observe elephants giving birth; drive along the plains while the herds of zebras, giraffes and wilde-beests made their trek to the Masai Mara before this world vanished.

Horne was finally free to travel and would no longer be subjected to the intrusion of the media. They had initially portrayed his actions at Winterhaven as heroic. When he'd clammed up and refused to pose with his rifles, the reptiles and their cameras had dispersed. Unfriendly to the media, he was exposed as a former big-game hunter who had once been charged with murder in Tanzania.

Legal depositions, with a full tasting menu of state and federal authorities, also came to an end. Teams of expert forensic specialists had diligently examined the "battle scene"; photographed it, video-recorded it; taken statements from the exceedingly cooperative survivors of Winterhaven. The young gate guard sold his story to a tabloid with the connivance of a celebrated lawyer who claimed his client had been brainwashed by Magnus.

Magnus Von Winter, a.k.a. Martin Summerfield, had been found and identified. But American passport authorities had no records and photographs of him, nor did the DMV. His very existence would remain shadowy. The Austrian government had never heard of him, nor was he listed in any war crimes dossiers.

The skull of his prominent son was found amid the lion preserve; dental records confirmed that they belonged to Harry Summerfield, the celebrated architect. Yet the most elemental and destructive aspect of the Von Winters' history remained cloaked in secrecy.

As for the Benjamin family history, Butch, Tommy Haggerty, and the Leopolds were privy to the horrors visited upon Lilli Benjamin, and their compact of silence would never be broken.

The Swiss corporation that owned the Von Winter estate was also a mystery. Notwithstanding the enormous value of the land, no one came forth to claim it. There it rested, as an army of befuddled state and federal civil servants battled for jurisdiction. The lions were shipped to the San Diego Zoo and would probably be forced to live on horsemeat.

Horne's legal bill had reached an inflated level. In round figures, he had been into the lawyers for $340,000. Tommy Haggerty's eloquent pleading with his partners had failed. The lawyers had represented Horne during the investigation, and they *wanted* their money.

From the cab of a bulldozer, the wrecking-crew foreman was jawing with a building inspector about permits. Planted in the small front garden, a Roman-legion flag of property-conquest announced that Horne's residency at 99 Sycamore Place had concluded.

SOLD BY
DONNA SEYMOUR REALTY

Pulling up alongside the crane and bulldozer, a familiar Rolls Royce arrived, followed by a limo. This eccentric pairing caught the attention of the ambitious traffic warden.

Through months of rehabilitation, Rebecca had survived, barely. The gas had damaged her lungs. Surgeons had removed the glass splinters from her arms and legs. She owed her life to Butch. In a desperate last effort, he had performed a battlefield tracheotomy after Horne had left to hunt down Bruno.

Emergency doctors arriving at the carnage of Winterhaven had managed to stabilize her. With plastic surgery, the scar would vanish. But Rebecca was still undecided and thought she'd live with it as a badge of honor.

Jack and Paula waved at Horne. They were followed by Butch with Ingrid in a summery mini-skirt and décolletage that caught the traffic warden's attention. Haggerty also emerged from the back of Butch's Land Rover, his hand gallantly extended for a young woman, who for a moment, looked as though she had been cloned from the tragically murdered Taylor. He and Butch had downed their differences in fine single malts at The Viking, where good-looking, unattached young women found themselves entranced by the distinguished lawyer.

He left Glück asleep and walked downstairs. All he needed now was a runaway cat.

With her fiery red hair cut short in a shag, and the intravenous diet, Rebecca's figure had the statuesque gauntness favored by women's magazines. To Horne, she appeared even lovelier and younger than her years, as if she had just left her teens and wasn't in fact circling her twenty-fourth birthday.

"My God, look at that gorgeous man in his new clothes!" Rebecca exclaimed, then opened her arms to kiss him. "This can't be Tijuana's finest!"

"No, going Downtown is much too dangerous," he said. "People get shot there." He kissed Paula and shook hands with Jack. "Five big ones at Ralph Lauren without a scratch."

Jack looked him over with approval and aggressively pulled him aside.

"Have you discussed it with Rebecca yet?"

"No, but I will."

"It'll break Paula's heart if she doesn't agree."

"Okay, okay."

Rebecca had pardoned the Leopolds, though forgiveness did not come easily to her. Jack and Paula had visited her at Cedars-Sinai every day. Over the years, Jack's contributions had been so bountiful that he practically owned the hospital. *His* doctors had claimed Rebecca's case. There had been another, more realistic consideration from her standpoint. She liked the sound of their Steinway and practiced there for hours each day to build up her stamina.

Ingrid pulled at Horne and Rebecca. "I want you to meet Selena Hamilton. She may become the first Mrs. Haggerty."

The look of worship, seldom seen in the diminutive, successful, elderly attorney, was a confession that this *might* be true.

"If this happens, Tommy, I want a finder's fee," Horne said.

"You'll get it in my will, if she doesn't grab it first."

Rebecca, accustomed to crowd control, broke away from Paula and nestled her head on Horne's shoulder.

"Please, can Horne and I have a last walk through 99 Sycamore Place—alone?"

There was silence from the well-wishers as they watched Rebecca with her cane make her way up the steps.

"Sure. I wasn't going to do it without you."

"Our memories are upstairs...."

"Mine are here with you. Want me to carry you up?"

"No, I can make the steps." She had Rose's Malacca cane, and he walked alertly behind her. "Just don't get smart and poke your hand up my skirt."

"Since when do I obey rules?" he asked. "I'll do what I like."

They reached the patio and went inside the stark apartment, alien to both of them. Glück lay in a deep sleep on top of his bag.

"He never sleeps at this time. What did you give him?"

"I smoked a little weed and blew it at him. Second-hand smoke works. Calm him down for the flight." She backed away from him. "I also found one of Rose's old Seconal caps that I mixed in his water."

"Are you serious?...You're a dangerous mental case."

"Serious, no. Deranged, yes. I fed him some smoked sturgeon. It acts like a turkey at Thanksgiving."

She smiled adoringly at him

They stood at the window, shying away from the wrecking ball. The group of workmen sat on the lawn, talking baseball, eating sandwiches on their lunch break and occasionally looking up, waiting for them to vacate so that they could do the job and move onto the next one.

Rebecca looked around, and with relief saw her old briefcase.

"No, you didn't forget it, or lose it. Your scores are all there."

"I keep forgetting to copy my schedule on my Palm Pilot."

"You've got a very full load...."

Unlike Horne's refusal to be interviewed—short of a court order—Rebecca had spent a lifetime with journalists and knew exactly where to begin, pause, stop, and elaborate. Stardom had embraced her for all the wrong reasons, she thought. But her place in the limelight was assured. Salzburg in July; her official debut opening the fall season at the Vienna Philharmoniker; Amsterdam's Concertgebouw; performances in Paris, London, Madrid, Tokyo, and Carnegie Hall.

"Lilli called. They want me in *Berlin*!" She was elated. "Can you believe it?"

"That's great. Can you fit it in?"

"She's working on it."

"How's she feeling?" he asked.

"She's a lot stronger now. My grandmother's always been someone who thrives on work. She's left the university and taking on a couple of students privately, without charging."

"I'm glad she won't have to struggle over money ever again," he said.

In a gay mood, Rebecca dropped the cane and tentatively whirled around the room. Horne remembered his parents rolling back the carpet and dancing. His father had once sung Neil Young's "Wrecking Ball." In this room.

"You look worried," she said. "Is something wrong?"

"Would you close your eyes?"

Puzzled, she did as he asked. He took her left hand and slipped an emerald-cut diamond on her ring finger.

She was staggered. "No! Good God, it's gorgeous. The agony of spending so much money must have been sheer torment for you."

"Weeks of sleepless nights."

"Did it cost a fortune?"

"Don't ask." He kissed the tip of her nose. "Will you wear it when you play concerts?"

She was genuinely uncertain. "I'll have to see how it feels."

Horne had taken a post-doctoral seminar course from Jack in ring shopping. First threats at Cartier; a walkout at Tiffany followed; finally concluding with a slugging match at Harry Winston. He had threatened never to shop there again and beaten the jeweler down by 30 percent. To avoid almost nine thousand dollars in sales tax, Jack had had it shipped to a lawyer friend in Seattle who sent it by FedEx to Horne.

"Doesn't matter. I was just curious. It's not really a diamond. I bought it at this place in Tustin that advertises on TV at two in the morning. They have a thirty-day return policy."

She peered at the diamond and the sparkle belied his taunting.

"Don't worry, I'll flash it on every stage."

He held her in his arms and kissed her neck, her ears and her lips with exuberant passion.

"You better stop, you're getting me so excited."

During her convalescence, they had not been intimate and he wondered if this had promoted his depression or if had been a natural reaction to the Winterhaven massacre.

"Me, too. Damn, they're waiting downstairs."

"I'm sad to be leaving Sycamore Place. My nights of loneliness and grieving, Rose dying, then finally you appeared."

"Well, Rebecca, we're only leaving temporarily."

"How come? Aren't they going tear it down?"

"Yes...but...."

"What? Do you have some kind of scheme?"

"Jack had one."

"Jack! She said with a mixture of anger and gratitude, never quite certain of how she actually felt about him. Ambivalence ruled. "What sort of stunt has he pulled now?"

"It's not a stunt, all right. Call it reparations—war damages."

"He's been very good to me, but I don't trust him."

"I think you might after this."

Jack Leopold had purchased 99 Sycamore Place for three million dollars. Donna Seymour, the hustling realtor, had waived her commission from Horne on the sale and was signed to exclusively represent the new property, which would comprise eleven condominiums. Jack had already received planning permission to build them and they would be priced at a million plus. The 3,000 square foot penthouse would be Horne's and Rebecca's—free—and a studio would be designed to her specifications.

"I can't believe this. Is this reward money for Miriam?"

"Call it what you like. Jack just wants to look after us." Rebecca shook her head skeptically. Horne wondered if she was sharper than either of them. Or had she been born with a bullshit detector? "Okay, There is a kicker. When Jack recoups his investment, the profits go to us."

She was still suspicious. "And exactly what does he want in return for this *transaction*?" Horne knew that this posed a dilemma for Rebecca. "You don't have to stroke me."

"It's not so much a question of what he wants. It's more in the form of a request."

Her eyes were intent on his face. "Come on, out with it."

"He and Paula want us to get married on Valentine's Day 2001 at his house and give the bride—you—away."

She was too rattled to respond. Confounded by the implications, she paced around the empty apartment, snuggling the cat in her arms.

"Rebecca, I'm not going to press you or insist on this."

"Have you discussed this...this *offer* with Butch and Tommy?"

"Of course not. It's our business—our life."

"Why, *why* would Jack do such a thing? There must be a reason, something hidden and devious."

"Again, I'm not sure you're right about this." He reflected. "Suppose it's innocent and has to do with faith, being Jewish?"

She was pulled up short again. "Am I suddenly dense, have I lost it, or what? Explain this."

Scott's new wife was not Jewish. They had also discovered that she was infertile and proposed to adopt a child. Furthermore, Jack was relieved. As a recovering addict, the Leopolds expressed concern about Scott.

"What's wrong with them adopting?"

"The kid *can't* be Jewish—even I know that—unless the mother is." Rebecca's eyes filled with tears and Horne went to her. At moments like this, he was conscious of how deeply wounded they still were. "He wants our child—when we have one—to be brought up as a Jew. Frankly, it's okay with me. The ball's in your court."

She began to gasp. Horne panicked, afraid that he'd have to call emergency and get her back on a respirator.

"I'm all right. Just nerves." She caught her breath. "May God forgive me. I thought Jack was a monster."

Horne considered his own circumstances at Winterhaven, feeding Bruno to the lions.

"Maybe there are times when anyone can be one."

The car horn beeped downstairs. They went to the window and Butch shouted up: "Your flight!" This was followed by the grinding engine of industrial machinery, and they eyed the swinging wrecking ball in front of the window.

The voice of the foreman outside boomed over a bullhorn.

"Folks, you must vacate. We're on a time schedule. Please come down now!"

Horne squeezed Rebecca's hand and gave her a tender look before packing the cat inside his bag. She picked up her briefcase.

"I won't need Rose's cane any longer." She fondled the jade cat's-paw handle. "Shall I leave it?"

He brooded over this. "Yes, I think it would be right. Tommy sent her ashes to Lilli. We'll sprinkle them together on Miriam's grave at the service for her in Vienna."

"Yes," she said, tears running down to her chin.

They walked down the flight of stairs, gazed back at the house, turned away and stopped by the limo.

The group waited for them. Tommy, his girl, Butch, and Ingrid were all laughing and had already begun passing a flask around. Standing to the side solemnly, Jack and Paula stared at Horne, waiting for a signal.

Rebecca went to them, hesitated, clasped their arms, kissed Paula first, then Jack.

"We'll see you in Salzburg in July for your performance," he said.

"I wouldn't give one if you weren't there."

"Have you made a decision...?" Paula asked with newfound timidity.

Rebecca hesitated. "Of course. Our wedding at your home will honor my sister's memory and be the beginning of a new life for Horne and me."

Amid more kisses and farewells, she and Horne drove away in the back of the limo.

Horne held her tightly. Rebecca's eyes closed. For an instant she saw herself playing the piano at five, with Miriam, aged nine, accompanying her on the cello in the music room at the house on the Berggasse.

"Did you see something?" Horne asked in alarm.

Rebecca opened her eyes, smiled, and kissed him. "Just us."